Nameles
By Matthew

GW00870227

Dedication

To Julian, because you saw me better than I ever saw myself,
and to Peter, because without your help I wouldn't have written it

© Matthew Rossi. 2016
All rights reserved

Contents

Epilogue

Book One

You'll Never Be Alone

Chapter One

The Strange Hours

Thea woke up with a start when the tapping began.

She shook her head. Grit in her eyes, that sickened feeling from sleeping in her car. She blinked, pulled the seat upright, looked out the window.

Black hair, a lot of it. As black as hers was. She rolled down the window.

"Thea."

"Seria. What're you doing here?"

"I live here." Thea's cousin Seria looked a lot like her around the face – they shared the Rafiela crooked nose. Thea's mother had passed it down to her just as Seria's father had, that little sign of kinship. The two girls often didn't get along. Thea got the sense they weren't going to this time, either. "*Why* are you parked in our driveway?"

"Didn't have anywhere else to go." Thea popped the door open and got out of the CRX with effort. Seria backed up enough to let her.

"Why not go to Nana's house?"

"Because I haven't talked to her in a decade, Seria." Nana was a bit like Bigfoot – people talked about her but few actually saw her very often, and fewer still had any evidence. "Is Joe awake? I could use a shower."

"Yes, you could." Seria sniffed and Thea marveled at how effortlessly her cousin made her feel about an inch tall.

They walked up the duplex's stairs and Seria fished out her keys. Thea's stomach growled, and Seria shot her another look, but this one at least traded disapproval for concern.

"When did you last eat?"

"Sometime yesterday."

'What the hell are you *doing*..." The door opened, and Joe peered out with the same look of *I just woke up* that Thea had.

"Hey, sis. Cos." He blinked. "You sleep in our driveway again?"

"Yep." Seria hugged him. Thea felt that little stab of envy she always felt around them, the twins being so much closer even that normal brother/sister would explain. They would always have each other. Even after their parents died, here they were. Thea's parents had left her no one.

"Well, you at least willing to come in during the daylight hours?"

"Both of you stop being ridiculous." Seria pushed Joe in and Thea grumped in after her. Just being around the two of them made her feel so defiant, so... *ludicrous*. She was eighteen, almost nineteen, not the child they made her feel like. Seria was in college. Joe was in college. She'd barely graduated high school.

They ended up seated at Joe's flimsy coffee table while Seria made omelets. She'd flown through the kitchen, catalogued available food and swept into cooking. Thea felt oily, her hair lank. Joe and Seria had the Rafiela hair too but somehow she always felt like they wore it better than she did.

Thea was jarred from her self-derisive assessment of her hair when Seria slid a plate down in front of her. An omelet, cobbled together in the time it had taken Thea to get a good sulk going. *Well, no point in not eating.*

Thea luxuriated in the novelty of eating. It had been more like *three* days. The taste of provolone and diced up ham, even the cheap stuff Joe bought, made her remember weekends as a child running around her house, with her mother cooking. Before that had all ended. "This is fucking *amazing*, by the way. You should go to Johnson and Wales."

"I just cook for family." She seemed pleased by the compliment. Thea loved Seria – when mom died, she'd been there trying to be a shoulder to lean on. Thea'd given up on her understanding. Seria just would never see the world she did but she still loved her. "You need to stop trying to live in your car." Seria's face was that particular flavor of upset it got when she wasn't sure whether to be angry with you or protective of you. "Thea, you have a perfectly good house to sleep in!"

"Hey, ease up." Joe tried to calm his sister down. "I'm just going to put it out there that maybe she doesn't want to stay in the house her dad died in."

This wasn't even slightly true, but Thea held her tongue. If Joe wanted to draw the dragon onto him, he was welcome to her. She was his twin sister, after all. Thea was just their cousin.

"If she can't stay there, she can stay with Nana Raffy, or with *us*." None of this sounded like a good idea to Thea. She was two years younger than her cousins, and they absolutely never let her forget it. Nana was out.

"I'd need to hire Sherpas to find Nana. And I'm sure not moving in here." Thea stood up from the kitchen table. "You get too involved."

"What's that supposed to mean?"

"It means, Seri, that you jam your nose so far up into my business I'm surprised I'm not in stirrups." She walked over to the fridge and pulled out some OJ. She drank it from the carton just to annoy Seri.

She knew they both thought she was grieving her father, and that was fine, let them think that. She'd learned her lessons when she was twelve, after her mother. Her father had spent the last six years killing himself slowly, and while she wasn't happy he was dead, she'd been expecting it. She mostly missed his few good days. Like the last one, the trip out to East Greenwich to visit the house he'd grown up in, now his brother's place. She didn't know the Mendel side of her family very well. Her uncle Anton had shown up at the funeral, said something, and left. She'd barely noticed.

"You can't keep sleeping in your car." Joe said as gently as he knew how. "As it is, you're basically moved into the driveway, why not move in here?"

"I repeat my earlier objection." She took another swig and realized the carton was empty, put it back anyway just to notch Seria up. In a way Seri was more her older sister than her cousin, it had been Seri who'd taught her how to put on makeup, how to deal with her period, all the mom stuff her own mother had been too dead to do. Seri and Joe's parents had died when they were much younger, typical of the Rafiela clan – only Nana seemed immune, everyone else dying young.

"All I did was tell Scott the truth."

"You told him to *woo* me, Seri."

"What's wrong with that?"

"I don't want to date Scott. I do not have to date a boy just because I slept with him once." She leaned back on the counter. Seria *had* dated the first boy she slept with, and was *still* dating him. David Kanmore, who never missed the opportunity to ogle Thea when he thought Seria wasn't looking. The problem was, you couldn't get much *past* Seri. Somehow David's wandering eye was Thea's fault.

Hate to tell you this, but your boyfriend's a toad.

To be honest, Thea and Seria looked enough alike – long black hair, roughly similar faces and eyes. Thea's were ice-blue while Seria's were more sky blue. They didn't dress alike, Thea being more eclectic in her tastes. But if you liked Seria, it would make sense that you'd like Thea; it wasn't that David looked that really bothered her as much as how classless he was about it.

Thea wasn't entirely without ego, and she knew what she looked like. But David was just such a pig about it.

"...at least that much." Thea blinked, knowing that she'd tuned out Seri at exactly the wrong time.

"I already said *I'd* go." Joe looked mildly amused at the whole thing. He was usually the one she teamed up with to annoy his sister, but occasionally he'd switch off if it would make Thea uncomfortable. The look on his face clearly indicated he knew she'd been zoning. "So now it's just you holding out, Thea."

"Right." She ran her hands through her hair. "What are we talking about again?"

"The *party*. David's brother just moved in with that girl he met, I guess they're pretty serious." Seria looked like she was telling Thea about a military strike team she was assembling. "David asked me to invite you both, just so there's more people he knows."

So he can stare at my tits, you mean. Thea groaned inwardly but managed to keep a nice, normal look on her face. A whole night of David Kanmore leering at her didn't appeal. But the idea of spending her night either alone in her car, or in that house… that was worse.

"I'll need to borrow some clothes."

"I have some that will fit you…"

"You have some *jeans* that will fit me." Thea corrected her. This was an argument of long standing between them.

"You can wear my shirts!"

"I can, but *you* can't after I have." Thea looked down then back up meaningfully, enjoying herself just a bit too much.

"Okay, okay, enough. Thea, you can use our washer/dryer to get whatever you need clean. Seri, tell David we'll be there." Joe stood up. "I have to get to work and then I have classes." It was just how it was in their family – after Seria and Joe's parents died, Thea's parents had taken care of them for a while, before *Thea's* mom had died. Everyone died young, everyone pulled together.

The death of Gregory Mendel had affected Seria and Joe almost more than it had Thea. He'd made sure they kept their parents' house, that the bills were paid and they finished school. How could she tell them that the man they'd relied on for years had been a broken, drunken ruin when they weren't there to see it?

She couldn't. They were the only real family she had left. They had other cousins, Nana Rafiela had been married three times and had a host of kids, but they were scattered all over New England and they didn't know them well. They were who she had. As much as she might enjoy tweaking Seria's nose, she didn't want to *hurt* her cousin.

"All right." She sagged a little. "On the condition that you stop telling Scott to keep trying, Seri. I mean it, okay? It's not going to happen."

"All right, all right." Seria held up her hands. Getting her way often put her in a better mood. "I have some shirts you might like in the closet in my room, and that pair of jeans I *know* you like because you keep stealing them."

"I borrowed them once."

"Three times."

"Like I said before, so far up in my business." Seria hugged her, an impulsive thing, and Thea hugged back. Joe was smiling, as always secretly sure he was behind everything. Sometimes Thea wondered if he was right.

"You can use the shower too." Seri added.

"Subtle."

"Why don't you go use it now?"

"You're lucky we're family." Thea mock-swatted Seria on the shoulder. But the truth was, a shower sounded amazing.

*

Thomas usually didn't sleep very well.

The sound of the crash ripped him out of sleep. He sat in bed blinking, sweating, looking around.

He was always surprised at how *loud* it was. He'd been sleeping in the back seat. He'd been asleep when the car jostled hard to the side.

A nurse told him that his seat belt had saved his life.

Half awake, he only saw fragments, flashes. The dull sound of impact as the driver side door caved in. The screeching of tires trying and failing to hold onto the road. The frame of the car crumpling around them. His mother's voice. Then the sound of the car plowing full into a pole, and then...

The dream always ended there. He'd hit his head on the roof of the car as it collapsed while the car twisted up around them, an empty beer can crushed by a drunk. The other car that had slid into them must have fled the scene. No one saw it.

If a passing car hadn't stopped, he would be dead. They told him that often, too. They seemed to like telling him how lucky he was.

He was living in a house made empty by their lack. It was a white Cape Cod style with plastic siding that his father had just replaced that year. They'd owned the house free and clear, no mortgage, and so now he owned it. He owned the house, and the contents therein. The farm, too, the last remaining bit of his grandfather, that was his now. He had everything of theirs but them.

Eventually he'd have to sell something, or get a job. And getting a job would interfere with the serious drinking he was doing.

Plus the reading. The reading was important.

The reading was going to fix everything.

He lay in bed after the dream and replayed the events in memory, trying for a glimpse of the other car. But there was nothing. He'd been asleep, and he'd missed it, and now his parents were dead and he didn't even know who'd killed them.

He staggered out of their bedroom. Down the stairs to the ground floor, into the bathroom to empty his bladder. His mouth so dry and sticky that he drank a glass of water after.

The house echoed. Every sound he made came back to him.

Neither of his parents had family to speak of – his mother's parents had both died within a couple months of each other, his father's mother the year before her husband. He could remember Grandfather Tom-Tom visiting when he'd been much younger, but not the exact circumstances of his death. He drank another glass of water after washing his hands, desperately tired of the taste of his mouth.

In order to keep the savings and the insurance settlement lasting as long as he could he'd taken to leaving the lights off as much as possible. The heat was set low, too, because he didn't want to try and replace the oil in the furnace. He knew he would have to around January, figured he'd worry about it when it happened.

He walked into the living room and looked at the tree standing in the corner. He'd left it up. It was plastic, it wasn't going to rot, and all the tinsel and colored glass globes helped him pretend it had never happened. It was October now. In less than two months it would be a year, but he refused to accept that. He hadn't tried everything yet.

Stumbling in the kitchen he remembered helping his father put up the island, the garbage disposal and stove top. He'd had to learn some wiring to help with it. His father's large hands as he wrapped black tape around the end of a junction. His mother's voice in the background.

He tried to remember it but it turned into her screaming again.

He walked to the fridge and pulled out a bottle of cheap beer. He wasn't old enough to buy beer, but he was big enough and the scar on his face made him look older. It wasn't that bad, considering they'd had to cut him out of the car with torches. Could have been a lot worse.

That was another thing people loved to tell him.

After he drank the beer he dropped and started the push ups. Aside from his face, he was in good shape. The rhythm of the exercise let him drift, almost mindless.

He stopped the push ups once his arms started to go rubber on him.

He was sweating, so he walked around and let the air coming in the windows cool him down. His neighbors had stolen the TV and VCR after his parents' death announcement. He'd been in the hospital. They'd kept him for a week because of his unresponsiveness for lingering damage. It had just been him not wanting to talk. What was there to talk about?

Sometimes he thought about going next door and getting his TV back. He didn't care that much, though. He'd seen the looks on their faces when he'd come back to the house. He'd always hated the Whatleys. They liked to brag about coming from old stock.

The knock on the door told him time had gotten away from him.

The door squealed when he opened it, another sign that he needed to start working to maintain it. Bishop was smiling. Taller than he was by an inch, which made him *very* tall, but narrower.

"Interesting choice of outfits."

"I just got up."

"It's six PM."

"Thank you." He stepped back and let Bishop come in. "There's beer in the fridge if you want one."

Bishop smiled and headed over. "You going to at least shower?"

"Probably should. Entertain yourself, then."

"Oh, how will I choose with so many options?" Bishop gestured to the empty living room attached to the kitchen. Or maybe it was the den, or dining room, he barely remembered.

He took a cold shower. He *had* hot water, but he chose not to use it. He enjoyed the way the water made his teeth chatter and his body shudder. It made him focus on something aside from the leaden feeling that enveloped him most of the time. He scrubbed with a bar of Lava his father had left behind, washed his hair with shampoo he didn't even bother to look at. He'd likely smell like fruit or flowers afterwards.

He tied a towel around his waist and walked out to find Bishop going through the pile of books he kept in the living room.

"*Three Famous Alchemists*, huh?"

"Famous for their time anyway."

"Weren't you a history major?"

"That's history." He didn't bother to correct Bishop. His major hardly mattered now. "Going to go get some clothes on."

"You don't have to hurry on my account."

"That would be more flattering if you were even a little choosy."

"I have excellent taste." He decided to let Bishop be smug and headed down the stairs. They creaked and groaned and he knew he should probably fix them. His parents had meant to get around to it.

He had more clothes than he knew what to do with now, all of his father's clothing as well as his own. He could wear most of his dad's shirts, at least. He usually chose not to. He threw on a black long-sleeved T-shirt with a cartoon skull on the front and a pair of black jeans. His hair was getting long again after they'd shaved him in the hospital. He missed having hair long enough to be harassed for it.

"So. Where are you dragging me?"

"It's a party." Bishop smiled. "Karen Aubry, remember her?"

"The girl in our CW class who turned in her fucking diary?"

"She moved out to Warwick, shacked up with a guy and she's having a housewarming thing. Kind of a Halloween party, but no costumes." Bishop saw the look on his face and barreled on. "Look, you're coming. You spend way too much fucking time getting drunk and hiding in this place. You need to get out into the world again."

"Sure. Whatever." He shrugged. Went to his closet and pulled out his leather jacket. They'd handed it to him as he left the hospital. It had been in the trunk, a Christmas present. *Merry Christmas, Son.*

He wore it a lot, even when it was too warm out. Tonight was October 30th, though. It would be fine.

He followed Bishop out to his car and made himself get inside. Strapped on the seat belt. Didn't scream. Told himself everything would be fine.

Didn't believe it.

Chapter Two

Drive Me Crazy

Bishop noted how stiff his friend was the whole ride. He deliberately avoided taking Route 10 to get to Warwick, even though that meant taking longer to get to 95, because while he thought that the whole '*living in the house of his dead parents and wallowing*' thing was unhealthy, he sure didn't want to stab him in his bad memories.

Getting him in a car at all was a minor miracle.

They'd first met at the William Blackstone library. Bishop was from money, a rich family living in Barrington. He didn't even know what his grandfather had *done* for the money, he just grew up with it. It wasn't until he'd gone to Blackstone that he'd realized that the way he'd grown up wasn't typical. Even now it was hard to remember. He'd tried to offer money a few times, lift some of the burden and let his strange friend keep his house, but so far all his overtures had been rebuffed.

"So I thought you and Aubry had a thing?" Bishop turned his head slightly, just enough to look at his friend in the mirror while keeping his eyes on the road.

"We did. It was nice. But she wanted permanence and I didn't." He shrugged, taking the exit off 95. "You were in London that year." Bishop didn't say *she was my rebound girl* because he sure as hell didn't want to get into who he'd been rebounding from.

"I told you that you should have taken that program."

"I don't like plays."

"I didn't either, until I saw them performed properly." He leaned back against the headrest and muttered softly to himself. Bishop could only make out a little of it. "...upon us, O King."

"You ever talk to that Delphy girl again?"

"I never have."

"Ever thought about it?"

"I have not." He didn't sound like he was lying. Sometimes Bishop had to work very hard to try and understand his friend. In a way, it was the first thing in his life that *hadn't* come easily to him. Born rich, tall and good looking, with a ready smile and, if he said so himself, a talent for reading people, Bishop rarely had to extend much effort to get what he wanted.

Then he remembered Evvie, the one who'd taught him that could be a bad thing.

"Well, maybe you'll meet someone tonight."

"I suspect I'll meet several people tonight, since I barely know Karen and don't know her boyfriend at all."

"Not what I meant."

"I'm ignoring what you meant." He tossed his head side to side, popping the joints in his neck. Bishop took the hint and let him alone for a bit.

After swinging around TF Green. they turned into the residential neighborhoods of Warwick. Same as most other cities and towns in the postage stamp sized state. Bishop hadn't realized how much growing up there had affected him until he'd gone out to California and realized people there thought nothing of a two hour commute to work.

In Rhode Island, a two hour drive put you an hour into another state. RI was less like a modern American state and more like a Greek city-state, run by a few powerful personalities, steeped in corruption below the surface, but small enough that you felt like you knew everybody. Even though there were over a million people all told and you couldn't possibly.

There were several cars lined up and down the street, parked in front of a nice little raised ranch style house. Probably a rental. The whole neighborhood likely dated back to WWII, when people were gobbling up local farmland to build as many houses as possible. Bishop had listened to his father sneer enough times about it. You'd think the concept of a Levittown was a personal affront to the Kramer family. The lights were on and he could already see people standing around and even dancing in front of a picture window.

Look at us, trying to pretend we're all grown up.

"We're here."

"Good, I was afraid you'd gotten lost and just taken us to some *other* party." The car groaned as they got out of it. Neither of them were small men. Bishop led the charge, of course, smiling and greeting people as they walked up to the front door.

"Karen, hey!" He wrapped her up in a hug. For some reason Bishop could just *hug* people. No one ever seemed to mind.

"Hey, Bish!" She turned to a man only an inch or so taller than her, wearing expensive looking thin-framed glasses. "Kevin Kanmore, this is Bishop Kramer, he and I went to WBC together."

"Nice to meet you." Kevin shook Bishop's hand. Behind Bishop, leather jacket squealing, Thomas did his level best to be ignored. It was often very easy to hide in Bishop's shadow.

"It is, isn't it? I'm amazing, everyone should get to meet me." Bishop laughed politely to make it clear he was kidding. "Thanks for the invite, Karen. You look great, cohabitating agrees with you."

Sensing this was going to go on for a while, he made his way around the knot of conversation and looked for beer. It wasn't hard to find – there were several people standing around holding bottles or cans, so he walked into the kitchen and sure enough there were several coolers. He fished a Miller out, looked at it with distaste, and then shrugged and opened it with his thumb.

"Neat trick, man."

He turned his head and focused on the speaker. He looked like the host of the party, but taller, broader. Almost Bishop's build, nearly Thomas' height but much lighter. Something about him set the teeth on edge even though he was trying to be friendly.

"They're twist tops. They want to come off."

"Sure sure." He was wearing a T-shirt with different colored sleeves and collar, what people called a baseball T. He reached into the cooler and pulled out a beer. "You got any weed, man?"

This question always pissed Thomas off. He'd skipped weed. Even when his dorm mates had offered, he'd never gotten much out of it. But people asked him fairly often, usually ignorant people, and his already low estimation of green sleeves T dropped another set of notches.

"Don't touch the stuff."

"Shit, I was hoping. My girl's coming and I wanted something to hopefully loosen her up a little. I'm David." The prospective pot enthusiast reached out a hand and he forced himself to shake it, not wanting to make a scene yet. He really only had the one friend left. He didn't want to lose Bishop because he'd snapped and beaten someone unconscious. "You a friend of Kevin's? He's my bro."

"I went to school with Karen."

"So, you sure you can't help me out?" The urge to just put his hand around the man's neck and drive his face hard into the refrigerator was getting intense. "It would really be a service."

"Afraid not." His neck was twitching.

"Daaavid." A girl with long black hair and blue eyes forced her way into the kitchen and put her arms around baseball T's neck, apparently very glad to see him. She was much prettier than the asshole deserved, in his estimation. Thomas took advantage of the distraction to snag another beer and make his way out of the kitchen as unobtrusively as possible.

"Hey babe."

"Who was your friend?" She was staring up into his eyes. If David Kanmore had been much for contemplation he might have wondered if he and Seria were on the same wavelength about their relationship, but he barely realized he was *in* a relationship. Part of the reason he'd wanted pot was the hopes he could get Seria and her cousin Thea stoned and see about moving things in a certain direction.

David Kanmore was nothing if not an optimist. He certainly wasn't a realist.

"Just someone Kev's girl went to school with. Where's Thea? And Joe, did he come?" David didn't really care if Seria's brother came, but he didn't want to just ask about Thea.

"Joe dropped me off. Thea insisted on driving her own car." Seria rolled her eyes. David had been subject to her complaints about her cousin over the past year, but he'd managed to keep them from dampening his enthusiasm for The Plan. He'd first conceived The Plan over the summer, before Thea's dad had passed.

"You want a beer?"

"I'm not much for beer. Maybe they have a wine cooler?" Seria's blue eyes caught the overhead light, and David moved to fetch that wine cooler for her. *Definitely need to get the two of them together.*

Joe and Thea had met up on the front steps and come in together. The house wasn't very large and there was already a significant crush of people, so they looked at each other.

"I'm going for the kitchen."

"I'm going to... mingle, I guess?" Thea shrugged. "Come look for me if you can't find her."

There was something strange about a house party where everyone was an adult. A certain furtiveness was lost when everybody was of age and the house belonged to the people actually throwing the party and not their parents. She had no idea if it was a rental or if they'd actually bought the place. Since she was in the market to offload her father's house, she found herself curious about it. She'd already been told she'd likely have to dump some money into her place just to sell it, which was a problem, as she didn't currently have a job.

I can always go work retail again. She'd quit her job at Ann & Hope the day after her father died. They would have let her take time off, but she knew there was no point to continuing, she wasn't going to be in any shape to work for a while. She'd graduated from Pilgrim that year, and she hadn't decided yet if she should try going to Reject or not. She certainly wasn't likely to find the money for anything better. Seria and Joe were both in college already, of course. Her father had still been functional when the time had come to get *them* placed.

She tried not to resent him for dying but it was hard. Being around so many people drinking and chattering on about their lives made her uneasy. It was as if he'd taken her entire future when he died. Now she didn't know what to do.

Not to mention the visits. She was *not* going to think about them.

She ended up outside, letting the air bite at her a little. It was 30 degrees according to Joe, who was compulsive about paying attention to forecasts. Her bare arms were pebbling up, and she was glad Seria and David were nowhere around because if she'd had to put up with David staring at her nipples she'd have punched him in the face. *Why* did he have to be so fucking creepy about it? Other people looked at her and it didn't bother her. She even liked how she looked; the black top suited her.

There were a few other people out in the yard. It was a fairly big yard, the kind that would have made sense with a pool in it. They'd rigged up some lights, and people were finding corners to do what people always did at parties, chat, cop feels, maybe get a little further.

And she was there alone.

"Hey, look who it is." She looked up, surprised as a familiar face stepped out of the house. He had a tepid little smile on, the same way he always got around her now. She fought back the urge to flee.

"Scotty." She'd managed to avoid Scott ever since what she liked to call *her moment of weakness*. It was cold, but what was she supposed to say? "Didn't know you'd be here."

"Oh yeah, Seri told me about it last week."

"That makes sense." *I am going to murder you, Seri.* She knew it was likely Seria had forgotten, but it was still her meddling and now Thea was stuck, there was nothing for it but to barrel through once he got started. *I should have just started sleeping in my car earlier.*

"So, uhm, I…" Scott swallowed. "I haven't seen you since… well, that night."

"No."

Silence between them corded with the tension of not speaking. Thea could hear the sounds of the party washing out from the house – the bass of the music muffled by walls, hushed conversations in the dark. She wanted this not to happen, felt like she was watching a plane crash. Scott's face, the firm jaw, topaz eyes, the ginger hair and beard. He was a handsome man, a lot of the girls in their class had a thing for Scott. She wished she did. It would all have been so much easier if she had.

"Did I do something? I didn't…"

"You didn't." She felt a hot rush of air and realized she'd been holding her breath. "I shouldn't have called you that night."

"I was glad you did." He stepped a bit closer. She knew he wanted to touch her, was so relieved when he didn't. "You sounded messed up."

"I was. I guess I still am. But I still shouldn't have called you. Much less let you stay over."

"Why not? I wanted to." Scott's face was all edges and angles in the faint light, she wished the moon wasn't behind trees. "I thought…"

"I know. I know, I *knew* what you were thinking at the time. But I was scared and lonely and miserable and I wanted a night's sleep and not to be alone. Can you understand that? That it wasn't to hurt you? Because I didn't want that, I don't want that." She looked him full in the face, trying to decide what the kindest thing would be.

"I just thought we…"

"There's no we." She hated how her mouth felt saying that. "There's no us. There can't be. It's not what I want, and I never should have let you think it was."

And there it was. The flickering across his face, the pain that she'd given him. Part of him had seen it coming, that made it worse.

"Why?"

"Because it's not there."

"It seemed there that night."

"Did it? Really?" It would have been nice to just cover her face in her hands so she didn't have to look at him while she said these things. "Scotty, you've been one of my only friends for three years. *Three.* Did I ever show the slightest interest in you that way? The whole time I dated Karl, after we broke up, *any* of the people I've seen since? If I wanted to be with you, I would have said something."

"Sometimes..." He actually shuddered and she knew this was probably the first time in Scott's life he didn't get something he wanted. He didn't know how to cope with this. "Sometimes people don't know how they feel right away. I didn't...I wasn't, when you were with Karl I never even thought..."

"I'm sorry." She made sure to keep meeting his eyes. "I don't feel that way about you. I'm never going to. I'm not even looking..." Over his shoulder she saw movement and her eyes went to it. In the dark, a man was standing up against the fence, his hands on the metal. He was staring up at the sky.

If he hadn't turned his head at that moment, she would have looked back to Scott. She meant to do that. But he did, lowering his head and scanning the yard as if looking for someone.

Thea could take in a person very quickly. She'd always been good at it. This man was tall, broad, arms and legs like tree trunks, a chest you could project a film on. Black leather jacket, black shirt, jeans a little frayed at the knees. A face that managed to look hard and soft at the same time, a square jaw, a scar on the left side of his face.

None of that mattered. It was just details, filed away. It was the eyes that went through her, caught her there and held. They were astonishing.

Thea had gone swimming a few times in Narragansett Bay, late at night. In certain places, you'd go in the water in the dark and there would be green sparks underwater, algae glowing and swirling around you as you swept into the dark. She remembered seeing her arms orbited by trails of bright green.

His eyes were that color, that bright sea green, huge and staring right into hers. She could see pain, loss, that emptiness that comes from so much fear that you can't feel anything anymore. She knew that look. She fought that look every day.

"Thea?" Scott's voice. She turned just enough to see his face while keeping her attention focused on those eyes over his shoulder.

*

Thomas finished his second beer, just as piss poor as the last, and left it on a table before walking outside. He didn't feel drunk. He hadn't actually felt drunk in months.

Why am I drinking if I don't get drunk?

He couldn't delude himself – he wasn't achieving anything by drinking. He certainly wasn't being a Dionysian visionary or even just getting buzzed. He was mostly just wasting his time.

The stars were hard to see with the light from the airport washing them out, but every so often a plane would fly overhead and those were almost as good. He watched a couple land and one take off.

Nothing matters. Nothing works. I can't... He hadn't tried everything yet. There was still one way he could try and fix it. He was just afraid. He'd been afraid ever since the idea came to him, and every mark he'd cut into the felt on the table had done nothing to ease it.

You can't even get drunk right. You slept through the accident. You've done nothing but read and drink for a whole fucking year. That wasn't entirely true. He'd spent a lot of time lifting weights, doing pushups, anything to exhaust himself.

There were no planes overhead. A few stars. He stared at those instead. None of it mattered.

If it doesn't matter why don't you just go home and get it over with?

Because I'm afraid. He hated to admit that, but he was. Afraid, alone, a year down the road and no solution, nothing but their absence. They were gone, and he was...

He looked away from the sky.

There were people around. He hadn't noticed them when he'd come out. He swept his eyes over the yard, his usual paranoia, and there she was.

If she had walked up to him and slapped him he might have been less surprised. There was a man there talking to her, he noticed this, but it didn't matter to him at all. She had eyes like a glacier calving into the sea, a blue that was almost white.

It felt inevitable. Like an answer to the question he'd been afraid to ask.

He was moving before he knew he was going to.

*

Three things went through Thea's mind.

Oh my God he's coming over followed by *Oh my God I want him to come over* and then *Oh my God I have to get rid of Scott now.* He was standing there, looking hurt and confused and she had no idea how to get him to go away.

Yes, Mendel, by all means chat up some stranger right in front of the guy who has a thing for you.

I didn't ask for Scott to decide he could save me. I don't want to be saved.

"So... that's it?"

She worked her mouth, trying to think of what else she could possibly say. Words came tumbling out.

"Yes, that's it. I can say I'm sorry again, and I am sorry. I'm sorry that I fucked up. But I'm not going to pretend. Ever. For anyone."

Another very long moment. Behind him, the man with the eyes was walking in their direction. He wasn't in a hurry about it. She wondered if he was waiting to see if Scott left. She wondered if he knew she was waiting for that.

Scott sighed, looked away.

"Yeah. Okay." He made a sound that might have been what was left of a laugh after you ripped all the humor out. "Well, I find myself single at a party. Guess I should go in, mingle."

"Guess you should." She tried very hard not to sound relieved. Some of it leaked through. "I'll be out here. Even with the airport you can see some stars."

He bobbed his head and walked off, preserving as much dignity as possible. She didn't watch.

What the hell am I doing? She turned to face those eyes, now out of the shadows of the trees, almost luminous in the light from the steadily climbing moon.

"Hi."

"Hey." He nodded, his hair shifting in the faint breeze. It was getting colder out, and she decided to blame the gooseflesh on her arms on that. "I didn't mean to interrupt."

"You didn't. I wanted that to be over." She held out her hand. "I'm Thea."

"Thomas." His hand touched hers and they both stared at each other, eyes locked together, unmoving. He managed to let go with an act of will. She wished he hadn't.

"Look at them often?"

"More now." He was craning his neck. It was a hell of a neck. "Had a telescope when I was a kid."

"See any interesting ones?"

"Well, there's Camelopardalis, over there." He pointed.

"Most of it's too faint to see like this. Too much light from around us. You could just see it from my grandfather's place."

"Seriously? You pick a giraffe to show me?"

"It's the one that came to mind."

"I have no idea why I'm here."

"Meaning the party or…"

"Either, but the party most of all. My cousin is dating the brother of the guy whose house this is. Somehow she got me to come."

"Ah. I think I saw her inside, in the kitchen." He grinned. "No offense but her boyfriend's a turd."

"None taken." She smiled back. "I'm not a fan."

"Not much for parties?"

"Not even a little fucking bit. What's there to do but drink and talk to strangers?" She pushed her hair back out of her face. "Yet here I am."

"You look cold."

"I am." She considered this. "Just a little."

"Here." He took off his coat, put it around her shoulders. There was a moment when her thumb brushed the back of his hand and they both almost locked up again, but she managed to get it under control and got the jacket on.

"You don't need it?"

"I never get cold."

"Suit yourself." It held a lingering trace of body warmth and the faint smell of sweat, not unpleasant, just very present. "So how'd you end up at this?"

"I went to school with the woman your cousin's boyfriend's brother is dating." He was looking at the back of his hand now. "I guess she's graduating this spring. That's when I was supposed to."

"Supposed to?"

"I took a leave of absence." She liked looking at his mouth, at the way the scar curled up to just graze his upper lip. He had surprisingly nice lips, just slightly curved. "Couldn't make myself go back."

"I keep trying to figure out if I'm going to go, myself. I just graduated high school."

He was staring and he knew it. She was beautiful, and that of course affected him. He wasn't dead, as so many people had helpfully informed him. But there had been other beautiful women over the past year try and talk to him, from Claire to Evvie. And he'd hadn't felt this *nervous* around any of them.

"You're at least eighteen, right?" She laughed at that.

"I'll be nineteen in a month." She gave him another once over. Without the jacket she could see his arms. She wondered what he looked like without the shirt. "You're what, twenty?"

"Twenty-one." He considered. "I'll *be* twenty-one. In two months."

"So there you go, although maybe you're getting ahead of yourself there."

"Never too early to be sure of things."

"And are you? Sure of things?"

"Sure of your age, that's one thing. The rest? No. Not sure at all." People were milling around in the dark, trying to find good places to be alone, or just not to be seen. The light from the party washed out over them in various colors, orange and red and green. "I wonder if Bishop has met anyone yet?"

"Bishop?"

"Friend of mine. He's appointed himself my keeper."

"You need one?"

"I'm bumming him out. You know how people are. We're friends so he thinks he has to fix me."

"Does he?"

"I don't think so." They were looking at each other again, the pretense of the starry night forgotten. "What about you? If you don't like drinking and you don't like talking to strangers…"

"I guess it's not that different. Something bad happened and Seri thinks she can mother-slash-nag me into getting over it." She took a half step closer to him, wondering if he wanted his jacket back. "But I have to put up with it."

"Have to?"

"She and Joe are my last family. Well, there's my Nana

Rafiela, but she's practically the Loch Ness Monster for all I ever see her. My dad had a brother, but I barely know him, and I get the sense he didn't approve of my mom, and by extension, me."

"Both my parents were only children."

They were touching now. She didn't know when that had happened, but her head was against his shoulder. *You don't know him, you don't know him at all, you just met him Thea.* The voice of Thea's conscience often sounded like Seria. It was accurate. She didn't know him. He could be a maniac, or a...

She felt him shake, just a little.

"Cold?"

"No." He shook again. "Not used to talking this much." His hand came up and he was wiping at his eyes. "How long?"

"My mom died when I was twelve. My dad was late July. Everyone thinks he drank himself to death."

"You don't."

"No, I don't. Oh, he did drink. Way, way too much. Had been for years. But he was functional, which was worse. Harder to see. He was... Seria and Joe pretend like they're fine, but they're *not*. He raised them, he was as much their father as he was mine, and he's gone and... they didn't *see* him. He was *Uncle Greg*, he couldn't do wrong to them. I saw it, I saw it all, he *wanted* it." She swallowed to keep from spitting.

He had no idea when he'd put his arm around her waist, just holding her, listening to her talk.

"They wouldn't believe me if I told them. You wouldn't, either." He knew what she wanted him to say. But he didn't quite say it yet.

"I don't know if I would or not." He closed his eyes.

"All right." She shifted in his arms and now the top of her head was resting against his throat. "My mother killed my father."

She waited for the questions. When she'd tried to explain it to Scott that night, he'd just stared at her and told her it was a nightmare. Seria had dismissed it as hysterical babbling. Joe just humored her. *Your mom died six years ago, Thea, it was just a bad dream.*

"How'd she do it?"

She turned to look up at him. He looked interested, a little curious.

"She can appear. Some nights, not all nights. I can see her. Dad couldn't unless he was drunk. So... he drank more. Like I said, he wanted it. She would... go to him."

"Some nights. Were their nights *he* could see her, but you couldn't?"

"Maybe? He didn't tell me, I just saw it." She watched the muscle twitch in his jaw. He was considering it. Turning it around in his head.

"When did you first start seeing her? Immediately after she died?"

"A year later, I think? Seri was still with us, but she never saw her. Or if she did she did a job on herself to make sure she wouldn't remember." Thea finally had to ask. "Usually people blow me off way before this point."

"I've seen a few things." He was looking full into her eyes. "Christmas day, last year. My parents took me out to dinner, I'd just gotten back into the country. Spent a year abroad studying. Theatre. It was an excuse to live in England for a year. I was asleep. The car got hit, driven into a guard railing, they were both killed. I was in the back seat. Car wrapped around me. Everyone said I should have died too, that it was a miracle."

She didn't say *I'm sorry*, just as he hadn't said it to her.

"The day I woke up was January 1st. They'd been dead since the 25th. And they were in my room." He wiped again at his face. "So, maybe you're wrong, maybe you're hallucinating, but I'm not going to just say *no, it didn't happen* just off the bat."

"Thank you." They were facing each other now. His arms were around her waist. Hers were around his back. It felt comfortable, like she'd known him for years.

He swallowed, unable to believe what he was about to suggest. Finally he forced the words out.

"Do you want to see if we can find out for sure? I should warn you. It's going to be weird."

Her eyes, the light blue that looked almost white in the starlight, narrowed.

But she nodded.

*

Seria Rafiela was starting to get tired of several things.

One, she was tired of Thea's attitude. Uncle Greg's death had hit her hard. Her own parents had died when she was ten, Aunt Paola when she was fourteen. Even after she and Joe had moved out, Seria had depended on Uncle Greg. He was a steady, comforting presence in her life, he'd listened to her complain about school and work and boys and now he was gone and Seria just wanted someone to talk to about it.

He wasn't your father, though.

He was close enough. Thea acted like she was fine, like she'd expected it all along, and that made Seria furious. If he was that far gone and Thea knew it, why hadn't she told them? They could have dumped his booze out, or tried to get him some help, or…

She didn't know, of course. But something, she could have done something. It was starting to claw away at her. Everyone she loved died. Her mother, her father, Aunt Paola, now Uncle Greg… and Thea acting like nothing bothered her, Joe more and more off in his head.

Second was David.

She was struggling with what she and David were. Watching him in the kitchen, holding court with people she didn't know, his hand around her waist she remembered the good times – that year the two of them worked together at Rocky Point, making love for the first time in his car on her sixteenth birthday, the ups and downs of a relationship that had survived this long. They were both twenty, it had been five years, surely it meant something.

He stares at Thea.

She watched him laugh at something, the way his face lined when he smiled. He was still very handsome. He'd always been handsome, dark hair, a smile that lit up his face, tan and dark eyed.

He had a way of putting all of his attention on you when you spoke to him, it had always made Seria feel special. Less so lately, though.

Not just Thea, either.

She sipped her wine cooler and then saw Joe talking in the corner of the living room, across a sea of heads. Joe was a little taller than her, a little shorter than Thea, and for whatever reason the two girls had somehow come to the conclusion that Joe needed to be protected from the world. Right now he seemed to be…

"Hey, Davy?"

"Yeah?" David turned one of those smiles on her, the kind that would have melted her a year before. She didn't know why it didn't anymore.

"I'm gonna go check on Joey. I'll be right back."

"Okay. I'll be here." He kissed her, and that still made her tingle. David was a very good kisser. There was a bit of a bounce to her step weaving through the crowd to get to Joe. He looked up and saw her just as she got around a pack of girls earnestly discussing rent in Providence vs. Warwick.

"Hey, baby brother."

"Seri." He kissed her on the cheek and put his arm around her shoulder, drawing her in. It was the one thing she and Joe had always had, and why she worried so much about Thea – No matter what, she and Joe had each other, they were twins. "This is my formidable sister, Seria. Seri, this is Bishop. Apparently he and Karen used to date."

"*Dating* is a bit strong." Bishop was very tall, taller even than David, with a broad smile full of perfect teeth and blond hair and beard messy in the way that takes money to arrange. "We spent some time together, that's all. She seems very happy now though."

"Kevin's a nice guy." Seria didn't really know David's older brother all that well – they didn't run in the same circles and he was a year or two older than she was – but he'd always been polite.

"One of the Kanmores had to be." Joe said.

"Hey!"

"Seri, you know I love you." Joe was looking over his sister's head into the kitchen, where her boyfriend was expending a lot of effort to entertain a group of mostly women. It made him scowl. "Before we get into an argument, have you seen Thea? I lost her once we got here."

"I was just going to ask."

"Does she look a lot like you two, very dark hair, blue eyes, a bit taller than either of you?" Bishop said, covering the lower half of his face with his hand but not quite concealing a grin.

"Yeah, why?" Seria turned her head to see where he was looking. Sure enough, there was Thea, coming in from the backyard. She was wearing a leather jacket that was significantly too big for her, which wasn't the part that had Seria surprised. Thea's approach to clothing was *'I can get it on, good enough'* at the best of times.

No, what had Seria surprised was that Thea was holding a man's hand.

He was massive. She didn't know if she'd ever seen a man that size in real life, he looked to be almost twice as broad across as Bishop. He wasn't attractive, exactly, but he had presence. A quality Thea shared, really. People were moving out of their way without either of them having to say anything. Thea's face was grim, her eyes challenging people to say anything, and Seria noted that she at no point let go of his hand.

Thea is holding a boy's hand.

This was not something Seria had ever seen in her life. Thea was leading him and scanning the room, and her grim look went almost mutinous when she saw her cousins and started heading their way.

It was Bishop who spoke up first.

"Hey, look at *you*, you forget you're supposed to be brooding?"

"Stick to the life of the idle rich, comedy isn't your thing."

"You going to introduce me?"

"Hadn't planned on it."

"My best friend, ladies and gentlemen." Bishop made a sound, a pleased snort. He turned to Thea. "You'd be Thea? Your cousins here have already let your name slip."

"And you'd be his self-appointed keeper, Bishop."

"I am the bitter name." He nodded. Neither Seria nor Joe had managed to put words together at this point, so Thea turned to them.

"We're taking off."

"You… I mean, where?" Joe tried to act like this was something that happened and that he wasn't desperately curious.

"We're going to the house." Thea turned to Seria. "Don't."

"I didn't do anything!"

"Good." She softened incrementally, kissed her cousin on the cheek. "I know. But I'll be okay."

"You going to be okay for a ride home?" Bishop asked.

"She'll take me home." He looked to her for confirmation and she nodded. "You can always drop by tomorrow and make sure she didn't bury me in a shallow grave somewhere."

"If you go that route, my advice is to use a backhoe. Ground is hard to break up when it gets this cold." Thomas clasped hands with Bishop, nodded to Joe and Seria, and was out the door following Thea before anyone else could say anything.

She broke out into bright, musical laughter as they walked down the street to her car. He immediately wanted to listen to that, wanted to hear her laugh again.

"I think you actually managed to stump my cousin."

"Which one?"

"Seri. Joe… he always keeps to himself until he's sure of what he wants to say, but Seri usually jumps right in with the interrogation." She had her keys out and was popping open the lock on an old Honda CR-X. He looked at it dubiously. There were a *lot* of books in the back, some he recognized – A.E. Waite's *Book of Ceremonial Magic*, Colin Wilson's *The Occult* – and others he didn't.

"Interesting books. What's that one?" He pointed to one named *The Archaic Revival.*

"Terence McKenna. Hurry up, get in, we can compare reading later."

"I am not going to fit in this."

"Sure you will. Just not comfortably." She got in the car, leaned over and popped the lock on the passenger door. "Slide the seat back before you try and get in."

It was a cramped fit but he did manage to get in. The car didn't actually have a back seat, so there was only so far for him to go. He was definitely uncomfortable. How much of that was the car versus her, he wasn't sure.

The little CR-X pulled out with a bit of a groan of protest, or perhaps he just imagined it.

"So where are you from?" She was watching the road. It was easier to talk to him when she couldn't see him.

"Family house is in Cranston. My grandfather's farm is on Wolfshead, out in the bay."

"You're a farm boy?"

"Spent summers there. Did a lot of chores. Wouldn't actually say I was a farm kid." He looked out the window. They swung onto Post Road, and he watched headlights and tail lights without much thinking about it. "You said you went to Pilgrim?"

"Yeah. You... Cranston East?"

"Yeah. How'd you know?"

"You're not a big enough shithead to come from West." She laughed again. "Never met anyone from West who wasn't a total Guido."

"Aren't you half Italian?"

"Who isn't? I bet you are."

"My dad was. I'm more like a quarter." He smiled. "My mom called me a Heinz 57. I'm a little of everything."

"I'm Russian and Italian." They swung off of Post Road and ended up in another residential neighborhood, he had no real idea where. Eventually they pulled up to a nice little house, in better repair than his own. He noted she didn't pull into the driveway, where an old Ford pickup sat.

"My dad's truck." She was busy shutting the car down, her tone brisk. "Haven't found a buyer yet."

Both his back and the Honda groaned in relief when he got out of the car. He followed her up the walk, and noticed without paying too much attention how her hand was shaking. He wanted to offer her reassurance, but didn't want to push himself on her. Too many people did that to him.

Chapter Three

The Phantom World

Inside, the house smelled that particular brand of stale that came from a person barely living in it. He'd snapped after four months and done a clean. That seemed to be his limit. Hers wasn't as bad as his had been at three months, she could probably go longer.

"I haven't slept here in…" She was counting backwards in her head. "Two months."

"Where do you sleep?"

"Mostly my car." She shrugged, put her keys in her pocket. "So what now?" She took his jacket off, hung it on a hook near the front door.

Inside she was screaming at herself. It was the middle of the night, less than an hour till Halloween and she'd brought a man she didn't know to her house hoping… what? That her mother's ghost would appear? She *wanted* that now?

"Where's your kitchen?"

"You're hungry?"

"Yes, but that's not why I asked."

"This way." She led him in, flicked on the light. Was a little relieved it still worked. Had she remembered to pay the bills this month? Maybe Seria did it. It was a faded yellow kitchen, Thea had no idea who'd picked out the color or what it had looked like new. At present it was washed out, like a daisy held up to the sun. He looked around, found the large round salt container and shook it in his hand.

"Salt?"

"Yeah." There was a lot of room in the kitchen, it was designed around an open plan and as a result there was never enough counter. Her father had died where the dining table had been, so she'd made Joe help her throw that out – she didn't know if she should tell him that or not.

She watched as he walked right to where the table had been and dropped down to his haunches.

"What're you doing?"

"This is where he died." He put his hand on the floor. "She died in the basement?"

"Yes. How do you know that? I didn't say anything about that."

"I was born with a caul."

"Come *on*."

"I was, but that's not actually how I know." He took a deep breath. "You said your father drank so he could see her. I could go on and on about Dionysos and alcohol intoxication in ritual, but I don't think I have to. I think you already get it." He began drawing a large circle on the floor in salt.

"I read."

"I bet." He stood up and stripped off his t-shirt. Handed it to her. "Put this somewhere away from the salt line, please. Then come back and step over it, please don't break it."

She walked to the mail table, put the shirt over it, then walked back. As weird as it was, she took the moment to check him out. A little thicker than she was used to, but *nice* shoulders, a back that looked like he could pick up a car. He reminded her of statues she'd seen when her class had taken a day trip up to the MFA in Boston, carved and strong.

She wanted to touch him.

"This is going to sound weird."

"I think I've probably earned that." He was smiling, but he also looked a little embarrassed.

"You're... damn." She felt like her face must be glowing. "You have a *nice* back. Front's good, too."

"Thank you." He was very quiet now, ducking his head. "I, ah, there's a reason. It wasn't just..."

"Yeah." She was now standing in the circle with him. Remembered when they were standing outside, her head against his neck. "What now?"

"Don't break the circle, don't step outside of it." He stepped outside of it himself.

"You just said..."

"I need to be outside." He walked more fully into the kitchen, found a bowl in her cabinets and put it on the counter. Then he took a knife out of her cutlery drawer, checked it with his thumb for sharpness, discarded it and found another. "Okay. This is going to be messy and I'm going to stay over here, away from you. Whatever you see, *don't step out.*"

"What are you..." He didn't wait for her to finish asking. He took the knife in his left hand and slashed it across his right, hissing as it cut along the inside. He'd hit the vein, and bleeding was immediate, dripping into the bowl he'd selected. He shook his head before she could come out of the circle.

"**Don't**. I know, but I'll be fine." He concentrated, seeing the same trails of fire in the air he'd seen the day he woke up, the shimmering awfulness of things he shouldn't know. Let his arm bleed for three more heartbeats, and then released his breath in one guttural burst. *"Zhro."*

Blue-white flames erupted from his arm as the blood ignited, lighting the whole room in fluorescence, and when it was done the cut was sealed. Thea's eyes were wide, but he could tell she wasn't shocked. Surprised, yes, but not shocked.

"You slashed your *arm.*"

"Odysseus needed blood to compel the shade of Achilles to speak with him. The dead, one way or another, they need life to manifest. Someone else's, since theirs is gone." He took the bowl with his blood in it and put it down inside the circle with Thea. "You're going to have to do the talking. I'll be busy."

"Doing..."

"You'll see. Don't come out." He stepped back, his arm still seething, and traced a symbol, a star with an eye in the center on the floor. There was silence for a long moment, but she knew better than to speak. It was as if she could feel what was about to happen before it did, see it as it formed.

The ghost had always just appeared in the past. She'd see it walk through a wall or come up through the floor, it would just be there. This time there was a gloom that ate the light, a darkness that wasn't absence but rejection. And then there she was, inside the circle. Silent, staring, an expression equal parts horror and exultation on her face.

"Offer her the blood." Outside the circle he was standing facing away from her, staring into the darkest corner of the house. In the year since he'd failed to die, he'd spent a lot of time looking for truth, only to decide that truth was subjective, but there *were* things to be afraid of. He heard the spirit gasp, the sound of greedy drinking and fought back nausea. *She was drinking his blood.*

He had no idea why he'd done this. Why he'd come here, knowing what he'd find, someone else's horror story. The darkness swirled before him and *it* began to form, malign and terrible. Hungry, so very hungry, a parody of form and shape that laughed at time. Laughed at *him.* Four paws padded on the wood floor.

"*Ohooohatan. Yahoeloj. Thahebyobiaatan. Thahaaotahe.*" Each word came out with a flare from the burning fire on his arm, flaring forth to light the room. It snicker-bark-growled at him, but could not come forward, could not manifest as long as he held the light.

As long as he burned.

The pain made him want to drop to his knees but he held on. *If you can't do this now, how are you going to when the time comes?* He held the knife the way his mother had taught him, blade between him and the darkness. *This is always pointed at what you want to stab, never at yourself.*

He wanted very much to stab into the mockery dripping drool from a gaping maw made out of night, but he made no move on it. His arm, and the blood on the knife glowed.

"Thank you." Thea stared at Paola Mendel née Rafiela as she finally finished greedily licking the last traces of blood from the bowl. She looked less insubstantial, and Thea was disturbed to see a trace of his blood at the corner of her mouth. Like a child who'd drank the milk from a bowl of cereal. "You're grown now."

"Yes." Thea could see light and movement outside of the circle but didn't move, kept her eyes focused on her mother, or what was left of her. "Why did you kill... why? He *loved* you."

"And I him." Her voice was just a voice. Thea had expected a rustling wind or the scraping of a tomb door, but it was almost normal. "He wanted... he *called* to me. I warned him. The price... but I couldn't stay away. Trapped by *her*. He was my release." A line of blood trickled down from her eye, stained her face. Thea watched it, knew it was the blood she'd just consumed, that it was all that kept her here and when she used it up she would be gone.

"Who is *her*? Who trapped you?"

"I can't say. She has a piece of me, has me pinned here between. Won't let me." She wiped at her face, saw the blood on her fingers and placed them in her mouth, cleaned them. Thea fought to keep from throwing up. "Greg at least is free. She couldn't take *him*. But you... Seri and Joe and you, she can take you. You have to hide."

"Hide from *what*? I don't..." Thea took a breath. "Tell me everything you *can*, then. Everything she hasn't forbidden you."

"She's old. Older than she looks. She came here after her family was killed. We're *food*. She eats us to stay. She had a lover, once. But he turned away, wouldn't... she hates him, loves him, would have made him immortal. Like she is. Instead she's alone." The ghost hissed. "She knows I'm not where I should be. She'll try and put me back soon."

"How?"

"I don't know. I never learned. Wouldn't let any of us learn. If we learn... *you* have to learn. Learn everything. Wake fully and see. If you do, you're of no use to her. But a threat, you'll be a threat, she'll move against you." The ghost of her mother was fear and defiance as she turned to look where the black shape stalked the corner of the room. "Her hounds chase after me even now."

The man with the fire in his blood was sweating now. The pain was growing. Before the night he hadn't died, he'd probably have broken long before that point. But being shattered had left him with a deep capacity for pain, for trading pain for power. He snarled, took a step forward, brandishing the blazing knife in his hand.

"I can't stay. I love you, Greg loved you. Don't hate us for dying. It was *her*. I would have stayed."

"Mom..." Thea knew she was weeping now and she didn't care. She reached out a hand, touched air. There was no flesh, no substance, and yet she'd hoped. "How do I save you?"

"I don't know. But you will. Learn." The bowl fell to the floor as Paola Mendel vanished. As she did, the oppressive darkness trying to devour the unnatural light went with her, and the mockery prowling in it faded away, leaving with a groaning cackle, a bark that laughed at life.

He relaxed and hissed a word. "*Uaaah.*" His arm stopped glowing, the flames dying down. There was a scar on his arm where he'd cut himself, but that was all — it looked a long ago thing, and not something recent.

He put the knife down. There was no trace of his blood, burned for power. He felt like an intruder, having overheard what they'd said to each other, but without him *it* would have been free to advance, and he wasn't that sure of the salt circle.

Finally she looked up at him.

"Was it like that for you?"

"It's different for everyone, I think. Mine weren't..." He sighed. "I'm sorry."

"Yeah." She felt cold and alone. "Can I..." She indicated the salt with her feet.

"Yes, it's fine." She stepped over it and hugged herself.

He didn't even realize he'd stepped closer to her until his hand was on her shoulder and then there it was, and when she looked up at him he drew her carefully into his arms. He didn't know if it was the right thing to do, but if she was as afraid and angry as he'd been, he wanted to do for her what no one had done for him.

They stayed like that for a while. Eventually she slipped into awareness that she was embracing a large, shirtless man in her kitchen. The fact that her body was responding shocked her – *you just found out your mom's ghost is food for something she couldn't even tell you about, that can send monsters after her and you're feeling him up* – but it felt good to have something real, warm and alive to touch. Her fingers splayed out against his shoulders.

"Thank you." She stepped back with a little effort.

"Not a problem."

"I very much want not to be here anymore." She walked over to the mail table, looked at his shirt. Wondered if there was a way to not give it to him, but finally decided to. He took it, pulled it on and while he did she looked at his chest and arms without him able to see her doing it.

Seriously, girl. She couldn't make herself feel too bad about it. Being alive was infinitely better than what she'd just seen. She wanted to remind herself of it so badly it made her ache.

"I'm fine with leaving." He was a bit envious of how well she was taking it, compared to the screaming, weeping mess he'd been his first night, but everyone was different and she *had* been seeing the spirit already. *Or maybe she's just that strong.* He kept stealing glances at her, at her face, the track of tears drying under those pale blue eyes. Like moonlight set in a face. She caught him at it and smiled.

"Where should we go?"

Chapter Four

Perihelion

They ended up driving up through Providence. He felt a twinge when they went past the exit onto Route 10, but thankfully she didn't take it. Neither of them really knew where they were going, it was more a case of just putting distance and space between them and where they'd been.

"I have no idea what I'm going to do." She had an arm out the window, letting October come washing in over both of them. The cold air felt so much cleaner now that they'd left the house. The house she knew she'd never live in again. "Could you hear what she said?"

"Yes."

"I should be freaking out." She switched lanes. "But I was *right*. Why does that matter so much?"

"I wish I knew." He was making himself not look at her. "I have some books at my place. You should probably read them." He tried to smile, actually managed to pull it off. "Based on the books you already have, it won't be new to you."

"Sure. After all, my mom's ghost just gave me homework." She ran a hand through her hair, feeling the air rush through the remains of flop sweat. "Where do you live, exactly? I was supposed to take you home. Are you in a hurry to go home?"

"Not particularly."

"I'm going to get us some food, then." Satisfied that she'd made a decision, she switched lanes again, heading right to take the next exit. "Did you know the arm thing would work?"

"Nope."

"Were you showing off?"

"Yes." He nodded slowly. "I was absolutely showing off."

"Cool." Her smile was a feline thing and he realized he was

falling, and falling fast. The lurch in his guts was free fall. He remembered the last time he'd seen Delphy, on his birthday the year before, her telling him she couldn't love him. It had been the beginning, he realized that now, if he hadn't come home with his heart broken...

Not again. We can't do that again. It's why they died, because they wanted to cheer me up, it's why it's my fault. Can't can't can't.

She was nothing like Delphy. Nothing at all.

They ended up in a diner in Johnston, just off of Route 6. He'd never been there. She seemed to know the menu, ordering a plate of hash browns and two eggs. He got the chicken fried steak, even though that never worked out for him.

"So you've only been doing this since last year?"

"Yes." He had his jacket off, the diner was kept warm by the kitchen. "My parents... I have no idea how they met, what convinced them to get married. They both had some weird beliefs. Maybe not so weird. Apocalypse cult stuff. They were getting ready. My grandfather's farm is stocked for 2000. Then 2012, if that one doesn't work out."

"Really?" Thea's eyebrows went up. "They were into the whole Mayan thing?"

"Yeah. You know about that?"

"The McKenna book. He wrote a computer program around it. Seems like bullshit to me, but fun." She grinned, licked her lips and he couldn't tell if she was doing it on purpose or not. "Machine elves."

"My dad built a bunker, there's a ton of canned food there. Good for years. A shitload of guns in the safe, more in the bunker. Ammo, knives. My mom taught me how to knife fight, hunt, all that kind of thing." He took a sip of water. "I guess we were those crazy survivalists you read about."

"Huh."

"That's why I don't say I was a farm kid. It wasn't a working farm. It was Baby's First Branch Davidian Compound. Except my dad and mom didn't want a lot of people there."

"So you're not…"

"If the world's going to end, there's not much point to freaking out about it." He shrugged. "Things like we saw tonight… we might as well live while we can."

"I guess." A cup of coffee came for her, and a coke for him, and then their food. They both ate quickly, more hungry than they'd want to admit. He'd lost blood, was feeling his body try and make him shut down and rest.

"I'm making up a lot of this shit as I go."

"Well, it looked like it worked tonight."

"I'm just saying, if there's a secret cabal that has the true wisdom out there, none of them came by my house or anything. I read some books, try to adapt what I can."

"It's like Jeet Kune Do."

"Huh?"

"I took some martial arts as a kid." She flexed an arm. "Met a friend through it. He might not be my friend any more, especially after tonight."

"Why not?"

"He and I… I fucked up." She took a breath. "It's kind of personal, but I'll tell you if you want."

"It's up to you, I'm not trying to dig up your secrets."

"Okay. Quick and dirty version – he's always had a bit of a crush, I ignored it, after my dad died I… didn't ignore it as well as I could have." She drank her coffee, looking at him to gauge his reaction. His expression hadn't changed. "So, yeah. Tonight was the first time I saw him in a while, and he seemed to get that I'm not looking for that from him. But I still feel bad." She put her coffee back down. "But he's the one who got me started in *Jun Fan*. That's the martial art. *Jeet Kune Do* is the philosophy of it."

"I took a year of Judo at the Y, that's about it for me." She laughed.

"You look like you can fight."

"I don't really like to." He remembered his mother drilling him. "But I can if I have to."

"Anyway, I'm no expert, I just took it for a couple of years. I just remember the idea was that you didn't want to rely on a style, you used what worked, reacted to the situation."

"Makes sense. I guess it's like that." He chewed, swallowed. The light was yellow, dingy, and he could smell years of smoking practically embedded into the wood of the booth bit the food itself was surprisingly good. "Where'd you find this place?"

"Here." She grinned at him. "I'm pretty sure this is where it was."

"Cute."

"I like to think of myself as *striking*." She ate a few mouthfuls of fried potato. "I had the typical acting out phase, dated a lot of people I shouldn't have. Fourteen and riding around in a car with people, going nowhere in particular. This is one of the places we'd go. I ended up liking it."

"I grew up not all that far from here and I've never been here in my life."

"You missed out." Thea kept looking at his hands. Her own hands remembered what his shoulders, his back had felt like, and when he'd held her and she'd let herself cry she'd pressed full up against him. The longer she knew him the more she liked his face, that broken nose, his huge eyes. There was a softness in him that was at odds with the way she'd seen him stand in the dark brandishing a knife at blackness, growling at it. "Where'd you hang?"

"Between here and Bristol, mostly. Went to school at William Blackstone. Before that, when I was in the city we'd mostly hang out Downtown. Kennedy Plaza, thereabouts. Sometimes down around Reject, I had a friend who lived down there."

"We should really call it CCRI." She snorted. "Name's been CCRI forever."

"Reject just sticks. That's probably why they changed it."

"I may end up going to Reject." She considered it. "If nothing else I could use the library."

"Not a bad way to go. I went to WBC because my dad went there. Knew some people."

"Okay, I'm done eating." She stretched. "We still have no

destination and it's getting late."

"Two in the morning."

"I guess I should take you home."

"I, ah… yeah." He dug around in his wallet, pulled out some money.

"I can pay for my own meal."

"If you want to." He made no move to pick up the money. "The first time I met Bishop, he took me out to eat. Paid for everything. Sometimes a meal is just a meal."

"Sometimes." She stood up. "Let's get you home before I decide to just chuck it all and drive west as far as I can go."

"I've never been to Alaska. Always wanted to go." She arched an eyebrow at that while watching him put on his jacket.

Once they were back in her car he directed her. It wasn't hard – take the 6 to 10, take the 10 to Pontiac Ave, follow it to Colonial. Typical residential neighborhood. His house was a white Cape Cod, the grass had been getting long before it started getting cold enough to brown it out. The air felt like snow was coming any week. She pulled into the driveway, was surprised to see a green muscle car parked in front of the garage.

"Yours?"

"Yeah." He looked nervous. "I can't really make myself drive anymore."

She nodded. It made sense to her. His driveway was *very* close to his neighbor's house, the lots not lined up particularly well. She barely managed to get out and it looked like he'd invented a new dance to get himself upright, then she waited for him to walk ahead and followed him to his back door. He was taking out a key.

"It's kind of a dump."

"Looks okay from out here."

"Well, I tried." He popped the door open and they walked inside. It wasn't nearly as bad as she'd feared it might be, considering he was a single man in his early 20's living alone. No huge piles of mess anywhere, just a general sense of things being picked up and put down wherever. The kitchen was more modern than she'd expected. The den was off from the kitchen, with a couch and a love seat facing a blank spot on the floor.

"Neighbors stole my TV."

"You *know* this?"

"Yeah." He shrugged, taking off his jacket. "I could get it back but I don't much care."

"I figured this place would be piles of empty beer cans, or bottles. Maybe hard stuff."

"I clean up." He sniffed, laid his jacket on the counter.

"You're not denying the implication."

"You said your dad drank too much. You probably know the signs." This time he sighed, ran his hand through his hair. In the overhead light she could see a faint trace in his hair, probably the companion to the scar on his face. "Yeah, I'm a drunk."

"Are you?" She decided to sit down at one of the stools so she could face him across the counter. "I mean, if you had to go a week without, could you?"

"Probably." He held a hand out, palm down. "I don't drink because I feel like I need to."

"Why do you, then?" When he looked at her, clearly confused, she rested her head in her hand, her elbow on the counter. "You got to see my major problem. Your turn."

He thought about that. Walked over to the fridge, opened it, took out two bottles of Pepsi Bishop had left there. Gestured to her. When she nodded, he handed her one and opened the other.

"For future reference, I'm a coke drinker."

"Sorry." He drank about half the bottle, thinking. "Did I tell you I was asleep? When they died?"

"You mentioned it."

"I woke up when I heard the sound." He was using the bottle as something to stare at, to unfocus his eyes. Let the memory come. "The car screamed, tires screeching, my mother's voice... the one thing I never heard was another car. Something hit us so hard that the car collapsed, flew sideways into the guardrail, eventually hit a pole, and there wasn't anything *there*. I've gone over and over it, checked my memory. No one saw the accident. No one saw anything. But I *know* there wasn't another car. Whatever hit us..."

He trailed off. Drank more to get the tightness in his throat to go down.

She didn't say anything. He hadn't immediately believed her, but he hadn't dismissed her either, so she sipped at the too-sweet soda in her hand and listened, and thought to herself that when he wasn't trying to look brave he was almost delicate, soft and a little like a hurt child, and she found it beautiful. Those huge eyes of his, he'd make a terrible liar. Everything he felt at a given moment was in those eyes.

"Hit my head. Got this." He ran a hand along the scar. "There's another…"

"Under your hair. I noticed it."

"They had to cut me out of the wreck with torches. I was in a coma for days. When I came out… they were waiting for me." He met her eyes, hoping she could believe. "I drink to forget the way they looked."

"Does it work?"

"Hasn't yet. But hope springs eternal."

"I don't think it will. I don't even think…" She stopped. It was ego to tell him what to do, who he was. Even if she felt it in her bones it wasn't her place. Was it? "Well, it's up to you. I'd like it if you didn't so much."

"All right."

"That easy?"

"It doesn't work anyway, why keep doing it? It was mostly habit before now." He stretched, still feeling fatigued from earlier. "Plus, and I'm pretty sure you know this because I'm terrible at being subtle, I'm thinking getting hammered in front of someone with your story wouldn't be very impressive."

"And you want to impress me?"

"Yes." He didn't quite whisper it. She couldn't keep from smiling.

"Here I am in your house. Despite what Seri thinks, I don't do this a lot."

"I don't get it."

"My cousin thinks I bed hop." She snorted. "Maybe because

Daaaavy has a wandering eye and I'm one of the people it wanders over."

"He's got good taste at least."

"Oh, he's not picky." She was using the mostly empty bottle a bit like a conductor's wand now, emphasizing certain words. "I think *he* thinks he can sleep with me and somehow keep Seri, or maybe even have us both. He's very *oily* about it. And maybe Seri thinks I encourage it. Hell, maybe I *do*."

"You don't."

"I don't."

"I don't get that sense from you."

"We just met."

"It's been an eventful night. I feel like I have more insight than I might otherwise."

"Point goes to the man." She finished off the soda, put it down. "Cards on the table, then. There's a thing, you and I, I'm not just imagining this."

"If you are, I am too." He was watching her face in the bright white overhead light he usually kept off. Watching her think, and thinking about it himself.

"Can I use your phone?" She stood up. "I have to call Seri and Joe, keep them out of that house."

"Yeah. It's over there." He pointed to the wall. "I'll let you have some privacy."

"It's your house. I didn't mean to drive you off."

"It's fine. It's a nice night. Just let me know when you're done." He smiled and nodded and she smiled back, liking how it felt. He didn't bother to get his jacket, just stepped out onto his porch, closed the door behind him. She walked to the phone, picked it up and dialed.

It rang three times.

"Hello?" Joe sounded a bit muffled.

"Were you asleep?"

"Huh? No... I was, ah..." Thea grinned so hard Joe could feel it on the other end of the line. "I'm awake. What's up? Where are you?"

"I'm at his house. Cranston."

"What the hell are you doing there? I thought…"

"Is Seri there? In the apartment, I mean."

"Yeah, she left David at the party, hitched a ride home with us."

"Uh huh."

"Don't *uh huh* me."

"I'm just saying everyone thinks *I'm* the easy one."

"Enough subject changing, what are you doing at some strange guy's house?" In the background, Thea thought she could hear a man's voice say *'you liked me well enough and I'm a very strange guy'* and then heard Joe make a choking sound.

"Look, just tell Seri I'm in one piece, I'll talk to you two tomorrow. I'm sure Bishop can tell you all about him, if you're that curious. I'll be fine."

"Thea…"

"I'll be fine, Joe, really." She looked out the window at the back of his head. "I know."

"You know what? Thea, you're acting weird even for you."

"Oh, strap in, cos. You have no idea." She laughed. "Have a good night." She hung up the phone, a decision made. Walked over to the back door and opened it, stepped outside. He was looking at an old in-ground swimming pool, the liner torn and stagnant water only reaching half way up the deep end.

"You done with…" She put her arms around his neck while he was talking and he stopped, looking at her, his mouth slightly open. She was glad she was tall, she easily reached his lips just by standing on her toes. They were softer than she'd expected, then his hand slid around to cup the back of her neck, the base of her head. The warmth as he opened and she slipped inside, grazed his tongue with hers. The taste of soda and copper, he'd bitten his tongue at some point. His body hard against hers, a quivering in his limbs.

She didn't want to stop, their mouths parting and coming together again, her leading and then him, trading. She was *hot,* her clothes felt ridiculous, obstacles. Wherever their bodies touched she wanted to be naked. But she didn't do that, not yet.

They hit a lull, her hand cradling his chin, his mouth against her forehead. The sound of his breathing like he'd run, chasing her, or fleeing her.

"That was…" He swallowed.

"Can I stay here tonight?" She looked up, looking at his face in shadow. His right side was visible in the light of the moon.

"Yes."

"Good. I was afraid you were going to say no."

"I don't think that's possible."

"Looks like your friend Bishop is having his way with Joe tonight."

"Good for him." He bent down and brushed his lips against her throat. She arched to let him, her fingers now in his hair. "Should we go inside?"

"We should." She was already reaching for the door.

Inside, he felt a moment of absolute panic. He hadn't been with anyone since December of the previous year, had essentially given up on the idea. His room upstairs was a mess. His *parents* room seemed impossible.

She bit his neck, just hard enough to make him groan and pushed herself up against his erection. Thought became an impossibility. He lifted her in his arms as she wrapped herself around his waist, her legs squeezing, her mouth descending on his and they ended up in what his father had called "the guest room" – it had a bed, and at that moment that was all that mattered. He could hear the furnace in the basement below them, then he dropped onto the bed, making sure to keep most of his weight on his elbows and knees while she took his head in both her hands and teased his lips with hers, slid her teeth gently against his bottom lip.

He surrendered to her. She pushed her tongue into his mouth, found his, rocked her hips into his and rolled them both over so that she was straddling him. Pulled her shirt off in one fluid motion, then began working on his, his back arching to let her. He was staring up at her. In the dim light coming in from the open door she almost looked bronzed, her skin edged in light. She was reached behind her back to take off her bra, half her face hidden by her hair, her smile arrogant and yet just a little tentative. He doubted many people could see that, was amazed he could.

His hands were on her hips now, not holding her in place, just resting. She could leave. Even when she threw her bra on the floor she knew she could leave, if she wanted to. Instead she looked at his face, saw the way his eyes were wide, his mouth just open enough. She lowered herself so that they were touching, bare skin to bare skin. She felt so hot she wondered if she'd burn him, felt the start of sweat where they were together.

"Ready?" Her voice echoed off of the wood paneling, sounded impossibly loud. Her hands were trailing down his chest, to his pants.

"Absolutely not," he responded, his hand coming up to touch her face, as he arched up to kiss her again. "But please don't stop."

From there it became sensation. She peeled his pants off, and then hers, and then they were gliding against each other, his skin cooler than hers, softer than she'd expected. His beard tickled the inside of her thighs, his lips and tongue insistent against her and when she came the first time he thought she might break his neck with her legs. It didn't stop him. She took her time with him, made his last, watched him grab hold of the windowsill and thought he might rip it right out of the wall. She enjoyed knowing it was for her.

Afterward they lay against each other, breathing heavily, her head resting on his chest. She didn't feel *done*, just unable to keep going. They didn't speak for a few minutes before he finally shifted.

"Not to break the mood..."

"You have to pee."

"That's the case, yes."

"Hrrrrr." She rolled off and lay on her back, aware of how naked she was, of how naked *he* was as he got up and walked around the bed. She looked at him critically. His back and ass in particular were his best features. He walked out of the room and immediately turned to the left.

"This is the bathroom, by the way." He called out.

"Good to know." She leaned back in the bed. It had been made at some point. Now the blanket and sheet were bunched up on the floor and she wasn't feeling motivated to pick them up. She didn't want to give him an excuse to cover up yet. She heard the sound of a faucet running and closed her eyes, listening to the aftershocks in her body.

Okay, so that happened.

Thea wasn't a virgin and wasn't particularly concerned about what people thought about it. Sex was sex, it wasn't love. Rarely was it like *this*. She'd felt pulled, almost driven, wanting to... what? Mark him? Claim him? Maybe it was just a fuck for him.

"Sorry." He came back in.

"Not a big deal." She opened her eyes and watched him lie back down. He was surprisingly quiet for a big man. "I don't feel much like sleeping yet."

"Me neither." He lay back next to her, their faces only a couple of feet apart, and looked at her directly. The night sky was visible just above them both, the bed right up against the window. "That was... I thought the bed was in trouble."

She couldn't keep from smiling, fought back the urge to cover her face with her hair. She rolled over to press against him, her breasts flattening against his arm.

"I'd hate to wreck your bed."

"It would have been worth it." He was taking shallow breaths and she let her arm trace the hair on his chest. "I haven't... not for a while now."

"You didn't seem rusty."

"I was motivated." He hitched as her fingers traced over his abdomen. "If you'd want to stay, I would like that."

"And if I don't?"

"Then I'm glad that I got to meet you." His face was half shrouded in shadow, but she could see his eyes. Could see something in them that felt like déjà vu. "I would miss you when you left."

"I..." She took a moment and leaned her face against him, just breathed. "I'd miss you, too."

She wasn't sure when they fell asleep. Just that his arm was still around her when they did.

Chapter Five

Scraps

The sign over the old yard read *Morgan Williams Salvage*, but the man standing over the car in the round garage wasn't the Morgan Williams the sign meant.

"Jimmy, get your ass over here." He was looking inside the engine. The car in question was a 1977 Pontiac Firebird, painted an awful shade of green and with a body more constructed of bondo than metal.

"Just my ass?"

"Don't." He looked up. "Do not test me."

"You sound like an ass when you talk like that." The two men were similar in build, although the one named Jimmy was a fraction taller and thinner, with long brown hair and a case of stubble threatening to erupt into a beard. Morgan Jr. was pale, light blond hair, eyes the color of a robin's egg. "What's the problem?"

"Look at this." Jimmy did as his elder brother ordered, bristling slightly. He never liked being ordered around even though Morgan did it constantly. *The old man left the place to both of us, not just you, asshole.* "And where's Byron?"

"He's in the main building."

"You just left him alone in there?"

"What was I supposed to do?" Jimmy bent over. The inside of the car's engine compartment was full of what looked like bird shit. "What the fuck..."

"Yeah." Morgan moved his head to the side. "Look over there."

The fence that surrounded their salvage business (really just a shitty junkyard, if they wanted to be honest with themselves) was an unremarkable chain link fence most of the time. It did its job and screeched when it opened. Today, it was also home to a great many seagulls.

"What the fuck." It wasn't a question. Jimmy stood up from the engine, looked over. "Did you do something?"

"Did *I* do something? You're the fuck up in the family." Morgan slammed the hood of the car. "Now we're going to have to go see what she wants."

"I vote we just burn down that fucking rat trap she's living in and call it a lifetime."

"You want to try it?" Morgan had gone very, very quiet. "She kills people she *likes*."

"Needed us for that accident." Jimmy met his brother stare for stare. "And that was what, last year? Haven't heard shit out of her since, so..."

Morgan considered that. They'd handled that one just fine. Why *did* she want to see them? His skin was beginning to crawl. He didn't hold the old bitch any dearer than Jimmy did – all he had to do was look at the ruin she'd made of Byron – but he knew they needed more than hate to get around her.

"Go get Byron."

"Shit, you want to bring *him*? He'll freak out once he realizes where we're going."

"If we don't bring him and it turns out he's who she wanted to see..."

Jimmy didn't say anything, he just spit on the ground, gave Morgan the glare, and walked into the office to get Byron. If they were lucky the big man was watching *Sesame Street*. He was always easier to handle after that. Morgan walked over to the work bench, picked up a sledgehammer with a shortened handle, and carried it over to the truck, all the time watched by the gulls.

He turned and threw the hammer end over end into the fence, sending them scattering. They screeched and whirled in the air above the yard.

"Fucking rats of the sea."

"Feeling better, big man?" Jimmy had Byron, and for once he didn't even have a rope tied around the man's neck. "Hey, buddy, hop up in back, okay?"

Byron was easily seven feet tall. Grotesquely muscled. The expression on his face was dull. Whatever she'd done to him had left him unable to care for himself – he didn't talk, would only eat when directed to. He stepped up on the back of the vehicle and it dipped as he got settled, his back against the cab window. Luckily the truck had side windows because there would be no seeing out the rear view with him up there.

Morgan walked over and picked up his hammer. Spit onto the ground, his mouth sour. Seeing her always did that to him. He wanted to bash Jimmy in the head, maybe almost as badly as Jimmy wanted to do the same to him, but neither of them wanted to be responsible for Byron, or answering to the old woman, alone. It was like being cattle that *knew* it was cattle. They did what they did to keep off of the table. They didn't have to like each other to want the same things.

He jumped in the cab. Jimmy was already inside, looking out the window at the birds wheeling above them.

"An hour in the truck with that shit following us."

"You must think I'm planning on driving like you." Morgan put the truck in gear and let out the clutch, feeling the gears catch with his foot. "Half an hour tops."

Despite his best effort, it was 36 minutes later when the truck pulled down the dirt road in Little Compton and up the hill to her house. She lived close to the beach, and Morgan saw her sitting on the porch in an old swing chair, staring out at the water.

"Well shit."

"She don't look happy," Jimmy agreed with his brother for once. "Let's leave Byron here."

Morgan nodded. If the big man got agitated, she'd hold it against them. His mouth was so sour now it felt like he'd been puking. He decided to leave the hammer in the truck as well. He gestured and got out, not wanting to risk talking and sounding like he felt.

The two of them walked up to the porch. For all his mouth, Jimmy was a step behind him the whole way. That didn't surprise him.

"Boys." Her voice stopped them in their tracks more effectively than a slap would. "I'm pleased you thought to come see me."

"Got your message." Morgan managed to keep his voice from breaking with an effort. "Thought we'd stop by, see what you wanted."

"Such polite boys." She turned those black eyes of hers on them. Morgan knew they were probably just brown, but they *looked* black, like obsidian. "Do you remember last Christmas? I had you do an errand for me?"

"Yes, ma'am."

"Did I explain it to you?"

"You did not." Morgan wanted very badly to spit now.

"Because I don't usually *have* to explain myself to you, do I? I don't explain myself to my shoes, or my front door. The same with you." She was still rocking away in that swing chair like they were having a perfectly nice chat, her voice never going up in pitch. "I even praised you, didn't I?"

"Yes you did."

"That turns out to have been premature." She looked down at a table next to her chair. On it a pigeon lay pinned down, sliced open neatly as any instructor could hope for. Morgan noticed there were no flies, which in November might not be *that* surprising. She reached in a hand and pulled out something, he had no idea what, and stared at it with those black eyes. It took him a moment to realize the difference between how she looked at the bird's innards and him – she paid attention to its guts. They mattered to her. She put the raw chunk of viscera down and wiped her hand on a cloth on the table, clucking her tongue.

"Someone is attempting to do things I do not want them to. You're going to go stop it. You brought your younger brothers? Good. Bring them both. The special one, use him."

"Who..."

"The one you failed to kill last year." She waved a hand, letting him know he was dismissed. Morgan nodded, jerked his head to Jimmy and they walked to the truck together in silence. For once Jimmy was smart and waited until the truck was running and they were well on the road back north before he spoke up.

"What's she talking about?"

"The job last year."

"That shit was *totalled* when Byron..."

"Later." Morgan rolled down the window and spit. "We're going to the library. Checking the papers. It's not a big state and we know the date and time."

Chapter Six

Ordinary

Seria was sitting in Tony's Pizza on Pontiac Ave waiting for Thea, wishing she could chew on her nails. She couldn't, because they were painted a bright red, and it had taken her a few hours to get them all even. The whole reason she painted her nails was to keep from chewing them.

Right that moment she wished she could.

She saw Thea's CRX pull up outside, Thea get out and start walking towards the door, and relaxed. She saw Thea nod to the man behind the counter as she walked in, saw that she was wearing a black button-collar shirt with a fairly deep neck, it wasn't a shirt she recognized. She got up and they kissed each other's cheeks, giving Seria a chance to look her cousin over.

No bruises or marks, except a fairly livid one on her neck that pretty obviously came from a mouth. She had a faint but unmistakable smile on her face and her black hair was pulled back in a braid, which was unusual. Thea usually just let it fly.

"I'm *fine*, mom."

"It's been a week, I worry."

"I called Joe three times."

"You deliberately called late so I wouldn't be home or would be asleep."

"True, but you knew I was alive." Thea sat in the booth. "Did you order yet? Pizza's good here, like that place we used to go in Olneyville."

"No, I was waiting for you."

"Okay, hang on, I'll go take care of it."

"Thea..."

"I promise we'll talk after I order. You still like the same?"

"Yeah."

Thea patted her hand and walked up to the counter. As far as Seria knew Thea'd never been to this neighborhood before last week, but the guy behind the counter acted like she was a regular.

"Okay, I got a medium, sausage, pepperoni and green peppers for you, extra spicy for me." Thea slid back into the booth. "So, I was thinking you could come pick me up tomorrow and we could head back to the house, empty some things out."

"Like what?"

"Like anything you or Joe might want to keep. I'm going to sell the place, so..."

"Oh, no, I couldn't..."

"I know you miss him too." Thea was looking out the window at the overcast sky. "He raised you two. I just want to be fair."

"We can go through it if you want. Maybe there's things you want to keep."

"There aren't." Thea didn't get teary or visibly emotional when she was sad, at least not unless she was *really* sad. She got quiet. Her voice sounded very far away. "I just want it gone."

The man from behind the counter showed up at their table with a red plastic pitcher, with water droplets forming on the sides. He poured them both glasses of water then retreated. Seria waited a bit, sipped her water, then turned her attention back to Thea.

"So..."

"So."

"You've moved in with this guy?"

"Not officially. He just hasn't asked me to leave yet and I haven't felt much like leaving."

"Do you have a key?"

"Yes, I have a key."

"So he gave you a key."

"No, I stole it when he wasn't looking and made a copy. Yes, he gave me a key. It's easier for me to get in and out that way."

"And you've been sleeping there."

"The way I see this going, you incrementally ask me questions getting closer and closer to asking if I'm sleeping with him until, in about an hour, we finally get there." Thea was flat out smirking at her now. "Yes, Seri, I'm sleeping with him. We are indeed having sex."

"Is he good to you?"

"I don't follow."

"Is he kind? Are you okay there? I just..." She sighed. "I remember when it was all new and exciting and fireworks and I couldn't keep my hands off of David, and I... well, I ignored a lot. That I maybe shouldn't have."

"I'm starting to think this is more about *you*." Thea reached out, put her hand on Seri's. "Is David... did he do something?"

"No, no, nothing like that, I..." She sighed. "I know it's not the same. David was my first, this guy *definitely* isn't yours, but I just worry. You're moving really fast."

"In some ways. We're not engaged or anything, Seri."

"I have a hard time imagining you engaged."

"Stranger things."

"David and I... his eye wanders. I know, I know, but it's not just you and now that I notice it, it's hard not noticing it." Their pizza arrived, served on a metal tray with parchment paper lining. Seria snapped her mouth shut. "I know I gave you shit over that..."

"Yes you did."

"So I'm trying to apologize."

"I accept."

"You are such a brat."

"And you love me."

"And I love you. Just be careful with this guy. What's his name, anyway?"

"Thomas." She lifted a slice of pizza, the cheese reaching from the tray before snapping, steam coiling in the air from it. "Don't call him Tom."

"Why not?"

"Cause I don't like it." Thea took a bite, grimaced as the cheese burned the roof of her mouth as it always did because she always did that, and chewed it fast so she could take a big sip of cold water. Seria chuckled. "Besides... woah, hot... you're coming by after."

"After what?"

"After this. You're coming by the house."

"I am? You could maybe have just asked me to drop by."

"If you were being a raging pain I wanted an out."

"I'm *never*..."

"You invited Scott to that party."

"I forgot."

"It was wicked awkward, Seri."

"I said I... huh, actually, did I say I was sorry for that?"

"No, because we haven't talked in a week. All's forgiven now."

"I am sorry. I just always liked Scott."

"He's a good guy." Thea was feeling agreeable. "He's just not the right guy."

"And this Thomas guy is?"

"We're weird in complementary ways." Seria realized that Thea was actually getting a little color on her cheeks when she asked about the boyfriend. The boyfriend she met and moved in with less than a week ago. It occurred to Seria that her cousin Thea, who chewed through boyfriends, and at least one girlfriend, like a wood chipper through fireplace logs was actually sweet on someone.

"Wow."

"Wow what?"

"Nothing."

"Oh, don't get superior on me, Seri."

"It's just that I've never seen you in *wuv* before."

"I'm..." Thea opened and closed her mouth. Really thought about it. Polished off the piece of pizza and drank more cold water to give herself time. "So how would I know?"

"Oh my God." Seria was eating as well, the smell of the peppers having gotten to her. "You don't know what love feels like?"

"Well, it's not like I ever did this before!"

"You started dating when you were thirteen!"

"That was different. That was just wasting time." Thea put her hand under her chin. "He's interesting. We talk about books we're reading, ideas, places we've been – I told him about our trip to California. He's been to London. He's got such a nice ass."

"Thea, that's…. how nice?"

"Really nice. I like to dig in with my nails and feel the muscles tense up." She sighed. "I do not want to be one of those people who talks about their guy all the time."

"I would be surprised if that happened."

"So how did you know? When you realized you were in love?"

"I don't know that I ever have been." Seria admitted. "Or if he ever really loved me."

"Oh, Seri, I'm sorry."

"It's okay. I'm okay." She picked up another piece of pizza, ate it to avoid thinking about what she'd just admitted. "All I can say is, let it happen, don't fight it or force it."

Thea took that in while eating another slice, which was about her limit.

"I'm going to get this boxed up?"

"Makes sense." Seria was feeling full after two. "So do you need help getting your clothes out?"

"I wasn't…"

"Thea. Come on. You live there now."

"Maybe?" She laughed. "Would you mind?"

"No. To be honest, I didn't want to say anything but I hated the idea of any of us living in that house anymore. It just feels wrong."

You have no idea, cos. Thea just nodded.

*

The basement hadn't been finished before they died, and he certainly wasn't motivated to finish it now. The walls were bare concrete, the floor likewise. There was a bulkhead exit in the large room his father had used for storage down there. It was held closed by a padlock and chain, and he'd reinforced it by filling it with old furniture. Since the doors opened outward, it wasn't much of a reinforcement. He guessed if nothing else anyone who managed to rip the doors open would be annoyed by a dresser in the way.

It didn't really matter. What mattered was sitting on the pool table, golden urns against the green felt.

He didn't play pool. Neither did his parents. He had no idea why they'd had a pool table, but it had always been there. He stood leaning with his palms on the felt, looking at the books he had scattered around on the table, trying to figure out a way to make it work. Next to *Comte de Gabalis,* his father's translation, and a bunch of old mass market paperbacks – *Le Matin des Magiciens, Passport to Magonia, Three Books of Occult Philosophy, An Encyclopedia of Occultism* – he had comic books, textbooks, novels, even an old copy of the Player's Handbook his mother had gotten him for his 11th birthday. One of Thea's books, *Food of the Gods.* He'd been flipping through it.

He had two of the comics open. In one, a man with a hell of a mustache and a red and blue ensemble that would turn heads at Mardi Gras was invoking gods with names that would have struck Lovecraft as being too ridiculous. In the other, a fellow with a golden helmet that looked like a bell was calling upon the Egyptian gods to banish someone from existence. They were both ludicrous.

It was all ludicrous. All of it. From Henry Cornelius Agrippa to John Dee to de Villars, none of it made any fucking sense. Steve Ditko and Keith Giffen fit right in.

He looked down at the scar on his arm, the one he'd made a week prior. The one that had healed as soon as he'd stopped setting his blood on fire for power.

None of it made sense but it *worked*. That was what drove him crazy. That, and the words the ghost had said. He'd heard Thea speaking to her. Someone was after Thea. Someone wanted to hurt her. Someone who could torture you after you were dead.

He understood that he'd only known Thea a week. That morning, he'd lay in bed just looking at her while she slept, trying to understand what was happening. Other people met, they went on dates, they eventually moved in together and maybe got married and here he was living with a woman he'd just met.

He was terrified she would leave.

Why wouldn't she? Everyone else did. Delphy, Evvie before her. He'd thought things had gone fast with Delphy, but they'd taken two months to have sex, another to move in together. He'd done both with Thea in one night and the only regret he had was that he couldn't stop being afraid she'd leave.

He looked up at the urns again. They sat there, squat little golden reminders. He'd made a promise to them and now he didn't want to keep it.

"I think you'd like her."

The ashes in the urns didn't reply.

"I really..." He stopped. *I like her* didn't sound true enough. It was the phrase you used when you thought love was too soon, or too big. Maybe it was both.

He picked up one of his father's favorite books, Bill Whitcomb's *The Magician's Companion*. It was just like his father to think that great secret truths could be found in a second hand bookstore. He remembered again calling forth the four Elemental Kings, feeling their power throb through him. He'd used this very book to find their names. Things that couldn't possibly exist.

"Maybe I could do it." He put the book down. "Fuck me if I know how, but I could. I could do it. I know it'll fuck me up, if what I did hurt, doing this will probably..." He trailed off. He had no idea what it would cost. Would they want this? Did he want it?

He heard footsteps and knew Thea was back, could tell by how she walked. There was someone else with her. Likely the cousin she wanted him to meet. His heart didn't skip a beat, he didn't float or feel hearts or flowers orbit his head.

He just felt like he was real. When he knew she was there, it was where he wanted to be.

He turned and walked away from the table, from the urns. He stopped in the laundry room, pulled a shirt out of the dryer. He'd taken to doing laundry since Thea came to stay with him, not wanting to seem too awful, although frankly she was almost as bad as he was. She'd gotten him into the shower a few times. That he enjoyed quite a bit.

He tried not to be blushing when he walked up the stairs and opened the door, stepping out into his kitchen/den area. There were two women sitting in the den, Thea on the couch, Seria on the chair facing it. They shared a significant resemblance but he could tell them apart easily – Thea wasn't so very thin, she had more muscle tone and height than her cousin, and her eyes were a far lighter blue. Their features were very similar, but to him Thea was the more attractive.

Perhaps I'm biased.

"I told you he'd be up here as soon as he heard us walk in." Thea stood and walked over to him, put her arms around his neck. "What were you up to?"

"Reading." He had no idea how much she was telling Seria, decided to let her take the lead. "The thing we talked about last night."

"Oh, that." She slid in and kissed him, and he lost track of everything, lost in the feel of her in his arms. He could easily lift her, but she felt solid and strong. It felt like she could lift him, or that she was. The feel of her mouth against his, soft, but urgent and demanding, he could feel her wanting him and it made him want to begin peeling her clothes off. But he could just barely remember that they had company. She was breathing against his face when they parted. "I had an idea about that, we can talk about it later."

"Okay." He swallowed. Refocused his eyes to look at Seria, who was watching them both without even trying to conceal it. "So, uh, hi."

"Hello." She had a very faint smile on her face. "So you're Thomas."

"Yes." Thea had slid her arm around his shoulders and didn't seem inclined to disengage, leaning against him to face her cousin.

"This is my Seri. She's awful, but you'll get used to her."

"How am I awful, exactly?"

"You like to insert yourself into other people's problems, lives, business in general. You know that, it can't be a surprise."

"Thea is the brat of the family and she likes doing whatever she pleases." Seria said that with an arch of the eyebrow that was almost artful. He wasn't sure yet if he liked Seria, but he respected the clear intelligence in her gaze, weighing him. "Your house is nicer than I expected."

"I didn't have much to do with that."

"So she tells me." The two of them, still arm in arm, made their way into the den and sat on the couch together, both facing Seria. Thea gave his arm a squeeze, and he realized she was trying to be reassuring. He looked at her face, really looked at it, wondering. The worst thing about life was never really knowing what the people you care about were thinking, and he felt it keenly. She was so beautiful, those eyes, the cast of her lovely nose, the sweep of her lips. And inside, locked away, depths he couldn't even guess at yet. "My parents passed when I was... ten?"

"About that." Thea's voice was somber. "My mom died four years after. So it was just us, Joe and my dad."

"Uncle Greg raised us." Seria's voice was husky and Thea felt a deep pang of guilt. She'd completely ignored how much Seria was hurting. Wrapped up in her own feelings. Her own selfishness. She didn't like that. "So it's like you're dating my baby sister."

"Ugh, this again."

"You're two years younger."

"A year and a half." Seria just gave her the look and Thea fought back the urge to stick out her tongue. "Aaanyway..."

"I get what you're saying." Thomas' voice always made Thea's spine hum, the depth of it, how it rumbled through him and into her when they sat this close. "If it helps we're both aware it's gone very fast so far."

Seria didn't say anything to that, just leaned back in the chair. She'd been watching their body language, both the obvious displays and the ones she didn't think they knew they were doing. Thea was not touchy feely by nature, she didn't hug much, she only kissed Seria and Joe because she really thought of them as family. Seeing her sit so close to Thomas, her leg against his, her hand on his, this was new behavior.

"So, protracted silence, so awesome."

"I'm thinking. I mean, I don't approve, but I'm not going to tell two adults what to do. Even if you're barely an adult."

"Nineteen in three weeks."

"I'm twenty-one and I have no goddamn clue what I'm doing." Seria looked at him. "Please don't hurt my cousin. She's very vulnerable underneath the spines."

"Oh my God."

"I'll try not to." Thomas replied.

"Good. All I can ask." She looked down at her hands. "Also, when she inevitably hurts you, try not to take it very seriously. She never means to hurt people she loves."

"I am seriously going to gag." Thea ran her hand up and down Thomas' arm, squeezed it slightly. *Is that what this is? What if it is? Do you...*

"Okay, now that I've played the part of older relative, what do we do now? Board games?"

"I don't actually have any."

"You could tell us about what's going on with Joe."

"He's apparently frolicking with the blond from the party. Your friend." She aimed that one at Thomas. "He's been over a couple of times."

"Bishop?" Thomas' eyebrows went up. "Huh."

"Why 'huh', this is my baby brother we're talking about. I don't like 'huh'."

"He's three minutes younger than you."

"That's important." She turned back to Thomas. "Is there something I should know about him?"

He considered this. On the one hand, Bishop was his best friend and the only one he'd managed to keep after last Christmas. On the other, this was a chance to get in good with Thea's cousin. Finally, he decided on cautious truth.

"Bishop had a really bad relationship, or at least a bad breakup, a while ago." His hand was now firmly clenched in Thea's, feeling her fingers grip him. "This is the first time I've heard of him seeing someone more than once since I've been back."

"Is he some kind of man-whore?"

"Seri."

"Thea, please. You can apologize for me later."

"No, he's not. He's only dated a few times since it happened. He just generally gets gun shy after the first date. Without actually talking to him I can only assume he really likes your brother."

"He should, Joey is wonderful."

"Despite Seri's lack of objectivity, I do endorse Joe. He's kept me sane over the years dealing with her."

"Bishop put up with me after... well. Everything." He shrugged, the couch shaking. Seri kept realizing just how large he was. Seri was nearly six foot, Thea was slightly over that, and he was at least a head taller than she was, easily six foot four. And he took up most of the couch sitting there. Thea usually dated slight pretty boys like Scott. Seeing her with this walking oak tree was strange. *Maybe this one might actually keep up*. "Even if it doesn't work out, he's never an asshole about it. He's friends with everyone he ever dated except one."

"The bad one?"

"I didn't catch the details, I was in London when it went south."

"What were you doing there?"

"Studying. I was in the theatre program at William Blackstone." He felt a little awkward remembering that with Thea there, they still hadn't talked much about their previous relationships. "They do a study abroad program. It's really the only reason I took theatre at all."

"Were you an actor?" Thea was watching them both, interested in how Seri just asked him any damn question she liked. As much as it was annoying when it was *her*, she had to admit it was useful now. They hadn't talked much about the past.

"No. I was in a production of *The Misanthrope* as Alceste once, that was it."

"I was in *Tartuffe*." Seria was smiling now. "I played M. Loyal. It was an all girls production."

"She was pretty good." Thea was still leaning against him, and he bent down to brush his lips against her cheek, smiling when she turned to face him. She brought her hand up to touch the side of his face, feeling the beard under her fingers. They stayed like that a while, until Seria finally cleared her throat.

"Okay, you two are disgusting." She shook her head. "Just awful."

Thea fought back the grin. Something about Seria being there made it feel real and sudden and huge, like showing something you had cupped in your palm to a friend. She exhaled against his cheek, liking the way she could feel his response in the hand on the other side, the way he trembled.

"Just ignore her, she's always been like that." Thea didn't really want to pull away but felt like she had to or just start pulling clothes off. She didn't want Seria to see *that*. "Maybe we could all go out somewhere. We just had pizza, but by the time we get somewhere..."

"We could do the clothing thing." Seria offered.

"Clothing thing?"

"Most of my stuff is back there." He didn't need her to tell him where *there* was. "We haven't talked about it..."

"I gave you a key." He was a bit shaky on the laugh.

"So it's not a problem?"

"I'll come help if you like." He stood up and offered her his hand. "Plenty of room here."

*

Morgan Williams was sitting in his pickup truck watching the house.

"Are we sure this is the place?"

"No, that's why we're *watching* it, asshole." Jimmy Williams shot a snotty look his way, but Morgan didn't take his eyes off the house. He saw as two cars began backing out of the driveway, and a big motherfucker came out the front door, getting in the shitty little car. The Pontiac followed, heading down Colonial towards where it became Aqueduct for no real goddamn reason at all.

"Jesus, that guy's a moose."

"Byron'll handle it."

"He didn't last time."

"He fucking smashed that car right off the fucking road."

"And our boy here survived it, didn't he?" Morgan was drinking a cup of coffee from the Dunkin Donuts on Reservoir. "The bitches have me concerned."

"Why?"

"They reminded me of something." Morgan was putting the truck in gear. "Let's see if we can follow them."

It took a little time to turn. They'd had to park the truck around the corner on Autumn Street, but the two cars weren't moving all that fast and it wasn't hard to catch up at the light where Aqueduct met Reservoir. Morgan slid the truck in behind the Pontiac.

"Jesus, crawl right up her ass." Jimmy muttered.

"Might not mind."

"Ah, for fuck's sake."

"She's a piece, even you must have seen that." The light changed and the procession began. Morgan was annoyed that they went left, but it wasn't a surprise – if they'd been going right, they would have turned while the light was still red.

"I wasn't looking."

"The one with the gorilla in her car is nice, too." He was tapping his fingers on the wheel. "They remind me of someone but damn if I can think of it."

"Fuck, a couple of Guidos south of Federal Hill, not that uncommon."

"What was our mother's maiden name again?" Morgan waited, but Jimmy didn't rise to the bait. "Didn't think so."

In the CRX, Thomas was watching the road move past.

"We're taking the long way to get to your house, aren't we?"

"Yeah. I wanted some time." Thea didn't look away from the traffic as they drove past Garden City. "You all right? Seri can be intense."

"I'm fine."

"She didn't scare you off?"

"I don't scare easily."

"Good." She smiled. "It's how she shows her love. She's very protective."

"It's strange, I don't see you as the type who needs it."

"I'm not." They were turning past the Training School, essentially juvie. Thea remembered it from visiting Karl. "Okay, so, I'm not used to wanting to know about people's pasts. I don't know how to ask about it. Usually I don't really care."

"Do you now?"

"Yes." She waited for them to hit a red light, then turned to look at him. "I have a past. It's not a great past. If it's going to be a problem... and that night, at the party, the look on your face." She saw the light change and turned her attention back. "I figure you have some things you're not happy with, and I want to know about them."

"Okay." He rubbed at his neck. "It doesn't have to be in song, right?"

"What now?"

"I used to have a song."

"You're serious?"

"The song existed, but I don't remember how to sing it."

"You're a huge tease."

"Out of the blue of the western sky she comes, it's Beth!" He warbled. "Met in third grade. Were friends for years. My first kiss, first crush. Actually started dating Junior year. Got to Senior Prom, broke up because we were going to different schools, different lives." He smiled ruefully. "Oh, and she'd been fucking another guy for like the whole of Senior year and he and she got together when she went to UMass with him."

"She was fucking you both?"

"No, just him."

"*Why*?" Thea seemed actually offended. This made him snicker.

"We were better friends than anything else. Not a lot of chemistry. She likes skinny guys who wear tight clothes and read poetry." He shrugged. "She came to the funeral. Different guy now. I blew her off pretty hard, wasn't interested in the pity."

"Is it my turn?" She was turning onto Rt. 37 now, and he nodded. "So, my first. I was like thirteen. He was sixteen."

"Precocious."

"My mom died the year before, I was just getting my period, started seeing the ghost... my dad didn't know what to do with me, I was, er, 'developing' that year." She gestured around her chest. "He had a car and his older brother was in the Training School, it was all very designed to piss *someone* off. I was never really sure who, if I wanted to irk my dad or Seri." She leaned back in her seat. "It worked either way."

"How'd it end?"

"Disastrously, as you'd probably expect. I turned fourteen, he got sent to Juvie himself. Shoplifting. I visited a few times when I could get Seri to drive me, which wasn't often, but... Karl, his name was Karl, he just fucking hated *everyone*. His mom was a wreck, his dad long gone, his brother dealt weed and he wanted to fight all the time."

"Is he the one who you mentioned?"

"What? Mentioned when?"

"We were talking at the diner, you took Jeet Kune Do?"

"Oh, no, no. That was after I broke up with him. He got weird, clingy. I got Seria to help me find a place that offered classes, little place near the airport. That's where I met Scott, but I think you owe me one now."

"I do?"

"Fair's fair." He was distracted by the way her lip curled when she smiled.

"Okay. Well, I dated Evvie for a little while. Met her at William Blackstone. Smart, funny, pretty, we were in an Autobiography class together. Read Loren Eisley. *All The Strange Hours*. We were together for a few months, until I went to London."

"Why'd that end if she was so great?"

"Long distance, she was into Bishop..."

"Oh. Uh... sorry. I know he's your friend, I didn't mean..."

"It's fine." He shifted his shoulder. "We broke up before they got together."

"Was she…"

"The one who broke his heart, yeah." He sounded sad about it. "No idea what happened there, it's… I can't ask him, you know?"

"I think so." She exhaled, dreading this one. "Okay, so… despite what Seri thinks, this next one is the only other serious *anything* until last week. I dated a few others, but nothing major. But I was in my JKD classes, I took them more seriously than high school. They were *harder* than high school. And that's where I met Scott."

He didn't say anything, just waited. They were almost to 95, which meant not very far from her old neighborhood.

"Scott really liked me. I don't know why. I was a bitch to him, like, every time we talked. But he was always nice to me, and I… didn't have a lot of that, back then. I wasn't very popular at school, the burnout who dated a kid in juvie, everyone thought… well, you know, you get a reputation."

He nodded. *Crazy Willrew*, they'd called him. Or worse. He'd gotten into a *lot* of fights in high school. Neither of his parents really the kind to know how to help him fit in. At least his mother had shown him how to fight.

"So, we were friends. Just friends. That was all I wanted from him, and I thought that was what *he* wanted…" She swallowed, hating this part. "Then my dad died, and Joe and Seri, I mean, I know they were hurting too, but I was… I was jealous of them, they were off, settled, they had each other and I've always… I'm the outsider in the group, they're twins, they share everything, I don't, I'm not *part* of it and when their mom and dad died they got to come in to *my* family and push me out." She exhaled. "It's not fair. I know they do love me, I hate that I feel this way."

"It's not wrong to want to hold onto something for yourself."

"Anyway, that's how I fucked up things with Scott. I was home alone, and *she* kept coming by, but no one but me seemed to see her, so I thought… if I wasn't alone, she'd go away. She wouldn't come if I wasn't alone. So I called Scott and… well. I wasn't alone that night." She was looking at him side-eye while turning the car around the exchange onto Post Road.

"I didn't think you were a virgin if that's what you're waiting for."

"You didn't?" She fluttered her eyelids at him and they both laughed. "I shouldn't have... *anybody* but Scott. We were friends before that. Now... I don't know if he'll ever forgive me for not being in love with him."

"Speaking from experience, when he meets someone else he'll stop caring as much."

"But not entirely?"

"Well, who knows? In ten years he'll probably be over it."

"You're very comforting."

"I do my best." He looked out the rear view mirror, saw that salvage truck he'd noticed on Reservoir was still behind them. That bothered him. "So, I guess I'm up again."

"Ooh, three to my two."

"You left out a few unimportant ones. So have I, really."

"You weren't a virgin *either*?" Another shared laugh. "I so wanted to be your first time."

"Sorry to disappoint." He snorted. "Okay, so the last serious one was Delphy. Short for Delphine."

"Delphine. I hate the bitch already."

"That was quick."

"I would pretend I feel bad but I don't at all." She sniffed. She actually enjoyed how much she instantly hated the woman without knowing anything about her. "I take it the bitch was French?"

"Ethnically. She was from Andorra."

"Isn't that the planet the Death Star blew up?"

"I want you so badly right now. No, that was Alderaan. Andorra is a postage stamp of a country on the border with Spain, with a small French minority. Her family moved to England when she was sixteen. They worked for BP. She was very rich and very spoiled and we got drunk together and made fun of bad poetry."

"What, like, you'd go to the library..."

"Slams. We met at a poetry slam. I read a truly *awful* poem about being on life support, she read a pretty average one about winter in the mountains. Most of the others were even worse than us. We mocked ourselves, them, and drank too much." He shrugged. "I think we only got together because she was tired of being chased by Dyson. Yes, his name was Dyson. Very English fellow."

"So that was the whole relationship? Getting drunk and making fun of people?"

"More or less. I moved in with her for a while, but it was only a year study program and my year was up. Had to decide if I was going to stay. She offered to let me, but..." They were pulling up to the house now. It looked very average in daylight. "I wasn't big on her terms."

"Which were?"

"She was in love with this Welsh guy, Griffin. I never met the dude. He was engaged to some girl in Cardiff, but Delphy was just... she couldn't get over him. Didn't really want to. And I wasn't down for a permanent gig as 'Mister Good Enough'."

"Seriously?"

"I wouldn't make up that one." He grinned, lopsided, and she could feel the echo of pain in it, the way he'd felt at the time. "So I said sayonara to London and came back home, and two weeks later my parents were dead and I was *actually* on life support."

She reached out and took his hand, squeezed it. They ended up staring at each other, the way they had the first time they met.

"Whatever else happens, you're not Mister Good Enough to me, okay?"

"I..." He swallowed. "I haven't really felt like this before."

"Me neither." She undid her seat belt so she could get closer to him. "And it kind of scares me, a little bit."

"You don't strike me as the type there either."

"Oh, I get scared." They were still holding hands, and she found herself brushing hair out of his face. It was the eyes, she decided. The nose, the jaw and face as a whole, they weren't ugly but they weren't what compelled her. It was the eyes. Those beautiful glinting green eyes of his, like the surface of the bay when lightning cracked and flashed out over the water.

She kissed him, sliding almost half into his seat, twisted up to reach him. *I need a bigger car.* He let himself slide into the window in order to make room for her and she felt the urge to just *bite* him, not hurt him but leave teeth marks on his skin, make sure anyone who looked at him knew. She wanted to get on a plane and find his ex and just *slap* her, find the woman from UMass who'd had him and fucked around on him and point and laugh. *He's mine.*

She let him go knowing Seri would come knock on the window soon. She was taking deep breaths, liking how he smelled, how they smelled together. That was new, too, the sense of their scents mixing, like fresh cut grass and faint smoke in the distance.

"We should go in before I try and do something this car simply wasn't designed for."

"I should give you the keys to mine." She arched an eyebrow and he laughed. "It's got a lot more room inside than this."

"You'd let me drive that car? It looks…"

"I spent a lot of time restoring it. But yeah, why not?" He was smiling, and there was a thrill of shock that ran through him when he realized that this was what it was like to be happy. That he *was* happy, with her.

He hadn't been happy in almost a year. He wanted to resent it, but he couldn't. Looking at her, at those eyes so blue they were almost glowing, the slight flush on her tan skin, she was beautiful and she was there with him and he was happy.

They managed to get out of the car and were waiting next to the pickup truck when Seria finally showed up. She pulled up in front, behind Thea's car. Thomas noted that nobody seemed to want to park next to the pickup. He looked again at Seria as she got out of the car – the two women really did look like sisters instead of cousins. Their faces were *very* close.

"So." Thea walked over to the door and unlocked it, and they walked up the stairs into the house. He remembered the last time he was there, but he didn't feel anything that concerned him this time. "Seri and I will go pack up some of my clothes. I don't really have that much."

"Two bags tops." Seria looked disapproving.

"Anything you want me to do?"

"Carry shit, mostly." Thea laughed. "You could probably pick up my old bed by yourself. Don't worry, I'm leaving it."

"I might go through the kitchen, if you're still okay with…"

"Take whatever you think you or Joe might want." Thea nodded. "I'd like it if none of us ever had to come back here again."

An hour later, Thea and Seria were in her old room, packing the last of her clothing into a red piece of luggage she'd bought for the trip to California. The two of them barely managed to wrestle the bag onto the bed and zipper it shut.

"And that does that." Thea laughed. "Two bags, like you said."

"We really should have gone with three."

"I never shrink from a challenge."

"You're really sure about this? You can come stay with me and…" Seria stopped. "Forget it."

"Seri, it's okay."

"I just worry." She pushed hair back out of her face. "But after seeing you today I think I'll worry a little less."

"Thank you." Thea felt embarrassed that it mattered to her what Seria though, but it did. "Maybe you can get Joe to come hang out? I'd like them to meet. Well, more than just at the party."

"I will ask him." Seria nodded.

"Hey, another bag to carry out." Thea leaned out the door of her room, and Thomas dutifully walked in and lifted it with one hand. Seria waited for him to be gone before turning to her cousin.

"I didn't think you went for that."

"It has its advantages." She smiled softly. "Nothing I think you'd want details on."

"He's not *that* much bigger than David is."

"Not taller, no." They walked out of Thea's room, and she stopped to look back for a moment, remembering. It hadn't felt like home in years, but now that she was leaving it for good, there were still memories to push down. Weeks spent trying to water down her father's booze without him noticing. The sounds coming from his room that weren't possible. Seri and Joe coming back for visits, everything fine on the surface.

The downstairs, where her mother had died. Thea had no

idea, hadn't even thought to ask if it actually had *been* suicide. Now she'd never know, she supposed.

It had taken two bags – bigger ones, and absolutely overstuffed with clothing – to get Thea out of her house. Thomas was loading them into the CRX. He was also looking around, with a clear frown on his face and she could almost feel his tension. It wasn't related to Seri, he'd seemed fine around her all day.

"Something wrong?"

"I'm not sure. A feeling." He rolled his shoulders, his arms taut. He was ready for something to happen. She wasn't sure if it was related to what had happened the last time they were there or not, but decided to wait until Seri wasn't there to ask him. "You all set?"

"Pretty much. Seri, you still want to go through the kitchen?"

"Maybe this weekend. You and Joe can come out." She yawned. "It's getting late and I have class in the morning."

"Seri's going to be a lawyer."

"I haven't decided that yet."

"Trust me, or a cop."

"You could at least let him get used to me first."

"Nobody gets used to you, Seri." Thea kissed her cousin on the cheek. "You going straight home?"

"Probably. David's busy with his friends." Thea deliberately let that go. She didn't like David Kanmore, was never going to like him, and didn't see much point in pretending. She took Thomas' arm and waved as Seri got into her car and drove off.

"Okay, so what's wrong?"

"Thought I saw a truck following us earlier, and ever since we got here I've felt exposed." He dropped to one knee behind her car, like he was peering into the trunk, and spit on the ground. Then he began tracing a symbol, like three curving fangs interlocking. Thea watched, fascinated.

"What's that glow?"

"It's the weird shit happening." She saw him smile. "So far you're the only person who can see it. Bishop can't, even when I do stuff in front of him."

"It feels like I could do that."

"You probably could. When we get home remind me, my Whitcomb has lots of symbols you can use. This one I actually made up myself." She watched as it flared, throbbed and caught the light. She could see filaments of caged fire surrounding her house, like a glowing web. Thomas ran a shaking hand across his forehead. "Okay, if someone comes in here I'll know it."

"If you changed it here," Thea pointed to the edge of the symbol. "You could make it hurt anyone who did."

"Yeah." He steadied himself against her car's bumper. "But I'd need to provide more of myself to do that."

"Maybe." She considered it. "Let me think about it. Can you include me in this?"

"Sure. You just need to attach yourself." She placed her finger near the symbol, traced several lines around it that seemed right, based on what he'd done. It wasn't hard, but the feeling of it was sharp, like slicing her finger. She flexed her hand in surprise as she felt the filaments settled around her, then spread out over the house. "Like that, yeah."

"I just did that." She grinned at him. "I just did something magic."

"You did something magic the first time you saw your mom's ghost."

"This is the first time I *decided* to." She straightened up, feeling a little dizzy. The throb was gone, everything looked normal now. She scanned around. "I don't see anyone watching us."

"Quite a few places they could have parked and come back, we were in there for a while. Just wanted to make sure."

"If someone's following us..."

"My house has a lot more than just that one thing on it. Now that you're looking you'll see it."

"Is this how you learned it?"

"No one showed me anything. And I don't think I'm a natural to it like you are." They got into the car and she started it. "I think I had to actually die, or almost die."

"Thought you were born with a caul?"

"Sometimes a caul is just a membrane stuck to your face." He reached into his pocket and pulled out his keychain, a rather elaborate mess of keys and tags. He removed two and handed them to her. "To my car. If you ever want to use it."

She took them, pocketed them since her keys were in the ignition.

"Thank you."

"Like I said…" She reached over and put a finger on his lips.

"Just say you're welcome."

"You're welcome." She liked how his voice felt with her finger there.

"Let's blow this pop stand." She put the CRX in gear. Drove out of the driveway, still just able to see the lines of fire reflected on the hood of her father's truck.

Chapter Seven

Shadows

"Okay." Jimmy Williams said as the car drove off. "Let's go…"

"Nope."

"What? Why not?" The two men were crouched behind a bush two houses down from Thea's house. Morgan stepped out and walked slowly towards the house, scowling. He stopped well short of the driveway. Put a hand out and stopped Jimmy.

"You're the one who said you wanted to…."

"Look, idiot." He pointed to the house. "They did something."

Jimmy squinted. He wasn't as good at this shit as Morgan was, but they both could see – it was why the old bitch kept them around. So he eventually saw it, wriggling somethings that made his teeth itch.

"What the fuck is that?"

"Fucked if I know. But I'm not risking it." Morgan had already turned on his heel and started walking back to where they'd parked the truck. "I bet the house he lives at is worse."

"I didn't see anything there."

"Me neither. Doesn't mean it ain't there." Morgan didn't say anything else, chewing on the inside of his cheek while he thought. It was an old nervous habit, and he was plenty nervous. He didn't like *any* of it. Once they reached the truck and climbed in, he spoke.

"We're probably going to have to bring Byron next time."

"I told you to bring him *this* time."

"Cherish this moment then. You get to say *I told you so.*" Morgan considered smacking the stupid out of his brother's mouth. "We're going to have to go see her again."

"Ah shit." Even the momentary lift of putting one over on Morgan crumbled with that notion.

"She's going to want to know about these bitches and that house. That at least one of them can do that shit."

"Yeah, well, you're the older one, *you* can talk to her."

Wasn't planning on letting you, you gung ho shitbag. Morgan started the truck, listened to the engine run. He had no idea what she'd say or do – he was going to have to eat more shit than *ever*, and it's not like this mess was his fault. But he could imagine that voice.

If you'd completed your task there wouldn't be complications.

He waited until his hand wasn't shaking any more and then put the truck into drive.

*

He enjoyed making the bagels.

He could just sort of zone out and work the dough without much thinking about it. He was thinking about the lighting rig up at the Farmhouse, about his classes, about whether or not he'd finally get the chance to go to London this year. He had the money but he'd always found a reason not to go and now he was half way through Junior year.

Christ, I'm going to graduate soon. He put the tray with the raw bagels in the oven, stepped back to clean up the kitchen a little. The shop (creatively named *The Bagel Café*, because that was what they made) was busiest in the morning and at noon, and almost dead otherwise. Sally, the middle aged woman who owned the place, came in around five AM and worked till one in the afternoon, and then usually left the closing to him or Mira, because it really didn't matter. Breakfast and lunch were their money hours. So Joe used the afternoon mostly to just think about stuff, make what few bagels needed to be made for the stragglers who came in.

Right now there were two people there, a woman drinking a coffee and very slowly eating a sesame seed, and an older man who came in every day, had two toasted wheat bagels with roast beef and cheese and read the newspaper. Joe was obsessed with his beard. He made up stories for them in his head, imagined scenes for them.

God, I'm going to have to get a real job.

He had a year to go on that, of course, but it still reached up and slapped him sometimes. He was going to graduate with a fucking *theatre* degree. A Bachelor of motherfucking Fine Arts. Holy shit, what was he going to do with that? It's not like there was a huge market for playwrights, and as for hanging up parcans up around the inside of a converted farmhouse, that was a skill with limited application outside of the incredibly insular world of theatre.

Once his counter space was clean he busied himself with minor chores. The woman with the sesame seed was finally finishing up and leaving. Newspaper wasn't even close to done. Joe knew he might well sit there until whenever the shop finally closed. Mira would be in soon and then that would be her problem – stay open until six or close early, it really didn't matter.

The bell chimed and Joe looked up to see a now familiar tall blond man walk into the shop. He'd known Bishop for a while in that *'I've seen that guy around campus'* way, William Blackstone not being a huge school, but he'd never spoken to him before the party.

They hadn't really talked all that much that night either.

"Howdy." Bishop managed a drawl despite being from Barrington. "Thought I'd stop in, get a coffee."

"We do also sell bagels."

"I saw the sign." Bishop laughed. "I lived in this town for three years and I never once stopped in here."

Joe took a moment to really *look* at Bishop while he poured him a coffee. The night they'd spent together, there'd been a little drinking and he liked to keep the lights off when he had sex, so he'd only seen Bishop's face in what little light came in the window.

He was *pretty*. He had a square jaw, a perfect dimple on his chin, the kind of beard growth that just enhances the lines of the face. He'd age magnificently, be one of those grey streaked ageless men who could be late thirties or early sixties and you'd have no idea. His face lined up perfectly around his eyes when he smiled, which was often.

Only now Joe was noticing that the smiles didn't often reach the eyes. He handed Bishop his coffee, wishing he knew how to talk to people.

"So I was thinking…" Bishop began, sipping at his coffee.

"A vile habit."

"Right? And yet, I persist." A softer smile, more genuine. "I figured, there's places people go and consume food and have conversations, and we could do that."

"Huh."

"Huh?"

"Based on scuttlebutt, that's not your usual MO."

"Scuttlebutt? You actually use the word *scuttlebutt*?"

"I watch a lot of old movies." Joe couldn't quite stop the smile. "And it sounds better than 'Becky Hanscomb told everyone in the theatre department to stay away from you.' Doesn't it?"

"Becky? Why'd she do that?"

"I believe her exact statement was 'Bishop likes to fuck and forget.'"

A look crossed his face and Joe found himself fascinated by it, it was so utterly confused and even a little hurt. He drank his coffee for a little while, thinking.

"I had no idea she had a problem with me."

"I don't know if you noticed but she's a vindictive, spoiled little diva who thinks being the best actor in a theatre program with twenty-four people in it makes her Queen Shit of the Entire Universe." Joe flicked his eyes over to Mister Very Neatly Trimmed Beard, but he looked utterly absorbed in his newspaper. "She really hates your friend."

"She hates Tommy?" Bishop considered this. "Yeah, okay, I can see that."

"I'm told he was in the program."

"Just for the London trip. I don't think he was ever really serious about, well, anything. I can see that pissing off Becks." Bishop finished his coffee. "Well, that and he doesn't care about most people."

Joe considered this. The idea of Thea dating, or whatever the fuck she was *doing* with Bishop's surly friend made him uncomfortable.

"So, has Becky put you off me, then?" Bishop gamely soldiered on. "Or can we get that meal?"

"I suppose I could eat." Joe fought back fluttering in his stomach. Being this open in public, at his place of employment, made his years of Catholic school act up. He and Seri had both gone to La Salle in Providence, while Thea had insisted on going to Pilgrim near the house in Warwick. Being gay at a Catholic high school hadn't been as bad as Joe had feared, in part because whatever his other problems, Uncle Greg was pretty understanding. "Where and when?"

"When are you done here?"

"My shift ends at three but I'd want to go home and that takes me until around four if the traffic's bad so... let's say six? Time enough to shower and get cleaned up."

"I think that's a plan, then. It'll give me time to figure out a place to go." Bishop smiled again. "Maybe we can go hang out and I can meet your cousin for real this time."

"Thea?" Joe considered it. "I guess I really *should* make an appearance, I've just been..." He went quiet, but Bishop just laughed.

"You've been riding it out."

"I'm not good with new people."

"You're doing okay with me so far."

"That's entirely different." Joe's face was hot and he cleared his throat. "Anyway, gotta pretend to work now."

"All right." Bishop looked around and seemed to finally notice newspaper beard man. Instead of coming in for a kiss, which he might have otherwise, he chose to give Joe a nod and a smile and walked off into the November cold. It was sub-freezing but at least no snow yet this year. He stood for a moment and looked at Bristol, the town a weird contradiction of old buildings with trendy crap like a bagel shop or a record store – not even a *music* store, an actual *we sell vinyl* store – trying to part incoming fools and their parent's money.

Of course, Bishop had dropped plenty of money in that record store.

He walked down towards the water, where he'd parked his car. He was drifting a little, trying to figure out Joe's reactions. Actually trying to *date* another man was new for him. For all that he'd come out as Bi back in freshman year, he'd never really put it into practice before. Hell, after last year he'd decided casual hookups were his default setting.

Not really paying attention, he didn't realize he'd crossed the street at the corner with the post office and the upscale book store. That was a bad corner. If he'd been paying attention, he wouldn't have gone anywhere near it. At that particular moment he was thinking about Joe's rather hauntingly blue eyes. He got the sense that Joe noticed a lot more than he let on, and that intrigued him, the idea that he might be giving away more of himself than he meant to. It made Joe a risk.

Lost in these thoughts Bishop didn't see the two women outside the bookstore smoking until he was almost past them and the one with the short purple hair and small nose piercing looked up.

"Bish?"

He stopped. He didn't *want* to stop. He wanted to put his head down and keep walking like she wasn't even there.

"Evvie." He was very proud at how genuinely friendly he managed to sound. "Wow, it's been, what, over a year?"

"Since I graduated, yeah." She took a drag, using the smoke to fill the space between them. That was Evvie all over, theatrical. No wonder Tommy had gone for her.

No wonder Bishop had.

"Hey, I gotta go back inside…"

"I'll be in soon." Evvie said to the girl she'd been talking to. "Just tell Stuart I'm out here if he needs me, okay?"

"Yeah, sure." Bishop took in the girl he didn't know – Asian, mid 20's, probably a WBC student, maybe the Architecture or Law Schools. Hair streaked with purple and blue. Thin glasses perched on her nose. He didn't recognize her.

"So." Evvie used the cigarette to gesture. If there was one thing Bishop had loved about Evangelyn Fraser (and there was more than one), it was the way she used her whole body to talk, her arms always in motion. "You look good."

"Hard for me to look otherwise."

"Right." Another drag on the cigarette, and he felt like his temples were being squeezed. "I heard about Tom's parents. Saw him when he came up to drop out. Tried calling him."

"He was in a bad way for a while."

"Which we didn't help with."

"No, he was... surprisingly okay about all that." Bishop had feared that she'd bring this up. He and Evvie had met at the Cavern, one of the more regrettable of the college bars in Bristol. Actually, he'd met her the night Tommy had finally worked up the nerve to ask her out.

"Really? So you told him..."

"I told him that we were dating. I didn't tell him we'd started while he was still *here*." He exhaled. "Come on."

"I just think it's weird that he won't talk to me."

"He hasn't really been talking to *anyone*."

"Is he going to come back? Not a lot of credits left, he could be done in a semester if he wanted to." Evvie exhaled smoke, watched it trail off. Bishop wanted to say *look, if you're so curious about what he's up to, why not go ask him?* But every part of his brain said not to.

"I don't think he's really focused on that right now."

"You ever finish up?"

"I did!" The very fact that they'd switched topics off of Tommy made Bishop perk up. "Actually got it all done over the summer."

"I'm sure your parents were thrilled."

"I had some sudden free time, so..."

"I suppose you did." She turned and stubbed her cigarette out on the wall. "How is it I'm always the bad guy in this?"

"Evvie..."

"No, I mean it. I didn't make you do anything, you chased

after *me*."

"Can we not?" He lowered his head. "I know I shouldn't have, we both shouldn't have, especially not behind his back. There's nothing I can do about it now. And you *did* dump me."

"We weren't working." She turned to look at him. "I told you when it started it wouldn't work if..."

"Yeah, you did." He nodded. "Doesn't mean it felt great."

"Fucking someone over rarely feels great." She straightened up. "Funny how I'm the one who gets labeled the cheat."

"Okay." He shrugged. "You can think I went and told him some story about you if you want. I didn't. Believe me the last thing I like to do is bring that whole fucking train wreck up, okay?"

"So you what, didn't say anything?"

"I told him that you and I dated and that it didn't work out. That's all I did." He sighed. "He didn't seem surprised."

That deflated her a little bit. Bishop always wondered what was going on behind Evvie's eyes. He hated himself for still feeling something in her presence.

"So what are you doing now?"

"Living off my trust fund."

"I don't think you're supposed to be proud of that."

"I'm not. Not ashamed of it either. I have money, I don't really have to work. So I don't." It wasn't quite that rosy, but he didn't see any reason to tell Evvie that. "You're still here."

"Yeah, not a lot of jobs for that writing degree."

"You still..."

"Yes, I'm still working on it." She bristled. Evvie hated talking about writing with him, said his tastes were too parochial. This always made him laugh, which hadn't helped anything. He'd always been a little too quick to laugh at Evvie. "I'm hoping to get the second draft done soon."

"Good luck." She quirked her mouth at him. "Well, you don't like talking about it, not a lot else to say there."

"Okay. Okay." She rubbed her forehead. "Maybe I'm... look, I don't want us to hate each other."

"I don't hate you." He smiled, because it was true. "I just

regret how it went down."

"Well, I guess that's something." She shivered, her shirt and apron no match for the cold. "I have to get back inside, Stuart'll freak out."

"Yeah, he was always very tightly wound." Relief at the conversation ending flooded him.

"Goodbye, Bishop." He watched her turn and walk back inside.

Inside, Evvie felt colder than she had outside. She hadn't seen Bishop, hadn't wanted to see him, since they'd ended things. It had been six months she'd regretted, more if you counted when she was dating Tom and took up with him. She'd made all kinds of excuses about it – they hadn't been exclusive, he was moving too slow – but in the end she'd chosen to do it. Sure, Bishop had dropped a ton of hints that he found her attractive, but she could have avoided it.

She walked behind the counter. Miki was already tallying the receipts.

"So, friend of yours?"

"Not anymore." She looked over the list of pre-orders to give herself something to do. "Ex-boyfriend."

"What's wrong with him?"

"Nothing. Why?"

"Ex. He wouldn't be ex if there wasn't, right?"

"It's a long story."

"I normally wouldn't pry." This was probably true. Miki had worked there for almost a year and while she and Evvie had a solid working relationship they hadn't really talked much about their own lives. "But you look really down."

"I'll get over it." She took a breath, saw a customer walking up, and put on her best *Can I help you* smile. "Yes, sir?"

"I'm looking for *The Auden Generation*." He had a close cropped greying beard, carrying a newspaper under his arm. "I forget the author."

"I can look that up for you." Evvie let herself focus on work. Work didn't take much of her time. It wasn't hard. It didn't make her think about why she'd done the wrong thing.

Chapter Eight

Cannot Stand the Light

Thea was looking intently at the two urns on the pool table, at the patterns and symbols he'd drawn around them. Some seethed in her eyes, others were inert.

"What are these?"

"Alchemical stuff." He traced a symbol that looked like a number four with a boat anchor mixed in. "This one stands for rotting or decaying. The one next to it, the almost pyramid, that means *not fixed*."

"And this one?" She indicated a circle with two lines on the top and the bottom.

"That's a lantern." He looked sheepish. "It's not alchemical. It's from a 40's comic. *First to bring life, then to bring death, then to bring power.*"

"You are such a nerd." He'd been lifting weights in the corner while she looked over what he'd done. She liked looking at him post workout, shirtless, sweating a little and flushed from exertion. "What is this all supposed to do?"

"Make a trade."

"What's the trade?"

"I'm... okay, I came up with this before us."

"Yes, I'd gathered." She stood up and for a moment he lost his train of thought watching her move, her torso not quite covered in a very old T-shirt of his from before his teenage growth spurt. He'd gone from five foot five and around a hundred pounds to what he was now, so the shirt – a pale green shirt with yellow stripes, a rugby style T – no longer fit him. It didn't really fit *her* either, but he was okay with that. "I take it I'm not going to like it?"

"I was... adrift. I mean, I always knew they'd die *someday*, but not like that. And I had no idea what to do with myself. I was seeing things, hearing things – they came to visit me at the hospital, but I couldn't understand what they were talking about. *He stands between forevers.* But my dad had all this shit lying around. So I started reading it."

"Wow, this *must* be bad with this much build up." She walked over to him, put her arm on his shoulder, looked up at him. "Just tell me already."

"*First to bring life*," He pointed to the lantern symbol. "That will bring them both back from the dead. The symbols in the ring are for transmutation, to turn the ashes back into, well, *them*."

"What." She blinked. "You… can *do* that?"

"I don't know. This was the first time I'd try."

"Then let's *go*!" She got excited, then stopped. "Wait. What's the bad part? *Then to bring death*. Why is that there?"

"Remember what I told you. The dead need life and they don't have it anymore. I'd have to get it for them."

"Get it *how*?" She arched her eyebrows. "You don't even like thinking about where chicken nuggets come from."

"From me." He exhaled. "They'd get it from me. *Then to bring death* means they'd live, and I'd…"

"Okay, well, *that's* a terrible plan, we're not doing *that*." She turned back to him. "You were that bad?"

"I didn't really see much point to my life. But…" He rubbed the back of his neck. "Even then, I couldn't make myself do it. It's one thing to think your life is meaningless, but when you're down here, holding a knife, trying to… and I *did* love them, I did, but I…"

"Hey, hey." She took his hand without really thinking about it. "I know you did."

"I don't want to die. Even before I met you I didn't. Now…" He shrugged, feeling naked. "So I couldn't ever make myself finish it."

"Is that why only some of it is glowing?"

"Yeah. The last part of the symbology isn't in place, the price not paid. Until that happens it's inert. Waiting. I guess I should destroy it."

"No."

"No?"

"We can think of a better way to do this." She had no idea why she was so certain of that, but she really was, it was just out of her reach, tantalizingly close. "I just need time to think about it."

"The power has to come from somewhere."

"You're too quick to sacrifice yourself. Life, blood, these are strong, but they don't always have to be taken, wrenched. The price doesn't always have to be pain." She kissed the side of his face, put her arm up to turn his head. "There's another way. Trust me."

"I do." He let her draw him into the kiss, let himself relax. It was a languid heat, slow building and gentle this time. He could feel her body right through the shirt. When they stopped to breathe she slid her mouth down the side of his neck to the base of his throat. Bit down just enough that he sighed in pleasure.

"Let's... go upstairs." She finally exhaled. "It's a little weird making out down here."

Once they were upstairs he had that little moment of disorientation he always did seeing her influence. She'd taken it on herself to get the living room looking organized, had put away the Christmas tree and vacuumed and dusted. Thea could be a bit of a slob herself, she tended to leave food out until it went bad, but she couldn't abide clutter the way he did. The room they were sleeping in, the former guest room, now had clean sheets on the bed.

She hadn't touched upstairs. Neither of them went up there much, unless it was to get books. The first floor was enough for them.

"You hungry?" She was already in the kitchen.

"I could eat."

"So, what should I do? For my first thing, I mean."

"Whatever it is it should be important enough for you to be willing to bear it." He flexed his arm, remembering. "It can hurt."

"Some of that Crowley suggested you can use pleasure instead of pain." She looked at him over her shoulder. "I'd definitely like to experiment with that."

"He did?"

"I think *someone* gets embarrassed at the sex parts."

"Maybe a little."

"I'll fix that."

"You've made great strides so far." She grinned at him and went back to the fridge.

"Okay, we have eggs, some cheese, green onions, I can make this work." She began digging things out. "So, how the hell is it that you have clothes this small? You're a *tree*."

"I was shorter than you until I was seventeen."

"Get *out*."

"It's my house!"

"You're kidding me."

"No, really." He watched her start chopping the onions, impressed. "You're good with a knife."

"Karl had his uses."

"He taught you how to use a knife?"

"His dad was a chef. He taught me how to cook." She moved her neck in a way that might have been a shrug. "Honestly, he wasn't as bad as Seri thinks he was, it was just too much for me at that age."

"At that age being what, four years ago?"

"Five." She laughed. "In four days."

"Shit. I keep..."

"We just got together, relax." She was bouncing around the kitchen. "I still don't remember yours, either."

"That's because I didn't actually tell you."

"Why not?"

"It's embarrassing." He was fascinated watching her whisk the eggs with a fork. She did it fast, much faster than he'd have been able to.

"What's embarrassing about a birthday? When is it, already?"

"December 25th."

"Oh, damn. You must have gotten *screwed* on presents as a kid."

"Well, my grandparents were all dead by the time I was old enough to really care, and both of my parents were only children."

He leaned on the counter, resting his face in his hands. "In a lot of ways my parents were my entire support system growing up. I didn't have a lot of friends."

"Me neither." She got husky when she tried not to be sad. "Just Joe and Seri."

"You really love those two."

"I... yeah." She turned to look at him. "Don't tell them."

"They probably know."

"Well, let's not *talk* about it. I'm not the 'I love you' type. Words just... it's like, you feel all this, it's in you and then you start *talking* about it and it gets sprayed all over the place. Better to just keep it." She didn't know if she was talking about Joe and Seri anymore. She busied herself with getting the pan on the burner. "Speaking of those two, uh, Seri sort of asked me if you wanted to come with, I mean, they're doing Thanksgiving? This year? It'll just be the three of us, probably Seri's awful boyfriend, no idea if Joe's bringing a date."

"I... huh." The last time he'd had Thanksgiving was two years prior, he'd been in England for what would have been the last one he could have had with his parents. "I mean, if you'd rather I..."

"I'd like it if you'd come." She was quiet now, putting a pat of butter in the pan. "If you want to."

"Well, then I'll skip a meal that day."

"You eat like two people as it is."

"Growth spurts, man." He gave her a lopsided grin. "They take a lot of fuel."

"I'll tell them you're coming." She turned so he couldn't see her face, the hot flush she could feel on her cheeks. *Oh fuck me, why does this make me so goddamn happy? It's just...*

She shook her head. It wasn't just anything, she knew that, even if it made her so goddamn confused she couldn't tell if she should be laughing or crying. She just knew he was *hers*, she'd seen him and just *wanted* him and now...

Now you're making eggs. Just make the eggs. Words just ruin everything.

"So what's wrong with Seri's boyfriend."

"I mentioned him before? He wants to fuck me." She hadn't thought about that until she said it. There was a noise as he stood up, she turned and looked to see his arms and neck *corded* and realized he had growled. It was a *very* deep sound. *Damage control!* "I'm *not* interested in him."

"Never said you were." He still looked like he was getting ready to kill somebody.

"He's just a lech, that's all. I just don't like it."

"I can explain this to him."

"If I wanted that, I'd have done it." She was torn between wanting to calm him down, enjoying this rare show of jealousy and wanting to make sure he understood she didn't *need* that. "Okay?"

"I'm fine."

"You're not." She let herself smile. "You got a little possessive there."

"I, ah… yeah. Sorry." He sat down.

"No real harm. I don't need rescuing, though." She flipped the omelet. "You want cheese on this? I like cheese on mine."

"Do we have cheese?"

"You know I've been buying groceries, right? That's where all this food came from?"

"I was kind of hoping the cold box finally got a new shipment in."

"No such luck. Yes, there's cheese. Do you want some?"

"I would like some cheese, yes." He arched his neck.

"Something wrong?"

"I still really want to punch Seri's boyfriend."

"You were bound to want to do that eventually." She was getting cheese slices out of the fridge. "It's weird. I've never been the jealous type myself, but I still kind of want to go kick all your exes in the lady parts."

"You do?"

"All these bad ideas about yourself you have." She stopped and ran a finger along his nose, tweaked it. Enjoyed the look on his face. "I expect I'll have to spend some time breaking you of these bad habits."

He didn't say anything, just looked at her, and she decided not to slide across the counter to kiss him again. She'd burn the eggs.

The rest of the prep went quickly, each of them a little distracted. He was thinking about that surge of rage, about where it had come from. *You don't own her, Willrew. She could leave any time she wants, we haven't even said the words 'boy/girlfriend' yet.* But it didn't *feel* casual. He'd shown her... well, shit, he'd shown her his crazy magic suicide kings ritual. And he was starting to feel like... well, like maybe it wasn't just him. She'd asked him to spend a holiday with her family, that had to mean *something*.

She was busy being afraid that it did.

Flesh could only be pushed so far.

Her name had been Robia Dassalia when she'd been born. She didn't remember this, but she'd been told it by a camp guard. She and her sister Raifa, twins, a prize. What they did, Raifa didn't survive.

Robia had, somehow. She didn't know how. Thinking back on those years was impossible, an abyss, black and looming. But one day it had ended. Russians, who had no more love in their hearts for a walking corpse, had liberated the camp.

Liberated. She did not laugh at this word. Nor did she spit at it. It had been a liberation, of a sort. Robia had found herself being cared for in an army hospital, by a doctor who spoke Italian. She had been born in Italy. She wasn't Italian – they called her *Zingari*, and shunned her. But he didn't. He'd seen other camps, he knew what she'd experienced, some of it.

To this day he was *the man*. Robia didn't love him. She didn't think she could love. Not after Raifa died. But she had known he was caring for her, that he was going beyond what was expected of him. As she mended, grew stronger, recovered and hated herself for doing so he was there.

She'd felt *something*. That was a complication.

There is an awful, horrible truth to life, that you can survive things that should not be survivable, endure the unendurable. Robia's parents had long since died, killed as unimportant, not worth keeping alive as she and Raifa had been. There was no one left.

The man offered her another life. He pulled strings, made arrangements. Got her to America. And never asked anything from her. In the camp she had often been expected or forced to do things, that last bit of herself stolen. He didn't ask. One night, more than five years later, she had asked him why – why didn't he seem to *want* anything?

You've lost enough. I'd never take anything from you.

So strange now, to remember it. She'd taken something from him, after all. If there had been anyone she'd have been willing to give to, it would have been him.

He was married. He had a child not long after. She found herself eventually marrying as well. Her husband was a simple man, he welded submarines at Electric Boat. He died in an accident after their second set of twins was born.

Perhaps not an accident. By then, Robia was making plans for the future.

She was sitting on her porch now. Things were progressing faster than she'd anticipated and she was old now, past seventy, and while her mind was sharp and her power was intact her body could barely feel the cold breeze blowing in off of the grey water, frothing from the wind. She liked being near the water. Watching it churn and writhe against the air.

She had a pile of mandrake root in a large orange bowl. Methodically, she shaved it with a knife, slicing away the limbs first. Each root looked vaguely like a man. She muttered, chanting under her breath the words of a play. *Behind the door on my right hand there lives a judge so bovine that he must have learned law from Boëfius.*

She chuckled to herself. There were days she had trouble remembering her own name, but this never escaped her.

When she had enough mandrake shaved away, she lifted a large pestle and began grinding it into the bowl, crushing and mashing the root flesh into pulp. She did this careful not to get any on herself. There was no hurry. She would be finished when she was.

When she was done, she took the bowl inside and placed the mash into a pot, already simmering on the stove, and set it to boil. This would take time. There were other ingredients to prepare.

In the darkness of the house, eyes waited.

"You'll eat when I'm ready. And not before." She said.

She'd panicked before. When *the man* had died, she'd thought perhaps everything would be well, that there would be no harm in anything she'd told him. It had been weakness, and memory, that had led her to him at the end of his life, to make the offer. But it had worked for her, and she didn't wish for him to go. He had shown her the closest thing to pure kindness she'd ever seen. But he had said no, had said she should leave.

It had made her angry. She regretted that. Anger made her blind and stupid.

But after that, she'd been calm. Everything in the eye was calm, she could watch the water and know she had them all placed. She remembered the screaming the first time she'd done it. Too young, she'd been too young. You had to let them grow and replace themselves before you reaped your crop. She was a poor farmer then.

Why did you have to tell them? Warn them? Now I have to kill yours too.

She sighed and walked into her living room. The blackness with eyes swirled around her feet, not tame. Never tame. She knew what it would do to her if she ever let it. That was part of the price she'd had to pay, over and over again. And she'd paid it.

She felt the truck on her land before it was visible. Reached out and felt the birds, saw it through their eyes. She hadn't expected it, and it had been a long, long time since Morgan or his brothers had done anything that had surprised her. Ever since she'd put Byron back together broken, the way she'd been put together.

She walked to the door, watched them drive up. Morgan was alone, his features a mask. It was almost going to be a loss when she finally was done with him. He'd grown capable, in his way. Unlike James, with his petty streak, using the gift for empty, foolish things. If James were not such a goad and a spur to Morgan she would have unraveled him years earlier.

She waited until he got out of the truck. He had a gun. This amused her – he knew full well she knew he had it, that it was in the waistband of his jeans where he could get to it. He didn't expect it to save him. He just had it just in case he was wrong.

"I'm afraid I didn't make enough dinner for you." He stopped dead. He hadn't seen her standing in the doorway, in the shadow that swirled around her.

"That's all right. I'm not hungry."

"What brings you to see me twice in a week?"

"He... the one you wanted dead. He's got these women, two of them." He swallowed, working his throat like there was a lump of something foul in there. Robia understood this. Fear did indeed taste vile. She remembered choking on it. "There was something familiar about them. And they... I don't know which one, but one of them *did* something."

She narrowed her eyes. Ordered the shadow hound back in the house. It obeyed, sullen.

"Come closer."

He didn't like that, but he did it anyway. Walked up the stairs, and if you didn't know to look for it you wouldn't have seen the slight tremble in every step. She held out a hand, scraped a yellowing nail across his cheek, just enough to leave a mark.

"What did they do?"

"I don't know. Never saw anything like it before. Not even here."

She considered this. Morgan was hardly well educated. The last thing she wanted *any* of them to be was trained. She herself had only picked it up in pieces. She enjoyed feeling him struggle to keep his face calm in his looming certainty that she was going to kill him. He'd kept Jimmy away, partially out of fear of what his younger brother would say, but another part of him actually wanted to *protect* the younger Williams. It was that strange streak of familial duty that fascinated her. She knew what it felt like to want to save your sibling from themselves.

"Tell me everything you saw," she exhaled like a rusty hinge.

Inside, her concoction continued to boil.

Chapter Nine

Abominations

"I'm running a bit late," David Kanmore said into the cell, leaning over towards his end table to see the time. It was two PM, which was more than *a bit* late – he'd promised Seria he'd be over at her place by noon to help out with the table. "I just needed to check in with Kevin, see what's up."

"Well, at least try and get here before we eat." Seri's voice was clipped, and David realized he was on the edge of being in deep shit.

"I will, I promise."

"Uh-huh." She hung up on him, which was a serious sign that he was in deep. Sighing, he rolled out of bed. He'd been out with his friends from Salve Regina. David had graduated already, but he hadn't settled on much of anything for his future yet. His parents would have been on his case about it if they weren't spending the winter in Florida like they did every year, leaving him and Kevin to their own devices. *Kevin* was the good son – already working a 9 to 5 for the city, shacking up with the girl he probably would end up married to.

David had no idea why the idea of that made his throat close up.

He walked down to the bathroom. One benefit of his parents being out of town for months was he could use their place with impunity. He wasn't even bothering to rent a place this year.

He started up the shower, waited for the water to get warm, and thought about spending Thanksgiving at Seri's place. He felt a little guilty about it. Seri tried *hard*, she clearly cared about him, and here he was not trying at all.

But he liked things how they were. He liked his life – some people would call it coasting, but he didn't care. He liked Seri, he really did, he just wasn't ready for settling down, marriage, getting real about life and all that shit. He was happy how things were.

He got into the shower, thinking about who would be there. Joe obviously, and that was a problem – Joe didn't like him. Did not like him at all. Wasn't shy about it, although he also wasn't in his face about it either. Joe was hard to figure out. David probably would have liked him more if he wasn't dating his sister. Joe definitely didn't give the sense that he thought David was good enough for her.

If you were her brother you wouldn't either.

The water was now hot enough. David liked a hot shower. He was soaping himself up when the other probable guest popped into his head and he started to get a little hard.

She'd been fourteen when he'd met her. She'd come to the park to get in free and Seri had introduced her. She was jailbait then, dating that weird albino kid and *Christ* but she'd turned David's crank. She was like what Seri could be if she'd relax for a few seconds, plus she had curves that had stuck in David's imagination all fucking night. He'd never gotten past it.

As far as he could tell, she didn't like him either. It was hard to be sure – she rasped when she talked, a legacy of smoking for a few years, and it turned everything she said into a come on in David's mind. But she always made herself scarce when he was around.

Maybe she just doesn't want to make trouble with Seri. His hand was busy now, imagining what Thea had looked like that time he'd taken them all to the beach. She'd worn a bikini top and a pair of cut offs, and was finally legal. He'd been ragingly hard all day, had even managed to get Seri in the changing rooms to take care of it.

He made himself come imagining it had been Thea in there with him. Somehow, the idea that she didn't like him only made it better.

He had no idea who else would be there, but Seri had said 'guests' so he expected she'd invited someone else. Maybe someone from school who didn't have family to go home to, Seri was always trying to adopt strays like that. Usually they'd make themselves scarce after a while, David had no idea what was up with that.

He finished up in the shower, got himself toweled off and otherwise prepared – mouthwash, deodorant, brushed his hair and teeth – with his thoughts returning to Seria. He realized he didn't actually want to let her go. He didn't want to get married yet, or even engaged – they were barely into their twenties. But he did have feelings for her. He remembered working with her at Rocky Point, graduating high school with her. In his way he really *liked* Seri. He knew she was beautiful and smart and frankly, better than he deserved.

You're just a dog, Kanmore. He looked at his reflection to make sure his hair was even, then walked off to get dressed.

*

Half an hour later he was parking in front of Seri's place.

Seri and Joe were renting half a duplex near East Greenwich, just off of 95. Joe went to school and worked in Bristol, so he often liked to drive south and take the bridges across to Newport for the scenery. Once or twice David had hitched a ride with him in the morning and had Seri pick him up at night, since Salve was on the way.

They'd had a house – their parents left it to them – but they'd sold it. Too many memories, he guessed. Sometimes he wondered if he'd even notice if *his* folks died. Kevin probably would. He was the heir. David was the spare.

Oh, boo hoo, mommy and daddy don't love you. They pay for everything, that's better.

He'd picked up a bottle of wine – nothing fancy, just a bottle of Carlo Rossi – and he grabbed the real reason for his trip to the Almacs, hid it behind his back. He walked up to the front door and knocked. There were a couple of cars he didn't recognize in the street, a nice blue Toyota coupe and an old muscle car, maybe a Firebird. He didn't know much about old cars.

Seri opened the door and he took the flowers out from

behind his back, presented them with a slight flourish.

"Carnations," Seri smiled ruefully. "You're still late."

"But you love me anyway."

"I suppose I must." She sighed, took the flowers. He went in for a kiss and for a moment remembered being under the roller coaster with her, the smell of popcorn in the air. His first real girlfriend. Unless you counted Shonda Camarelli, but that had been a crush.

"Can I come in?"

"Yeah, get in already." She stepped aside and let him walk in, and he took his coat off and put it on the couch. Most of the half a house she and Joe shared was decorated by her, so the couch and chairs had flowers on them. Joe probably just would have gotten something off white and called it a day.

"Where's Joe?"

"He's in the kitchen. We're eating in there." She was wearing a tight pair of jeans and a blue blouse that matched her eyes, her hair tied back in a ponytail. Likely she'd been cooking since the day before. Seri liked to get things *just so.* He followed her in, expecting her brother and cousin. And they were there.

He *wasn't* expecting the tall blond guy standing over with Joe near the counter. David wasn't short. He'd played basketball at Salve, he was over six three. But this guy was taller, with long hair pulled back in a braid, and he was lounging against the counter like he owned the room. That wasn't the surprise for David. David knew that Joe liked guys. They'd never talked about it, because *man,* David didn't want details, but it was none of his business what Joe did with his life.

The surprise was Thea working on taking something out of the oven. She was talking animatedly to...

Is that that guy from the...

David had missed how big the guy was. He probably wasn't much taller than David, but he looked like he could weigh as much as all of the other men in the room put together. He was wearing a grey dress shirt that didn't fit him. David had been to enough fittings in his life to know this guy needed a tailor, off the rack was *never* going to work for those shoulders.

Between the two of them David actually felt small for the first time in his life. He didn't like it.

"Oh, you showed up." Joe said placidly. "I'm out fifty bucks."

"We didn't bet." Seri replied, almost prim.

"Well, no, you didn't bet." Joe replied. "Thea and I put some money on it."

"You can pay me later." Thea replied, now leaning against the behemoth. "Hey Dave."

"How's it going?" He put the bottle of wine down on the table. "We going to do introductions or…"

"What, I thought everybody knew you." Joe nodded towards the blond. "This is Bishop. Bish, this is my sisters *innamorato*, David. Oh, and that's Thomas, Thea's… I have no idea."

"He's just mine." Thea said. "That's all you need to know."

"Sorry, I left my tags at home." The big guy rumbled. He didn't move to shake hands like Bishop had, just stood there. David got the uncanny sense of what it would be like to piss off a mountain. He swallowed and decided to just let it pass.

"So what are we eating?"

"It's Thanksgiving." Seri came up next to him, took his arm. It helped a little. "What does anyone eat on Thanksgiving? We cooked a turkey."

"The better to celebrate how we stole this land from the Narragansett."

"Did anyone in our family get here before 1918?" Seria shot Joe a look. "Hell, I think Nana came after the war."

"Which war? There have been a few."

"Don't be horrible." She let go of David's arm after patting it, walked over to the stove and busied herself. "I feel bad we didn't invite her. She's just down in Little Compton…"

"Oh, *fuck me,* Seri." Thea snorted. "The last time I saw her she just cackled for like an hour. What do you expect from her?"

"We're her *grandchildren…*"

"Yeah, well, she's got like thirty, let someone else worry about her."

"Thirty?" Thomas spoke up.

"Nana was a bit of a slut." Thea smirked.

"She was *not*." Seria reached over and swatted Thea with an oven mitt.

"She got married like three times!"

"But she *was* married. It's not *her* fault that Electric Boat was a death trap."

"Our grandfather was her third husband." Joe supplied. "Her first died in like 47 or 48, sheet of metal dropped on him. Second guy got run over on his way home. And then after our grandfather got cancer she just decided to stop trying."

"We don't really stay in contact with the extended family." Thea was leaning up against Thomas, letting him support her. It felt nice to tell him things like this, let him see the three of them together. "Shit, we all have different last names, I don't even know half of them."

"It was just Thea's mom and our dad growing up, Paola and Paolo." Joe snickered. "Nana wasn't very original at naming."

"They were twins. Like Seria and Joe, actually." Thea snorted. "At least they dodged the 'basically the same name' bullet."

"I didn't know that," David said.

"Never asked." Seria was pouring the contents of the pot into a gravy boat. "And I didn't much like talking about it when we got together."

"I knew a pair of twins…" Bishop started, then stopped. "Actually, never mind, not a story for Thanksgiving."

"Is it dirty?" Joe elbowed him.

"It's absolutely vulgar." Bishop smiled and turned to him. "I'll tell you about it later."

Thomas felt very uncomfortable. He liked that Thea was in contact with him – the way she'd reach a hand to touch his leg or arm, light reassuring touches – but couldn't quite get the whole feeling of being a fraud out of his system. He felt ridiculous in the clothes he'd picked out. Over the past year, working out and reading had been his main outlets. He'd put on a lot of muscle mass, and now he felt like he was going to blow out the Dockers just by sitting wrong.

Watching Thea and her cousins had been wistful for him. He didn't have that. He'd grown up without any family except his parents. His grandparents had both died while he was still a child, and if they had any family he didn't know about it.

Also he wanted very badly to just kick the everloving shit out of Seria's boyfriend.

He knew it was unreasonable. The guy hadn't even been that bad so far, he'd given Thea a quick look, seen him, and pulled his attention right back. But it still bothered him, and being jealous at all bothered him more. He'd been confused when Thea'd said he was hers, at how he *liked* that.

The room itself was small for six people, the big table taking up most of the available space. Seria had seated him with Thea on his left and Bishop on his right. This put Joe on *Bishop's* right, and Seria on Joe's, and David on *hers*, which meant that David was on Thea's left.

You really need to calm down about this guy.

He forced himself to take a few breaths, thinking about the rite he and Thea had been working on for the past few weeks. He let his eyes wander looking at the plates and platters on the table, laden with food – squash, mashed potatoes, peas, the turkey, stuffing, canned cranberry sauce, all arranged by Seria's almost tyrannical instructions. The colors on the round plates, lit by the amber light above their heads, it called to mind the tree of life, the *otz chaim* from the Sephiroth.

You're too quick to sacrifice yourself. It doesn't have to be pain.

Thea kept making this point in different ways but it was hard for him to think that way. To him, growing up had displayed pain a lot more often than pleasure. Beatings at school. His grandfather's stories, told to a boy too young to understand them. Spending summers tending to chickens, sheep, pigs, even a few head of cattle and always seeing their lives end, eventually having to be the one to end them. He hated killing things. He'd done it more than he wished.

"Hey." Thea'd come in close. "You going to just stare at that or maybe eat some of it?"

"Oh, shit, sorry…"

"It's fine, I'm not mad." Her smile was a beautiful thing and he almost gaped at it. "But I think Seri'll freak out if we don't all eat and enjoy it on schedule."

"Sorry, I'm a little distracted." He closed his eyes, trying to focus on the thought he had going. Being here among so many people at once, feeling so exposed without all the layers of work he'd put into the house. "I wish we'd had a chance to ward this place."

"You need to relax. It's Thanksgiving, it's just a suburban house. We'll be fine."

"I don't like gambling on that." He took a breath, leaned in close to make sure no one else could overhear. "You remember what your mom said."

That made her frown. She nodded slowly.

"Okay. I've been doing my homework, will it make you feel better if I go do something? I want you to sit here and try and make pleasant conversation."

He nodded. Not that he wanted to do that, but it was better than the both of them trying to be unobtrusive at once. She slid her chair back.

"Hey, Seria, I'll be right back." She put on her best *I'm sad* face. "Just… kind of want to take a few minutes."

"Okay?" Seria didn't see that she'd taken the salt shaker with her. She walked by her cousin and kissed her on the forehead, ignored David staring at her as she did it. There were times that she wanted to sit David down and explain to him that he only ogled her because he was perennially chasing after what he didn't have instead of appreciating what he did. But that would mean taking time and effort out of her life to try and make him grow up.

She stopped at the front door and unscrewed the salt shaker, getting some in her palm, and traced a symbol near the door, a circle with a line dividing it like an equator. Inside it she drew four triangles, two also divided by lines. It was a simple enough concept, the four elements bound through the salt into the house. It wouldn't do anything unless a counter-force was applied, then it would flare into power. Quick and dirty, but serviceable. She set it, keeping the memory of the night before firmly in her mind, and felt it course down her arm and into the wood. She could see it rippling.

Pleasure works, love.

Satisfied, she walked out the door. It was cold, colder than she expected, and getting dark even though it was barely five. The sky was the color of a dying fire, clouds trailing along the edge of the sky between the purple and orange.

In the truck down the road, Jimmy Williams was staring at the door.

"One of them came out." He peered through a pair of cheap plastic binoculars they'd picked up at a sporting goods store. "Damn, it's not the one."

"Not the one what?"

"I like the one with the longer hair." He handed over the binoculars, and Morgan took a look through them.

"This one's hair looks long to me."

"I like sportier girls."

"Well, the old lady doesn't want us mixing with them."

"For fuck's sake, this is why we didn't have to tell her..."

"Get it through your fucking *head*." Morgan hissed. "Try and keep anything from her and when she finds out, it's *your* turn to need someone to walk you and feed you and change your fucking diaper, if you're *lucky*." Morgan put down the glasses. "If you think I like being her fucking personal bitch you're goddamn insane. Sometimes I think you want her to waste you."

"At least it would be over." Jimmy didn't even sound sullen or sarcastic, just quiet. "She's going to do it sooner or later."

"Might as well be later, then." Morgan hadn't given up figuring out a way to kill her. "Right now, she wants that motherfucker dead and the brother grabbed up. We'll take him to the yard until she says otherwise."

"Why not just take him right to her?"

"Because she doesn't want him there." Morgan hadn't

questioned her. Whatever that thing that had been following her around, it had made his brain scream to see it. He turned and looked into the bed of the truck, where a huge, vaguely human shape was crouching under a tarp, whining. "I guess it's time."

"Hope they finished eating." Jimmy was recovered from his brief burst of honesty and was back to being his usual self as he got out of the truck. "Byron doesn't leave much behind."

Morgan was looking at the house. There was something about it that bothered him. He stepped out of the truck, picking up a baseball bat from behind the seat. Closed the door and went around to the tailgate.

Byron was pulling on his collar. His face still looked more or less the same, but the rest of him had twisted. To Morgan's eyes Byron looked like several images superimposed over each other, primitive and feral things pushed inside his body. She'd been *playing*, he realized as he choked back bile. What she'd done to him was just to see if she could do it.

"Hey, buddy." He said in a soothing a voice as he could manage. Byron looked up, confusion and eagerness mixed on his face. "I need you to do something for me."

*

Seria was overall satisfied with the meal. Once Thea had come back inside and sat down, she'd said grace and then people started eating. Thea's boyfriend (because that's what he was, no matter what Thea or Thomas said about it) ate like three people. Bishop was very fastidious, but he seemed to grasp that you don't talk while people are eating and she'd been worried about that. Even David managed to keep himself in check.

After that they ended up in the back yard. It was divided by a picket fence between them and their neighbors, who were out of town likely at some relative's Thanksgiving – the duplexes around them were all rented by other college age people, and so were often deserted on holidays. They lit a fire in the brick grill/fire pit and sat around, David and Bishop drinking beer, Seria a wine. Joe,

Thea and Thomas were having soda, likely because Joe expected to drive Bishop home and Thea didn't drink much.

Seri was jabbing the fire with a poker, an old iron thing she'd picked up somewhere.

"So how long have you two known each other?" Joe was asking Bishop.

"Tommy and I met back in Freshman year at WBC." Bishop smiled. "Believe it or not, he actually approached me."

"He was reading a book I was interested in. Strindberg. *Inferno*."

"Never did get that book." Bishop drank his beer. "Anyway, so Tommy here basically walks up and says 'We're going to be friends' and that's how it worked out."

"Really?" Thea turned to look at Thomas.

"I was more gregarious back then." He smiled, a gentle, abashed thing and she resisted the urge to put hands on him. Opened her mouth to speak.

A tremor shot through her, something *wrong*. He could see it, like sparks climbing up and down her skin, and they both turned to look at the front door through the house. It was intact.

There was a sound coming around the side of the house. Thea wasn't a farm kid. To her, it sounded like the biggest dog she'd ever heard. To Thomas, who'd spent summers working in the family slaughterhouse it was the noise of a boar snorting and grunting, sniffing the air. And it was not. They both knew it wasn't natural.

Thea reacted, thinking as fast as she ever had in her life. Joe and Seria were there, they were *vulnerable*, they had to be protected. She visualized this need, how important they were to her, and as new as it was she could see it as clearly as the wood paneling of the house in the dimming light. There was no time for alchemical symbols, so she called out to the house itself, to the electricity that ran through its wires and the steam in its pipes, the Association of the Phalanstere and demanded it act.

Power crackled in her limbs. Despite the fear she felt *good*, and stood just in time to see it come charging into the yard. It wasn't... couldn't be... human, but it felt as if it *had* been.

"Get everyone in the house." Thomas had done something else. As usual, he couldn't believe in the idea of power from pleasure, power *as* pleasure. His voice was thick, deep bass that echoed. Whatever it was, it was wearing what looked like rags, snorting at the air, sensing them with its nose.

"What the fuck..." David's voice.

"*Get inside.*" Thea's voice was also different. Joe could see *something* looking at her, and whatever it was it compelled him to do as she said. He grabbed Seria and pulled her towards the door.

The thing pounded the ground with two huge fists. Thomas wasn't ignoring it, exactly. He remembered his mother taking him out to the barn when he was twelve. *You'll need to learn how to kill.* Put a gun in his hand, led him over to a bull lowering in a pen. *Sometimes killing is the end of suffering. Sometimes a cruel act, but sometimes it's mercy, Thomas. And you'll need to be able to do it.* So many summers spent there, little deaths and bigger ones. Chickens, pigs, cows, deer out in the woods. He'd wept the first few times.

Its eyes locked on him as he moved backwards, found the handle of the poker and slid it out of the fire. He remembered placing the .45 ACP his grandfather had left behind against that bull's head, the thick muscles of its neck. *Asterion,* the divine primal bull, slain for life by Mithras, slain for death by Ahriman.

Thea was hesitating near the patio door, wanting to come help him. He turned his attention just enough to be sure she saw him, shook his head. Her family came first. She followed them inside and he felt the ground shaking as it charged him.

It had a face like a boy's, unlined, weeping even while it roared. He stood with the poker held like a knife, point facing at it.

Mithras is Perseus is Theseus, killer of the bull, the star gorgon, the beast of the air. His panic forced associations. It leapt to crash down where he was standing.

He wasn't standing there when it came down. He rolled in the grass, came up with the poker and struck, taking it across the back. It shrieked, the voice terrifyingly childlike, and careened through the brick grill, destroying it as it stumbled through. The sound was familiar, terrifyingly so.

Waiting in the back of the car, the impact ringing. His mother screaming. Except she wasn't, was she? She was saying his name.

The screaming came from outside.

Sparks and burning wood scattered throughout the yard as it pulled itself to its feet. Fury on its disproportionate face. Red and yellow light flickering around them as it turned, the ruins of the concrete and brick and burning wood everywhere. Hard enough to smash a chimney.

Hard enough to push a car off the road.

He dropped and put his palm down, grabbed hold of a shard of burning wood. *You sacrifice yourself too quickly.* But pain was the only reliable source for him now. Bit back a scream as his skin bubbled away, blistering.

It charged again.

Inside the house Thea was crackling, lightning seeking a path to ground, the hiss of a boiler her breathing. She could feel the entire house, knew where everyone was inside it even without seeing them. David, Joe, Seri and Bishop were confused and afraid, both David and Bishop as inert as coal. Seri just a hint of fire, untapped, and Joe a little brighter, a little sharper.

She felt it just as it happened, the front door shaking then caving in. Two men, one with a gun, the other a baseball bat, both almost as tall as Bishop or David and *mean*, twisted up inside. The one with the bat swung it, cracking Bishop in the temple and sending him to the floor. The one with the gun pointed it at her.

"Bitch, get over with…"

He didn't get to finish.

The gun was a machine. Mechanism, springs, slides, all designed to channel the chemical reaction of the bullet. Each of these things happening as designed. Ordered. Inside that house, all fell under Thea's will, driven by need. The elves danced to her tune.

The ammunition in the clip exploded because she asked it to. The gunman had something, some trick, something he'd expected to protect him from her. But the gun didn't. He barely managed to let it go. Shards of metal grazed his chest, his face, because that was where Thea had asked them to go, and his trick turned them just enough to make it painful instead of lethal. He staggered back, staring at her.

The one with the bat came at her. He was bigger than her, broader, but he swung like she was a t-ball stand. Good enough to hit Bishop.

She stepped into his reach and slammed a knee into his stomach, just like in sparring. She didn't ask the house to electrocute or sear him, able to see whatever it was they had to shield themselves. She just let herself remember close-quarters in a small storefront near the airport and got her leg behind his while he wheezed for air, shoved him over. He hit the floor, back hard against the wood.

The one who'd nearly lost his hand came at her. David had by the this time realized what was happening and tried to tackle the guy, getting a hard fist to the face for his trouble that sent his nose blooming onto his cheek, a mess of blood. It gave Thea time to turn to face him, snap a kick into his liver.

Liver kicks are fucking horrible. Scott's voice. *You kick a man in the liver, he falls down.*

That was what happened. The first one was getting back up just as the gunman – darker hair, more beard scruff, but a certain lanky resemblance to each other – was dropped to the floor. He managed to smash a hand into Thea's collarbone and she fell back wincing, seeing him choking up on the bat.

"Right. She says she wants you alive, but she didn't say I couldn't tool you up."

His attention was fully fixed on Thea. He hadn't seen Seria pulling a large black metal flashlight out of the couch, and barely managed to turn in time to keep her from cracking it off of the back of his head. He took it hard on the shoulder and Thea shot forward, punching him hard to the side of the face, sending him staggering away from her cousin.

The one Thea had kicked in the liver had dragged himself up and he was pulling a small bag, like a Crown Royal bag, out of his jacket.

"Fuck this, let's go."

"Jesus, don't…"

"That's what she *gave* it to us for!" He threw the bag down on the floor and Thea could *see* that it was wrong, sick, something not to be. She reached out, but the connection to the house was weaker now, she'd been focusing on fighting them and not on it.

It hit the floor and shredded apart, as if talons tore it open from the inside.

*

Outside, Thomas wasn't all there anymore.

His burned hand was clutching the smoldering wood, time flowing slowly around him like syrup poured from a cold bottle. He could feel Thea doing *something*, something powerful that he didn't understand. Everyone approaches it differently, and in less than a month she'd already begun to forge her own path. He wasn't sure if being proud of her wasn't a little arrogant, but he was definitely impressed.

Focus.

Its arms were outstretched. It had already crashed through brick and concrete. His hand squeezed down tighter on that chunk of wood until it began to quiver in his fingers. The pain was crawling up and down his nerves, his spine, from the base to the top. He remembered those colorful plates of food on the table, imagined them spinning around one another.

Be Mithras or be Theseus, the Tauroctanator. Bullkiller.

He moved, not quite fast enough. One of those hands shot out and managed to slap him, grazing him with the edge of his palm, sending him skidding across the grass and into the house. Blood welled up in his mouth. He welcomed it, more pain, spit the blood out onto his burned hand and imagined the *Asterion*, the star-bull Taurus brought to earth. Housed in flesh.

His hand began to glow. He sank it into the ground, the soil, and pushed himself upright as it huffed and circled, confused that he wasn't dead. He looked at it with great pity.

That child-face atop its neck wrinkled as it heard a male

voice cry out. It turned, its attention split as his had been. His fingers curled in the ground, ripped up frozen soil and dead grass.

He shot forward.

Again those killing hands swept at his head. He dropped to his knees, slid under them, then up again behind it. Locked his arms around its neck, his own muscles corded like iron. Feeling the image of the star-born bull with its neck bent to the side, twisting inexorably. The thing screamed again, that scream that haunted his sleep. The noise that buried his mother's last words to him. He could see her mouth, her lips moving, the car hurtling sideways.

Sometimes it's mercy.

He twisted his arms as hard as he could. Bore it to the ground, struggling in his arms, which burned with stolen fire from heaven. He could kill it. He could absolutely kill it.

You're too quick to sacrifice.

Instead, he looked at it. Looked *inside* it. Things seethed, writhed, not human and not meant to claw and scrape and scratch for command of one. He was obsessed, livid with them, imposed from without. Stuffed full of souls like a bag fit to burst, like a rat king of beings.

His lungs were aching, his arms quivering. It was twitching now, trying to break free. Soon it would be and it would kill him. It would kill him, it would kill Thea and...

No.

He released it, pulling back the hand that glowed, and drove it inside. The flesh quivered and melted aside. Most of the flesh wasn't real, wasn't flesh. It was convulsing on the ground as he wrapped his hand around the things that found a home there and wrenched them out. His shoulder screamed, he bit his lip to push through the pain.

There was an explosion at his feet, like a sack of rotten meat splitting open. A smell he'd smelled before, putrefaction and waste. The *essence* of them, the platonic ideal of rot and feces. In his fist wriggled the creature, a mass of cords and tendrils woven through one another, visible only by what they weren't. He clenched his fist and then jammed it into the remnants of the fire, pinning it to the burning wood with the iron poker. It dissipated, slain by flame or metal.

Lying on the ground was a naked child, a boy, maybe ten or younger. He was quivering, empty eyes staring at nothing. Thomas fought back the urge to vomit at the idea of having almost broken a child's neck.

Then he felt the throb of *wrong* from inside the house.

*

Thea had a few seconds to act. Bishop and David were the most helpless, both had been hit in the head. The house spirits were shrieking in terror inside her head, incoherent sounds of panic as the blackness twitched and slashed itself into existence. A twisted caricature of an animal, a jagged rejection of what one would expect to see. Darkness that moved, slavered, hungered, *mocked*.

She bore down and forced them to her side, the caged lightning, trapped steam. Her heart was pounding. The last time she'd seen one of these things it had been on the other side of a circle, unable to approach her. She'd felt safe, that night.

It barked like laughter at her, padded misshapen paws on the floor. Swiveled those *not eyes* to look at the room.

She chose the weakest. Put cages of lightning around them where they lay prone. Hoped it was enough while feeling herself grow weaker. Her ritual had merely been meant for protection, alarm, and she'd twisted its meaning about as far as she could get away with. She cursed herself for being so *new* to it. Thomas might...

She felt rather than saw or heard his pain, felt the house shake from an impact. Managed not to turn her head. *So no Thomas*.

She tried to put herself between it and the others, walking slowly to the side, turning left. It twitch-shuddered and was suddenly just *there*, appearing out of the corner where the walls met. Another mocking bark, slaver sizzling the floor as it dribbled loose.

When Thea had been much younger, she'd really enjoyed cartoons. She and her mother would sit together and watch them, a rare moment of Paola/Thea time. No matter what else her mother had going on (and it had been a lot) she always made time for it. One of the shows had been about a singer, her band, and a computer that could turn her someone else. It had always been one of Thea's favorites.

It's all bullshit. But it works.

She pulled on the memory, used it as an icon, wrapped herself in the warmth of her mother's arms around her on the couch, watching the old TV. The creature wheezed in alarm as the world responded, pulled to her will. Colors swirled into being around her, orbiting her, like arcs of pure rainbow slicing through the air. Thea remembered her mother's faded remnant in the kitchen, begging her to learn.

She lashed out with the rainbow and missed, the jangling discordant *hiss* of the creature jumping to a corner, trying to come at her from another direction. She blazed, glowing every color, a fountain of light that forced it to veer or be plunged into pure brilliance.

"I'll hit you sooner or later," she panted, sweat dripping down her face and into her eyes. Bravado felt right. Let it fear her. She was outrageous. Truly, truly truly outrageous.

She flared up, lighting the whole room. It was like being inside a prism as big as the world. The void where light went to die contracted, spitting and snarling in outrage. They were just *meat*. Meat wasn't supposed to fight back, wasn't supposed to be so awful and bright.

Behind Thea, Joe and Seria were stunned. Seria didn't know what she was seeing, didn't want to, just wanted it all to end. She couldn't get to David with the lightning arcing around him, Thea was glowing, there was a thing in the room that made her shake just to look at it, and the worst part was that she was starting to feel like she could understand what was happening. She didn't want to. She wanted to go back an hour when they were still eating Thanksgiving dinner and talking and it was life, life the way it was supposed to be and not utterly broken and wrong.

Joe was fascinated. He could see what Thea was doing, but more, he could see how. Lines and patterns of things he'd always almost been able to see. Part of him, too, part of Seri, absent from the others in the room. Outside he could hear something horrific and astonishing happening, could feel tremors from it. The black beast scrabbling at the floor drooling and snarling, it bent the lines around it. Twisted them into new geometry. It was as simple as laying down a grid for a floor plan, as complex as actually running a production.

The blackness arched, splitting up and reforming in a corner provided by the kitchen alcove and leapt, tearing a chunk out of the light and ripping across Thea's arm as she rolled to the side. She spat out nonsense syllables as she came up, her arm bloodied from shoulder to elbow with twisted claw wounds. She flexed her arm, wincing. *Not too bad yet*. She ordered the light to close them, felt them resist but respond to her will. If it got its teeth around her throat...

It would kill everybody if it got past her. She knew this. She forced herself to stay calm.

She let the light dim. It wasn't hard – she was exhausted, her whole body aching. It wanted rest. She was glad they'd eaten such a big meal earlier because she felt like she'd run for miles, desperately pulling in air. She wanted to look helpless. Played up the arm, even though she'd healed it, maybe that wasn't obvious, anything to lure it in...

It vanished and reappeared from the corner behind Seria and Joe, leaping forward. Thea tried to react, but she felt like she was drowning in glue, not fast enough. But Joe was closer, and he'd thrown himself wide open. He'd seen it bend the lines, known where it was going to go. He turned and shoved Seria hard, pushing her onto the rug.

Then it was on him, those *not jaws* clamping down on his shoulder, *not claws* ripping into his chest. Thea saw it while she was still concentrating, and her fear and rage and her love for her cousin, her *brother* really, lashed out in an arc of seething light.

Tangled up in its attack, it couldn't part the world fast enough. It realized too late *why* Joe had let it hit him. What he'd seen, realized before it had.

It died with its last realization being that it had been tricked by meat. Thea's will ripped it apart, sliced it with edges of pure color. There was nothing left of it even as she ran to catch Joe as he fell backwards.

"Oh Christ, Joey *please*." Thea cradled him. He didn't even look *hurt*, there wasn't a mark on him, but his eyes were closed and she could feel him fading away. Seria was up, the lightning gone, the room utterly normal now. Aside from the damage to the front door and the three men all lying prone you'd never know anything had happened.

"What... what did, what..." Seria fought to stop babbling. "What happened to him!? Is he..."

"He's breathing." Thea cradled his head, listened to his heart. It was going *very* slowly. She was muzzy headed, so exhausted she felt like crying just from the pain of it. "I don't... I don't know what that *was*, I don't..."

"Calm." Thomas' deep voice as he walked in from the back yard, favoring his left leg. His face had been *smashed*, it looked like he'd taken a shovel to his cheek. There was blood dripping down his face and his hand was red from his own blood. He walked over and dropped to his knees, looked over Joe. "He got bit?"

"The thing, it came out of the wall, it came *out of the wall*." Seria was starting to panic, forced herself not to. "He pushed me out of the way, it was on top of him, and then Thea... I don't know what she did, or how she did it, or how you're still alive or what that thing outside was."

"Worry about that later." Thomas turned to Thea. "Did you see it bite him?"

"It bit him and it clawed at him." She sounded like she was about to pass out. He knew how she felt. "I couldn't hit the fucking thing."

"They're hard to get a bead on." He knew the typical path. Joe would sicken and die, and no one would be able to tell what had killed him. That was what his father's notebook had warned, anyway. *Beware the Hounds of Tindalos*. Its bite was destroying Joe by eating away at the time he lived in. He was so tired, it took him a second to force himself to think.

Bishop was groaning, holding his head. *Well, at least your only friend isn't dead. His potential boyfriend, the woman you... fuck it, the woman you love's cousin, he's gonna die unless you come up with something. No pressure.* Thomas dredged his head.

"Thea."

"I'm here, what do we *do*?"

"I don't know. He's going to die. There's nothing a doctor can do for him, they won't even know what this is, they won't *see* anything if they treat him." He bent so his voice only carried to her ears. "I don't know of a way to stop it."

"If you don't..." She stopped, her thoughts suddenly whirling. "Your ritual."

"That just trades one life for another..."

"That was you trying to bring two people back. We've got four here trying to save *one*." She panted it out, fighting the grey trying to swamp her vision. "We've got to try *something*."

"All right." He nodded, slid his arms under Joe's neck and back and lifted him like a child. "Follow me out back, we don't have a lot of time to set up."

"Shouldn't we..."

"He'll be dead before we get back to my place. And the longer someone's dead, the harder the rite is. Neither of us is in good shape right now." He tried very hard to sound confident, so that she'd feel like they had a chance to pull this off. Sometimes all this magic shit seemed like an elaborate case of the Placebo effect to him. Trick yourself into believing hard enough to pull the rug out from under life.

"Does someone want to tell me what the fuck is going on?" Bishop spit on the floor as he got up, blood from a bitten tongue from when he got hit. "What happened to Joe?"

"Short version. A monster bit him."

"A monster." Bishop followed them outside. "If I hadn't seen that thing come around the fence…"

He stopped talking when he saw the naked child in the fetal position in the back yard. Seria and Thea both stopped walking when they saw him.

"That's the thing that attacked us."

"It's a *kid*." Thea said. "Who would… they sent a *kid* at us."

"Whoever is behind this needs to die." Thomas placed Joe on the grass, in a clear spot not trampled or strewn with ruined brick or the remnants of the fire. "Thea, I need something I can write on him with, a marker or something."

"You want to write on him?" Seria said as Thea got up and went into the house.

"We have to do this quick, I don't have time for anything elaborate." He pushed on his forehead with his palm, trying to keep his head from aching. "Christ, what was the goddamn… Life, death, power."

"No." Bishop spoke up.

"No what?"

"You always get that one wrong. It's death, then life, then power. That's how I beat you on trivia night." Bishop had dropped to put his jacket over the unconscious child. Now he stood up. "What's that got to do with anything?"

"It's part of the ritual."

"A fucking *comic book*?"

"Anything that works." Thea came out of the house holding a marker, handed it to him. He began drawing the alchemical symbols on Joe's hands, which he crossed over his chest. "How are you feeling?"

"Probably better than you," she grunted. "Got it wrong, huh?"

"Guess it's a good thing we never tried it."

"Don't get it wrong this time, please." She tried to sound light. "He's my family."

"I know." He drew the lantern symbol last. Considered. He wished Bishop hadn't corrected him, it changed the whole thing around. Maybe that could work for them. Thea had killed the

Hound. That could be death. Next they needed to bring life. Maybe.

Awful lot of maybe so far.

He straightened up in time to see David stumbling out of the house.

"What in the *fuck* is going on!?" He was holding his face, still bleeding from when he'd gotten his nose broken. Seria broke and headed over to him, threw her arms around him. He hugged her back on autopilot.

"Are you okay?"

"I'm fine, my face hurts, what are you all *doing* out here, we have to call the cops…"

"And tell them what?" Thomas' voice was like granite grinding against itself. "What exactly did you see? You going to tell the cops that a monster attacked us?"

"No." Thea stood, put her arm on Thomas's forearm. "I'll handle this. You get back to work, we don't have time." He looked at her, at the intent on her face, and nodded curtly before turning back to preparing Joe. Thea rounded on David.

"Okay. I get that you're upset, and probably embarrassed."

"I'm not…"

"He kicked your ass." She said it flat, like an accountant handing over the bill. "You can salve your wounded ego later. Now isn't the time. Now is the time where we save Joe. Get on board or get out of the way because I dropped the dude who broke your nose with one kick, and I'll drop you just as fast if you make me." She turned to Seria. "Joe is going to need us. I need *you*."

Seria had never seen Thea this serious in her life. She nodded, wishing there weren't strange after-images when she looked at her brother, her cousin, Thomas – it was like they had more weight, more substance somehow.

"Seri, this is crazy!" David hissed.

"I know. Just… sit over there, I guess." She waved her hand at the few remaining chairs near where the fireplace was.

Bishop had lifted the unconscious child off of the grass and wrapped his coat around him as best he could. The boy was breathing but unresponsive, his eyes open and staring. He had dark brown hair, tan skin, blue eyes. Thea could see what looked like scars *inside* him, marks clawed into him, and the remnant of whatever Thomas had done spreading outward from a point on his back, a clean spot radiating into the utterly unclear scratches. Bishop looked up at her as she walked closer.

"He's alive. That's all I can say."

"Here." She put her hand on Bishop's shoulder. "Over here near everybody else so he's close at least."

"Is Tommy…" Bishop stopped. "This all doesn't, I mean, if I hadn't seen…"

"You did see, though. Just go along with it for now." She swallowed back a wave of vertigo, so tired that every gesture hurt. Bishop lay the kid down so gently you'd have thought it was *his* kid, which made Thea feel better about the whole thing. About trusting him to help with Joe's life.

"Okay." Thomas had pulled his shirt off. His arm looked *awful*, the hair burned off, scar tissue from the center of his palm. He'd healed it but not well. She wondered if she could fix it later. He had such gentle hands. "He's as ready as I can get him."

"So what do we do?"

"You'll have to actually do the rite." He turned to Thea. "You know him better, you care more about him. You'll be a better source." She nodded, accepting this, terrified of her own body failing.

"What about you?"

"I'll be occupied." He had a look on his face she'd seen the night they called up her mother. "This is going to attract attention. Whoever sent them… she's got juice, if shitty taste in servants. She'll almost certainly feel us."

"Does that matter?" Bishop managed not to sound utterly terrified. Thea still thought she could hear it.

"I don't know what she can do from a distance." He stood up. "Enough talking. We have to do it now if we're going to." Joe had hitched up, gurgled, and stopped breathing. Bishop saw it first and looked stricken, and Seria was openly sobbing. Thea walked over and took charge.

They got organized, Seria and Bishop to either side, Thea standing over him. Thomas reached a hand, cupper her chin in it, and kissed her softly for a moment. She blinked up at him after he pulled back.

"Why?"

"You were right. It doesn't always have to be pain." He smiled, clearly swaying on his feet. He leaned over to her ear. "I love you, Thea Mendel."

She felt like her eyes were the size of dinner plates when he stepped away, taking up a position away from them, watching. She swallowed, forced herself to focus on Joe.

Why did he have to say it now!? What the hell do I do with that, I don't… She calmed herself. *You know what to do with it. Save Joe with it. Worry after.*

*

Less than 20 miles away, a woman was shrieking.

She'd destroyed her living room, shattered everything glass in reach. Her hands were bloody, pieces of broken picture frames embedded in her skin. She shrieked and smashed and shrieked again, knocked her television over and the big curved picture tube exploded under the weight. She didn't care. She didn't watch TV much.

First she'd felt the breaking of the so, so *interesting* changes she'd worked on Byron. It had been curiosity that had bid her to see if Byron's flesh could host so many foreign spirits, a recreation of something they'd tried on her once in a less tangible way. He'd twisted and deformed but had changed, he'd changed into something useful. She'd been proud of that. When that snapped she felt it like a slap across the face, made worse because she'd *marked* him already. He was a sacrifice, she should have felt stronger, younger when he died.

But he didn't *come*.

Frustrated, maddened, and so hard to think she'd prepared to take action when the Hound died. That had been worse, much worse. It had been a long, long ritual to bind the Hound, to set it to her will. Placing it in the bag had been a risk but she'd gambled it couldn't possibly be harmed by them. How could they? It had taken her *years* to learn how to call the Hound. And yet it had died, it had *died*, her Hound was *dead* and the pain of her broken calling was rocketing up and down her limbs.

Then the fury took her.

Finally she simply ran out of screams. The boys had failed, the Hound had failed, and she had suffered. Yes, she'd suffered. Suffered, and suffering was useful. You could *use* suffering.

There were worse things between here and forever than just a Hound. She couldn't necessarily control them. She was old, and she'd used up so much already.

But she didn't *need* to control everything.

She raised her bloody hands up and rubbed them across her eyes, smiling now.

*

Thomas felt the draw on him when Thea started the ritual. What he'd said, what he felt was now a bond between them, she could use it.

He knew it was too soon, of course, and she likely didn't feel the same way. But he'd had to let her have that piece of him. She'd need it. She was new to this and she'd already used up more of her personal reserves than she really had, it was the only way. It was her who'd convinced him it would work.

Or maybe it's just another sacrifice.

Thea wasn't chanting. She was doing the work internally, thinking about the concepts of each symbol in turn. Decay, death, its reversal, purification, rebirth. The lantern symbol, death then life then power. Death was the wild card here. If Bishop hadn't corrected him he could just sacrifice their lives to fuel it, but he had. How was it...

He felt it and almost smiled. His unknown enemy had every advantage. They didn't know who she was, where she was, how to find her. But he was learning one thing about her – she was predictable in her vindictiveness. When he'd seen what she'd done to the boy, turning him into *that*, he knew she'd never let things slide.

He could feel the energies radiate out, sliding together from inside the house and from where he'd killed the defiling spirits. It was like watching tar ooze together, forming a lump of decay and awfulness, yoking that corruption together. It was a force of death, raw and aching to swallow life.

First to bring death.

David Kanmore sat terrified as the thing rose from the ground. He didn't know what it was, how it could possibly be, but he could see it. It was a mass of glop, covered in eyes and teeth and tendrils of oozing flesh. It reeked. It burbled a sound from orange beaks growing out of its sides.

"Tekeli-li." It didn't scream, it *sang*, a song that made David's blood run cold. Up till now he was managing to convince himself that it was all madness, that they'd had a home invasion and then everyone went crazy. He'd been preparing to pull out his cell phone and dial 911. But this couldn't be explained. The eyes, mouths, beaks all subsumed back into it and new ones formed as it heaved itself out of the ground.

Thomas watched it pulse and slither its way up. The time wasn't yet, and he didn't think he could fight it even if it was. But he didn't have to fight it. He'd ripped up the grass in fist sized circles, arranged in two rows of three and a longer row of four between them. Between them he'd made a thin curling line, as if climbing them.

Thea pulled harder on him. He let her, feeling his vision tunneling on the ooze as it began crawling at him, ready to crush him. He spoke as it slid its way out of the ground.
"And the Angel of the Elohim went before the camp of Israel, removed and went behind them, and the pillar of cloud went from before them and stood behind them."

The walls of the duplex began to tremble. The grass around them waved in no wind.

"And it came before the camp of the Egyptians, the camp of Israel; it was a cloud and darkness to the first but gave light by night to the second; and the one came not near the other all the night."

His head moved in erratic rhythm, his fingers twisting and pulling cord against cord without any cords actually being there. A ripple centered on him spread out along the ground, a shadow passing over his features.

"And Moses stretched out his hand over the sea, and the Lord drove back the sea with a strong east wind all night and made the sea dry land and the waters parted."

It oozed onto the first circle, representing Kether, the crown. That which was wholly of Atziluth, the world of Emanation, where the Limitless Light first became discrete. Thomas held out a hand and snarled as the cords in his hands all pulled taut.

There was a green light emanating from the grass now. The oozing monstrosity stopped, puzzled. It had never felt fear, or any reason to hesitate before. It *could* not feel these things. And so it flexed its fluid flesh to move forward.

But it could not.

The one could not come near the other. It could not approach him.

"She shouldn't have sent you." He brought his hands together, visualizing the path from Kether to Binah, to Chokmah, to Tiphareth and Yesod and finally Malkuth. The divine path. The lightning flash.

Lightning ripped apart the yard, crashing down from heaven above them, from clouds lowering that Thea had watched along the edge of the sunset. Now it was night and they answered the 72 fold name, driving their lightning like a sword from the sky.

The strike smashed its seething flesh into the rest of the circles, and the whole thing burst into flaming light as the death died. Thomas felt the power rocket into and through him, driven to his knees by it, barely able to keep conscious. His hand exploded in light, his arms, everywhere he was scarred or blemishes glowing as the power caught on him, his face lit up on the left side.

Thea had been calling, and waiting, and channeling their

love. Bishop's concern was still a new thing, a *what might this be*, but Seri's was that of a child who'd never known a life apart from Joe, her twin, her shadow and reflection. She loved Joe so purely that it made Thea weep. Tears streamed down her face at the force of it. And her own love, so much tinged with fear. Thea had pushed away love. Love meant you would lose the thing you needed, you needed them and then they were gone. Her mother. Her father – now, in this moment she couldn't lie anymore, her daddy was dead. It wasn't fair. It wasn't *fair* and she'd die before she let Joe go now. Everyone in the rite could feel it, feel *her*.

She knew absently that Thomas was working, could feel him too. He was part of her now, he'd opened himself and it was more than she thought she could bear. When the tide of death made life rushed over her, into her, she pulled Joe into it, pushed him full into the stream of it. Held him there. Every part of her felt it, rushing through her, and it was all she could do to hold on but she did.

Anyone else might have let go. Even Thomas probably would have. He was more experienced but he didn't know Joe yet, didn't have memories of him going back to infancy. And wasn't so thoroughly angry at the unfairness of losing someone you loved – he was still in shock, Thea realized, he'd scabbed over where they died. His scab was just coming off.

She was raw, still bleeding, still wounded. She used it now, held on tight, the power of the death sacrifice hers to direct. She held Joe in its path until, finally, it had rushed over and through and around him. She released Seria and Bishop.

Only then did she realize that she and Thomas were still linked.

Then to bring power.

They both realized their error. They were too tired to break the link between them, and so when the backlash happened, the power of the rite completed had nowhere to go, nowhere to discharge. Save in them. The rite as originally created had multiple Enochian watchtowers invoked to ground it.

This backyard version only had Thomas' crude tree of life, the ten spheres, the serpent and lightning flash. It wasn't enough.

Seria saw Thea crumple just as Joe jerked awake. She fell to the grass as certainly as if she'd been hit with an axe. Thomas dropped face first into the dirt he'd exposed.

*

Thea found herself at a carousel.

She was six. Her mother had rounded up Seria and Joe, both of them eight, and taken them to the park, because it was one of her favorite places. Thea hadn't know what her mother had done for a living then. It would be another few years before she knew what a 'clinical social worker' was. All she knew then was that mommy worked with people. When it got to be too much, she would grab Thea and sometimes the cousins and take them all to the park.

"My mom never wanted to come here," Paola would say, while getting Thea a bag of circus peanuts. Thea didn't like them, but she ate them so that mommy wouldn't be sad. When mommy got sad, usually after visiting her own mother, she would often go into the basement and wouldn't come out. Daddy called that her 'special place'.

Thea had very few memories from before she was six. The one that stuck the brightest in her memory was one of the trips to the carousel, riding the painted horses in her mom's lap. It was the first memory she had that she was sure of, the first one that wasn't a memory that could be a story someone else told her. No one but her and her mother had really known about that carousel. Maybe Joe and Seri, but they weren't up there. They hadn't heard her mother whispering in her ear.

"She said 'My Thea. My baby.'"

All around the carousel people stood, motionless. Thea turned to find the voice, found a woman with long grey hair sweeping behind her as she walked. She looked much like Paola had, much like Seria did, but older. Her eyes were calm, clear and blue like the lakes in the park near the Temple to Music. Her clothes were a long flowing dress and a peasant blouse, and she met Thea's eyes with neither fear nor hostility.

"You're not my mother."

"I am not." She nodded. "You've met Paola as she is now. I am not that."

"Aw fuck me." Thea wasn't sure if she was actually touching her head or just thought she was. "Is this going to be you spouting cryptic mystical bullshit at me?"

"I just wanted to see you." The woman swept closer, her hair and skirt flowing in counterpoint to each other. It was impressive and looked wildly impractical. Thea could imagine the weight of that much hair pulling on the back of her head all the time. Just having shoulder length was enough to make her want to cut it all off some days.

"Okay. Why?"

"Because my sister is going to make things very hard for you very soon." She stopped, a sad look on her face. "I'd say it's not her fault, but it is and I won't make apologies for her. What she's done is wrong."

"So you're sisters with whoever is trying to kill me?"

"Oh, she doesn't want *you* dead. She'd be angry if she knew how far you'd come already, because she doesn't want that." She made a face. "Goddamn it, Robi. She still has me bound, I can't..."

"What, like mom?"

"No, much worse." She sat down on the bench nearest the carousel, the painted horses a motionless blur of red and gold and white. "Compared to the slavery in which I toil, Paola and Paolo and the others are to be envied. I can only speak with you like this because she overstepped herself." The woman smiled. "You *hurt* her, little girl."

"Well... good." Thea sat next to her. "Can you tell me your name?"

"No, I cannot. Part of what she did. She did it out of love, which makes it profound in a way it wouldn't be otherwise. She won't let me die." A smooth hand reached out but stopped inches from Thea's face, then withdrew. "I'm sorry. This must be maddening. I'm trying to find what she didn't think of."

"Can you tell me what she *did*, why she wants whatever she wants? If she wasn't trying to kill me..."

"She wants your Thomas dead."

"What? Why? Because he helped me in the house?"

"She wanted him dead before you met." She smiled, a gentle thing. "She killed his parents. Just like she killed yours and Joe and Seria's. But they weren't of *use* to her, they *threatened* her." She stretched, made another pained face. "Ah, *that* she forbids. I can't tell you more about that."

Thea held her breath, counted to ten. She didn't want to scream at this woman. She felt stirrings of emotions she'd always wanted to feel around her, almost safe, comforted. She looked at the frozen people, searching for the particular way her mother had styled her hair back in 1984. She didn't see her.

"Why are we useful to her?"

"No, she won't allow that. But it's a good question." She seemed to think for a moment, smiled. "I *can* tell you to think about that, it's important. She hasn't forbidden that." She dabbed away at her eyes. "Robi isn't all there anymore, probably because of me, of my body."

"Can you tell me about that?"

"Robi and I were dying. But she found a way to keep us, both of us... in one place." She was looking down at her hands. "It was an awful thing to do. But we were dying, and neither of us wanted that. We were *young*, younger than you are now, it wasn't fair what they did."

Thea found herself touching the woman's cheek, and she looked up, brushing away a tear. Smiling again.

"And you think you're not kind."

"I'm not."

"I think you are, baby girl." She let out a little sob. "You look so much like Paola."

"Everyone says Seria looks more like her than I do."

"Seria looks like her father. You look like your mother. Although I can see Greg in you, in your eyes." She stood up, swift and graceful. "There's not a lot of time left. All I can do is tell you that you're closer than you think, you *can* find her. Stop her. It will hurt, but you can do it."

Thea wanted to speak, to ask more questions, but she could feel the air beginning to move around her, the music of the carousel speeding up. Suddenly people were everywhere in motion, talking and laughing and shrill little shrieks of a child running past.

She forced her eyes open.

"Thea, thank *God*." Seri had her head against her lap, was brushing her hair out of her face. Thea almost laughed, but the blinding pain in every part of her said that was a bad idea.

"Seri." She blinked and regretted it. Her throat felt like sandpaper. She saw a shadow, saw Joe bending over her with a glass of water. She smiled at him. "Joey."

"Here." He held the glass of water to her mouth. She drank it, her throat greedy for moisture. Swallowing it made her head ache. Some of it trickled down her chin but she didn't care.

"You're okay."

"If I am, it's thanks to you and your boyfriend." Joe knelt in front of her. "I had some very fucked up dreams. I'm not sure… I guess all this is really happening."

"Seems so." Thea managed to get herself sitting upright despite Seri making noises to the contrary. "How's Thomas, is he…"

"He's still out cold." Bishop's voice. Thea turned to look over at what had been the barbeque area, now a ragged, smashed in wreck surrounded by broken bricks and burned out wood. The grill was embedded in the ground some twenty feet away near the fence. She didn't think they'd be able to get it out. Bishop had Thomas propped up near where the kid was sitting, shivering in his coat, still looking almost blank eyed. Thea took a moment to remember that. *Right, a seven foot tall monster attacks and my boyfriend turned it into a pre-teen. Good night, everybody.*

She wanted to check out so hard in that moment. Just curl up in a ball and let this be someone else's problem. She'd done *plenty*. She'd talked to the spirits that made up the house, summoned a childhood memory of a TV show to kill a monster dog from beyond space and time, and raised her cousin from the dead.

Instead she pushed herself upright.

"Thea, you just *passed out*..."

"Seri." She reached over, put her arm over her cousin's shoulders. "Help me get over there." She didn't bother to argue. She knew Seri would support her. She'd been doing it her whole life.

It was sort of like a potato sack race as Seri held her up and they hobbled over. She slid her arm from around her cousin's shoulder and slumped to her knees in front of Thomas. Looked him over.

"There's something..." Joe said, then stopped. "Around his face?"

Indeed there was. Thea didn't know if Joe could see it now because of what had happened to him or because of who he was. The scar on his face was gone, as was the one on his arm that she'd seen him make the night they'd met, his ruined hand was healed. His beard had gone from longish stubble to an actual *beard*, and his hair was longer. She realized hers was, too, could feel the marks on her arm from the Hound were gone without even bothering to look. He wasn't hurt.

She leaned in close when the impulse took her. She decided to go with it, brushed his lips with hers, felt him respond and kissed him fully. Like she had on the porch the night they met. She broke it when she felt him groan, saw him blink into awareness much as she had.

"Thea?"

"I am she." She smiled, trying to be reassuring. Slid her mouth close to his ear. Felt a shiver go through her at what she was about to say, had never said to anyone who wasn't family. Not Karl, certainly not Scott. Her lips touched his ear. "I love you too."

He looked stunned, but it was hard to tell if that was from what she said or the after effect of the ritual grounding out in their bodies. She let herself collapse onto him, the two of them breathing into each other.

"Not that this isn't touching, but *what the fuck just happened*?" Bishop said, far too close for either of them. "Why did people hit me in the head with a baseball bat? How did you make

Joe not be dead because *he stopped breathing* and then there was lightning and..."

"Why is there a naked kid in a patio chair?" David added. "What was that fucking tower of ooze that..." He turned and retched, sickened just remembering what he'd seen. Seri moved to his side, rubbing his back and trying to be reassuring, and he *let* her, because he needed something that made sense.

"Later." Joe seemed surprisingly calm and lucid for someone who'd died from a monster biting him. "This place isn't safe. We have to figure out somewhere to go."

"I have a place." Thomas's voice rumbled through his chest and into Thea and she smile, letting herself just *feel* it. It was too soon. It made no sense. She knew that. She didn't care.

"Tommy, your house is..."

"Not my house." He groaned and sat up. "*His* house." Bishop's mouth snapped shut.

Joe was looking at his cousin and the man she'd picked, at the lines swirling around them. They deformed the world, made it bend. He didn't think he could do that, but he could *see* it, clearer than ever. Separately they were forces of nature. Together... he closed his eyes and saw them through his eyelids and realized he'd never know true darkness again. He could see everything around him, his sister and her concern and worry and fear, Bishop's incredulity and stoicism. Joe wondered if he was falling for Bishop, hoped for the man's sake that he wasn't. Saw David, almost broken, perhaps a venal man but no one deserved the kind of fear he was feeling now.

How do I turn it off? Everything went black. He felt panic tighten his gut, but then opened his eyes and saw again, saw people's outside faces, none of the lines.

"What do you mean by 'his' house?" Joe asked.

"It's secure, it's out on the bay. No one knows I own it. I rarely go there." He stood up, lifting Thea as he did. She took a moment to squeeze him and then stood apart, feeling herself getting stronger by the moment. "We can hide out there."

"I'm not going to some weird..."

"You shouldn't." Thomas cut David off. "No one was here for you. You and Bishop can probably go about your lives and be fine." Thea almost frowned, but it wasn't jealousy coming off of Thomas, maybe envy, but it wasn't about her. She realized he'd seen something too, and it was eating at him. "The four of us can..."

"Five." Bishop said quietly, forcefully. "Six if we count the kid, cause I have no idea what else to do with him."

Thea wobbled over and took a look at him.

"Thomas, what happened? Did you *change* him to this?"

"That's what he was inside all along." He turned his attention away from David. "See those black marks? The ones that are receding?"

"They look like the thing that bit me." Joe replied before Thea could. His hand was up at his throat now, feeling the skin. There were no marks, but he could still remember the cold of it smashing, biting down, the terror and the awful feeling of sinking into something so horribly old.

"He was infested." Thomas was now lumbering over and he lifted the child as if he was weightless. There was a small sound of protest, the child's eyes finally open and seeing.

"Hey." Thea tried. "Hey there. What's your name?"

He shook his head, moaned and curled up inside Bishop's jacket.

"Shit, he's even smaller than I thought." Bishop walked up. "Is he *shrinking*?"

"He's purging whatever she did to him." Thomas' voice cracked and only Thea and Bishop knew that it was fear. He was as out of his depth as any of them. She put her hand on his arm.

"Okay, whoever's coming, come on." She turned to Joe. "You two are coming, that's not negoitiable."

"We can't just leave, they *kicked in my door*."

"That part's easy." She cracked her neck. The fatigue was still there, but she felt like she'd been getting stronger every second, like she could do anything. "I'll ask the door to fix itself. Go pack up."

He was about to argue the point but Seria put her hand on him, shook her head. Whatever was happening, Thea at least seemed to have a plan. They went inside, and Thea turned to Thomas.

"You and Bishop can get him settled in the car? I figure he'll ride with us in case…"

"I got it." He nodded. Bent his head and they kissed, a gentle thing, and then he was turning and walking away, supporting the child's body with one arm. Bishop in tow, looking incredibly uncomfortable but with a narrow set to his eyes, a hard line to his jaw.

Thea waited for them to be out of sight before turning her attention to David. It was unusual for her to be alone with him, but she felt like it was necessary. He was sitting slumped, staring at the ground where the residue of the thing Thomas had killed was still pooled, cooling from the lightning strike.

We sure fucked up this backyard. She fought back a giggle. Now was not the time.

"David." He turned and looked up at her and she thought he looked broken, his lip trembling, his nose swelling up, two black eyes. She'd honestly never seen him like this. He wasn't her favorite person, but he was important to Seria. "It's okay if you go."

"We should *all* go!" He sprung to his feet, all nervous, almost frantic energy. "Jesus, Thea, this guy's a fucking nightmare, you should be running from him!"

"It's not about him. It's about us." She tried to stay calm and reassuring. Lashing out at David now wouldn't fix anything. "Me and Joe and Seri. They're after us."

"Seri and I were dating for six years and I never once saw *anything*…"

"Because we didn't tell you about it." Thea swallowed back some very unkind things. "Dave, I don't know your family at all, but are you seriously telling me you've told Seri every fucking thing there is to know about them? Hell, that you even *know* everything about them? I bet there's shit going on there that would freak me the fuck out if I knew about it. That's just life."

She let him glare at her. She didn't like it, but she didn't see the point in making an issue out of it. It occurred to her that it might have been the longest conversation she and David had ever had.

"My grandpa bootlegging doesn't fucking compare to *this*."

"I'm sorry you're not as interesting as we are."

He stopped for a moment and then laughed, maybe sobbed a bit. She decided to close the gap and put her hand on his arm, trying to be as supportive as possible. It was hard to know how to comfort someone you didn't actually like very much.

"You're *sure* about this guy?"

"Dave, don't even try, okay? Focus on your own love life." She heard Joe and Seri come down the stairs from inside the house. "I'm going to go fix the door. I think you should say goodbye."

He nodded, still looking utterly afraid and miserable. She felt bad about that, but he wasn't her problem, not really. She had enough to deal with. She walked into the house, saw them putting a few bags on the couch, was impressed with how quickly they'd packed.

"You got that together fast."

"Habit." Seria replied. "Always ready in case." Thea remembered the two of them showing up at the door that awful night. She'd been ten, they were twelve. They'd only had the clothes on their backs, her mom had driven over to her brother's house to get their things for them. She stepped up and hugged her cousin, cradling the back of her head.

"It's going to be okay, Seri."

"Maybe try that one later." She sniffed. "I have to go see David before we leave. Plus I don't want to see you do... that."

She just nodded, watched Seri head out back. Turned to Joe, who was watching Seri.

"Are *you* okay?"

"I'm not, no." He turned to look at her. "I'm trying really hard not to think about it right now."

"Do you want..."

"Oh, no, I'm not missing this." He tapped his face next to his eyes. "I definitely want to see it."

She dropped down next to the little salt image she'd left near the door. It was still there, mostly spent, but she could fix that now. She reached out her hand, stretched it above it and let her thoughts range over the concepts, the entities born of man that infused the house. Shaped and carved wood, metal, steam and sparks, the caged light and the hum of the mechanical.

The door flowed like wax. When she opened her eyes and stood away from it, it looked as if nothing had ever happened to it, even the frame restored.

"Handy." Joe had seen what looked like a whirlwind of small bits and sparks and embers and shards spinning around her as she willed it. He could see them clinging to her now, even as she wiped a hand across her forehead.

"After the big show earlier I'm still feeling a bit ragged. But it'll hold. Better than it was, even." She didn't bother to tell him she'd increased the ward. The house knew him and Seria, it would let them back in.

"Not every day you wake the dead."

"Joey..."

"Later." Seria and David walked in, his arm around her waist. She was a little teary but looked calm, more like her usual self. Thea tried not to notice.

"Let's go." Seria reached down and picked up her bag. "Call me after you get checked out, okay? Go to Kent, it's closer." She made a sad face. "I don't know when I'll get to call you back."

"Okay." She walked over and they kissed, and then she was out the door. The rest of them followed her outside, with Joe locking up.

"We'll take my car." Joe said. "You'll have four people to deal with already."

"Makes sense." She gave him a quick hug, was relieved that he hugged back, still felt like *Joe*. Then she walked over to Thomas' car, the one he wouldn't drive. He was leaning against the side, waiting for her. She took a second to look at the beard.

"I like the face fuzz."

"You know your hair is past your ass now?"

"Yeah, I'm going to need to get *that* taken care of." She arched an eyebrow. "So where are we going, exactly?"

"Bristol. We can catch the ferry there." They slid into the car. Bishop was in the back seat with the kid – he'd gotten a ride from Joe originally. He was frowning, looking the kid over.

"So there's a ferry involved?"

"I don't have a boat..."

"Yes you do."

"...on this side of the water."

"You've got a boat?" She started the engine. "What kind of boat?"

"My grandfather left it behind. Cabin cruiser. It's docked near the farm."

"Let's keep talking about this boat so that I can pretend everything's normal." She exhaled, put the car in reverse. "I like boats, I ever tell you that?"

"We had not discussed it yet." He smiled, rubbing at his chin. "If it's still in working order you're welcome to ride in it. By now Paul probably has it drydocked."

"There's a Paul?"

"He comes up and takes care of the horses and the property."

"There's *horses?*" Thea stepped on the accelerator. "Dude, you seriously should have brought up the horses *way* sooner."

Book Two
The Destroyers

Chapter Ten

Brute Anarchy

The truck rolled into the yard, the motor sputtering on fumes, about to stall.

They sat there inside the truck for a while after Morgan killed the engine, listening to it pop and gurgle as it cooled down. They didn't speak. Morgan's stomach and back both hurt from getting pummeled. Jimmy looked worse. He had marks from the gun going up in his hand, a bruise on his face and probably worse from when she'd kicked him and he'd flopped to the floor.

They got out of the truck and Morgan leaned on it.

"What the fuck do we do now?"

"I don't know."

"She's going to *kill* us."

"I know." Morgan had made Jimmy drive off but had doubled back, trying to find out about Byron. Had seen them come out of the house with a small child bundled in a coat, had recognized the curly dark hair on his head. "They broke what she did."

"What?" Jimmy had been too panicked to pay much attention to anything. When Morgan had finally showed up in the alleyway down the block from the house, he'd thought about just driving off, leaving his brother to fend for himself. He might have done it if he'd been thinking clearly. But he wanted someone to blame in case she came calling.

She'd going to.

"Byron..."

"Byron's dead, he has to be, if they're still alive..."

"He's not dead." Morgan turned and grabbed Jimmy's neck with both hands, pulled him close. His face was twisted up, spittle in the corner of his mouth. "I *saw* him. They were carrying him out the front."

"Carrying him? He weighs…"

"They broke what she did, Jimmy!" He let go, walked over to a pile of rusting metal, cars stacked on top of each other and kicked it hard. "Don't you fucking get it? I saw him! He's him again!"

That rang out, echoing between the towers of rusting trash around them.

"How?"

"I don't know how." Morgan sat against the truck. "I let them take him. He's better off with them."

"Listen to me. We gotta go get him back, give him back to her, before she…"

Morgan was up and slamming Jimmy up against the truck, making him squeal as his aching side contacted the door.

"No, we fucking do *not*."

"She'll kill us!"

"We're dead already." Morgan spat it in Jimmy's face. "You fucking idiot. Did you think either one of us was going to survive this? There's no way, no chance." He let Jimmy go again, stalked away kicking at the dirt. Thinking hard. "They broke what she did."

Jimmy was considering going for Morgan while his back was turned. Just bash his head in, dump him on the old woman's porch and run, drive until he ran out of gas. But he stopped when Morgan straightened up.

"We can kill her."

"…what."

"We can do it." Morgan turned on his heel. "Kill her."

"What the hell makes you think that?"

"We can see it, right? The old woman taught us how to see it. If we can see it…" Morgan's head was aching from fear and adrenaline. "We keep out of her hands long enough, we can figure out something."

"Great. Us two geniuses. That'll be great. We couldn't even take out them."

"She sent us in to fail. She didn't tell us what was there. And that bag? She wanted it to kill us."

"Well it didn't."

"So she was wrong twice." Morgan stalked away from the truck. "You want to live, little brother? We have one shot at this. Take her out before she takes us out."

Jimmy watched him stalk away. Craned his head around, looking for seagulls. He wasn't sure if he wanted one to be there or not, but he didn't see any.

*

The grass was dusted with snow.

Thea was staring out the window of the house, listening to the wind flow around the wood. It was strange to be so isolated when you were less than three miles from where you grew up. The bay did its job, she supposed. She could see the trees edging the property, and the water down the hill.

She put on clothes and a jacket, feeling the cold. The house wasn't really drafty, but it was old, hundreds of years old. The stairs up to the second floor were narrow, the basement had a dirt floor. She walked down the stairs carefully, listening to them creak. The house whispered to her, the wards she and Thomas had put up strong in the old wood. Unlike the duplex, this place seemed to have a personality, having seen people come and go over and over again.

It liked having them there. It felt useful again. She brushed a hand on the banister, acknowledging this.

Bishop was in the kitchen drinking a cup of coffee from an old drip maker. He nodded.

"You want a cup?"

"Sure. Black."

"Easy enough." He poured into a mug and handed it over. She let it warm her hands while she drank from it.

"You still..."

"Yeah, going back today."

"It's only been a couple of days, they might..."

"Can't hide forever." Bishop was staring into his cup. "Besides you'll need stuff from town."

"I was going to go back tomorrow for food."

"And because you're bored."

"So bored." She laughed. "I'm not the farm type. Although the horses are nice."

One of said horses was standing outside chewing at the tall grass despite the snow. It hadn't been a real snowfall yet, just something to remind you it was coming. December would soon be there. The big grey animal (Thomas told her it was a Percheron, she didn't know from horses) seemed content enough to keep cropping away at the lawn.

"I guess his folks had started to move here permanently after Tommy moved out." He shrugged. "They were trying to fix up the house in Cranston to sell it."

"He never said much about it."

"He's weird about his family. Then again, I guess they were pretty weird too."

"Must be hard." She sipped her coffee. Bishop snorted.

"Yeah, okay, point taken."

"What are we talking about?" Joe walked in the kitchen. He was wearing a too-short robe and not much else, and he stopped to put a hand on Bishop's shoulder. "Hit a fellow up."

"Here you go." Bishop handed him the mug he was already using. Joe drank without comment.

"You're sharing cups now?" Thea made a gagging sound.

"The two of you made the ceiling creak all night." Joe replied mildly.

"And when we got done, we drank out of separate glasses because we're not animals."

"The recording I made would beg to differ." Joe leaned over Bishop's shoulder, squeezed him. "How're you getting home from the dock?"

"Taxi." Bishop craned his neck. "I'll be back on the weekend, since this seems to be home base for a while."

"It's peaceful."

"Yeah. That's the problem."

*

He had been shocked by how old Paul was.

It shouldn't have been so surprising – Paul was old in his memories of the place, older than his grandfather had been. The two men had a kind of understanding. They weren't friends – Thomas Willrew the First wasn't a very friendly man – but they were comfortable with each other. Paul took care of the day to day on the farm, the old man paid him to do it, and everything was fine.

After he died, Thomas Willrew Jr. made a similar deal with Paul. It made sense to keep him on. But dad had wanted to live there, and so he was around more, watching how Paul did things, learning it. Paul seemed to appreciate this. He called him 'Big Tom' to distinguish him from his son, 'Little Tom'. Even after the growth spurt hit and he dwarfed his father he was 'Little Tom' to Paul.

"So Ramses is going to need extra sweet feed." Paul was showing him around the barn. He was wearing a red baseball cap and a denim jacket lined with fleece, thick work gloves over his hands. The man had to be approaching eighty, his face seamed with lines. "You got that?"

"Yep."

"You decided what you're doing with this place yet?"

"Can't afford it forever."

"The old man left money for upkeep."

"That's why it's still here." Thomas never really thought about what the old man had and hadn't done. He hated thinking about it. There was a stack of documents from Fleet in the locked safe inside the old house. He knew he had to look at them. It seemed hard to focus on the mundane with everything that had happened, but the world didn't wait.

"Your father and mom... they were good people." He was walking Paul to his pick up. Paul was a year rounder – he had a small house on the other side of Wolfshead, down where the Navy base had been. There were less than a hundred people living here full time and all of them were down to the other side, meaning that the Willrew property was as isolated as a medieval keep lording over the peasants. Thomas wondered sometimes if that's what the old man had been going for. "I'm sorry what happened."

"Thank you." He'd learned to say that. It cost nothing.

"So I'll come up Monday?"

"Yes, do. Make sure I'm not doing anything wrong."

"You worked here every summer, you know what you're about." He climbed into the pickup, turned to look over his shoulder. "Look, I don't know what's going on. None of my business. But I knew the old man for years." He started the truck. "You've got that look he had, around the eyes. Whatever it is, don't let it ruin you."

"Did he ever talk to you about it?"

"I never asked." He put the truck in drive. "Damn automatic, can't work a clutch anymore. My legs. It's an awful thing, Little Tom."

"You can just call me *Tom*, you know."

"Feels wrong." He smiled, cackled. "I still remember you running around in your underwear with that towel around your neck."

Thomas watched the truck drive away. Watched his breath trail away for a moment, December coming in cold. As always he was reminded that this was the month of his birth, looking up at the peak of the house he'd spent summers clambering over. Sitting on the peak of the house watching fireworks on the Fourth, or taking part in a bonfire, setting the old boats on fire and finding the melted lead afterwards, cooling into shapes. He'd found a piece that looked like a rearing horse. Still had it somewhere around here.

The pigs and cattle had been sold off, but John and Ramses were still here, and the chickens. He'd collected their eggs yesterday, would likely have to do so again today. The urge to murder the roosters was strong. They'd woken him up.

Instead he went into the barn, made sure John and Ramses' stalls were clean. When his father had expanded the place, he'd given them fourteen by sixteen stalls next to each other. The brothers were approaching twenty – they'd been born right around his second birthday – and he'd grown up seeing them, spending his summers tending to them, feeding them and mucking out their stalls. He remembered driving truckloads of their manure to the south end of Wolfshead, because people would pay for it to be dumped in their gardens. Not his favorite part of the job.

He did everything without really thinking about it, just letting the repetitive action happen. The two horses were out eating the grass in front of the old lodges, the three large stone buildings that looked like crude attempts to reproduce luxurious hunting lodges. They were collapsing. He remembered spending time descending into the tunnels beneath them, the access that allowed for underground travel between buildings when they'd been livable, hunting rats. The rats drew owls in at night, but there were no other large predators on Wolfshead. They'd all been hunted off years ago. So you either needed to get cats, or in some cases dogs, or go down yourself.

The farm was home to a cat now. He looked up and saw Balthazar, the cat his father had picked up for the place, watching him intently. Balthazar allowed Paul to feed him; he had no idea who this lumbering thing was, shoveling piss-soaked hay and horse turds into a wheelbarrow.

Thomas wished it wasn't cold so he could strip his shirt off. He was sweating. He wondered if he'd even need to work out after all this. He'd forgotten how much work it was. Once he had the two stalls cleaned out, he got new straw down, then put feed and water in for them. Next, he went up the pull-down metal stairs to the not quite finished hayloft, wrestled down a bale and forked half into the stalls, one for John, one for Ramses. By the time he was done, the sun was finally up.

It was familiar. And yet it was almost totally alien to him.

His hands were shaking. They were cold, even through his gloves, but that wasn't why.

Thea had told him what she'd seen when the vision ground itself in them. They'd taken the upstairs bedroom, lying spent against each other, her hand playing with his flanks. He'd needed the touch almost more than he'd needed what came before it, the sense of being alive and in contact with someone alive and real, something that didn't make his mind scream. She'd told him about the park and the carousel and the old woman. And he hadn't told her what *he'd* seen.

He checked the heater. It worked. It would keep the barn above freezing once the horses were inside. Satisfied with that, he walked out, feeling his sweat-soaked shirt underneath the hoodie, itself underneath the jacket his parents had gotten him for his birthday. Or for Christmas. Or both.

"Hey. Lord of the manor."

He turned his head to see Bishop walking up from the house, past the squat cement garage. The place had been used by the Navy before Thomas' grandfather had picked it up, so save for the old house and the stone lodges, everything else was a rectangular concrete block. The garage, the structure the barn was built on top of, and what he expected had been some kind of office and which was now full of old garbage to his right, built on a large concrete slab shot through with cracks. The plants were slowly winning their fight to reclaim that one.

"Something up?"

"Your woman is feeling domestic, so she's making breakfast."

"She likes breakfast."

"Most important meal of the day."

"There a reason you're out here instead of in there eating it?"

"Two reasons. One, she just started, so there's nothing to eat yet. Two, she told me to see if you were available to come eat it." It was always a bit of a trip to see Bishop on the farm. He'd never been one for manual labor, or roughing it. But genetics had conspired to make him look like a Hollywood Viking, so he seemed to fit on a rural outpost in the middle of the bay. "You seem to have settled right back in."

"Oh, no, fuck this. If I wasn't afraid Paul would see something he shouldn't I'd gladly keep paying him to do this." He rolled his shoulders. "I have no idea how someone his age can do that *every day*."

"Gonna cut the shit now." Bishop was looking across the farm at the harbor below it. "Are you… look, she's a really nice girl once you get to know her, but…"

"Are you kidding me?" Thomas pulled the hood back from his head. "Are you serious with this?"

"Look, you met her on Halloween."

"Technically the night before Halloween."

"Fine, Halloween Eve."

"Since Halloween is itself All Hallows Eve, you can't *have* a Halloween Eve. That's All Hallows Eve Eve, that's just weird."

"*Tommy.*" Bishop straightened up. "Since you got together with this girl…"

"Thea. Her name's Thea. It won't bite you."

"Since you got together with *Thea*, all this weird shit is happening." Thomas just stared at him. "Shit, I've known you for four years now and never once before did giant ooze monsters attack while I stood over my boyfriend's dead body."

"Ah."

"Ah? Ah what? What's 'Ah' mean?"

"Generally it's an expression of understanding."

"You going to share any of it, enlightened one?"

"You're not worried I'm going too fast with Thea. You're worried you're going too fast with Joe." Thomas watched as Bishop opened his mouth, then closed it, sighed.

"He's been having these dreams."

"I'm not surprised. You know, it's not like he was dead much longer than someone who gets resuscitated is. Heck, I was probably dead as long as he was."

"Yeah, but somehow CPR pales in comparison to calling down a lightning bolt to fry a snot monster over a homemade crop circle." He rubbed his hands together. "Jesus, it's cold out here."

"December."

"I know what month it is, thanks."

"All part of the service."

"I don't know what the fuck I should be *doing*." Bishop was looking down at his feet now. "Joe's a really nice guy, he's… sweet? Is it weird to say a guy is sweet?"

"Who cares? Just you and me here. If you think he's sweet, I'm not going to argue with you." Thomas gestured with his head.

"Keep talking, I gotta go check on something, you might as well come with."

Bishop fell in behind him as they walked down along a narrow path into the tree line.

"Maybe if I didn't know for sure it was real." Bishop cursed himself for wearing his sneakers instead of a pair of boots, not that he'd brought boots. "I mean, that guy David, I get why he freaked out. Because who wants to believe this shit?"

Thomas didn't say anything to that. He wasn't inclined to be charitable to a guy who wanted to fuck his girlfriend. Bishop just kept rolling with it.

"But I was part of it. Me and Seri, we were… it was *real*. We both know. But we're both just people, and you three are…"

"Seri has it too."

"She does? She's not doing anything."

"It's an act of will. Seri has the ability, she just doesn't want to do it, and not wanting means not doing with this." Thomas felt stiff along his back and shoulders. "It tends to run in families."

"Was your family…"

"I'm not sure. Maybe. Or maybe it's because I was born premature, or maybe it's the near death experience. I don't fucking know. I've done a lot of reading since, but… most of it is bullshit. I'm sure some of the stuff I've done has never worked for anyone before I did it."

"So how does it work for *you*, then?"

"Because I want it to badly enough."

"So you're telling me you're using the placebo effect?"

"Something like that." They stopped at a rude stone cairn, it looked out of place. The rocks were glacier polished, from the time the whole state had been buried in schist from the slow retreat of the ice. There was a plaque, just the name *Willrew* and the year 1984.

"My point is, I have no idea what I bring to the table now, you know? He's… well, he's like you, and her, he sees things I'll never see or understand, I'm just…"

"That kid." Thomas had dropped onto his haunches, looking

at the plaque.

"What?"

"The kid. The one that is probably sitting at the kitchen table right now watching everyone talk."

"What about him?"

"I left him lying on the grass. In late November. I was too busy, too self important, to really think about what I'd done." He picked up a rock, looked at it, added it to the pile of stones. "The first thing you did when you saw him was go pick him up, wrap him in your coat. Why?"

"Because he was mostly naked and going to freeze?"

"Because you *saw* him. None of us did." He lifted his head. "Bishop, this whole thing isn't the way life is supposed to go. It violates things. It changes you, in a real, fundamental way. It changed me. If not for Thea...." He took a deep breath, let it out. "I like to think I do the same thing for her. Keep her grounded. If we lose that, we become like whoever's hunting us, doing whatever bullshit we want just because we can."

"So I'm what, the conscience?"

"I was going to say the heart. But you need to get a monkey." He laughed at the look on Bishop's face. "You're not anything like that. But you saw that kid, and we didn't, and that's important. You know it's real, but you're not *in* it. You have perspective we lack."

"Why are we out here?"

"I was like seven when he died." He picked up another rock, stood up with it. "He used to come by the house, freaked out my mom something hard. They did not waste much love on each other. She loved his son, and so she couldn't really stand the man who'd ignored and mistreated him all those years."

"He was that bad?"

"He didn't beat him. At least that's what my dad told me, the one time it came up. He was just distant. Cold. My mom called him *The Statue*." Thomas tossed the rock up in the air, caught it. "He liked me, though."

Bishop felt a hundred responses, left them all unsaid.

"He used to come by the house and take me down to the

basement. There was an old chair down there, carved wood, devil faces on the arms. He'd brought it back from Germany after the war. He'd sit in the chair and hold me in his lap and tell me things. Stories. I was too young to understand them, but I knew to listen, just to hear him talking. He was my grandfather and I wanted to love him."

"What about? The stories, I mean."

"Concentration camps."

"...why do I ever ask you anything?"

"You know, that's a good question."

"What the fuck was he doing telling a seven year old about concentration camps?"

"He knew he was dying, or soon to die. He wanted someone to know what he'd seen, where he'd been, his life. And he'd alienated my dad so spectacularly that *he* wasn't going to do it, so it was me or nobody." Thomas put down the rock on top of the cairn. "Let me ask you a question?"

"Is it going to be a weird fucking question?"

"Almost certainly."

"Fantastic, let's have it."

"Is it okay if I let my parents be dead?"

"Is it... we don't have much choice, do we?" Bishop thought about what he'd seen a few days prior. "Do we?"

"I don't think I could actually bring them back. Maybe if I'd tried earlier. But I didn't know how then. I think maybe if they'd been dead a day, or a few hours, something like that... but considering how hard it was to save Joe, and he was a few minutes dead..." He made a gagging sound. "I felt like I was going to explode. Just shake apart into sparks and nothing."

"So you don't really have a choice..."

"I could still try." They were walking back towards the house, past the barn. The two big horses, Bishop didn't know their names, were eating grass to their left. "I could still set it all up, try and pull something bigger through, try and do it. I think I'd die, but I could..."

"Tommy, do you really need to make more trouble for yourself?" Thomas stopped walking, looked into Bishop's face in surprise. "Seriously, you're finally with someone who *gets* you." He took a breath, not wanting to talk about it, but feeling like he had to. "Look, first off, yes it's okay to let your parents be dead, they *are* dead. Some things you can't *fix*. You can regret them, lament them, hope to heal from them but you can't just slap a new coat of paint on them and say 'voila'. They're dead. They've been dead since last year. It's not your fault now, it wasn't then. You do have to let them gone because they're already gone."

That hung there for a while.

"But I could..."

"Get yourself killed trying to force something? You tell me, honestly, do you think you could do it?"

"No." He sighed. "I don't."

"So there you go." Bishop swallowed. "Tommy, I never... my mom and dad barely even notice me. And I'm usually good with that, because it means I can do what I want with my life. But you... nobody who knows you can doubt you cared about yours, no matter how crazy everything got. It's not failing them to live."

Thomas didn't respond. Bishop didn't know if he could.

"Okay. Good talk." Bishop felt nausea coming on him as he considered what he was about to say. "Look, I... it's been almost a year and a half since Evvie and I... and I never really admitted it, how I..."

"If this is going to be some confession that the two of you were fucking around before she broke up with me, save it." Thomas actually smiled at the look on Bishop's face.

"You knew?"

"Neither of you were very subtle. A lot of looks back and forth."

"Yeah." They were moving again, almost back to the house. "You're not mad?"

"I was for a while. But I was over there and you two were back here. I wasn't sure I was ever going to come back." He shrugged those shoulders, and again Bishop wondered at how little Thomas enjoyed fighting, considering how much he looked made to do it. "I had other shit to worry about."

"I suppose so."

"If you don't mind me asking..."

"No one has ever wanted to be asked a question that opened like that."

"What the hell *happened* with you two? I go to London, she dumps me that week. Then six months later you're telling me it's over."

"Evvie..." Bishop held himself very still. Having this conversation with Thomas was at once utterly easy, because the two of them talked about everything, and yet completely unimaginable since Thomas was the guy Evvie had been with when Bishop had first decided he loved her. "She does two things really well. Guilt and blame."

"Not that you're bitter."

"Oh, I'm extremely bitter. I'm not sure she's wrong about the blame, for one." They were back in front of the house, next to the parked car Thea had driven onto and off of the ferry. Joe's car was parked next to it, facing the other way. "I guess I'd better go get Joe..."

"Let me go get my keys. I'll do it."

"You're going to drive?"

"It's my car, I might as well." Bishop wasn't sure if this was one of those times where you said *but you hate driving* or you just shut up so he simply nodded. Thomas walked up the stairs and into the kitchen. At the table, Seria and Thea were talking to the kid, trying (and actually succeeding, slowly) to get him to eat some scrambled eggs.

"Hey!" Thea popped up. "You hungry? I made breakfast. Seri helped."

"Yeah. 'Helped.' Let's go with that."

"You shush." Thea popped around to him. She'd had Seri give her a haircut the night they arrived, down to a shaggy bob barely half way down her neck. It was beautiful on her, of course. Even if it wasn't he'd have thought it was. "So sit, eat."

"Actually, I'm going to drive Bishop down to the ferry." He snagged the keys from the hook on the wall. Turned to see the look on her face, a bit of a smirk.

"Can I come?"

"If you want, sure. Be nice to have someone to talk to on the ride back."

"I'm going to go get dressed." He almost said *you look good like that* but he'd learned not to do that. She went up the stairs and left him standing in the kitchen with Seria and the kid.

"He give you his name yet?"

"Not yet. I'm not sure he can talk. It's like he's a baby in an eight year old's body." She turned to ensure that he was eating, watching him trying to use a plastic fork. "He seems to understand, at least some of the time."

"Make sure someone spots you, it's not fair you have to handle him all by yourself."

"It gives me something to do. I'm in such trouble at school."

"You only missed four days, it's the Thanksgiving/Christmas season. Just get your exams done, you'll be fine." He said that as if they had any idea if it would be safe for her to do that.

"Yeah, well..." She sighed. "I'll get Joe to take a shift. He's better with kids than I am anyway."

"Everything all right there?"

"I have no idea." She looked at him. "I wish this was all your fault so I could blame you for everything. Thea tells me it's not on you though."

He heard Thea coming down the stairs. She'd switched out to a black long-sleeved T-shirt with a V-neck and a pair of black jeans. They were both likely Seria's. They looked amazing on her. He felt himself bend a little at the waist to keep from pitching an obvious tent in front of her cousin.

"Shall we go?" She looked around him to Seria. "I'll watch him tonight. Thomas and I need to cover some stuff anyway, try and figure out how to get us back to our normal lives."

"I'd much rather I watch him and you focus on that *completely*." Thea stuck out her tongue and then they were tramping outside, Thea pulling on an old high school varsity jacket she'd found in the closet. Green and white.

"Is this thing yours?"

"Yep."

"You don't strike me as the football type."

"I'm not. It's a wrestling jacket." She looked down. Sure enough, *Cranston High School East Varsity Wrestling* down the sleeve. "Just Junior year. They thought it would be a good outlet for my acting out. Exact words from the school therapist."

He slid into the driver's seat and Thea jumped in the back, letting Bishop have the front.

"You're coming along?"

"I told you I was bored."

"Cannot blame you." Bishop turned to Thomas. "What's the plan?"

"Well, I don't know if it's safe to go back to my place. Probably being watched. They may have already gotten past my wards. I haven't felt that, but I'm not feeling *that* confident."

"I'm pretty sure they're still intact." Thea was resting her arms between the front seats.

"Still, not going to risk it. What I need is a decent bookstore."

"Oh, fuck no." Bishop moaned. "Is *that* why you asked me..."

"Yep."

"Fucking *Stuart*?"

"He is a creepy little dude, but he's got a good selection." Thomas said mildly.

"I am getting the sense that we don't *like* Stuart."

"He's kind of awful." The car's suspension felt a little tight to Thomas. Then again, it was a fucking Camaro, it wasn't designed for dirt roads. "But that's not why Bish is freaking out."

"I'm not freaking out."

"You really are."

"I am at most mildly upset."

"Your lip is trembling."

"Stop looking at my lip and drive the car already."

"I don't have to look, I know your tells by now."

"I'd wish for a unicorn to appear and impale you, but with my luck that might actually *happen*, so I won't."

Thea was absolutely fascinated watching Thomas interact with Bishop. Sure, she and Seria got like this, but they were family. Watching the two men do it, especially when one of them was Joe's boyfriend (were they boyfriends?) and the other was hers was like being backstage at a play you were normally on stage for. She wondered if Thomas was so scrappy with Bishop to distract himself from the fact that he was driving for the first time in a year.

"Not to end this lovely game of tennis, but is someone going to tell me why we don't like Stuart, or why Bishop is actually upset, or anything relevant?"

"...fine. My ex works at Stuart's bookstore." Bishop suddenly got a sinister grin on his face. "Come to think of it, are you bringing her with you?"

"Of course I am."

"Oh, I almost wish I could be there for it."

"Wait, is this the ex that's *your* ex, too?"

"Yes ma'am." Thomas was driving, but he wasn't going very fast and there wasn't another car on the road and wouldn't be for another mile, so he let himself briefly look around at the grass, trees, and the bay to his left. But he could hear Thea's voice just fine, could hear the pitch change. "Her name's..."

"I remember her name." Thea wondered what she was feeling. At first she was pretty sure it was jealousy, but jealousy requires some insecurity and she wasn't insecure about Thomas. What they'd shared, what they'd *done* – there was no way some ex could compete with having touched the way they had, having channeled what they did. But she was burning. "I'm a little surprised you'd bring me along."

"I don't want to hide anything from you."

"That's a good answer. That'd get you on the board." She leaned back in the back seat, letting herself process what she was feeling. One thing her father had always told her, *you have the right to feel however you like, but not the right to act however you want.* She wished he was still around, that he hadn't... but he had, he'd clung too tightly to a ghost and he'd died. That wasn't going to be her.

The rest of the drive, waiting in the only store on the Island's parking lot, and then finally boarding the ferry were all uneventful. Thea liked boats, so riding on the ferry was fun, it was like being on a car on the water. Bishop got whey-faced, Thomas didn't seem to feel it much one way or another. She leaned forward again.

"Enjoying driving again?"

"No." He laughed. "I've lost my taste for it."

"I can do it if you'd rather."

"I'll do it today to prove to myself I still can. With what's going on... I don't think I can afford to not be able to do it."

"Makes sense." She came in a little closer to his ear. "So are we going to this bookstore first, or dropping Bishop off, or what?"

"I assumed we'd drop Bishop off first."

"Please do." They both heard Bishop swallow audibly. He was staring at a pack of seagulls... *is that what they're called? A flock? That band with the guy with the hair was A Flock of Seagulls.* One thing you never ran out of in coastal New England was seagulls. "It's bad enough I have to ride on a boat *again*."

"So you coming back down tomorrow?"

"I am." He nodded. "Might as well spend the weekend while you two fix all our problems for us."

"I like his confidence."

"It's reassuring."

Chapter Eleven

What Is Past Or Passing

It was the middle of the afternoon and Evvie Fraser was trying to get the day's tally to make sense. Stuart had gotten obsessed with some English kid's book about wizards; he'd insisted they stock it, and sure enough, the damn thing was selling like crazy. Evvie hated kids books, and wasn't a big fan of fantasy in the first place. She'd always said *if you can't write about real things, dreams and hobgoblins aren't going to help disguise the fact*. But she couldn't argue with money. Miki had left the register something of a mess, and she was reconciling it, her forehead pounding.

I need to quit this job.

"So how're things doing?" Her headache prepared to get worse as Stuart came out of the back office. It was rare he would do so this early. He preferred to sit in the back surrounded by the latest of his 'rare' book acquisitions. Usually some garbage – Charles MacKay, Maria Corelli (he loved *The Sorrows of Satan,* had a rare first edition) – mixed with stuff that wasn't even *that*, Time Life and Reader's Digest books, weird UFO collections, whatever he could get his hands on.

Tom had liked that shit too. Evvie could never tell if he was being ironic or not. Stuart absolutely wasn't. He didn't have an ironic bone in his body.

"Your nose for books people will flip out over seems to be working. We're sold out of that book you special ordered."

"Can we get more?"

"I already talked to Jill." She scribbled on the paper she was using to tally it all up. "Please consider spending some of the money on a computer."

"Those things are…" The bell up front jingled and Stuart got that *look*, the one he always did at the idea of customers. She had no idea why the man had started a bookstore if he hated *people* so much – people tend to be your clientele in *any* store.

She looked up, preparing to be bright and cheerful to a stranger who would likely ask her to find a book only knowing that there was a dog in it and it was blue. Instead, she found herself facing two people, one she knew *very* well, the other a complete stranger to her.

"Tom?"

"Hey. Been a while." He nodded and she remembered sitting in class with him, bickering back and forth about the lost generation writers (he liked Ford Madox Ford and hated Ezra Pound as a person. *He worked for the fucking Axis, I don't care that he was a better poet than I'll ever be or could be*) and looking at him now, she wondered...then she blinked.

"Didn't you have a scar? The last time I saw you..."

"I got better." He smiled. He looked remarkably boyish without the scar, even with the beard and long hair. Evvie wished they'd never dated. It wasn't even that he was a bad boyfriend, they were just unsuited to each other, they were too different and wanted different things. "Hi, Stu. How's it hanging?"

Evvie watched this exchange, not sure what was happening. Tom could go flat with people, just shut down almost all emotion in his voice. She'd never seen him do it to Stuart, though. He had always seemed to harbor a mild affection for the man's love of old books. She was seeing it now, though. Tom suddenly didn't like Stuart, actively.

It was hard to focus on it when the girl with the awesome hair was giving her the once over. She wasn't staring – with eyes like that, Evvie would have noticed – but she was definitely looking her over, and not in a *you're attractive* sort of way, which was frankly too bad in Evvie's opinion. She wasn't averse to a pretty girl, and this one was definitely that. She had the same hard, cold stare when she looked at Stuart, though.

"It's fine." Stuart, too, sounded cold. He was never a terribly friendly man, but now he sounded absolutely dead, as devoid of intonation as the voice on the phone when you placed a collect call. "What brings you back in? I'm pretty sure we sent your last paycheck along."

"I was actually hoping to take a look at the collection." There was a very long pause that stretched out, and Evvie knew from long pauses. This one was threatening to become an actual lacuna when Stuart finally blinked.

"Sure. Sure. You helped me put it together after all." He gestured, and started heading back. Thomas turned to the girl he was with. "Evvie, this is Thea."

"Hi." The look Thea gave Thomas was questioning and he nodded in return. Evvie could have sat and watched the two of them for an hour, it was filling up the notebook in her head with ideas for scenes. Tom's eyes were always his best feature, and they lingered on the girl's face before he turned and walked after Stuart. She watched him, then once he was out of sight turned to her.

"How long have you worked here?"

"Almost four years now." Evvie felt unwashed, even though she'd showered that day. Stuart didn't like to pay a real cleaning staff, so it was up to the people who suffered through working for him to dust the place, and with this many books that was a real chore. She'd been stuck doing it today because she'd managed to get Miki and Craig to do it the last week. "You from around here? I didn't think Tom was..."

"I'm from Warwick." Thea was looking very intently at her neck. It wasn't the way a girl found another attractive, the interest felt almost clinical. "Tom and I met at a party."

"He's going to parties? That's great, I know he was really messed up after his parents died."

"Bishop made him come out."

"Ah." *Of course he did.* Evvie wasn't sure if that should bother her or not. It's not like she wanted Tom back or anything, at least not as a boyfriend. But she was still very embarrassed by what she and Bishop had done.

"Does Stuart ever..." Thea seemed to reconsider what she was going to say. "Does he get up in your personal space a lot?"

"Stuart? God no. He doesn't like being anywhere near people. Why? Thinking of applying here?" Despite how incredibly awkward that would be, Evvie didn't hate the idea. It would be nice to have someone else to talk to, at least.

"Not making any plans right now." She turned and looked out the window. "My cousin works at the bagel place across the street."

"Yeah? Maybe I know him. Did he go to WBC?"

"He's got a semester or two to go, yeah. Joe Rafiela."

"Oh, yeah, I think… he worked on a play I went to see, I might have talked to him after. He does lights?"

"Yes he does." Thea's eyebrow was up. "Good memory."

"I remember people."

*

Thomas was tracing star symbols in his palm with his middle and index fingers as he followed Stuart back.

"So what the fuck *are* you?" Stuart spoke up once they were in his cramped, book-filled office.

"Whatever I am, I'm still alive." The symbol for The Head of Algol was very hard to trace with just two fingers, but he managed it. "I'm not so sure you are."

Stuart grunted at that. "Nope."

"The honesty's a nice touch."

"Normal people, I can see them in the dark. They glow, I can kind of tell where they are. Maybe because I need the blood." When they'd walked into the store and seen Stuart standing there, both Thomas and Thea had felt a shock go through them. He was *wrong*. People talk about obscenity, and usually they're talking about pornography, but it would take a truly depraved sexual act to even come close to the sensation of the obscene that Stuart created just by standing in a room, just out of the sunlight. "You look like a house fire. You and your little friend."

"You don't." The power of the demon star, the head of the gorgon, was trapped in Thomas' fist. He could gesture and blow the entire room up. But the books were there, and he didn't particularly hate Stuart. "You look rotten."

"Well, like you said. I'm dead."

"How long?"

"Forty years?" Stuart walked back behind his desk. "Since I ran into a dame in East Greenwich. It's not really important."

"It kind of is. It's kind of *very* important."

"Look, I get my blood from butcher shops and slaughterhouses." He pointed to a small cooler in the corner of the room. Thomas had always wondered about that. "I don't really have *needs* anymore, aside from that, so I just stay in here."

"Really?"

"Really. Hell, I might have bought from your folks back in the day. I stay in here, I read, and try and figure out how to fix myself." He leaned back in his chair. "I mean, I won't pretend I never hurt anybody, but I was just a kid when it happened. Not that that's your problem."

"Indeed."

"You going to kill me?"

"Thinking about it." He looked around the room. "You're awfully calm about it."

"I was born in 1930. Got bit in 1948. My older brother got himself chunked on some fucking island in the Pacific. When your number's up, it's up." He pointed to the book he had on his desk, Thomas Bucknell, *The History of the State of Rhode Island and Providence Plantations*. "You ever read this? Really dry."

"You read E.F. Benson."

"Benson's *Lucia* books are surprisingly engaging."

Thomas had always vaguely liked Stuart. Oh, he'd thought the man was awful – he hired young women entirely so he could stare at them, he always smelled bad (in retrospect, not all that surprising) and had the manners of a yak, but they'd bonded over weird books. He took the time to really look *at* Stuart. Having seen Paola's ghost, he could see similarities, but there were differences. Start was like a ghost *stuck*, trapped in a body that couldn't decay properly.

"I can't fix you. You're dead. Maybe if this had just happened."

"Okay." Stuart looked to be bracing himself.

"I'm surprised you're not trying to hypnotise me or something."

"Huh?"

"You know, Dracula?"

"I don't watch a lot of movies."

"Come *on*."

"I don't."

"Okay, you're telling me you've been a fucking vampire since 1948, you've been trying to figure out how to *not* be one, and you haven't *read up on vampires*?"

"It's not a subject I'm really interested in." Stuart was looking down at the book. "I always knew I was wasting my time. But this isn't... I don't eat. I don't sleep. I don't *age*. People can't stand being around me. If I want to keep my store I have to hide out in the back. I arrange buying pig and goat blood by convincing people I make a lot of blood sausage or just am a really fucking creepy pervert or whatever they think I'm doing with it, and that's my whole fucking life."

Thomas didn't respond.

"If you're not here to kill me..."

"You had a copy of Augustin Calmet around here. *The Phantom World*." Thomas scanned around. "I need to borrow it."

"I have a couple. There's a mass market out now. Cheap reprint."

"Seriously?"

"Yeah, it's over there." He pointed to one of the stacks. Thomas went over, looked through the books, finally picked out a copy. It was in decent shape. He pocketed the book. Turned and looked back at Stuart, sitting there, waiting for the hammer to fall.

"Look, I don't have anything personal against you, okay? If you're not hurting people it's none of my business."

"Okay." He nodded slowly. "You going to tell Evvie?"

"I might try and convince her to quit."

"She's pretty close to doing that anyway." He smiled sourly. "She's actually my longest lasting employee. Most people quit after a year or two. It just gets too much for them. Even if they don't *know* they can always tell, you know? I give people the creeps."

"The staring at them doesn't help."

"What?"

"You stare. Especially at girls. You stare a lot. I always thought it was..." He gestured, not sure what the gesture for *sexual harassment* was.

"Oh, I do? Shit. I guess... I mean, I was a virgin when, I never got to, and now I *can't*, so..."

"People are still going to be creeped out by you staring at their tits. Or asses. Or necks or whatever you're staring at."

"Necks?"

"Oh, for fuck's sake, Stuart, go look up some fucking books about vampires already." He traced a symbol in the dust on the bookshelves, a star with a three lobed burning eye, slapped his hand on the wall. The power of the Demon Star Algol flowed into it, crackled throughout the structure. If Stuart was lying... if he did anything to directly harm Evvie or the other people who worked for him... he'd know about it. And then he would act. If Stuart could tell he'd done it, he didn't say anything.

"You done, then? Take whatever you want."

"I'm done for now." He stopped in the doorway. "You realize this book mentions vampires several times?"

"I never got around to reading that one."

Thomas stared at him. Stuart shrugged.

*

Thea was leaning against the counter, waiting, thinking about fire. Thinking very clearly and precisely about fire, the pyramid symbol of it, keeping it very close to her at all times. She could think hard and burn the whole fucking building down in a rush if she wanted to.

She didn't like letting Thomas walk off with that thing. Didn't like it at all. In comparison, his ex was a delight to talk to.

"So, this is an awkward question."

"Actually, it's a statement." Thea leaned back and looked at the girl. If Thomas had a type, you couldn't tell by looking. She didn't look much at all like Evvie. The girl was slim, less than five foot eight, with dirty blond hair streaked with some Manic Panic red around the edges. It looked like she'd cut it short a while back and then just let it go. "Yes, we're dating."

"How's that going?"

"That *is* an awkward question." Thea couldn't quite keep from smiling when the girl blushed.

"I, uh, oh Christ this is…"

"Relax. I came in here expecting to hate your guts but… I don't."

"Really? Most people aren't fond of their current people's exes."

"I'm not saying I want to braid your hair or anything." Thea could feel Thomas building power, holding it. It sent warmth through her, like a note played on him resonating through her. She made sure to be ready in case he needed her.

"You have nice hair. I like the color."

"It's natural."

"Get out, really?"

"Yep. My whole family. Black hair, blue eyes." Thea looked around the shelves. "You must get a lot of reading done working in here."

"Well, no. I mean, it's dead now because Christmas break is coming up, everyone takes off after the semester ends. But usually we're pretty busy. Not much else to *do* in Bristol."

"They get rid of bars?"

"We tend to be closed when those are open." She waved her hands, something she did often when talking. "I used to work at Carl's Bad Cavern, it's one of the divier dive bars."

"Bristol blessed with a plurality?"

"There's a few. WBC doesn't attract the best students. I mean, it's not *bad*, the writing and theatre programs are good, there's the architecture school and the law school, but generally a lot of the students there are 'I couldn't do better' types." She craned her neck. "It's not Salve, though."

"I guess." Thea wasn't sure what to say on that subject. "I haven't decided if I'm going to school or not."

"I kind of wish I hadn't, but... I like writing. I'm glad I took those classes." Thea felt the shift when Thomas came walking out, holding what looked like a pretty ordinary paperback. The *thing* was following him at a respectful distance, stopped well short of the puddle of light coming in the windows behind her. She expected it would know that by rote. "Oh, you're back."

"I am indeed." He cocked his head to the side, looking at Thea. "Ready to go?"

"Are we? Going?" The flames leapt in her mind. So easy. Just *focus* on the greasy, sickening thing in the shadows and it would go up like dumping gasoline on a campfire.

"Yeah." He gave her a look that said *trust me* and since she did, she nodded. "You still working on that book, Evvie?"

"Huh?" She hadn't expected that. "I, uh, yeah, of course."

"You should consider focusing on it. Take a sabbatical, go somewhere quiet and just work on it."

"Yeah, well, bills and all that."

"You're always going to have bills." He turned and looked at her, and it was so strange. Tom had always kept walls up, with her, with everyone. It was what made him and this girl so strange to watch, the way they traded looks and understood them, Like they had a secret language. Now he was looking at her and it looked sincere, unguarded. "Just think about it."

"Sure. Sure." She considered what she was about to say, let her eyes flick over to Thea. "It was nice seeing you again. And meeting you."

He just nodded. Thea took his hand, gave Evvie a bit of a nod, and then the two of them were gone. Evvie looked over at Stuart.

"Was that weird?"

"Things always are." He looked *old*, for the first time that she'd known him. "I'll be in back if you need me for anything."

*

She hated leaving the house.

She'd lost the boys. Perhaps they were dead. Once she'd stopped being enraged, and had dealt with the wounds to her body (was it hers? Did it matter anymore?) she'd sent the birds to find them, but they weren't at the scrapyard. Another thing the Willrew boy had cost her.

Raifa was quiet for once. That didn't please her. Raifa only got quiet when she was fighting.

So after she stopped the bleeding and cleaned up the living room, slowly, her flesh protesting despite having been forced to mend, she sent a message. Two days later a note appeared in her mailbox. She'd felt them deliver it, but had no wish to try and intercept the messenger. The note merely said *Come alone.*

Now she found herself driving the old Impala that Gio had left behind. She'd almost regretted Gio. A simple man, but not a cruel one. She hadn't even deliberately done it. The cancer had come as a response, not because she'd called it. Too much tinkering with probability, and there had always been a chance he'd contract it anyway. Sometimes this consoled her.

It was still sunny out. She was wearing a black veil, a black dress, clothing she'd worn to a funeral last. It was partially because they were the best clothes she owned, and partially because she liked the subtle jest. It didn't hurt to remind them who she was from time to time.

The flesh of her right arm was bandaged. The wound was new, not one she'd made with her fit. When she'd felt her *second* sending destroyed, her rage had given way to fear. What was she dealing with? How was it possible he could do *that*? Or was it one of the girls?

It could be either of them. Girl children were necessary, but dangerous. If they woke too soon, learned what they could do, they became unsuitable but without them she'd have no way out. What

Morgan had told her before she sent him to his death had convinced her that somehow Willrew had made contact with them.

It almost made her laugh. It was like fate. *Like calls to like*. To think that after all this time he'd find them, or they him. If not for the danger to her plans, perhaps...

But she needed them. She had many, but she needed them all. The work depended on it, on them all, of them remaining ignorant. If they knew too much, if they could reject it, then they had to die and their essences returned to her. As Byron's was supposed to.

She drove the car up the Bald Hill Trail, her hands locked on the wheel like iron. She refused to shake. She was the master of the body. For as long as it lasted, it was hers, *hers*.

Eventually she turned, following a dirt road up a hill past trees. The sun was beginning to drop out of sight. They'd be happy about that. Superstitious creatures.

The farmhouse was quaint. Real farmhouses tend to have a lived in look, are often built piecemeal. They're expanded as the need arises. This one was perfect, constructed for looks more than function. There was very little farming done on this soil. Animals wouldn't abide them, even the ones folklore insisted. Rats, wolves, they know better than to stay where death lives. She shut down the car, stepped out, her long grey hair tied back behind her. She'd been a handsome woman, once. She looked at her face, at the lines time had carved. It was better than she had any right to look.

Raifa. She touched the reflection, fought back a moment of sadness. Of course her face was her twin's. It would have been anyway. Soon it wouldn't matter.

They were waiting on the porch for her, three of them. Younger ones. One of them, a lean limbed young woman, perhaps less than a century old, stepped forward.

"She said you can talk to me."

"Did she."

"She did." The dead woman was dressed appropriately for someone just out of college. She'd often wondered if it was hard for them to keep track. *All hail television*. The thought made her smile.

She'd destroyed hers, would have to replace it. Maybe finally get a computer. "So whatever you want, you can tell me."

"I *can*, yes." She stood and unwrapped the bandage on her arm. The smell of blood hit all three of them; she saw them jerk in surprise, then hunger. The young one held a hand up at them. It proved a wise act as the light began to leak out of the wound.

"I have put the sun in my blood." She kept the wound pointing away from them. "I can and will turn the lot of you into ash. Then I'll walk into that house and do the same to everything inside it. You go inside and you tell her that I will not speak to anyone less than myself. I did her the courtesy of coming alone. She'll do *me* the courtesy of a face to face meeting."

The two males on the stairs looked prepared to attack her. The woman pushed them back.

"She won't like it."

"I'm not concerned with what she *likes*." She took a deep breath, mastering her anger. "I'm old, and unlike you, I'm getting older. You're testing my patience. It's not infinite. Run along and do what I said."

The woman who'd been named Robia once stood waiting, light leaking through her coat sleeve. A minute passed. Then two. She was beginning to grow angry again when the figure appeared at the doorway.

Robia had been handsome, beautiful even. This was *beauty*, concentrated and preserved. Her face, her figure, wholly without obvious blemish or fault, unlined by age. Lips the color of a fresh rose, skin like gold, hair like a black waterfall. She carried herself with an air you could only learn if you had all the time in the world to master it, a completely conscious sense of her own superiority.

"You're feeling quarrelsome today."

"You knew full well you'd offend me. That's why you did it."

"Indeed, but I'm surprised you felt like making a point of it." Those astonishing golden eyes of hers, like a lioness, seeking her weakness. Looking for a way to drag her down. If Robia hadn't given up the idea of passion, her whole body would be on fire now. The wound in her arm throbbed, the captured sunlight seeking escape.

The veins visible under her skin were glowing now that she'd exposed the blood to the air. "What can I do for you, dear?"

"I require your eyes."

"I'm going to assume you mean metaphorically."

"Yes. You have people. I need to find someone." She fought back a cough on sheer will. The body didn't like being used thus. "Four someones."

"And you couldn't have told Mercy this?"

"I could have. But my pact is with *you*, isn't it? I left your people alone, assisted you when you needed my help. I dealt with Akivasha, not some child barely a century dead."

"So you did." Their teeth were white, even, strong but not pointed. She always found that disappointing. The movies had made her promises. She'd watched many movies, read many books over the years, seeking inspiration. The reality of them was so *mundane* in comparison. "I can certainly ask around. You understand it will take time? We're distributed. More food in Providence and around. Almost nothing here, everyone knows better."

"Why stay then?"

"Nobody looks, either." Akivasha smiled, and oh, it was a beautiful thing. "You know, if you're so afraid to die..."

"Just look for them."

"I will need details."

"Their names are Seria Rafiela, Joseph Rafiela, Thea Mendel and Thomas Willrew the Third." She reached into the purse, a small black clutch, and pulled out Morgan's notes. "This is what I have on them. I'm sure you can find out more."

One of the males, a tall one with close cropped hair, walked forward and took the papers. She made sure that just enough light hit him that he yelped before covering her arm again. He retreated, wary, and Akivasha frowned slightly.

"That was unnecessary."

"I'm not stupid enough to *trust*." Akivasha took the papers from her servant, looked them over. Robia had no idea how old she was, how many languages and alphabets she'd learned over the years. She got the sense it was a great many of them. "I want the two women and Joseph Rafiela alive if at all possible. Better would be if your people avoided them entirely and simply reported them."

"Oh, I'm not going to kill for you." Akivasha turned and put the papers in Mercy's hand. "It will be a few days. I have many children."

Robia merely nodded, and turned, walking back to her car. Akivasha stood there, watched it drive away, waited until the taillights were mere red dots in the distance.

"I want to know why she wants them."

"I'll take care of it." Mercy nodded. Akivasha smiled at her chosen, the first vampire she'd created in the new world.

"Thank you." She pressed a kiss to Mercy's lips. Mercy gasped and opened to her, thrilled. As they all were when Akivasha paid them any attention. Her beautiful, perfect ones. She loved them all. And she would not endure that old hag threatening a single one of them gracefully.

Chapter Twelve

Reminders

The car windows were completely opaque now. He could see his breath streaming off, and the leather was cold against his back. He'd had to twist his legs just to fit back like this. And he didn't care at all.

Thea was above him, her weight negligible, her presence all important. Her shirt was in the front seat with his jacket and t-shirt, her bra *somewhere*. She was biting down on his neck, almost hard enough to draw blood, her breasts mashed against him. She was keening, grinding into him.

"Thea..." he was moaning, so hard in his pants he thought he might pass out. The angle was all wrong, he couldn't get enough contact with her.

"You need a bigger car." She hissed in his ear. "Or just rip some seats out."

He didn't answer, reaching up to bring his mouth against hers, taste copper. She *had* drawn blood. He hadn't felt his skin break, didn't much care as her tongue slipped past his lips and against his. He was freezing and on fire, his limbs trembling.

Then he somehow rolled them both over and she was the one lying on her back, and she wriggled against him, her right hand against his face holding him to her while she reached down to open his pants, and then hers. Her hand wrapping around him, stroking him. He felt like he might die right there and had no desire to stop it, no *will* to stop it.

When they were done, his head and neck were sore from repeated impacts with the wall and roof of the car. She was straddling him again, both seated, her in his lap, him inside her.

"More room than *my* car, but still not enough." She flexed, making him groan in response, rocking her hips back slightly. "Oh, I love you, I *must* love you, because this was *not* the best place for this."

"No complaints here."

"You might have some when you see your neck." She leaned forward, pressed herself against him. "Where did my bones go?"

He felt like he might get hard again if they didn't get dressed, but didn't want to say anything or move, so he just closed his eyes and waited. Eventually she pulled off of him, began hunting for clothing.

"Such a bad idea."

"It was *your* idea."

"I didn't consider the space issues." He opened his eyes. She was mostly dressed now, pulling on her bra upside down and backwards, sliding it around. "Here."

She reached behind her and pulled his shirt and jacket off of the front seat, tossed them next to him. He took the hint and began to wriggle his pants back up.

"Awww."

"I could keep them off..."

"That would be distracting. And potentially bad news if we got pulled over." She was smiling at him, and it made him feel lighter. He reached up a hand, felt at his neck. She'd managed to pull blood out without actually breaking his skin, he could feel traces of it drying.

"Should I even ask what brought that on?"

"Sometimes I just want to. I love looking at you when you walk." She laughed. "You really have no idea what you look like, do you?"

"I know I'm not really..." She slid forward and kissed him, surprising him.

"You're not *pretty*. But you *are* handsome. You're very male. Just accept this, it'll go easier for you." She slid to look at his neck. "Oh yeah, that's going to leave a mark."

"Inspired?"

"Ugh, no, that guy was..." She shuddered. "He looked utterly *wrong*. Worse than the Hound did."

"Less scary, maybe."

"Oh, sure, less scary. Kind of pathetic, from what you told me. But just *gross*." She sighed as she pulled her shirt back on. "Dude's completely ruined my ladyboner for vampires."

"Did you have one?"

"I did. Nothing major. I may have discovered masturbation around the time Anne Rice starting writing full on smut." She was smiling again. "Don't judge."

"Wasn't going to. For me it was magazines." He struggled his pants up fully over his hips and fastened them.

"I feel bad for your ex."

"Evvie? Why? I told you, if he even tries..."

"No. Not that guy. She's just *very* lonely."

"Why do you say that?"

"Not many women are going to try and strike up a conversation with an ex's current someone. She even asked if I wanted a job there."

"If I hadn't just found out Stuart was a vampire I might encourage this." He pulled his shirt on, and Thea watched him stretch to do it. She loved looking at his chest, the lines of his ribs, his abs. Now that his scars were all gone she'd taken to exploring, looking to see if any were still there.

"Still kind of freaked out that vampires are real." He gave her a look, she stuck out her tongue. "Look, I get it, world stranger than we know and all that. I'm still not ready for the whole Universal Monster Mash."

"Shit. If vampires are real, it might *all* be real."

"And now you share my disquiet. Excellent! So, what're we doing now?" She checked the phone she'd borrowed from Seria. "It's close to five."

"We have one last ferry we can catch, or we could stay on this side tonight."

"I'm not stranding Joe and Seri over there with mystery kid all night."

"Probably a good idea."

"What *is* it with that kid? I feel like I *know* him."

"He looks like you." Thomas got out of the back seat, stepped around to the front, sat in the driver's seat. "Black hair, blue eyes."

"He does, a bit. I'd noticed." She belted herself in. "Those two guys... the ones who attacked. One of them had white hair, the other brown, but..."

"Blue eyes."

"Yeah."

He said nothing, his head bent. Thinking furiously. She watched him do it, looked at *his* eyes. Green, so green, like the sky flashing just before sunrise. *Christ, how can he not know? I could spend all day in those eyes.* Patience was hard for Thea, always had been, but she made herself wait.

"When we got hit by the backlash, when I forgot to ground..."

"We both forgot that. I was the one who came up with the idea, remember? Not just on you."

"Well, whoever we blame, when the backlash hit... I saw things. I didn't want to think about them, talk about them. Still don't. But if I can't tell you..." He swallowed, trying to lubricate a dry throat. "I saw her."

"You did." Thea managed not to whoop or shout. "I don't suppose she flashed her address or anything."

"No. It was... jumbled." He took another breath. "The woman you described? Long grey hair, kind of like an older Seria, or maybe you?" When she nodded, he took it as license to continue. "Take that, strip out everything *human* about how she carried herself, and that's who I saw."

"Huh." Thea remembered what the woman had told her. "It fits with the whole 'body snatcher' thing." She felt like she finally had to face what had been haunting her every second since she saw that face. "You know... she looked a lot like my grandmother Rafiela. I mean, I haven't seen her since I was sixteen and she was a raving lunatic that visit, but..."

"Yeah." He nodded. "In the vision *I* had, he called her 'Robi'."

"He?"

"My grandfather." He exhaled, remembering. "Just before she killed him."

The car felt very small and Thea felt trapped in it, looking at his face. His eyes. That night at the party it had been the eyes that had trapped her. His eyelashes. The deep green of the irises that almost glowed. It had all happened so fast. She remembered his voice in her ear less than a week ago.

I love you, Thea Mendel.

She put her hand on his.

"Can you tell me?"

He nodded.

"It was like I was him."

*

He'd buried Madeline two years prior. Their marriage hadn't been perfect, and most of that was on him, he accepted this. He'd loved her so much before he left for Europe, and then he saw war, saw men die. Almost died himself, felt bullets pass his head. Heard them hit others. He'd been a doctor, but he couldn't save people when they were torn apart, and often bleeding wouldn't stop. He'd been sent to Italy, because he spoke the language, learned it from his mother's family.

Then back to England in time for D-Day. The Willrew side had given him German, and so he was useful *there*, as well. Useful. He hadn't felt useful. Just sick and awful. A constant state of terror wore away at him, and the failures loomed larger than the successes.

He saw people die from typhoid, or starvation, or overwork and starvation, because he was asked to treat the victims at the camps. Feeding them killed them, sometimes. It was too much. They say you never know what you can endure until you experience it.

He found out what he could endure. That wasn't it.

When he met Robia, he was convinced she was going to die. It broke him, already on the edge of breaking, he couldn't take it.

She had to live. If she could live, if she could survive, it would mean he'd accomplished something.

"It was never about you." He spoke to the wind, because Madeline had been cremated. Her people were Episcopalian, but Madeline didn't observe. He was Catholic. He didn't observe, either. "It was my mistake. My sin."

He didn't know if he loved Robia. Her survival, her nearly miraculous recovery, these had pleased him. Her frankly brilliant mind had attracted him in a way Madeline had not. It wasn't that Madeline was unintelligent – she was if anything *quite* intelligent. But Robia seemed to understand everything, like she could see right into him.

They'd both seen horror, lived it. It was something he couldn't, *wouldn't* tell Madeline. The smell of a man shitting himself to death, the sound of the body still trying to live when a bullet has taken the top of the head off. An explosion that turns a man to mist. Children dying from eating broth. He couldn't tell Madeline, but Robia had been there. She already knew.

She eventually grew tired of waiting for him to seduce her and took matters into her own hands. And he'd secretly been pleased that she had, that he could tell Madeline that it hadn't been his idea.

Because he was a coward. Because he'd already broken once, and never put himself back together. Because it was easier.

Madeline never asked. He couldn't say she never found out, because they never discussed it. Walking next to the stone wall between the old lodges, he considered how their marriage had curdled, hardened into politeness. She couldn't divorce him with Tommy there, her son, so much like her but with his name. She clung to him, and as a result, he'd pulled away from the boy. From his son. And now that son had a son himself, a small child, and it hurt places he hadn't ever expected to hurt again to see the boy. So much like his father had been. All the things he hadn't said, hadn't done.

He let his eyes wander over the collapsing stone walls of the lodges. They'd been on the property when he'd bought it, built some time after the Civil War by whatever eccentric survivor had decided to waste his time on them. He felt like he could relate. It was why *he'd* bought the land.

"You were always this." Her voice. He hadn't expected it, and yet he had.

She was walking up the road. If she had driven, he had seen no sign, no plume of dust on the dirt road. No sound of rocks pinging off of the undercarriage. He was grateful he'd grown the beard, that she couldn't see his face clearly.

"Robi." He nodded. If his son had heard his voice, he would have been astonished by the emotion in it, how thick and tremulous it was. "I didn't expect you."

"No." She looked around. "This is where you chose to hide."

"I wasn't hiding."

"Weren't you?" She'd gone grey, in streaks, like clouds across a night sky. Her hair had been a lustrous black when he'd met her, but short, close to her scalp. She'd never cut it again, and so now it was trailing behind her, almost to her knees. He saw again that emaciated child, more than a decade his junior, starved and sick and scarred. He'd never forget it. "I got your letter."

"Ah. I didn't expect it to arrive so quickly. Or for you to read it yet. It was to a PO Box."

"I check it. Not much else to do there." She laughed, raspy. "Occasionally one of the children comes to visit. Most of them... they don't."

He nodded. Thomas never came to see him, after all.

"How many did you have?"

"Five sets of twins." His eyebrows narrowed. She laughed, delighted with him, with his unspoken consternation. As she always had been. Any time Robi could shock him, she did it. She'd shocked him often. "Four fathers."

"Four? I thought you married three times."

"I did." Her smile faded. "But I've known four men."

He took that in. Another way he'd failed her *and* Madeline. A stronger man would have chosen, would have... his breath escaped like a radiator gurgling and he coughed, hard. He wasn't a stronger man, had never been. There wasn't any point to fighting.

They stood there for a while. There was a strength to Robi, a rage that kept her from bending. He admired and pitied it. Robi *needed*, more than anyone he'd ever met, and some days he'd wished he could have… but there had always been the life before to consider, the wife, the child born to her. Robi was strong enough to do without him. It was more cowardice, but looking at her now, at those blue estuaries she called eyes, the sky reflected in the bay, he knew it was true.

"You don't look ill."

"The X-rays paint a bleak picture." He tapped his chest. "Riddled."

"That's how Gio died." She looked startled. "How?"

"I smoked. I drank. I was cavalier with myself." Here at the end he felt a strange willingness to just *talk* with her. It had been so long since he'd let himself have even that, ever since she'd sent the first marriage announcement to the office. Never to the house, of course.

"I can…" She looked away, out over the water. "You won't. Not you. You always came the closest to understanding, but…" She took a breath, held it, her back like iron. "I thought about killing your wife."

"I'm glad you didn't. None of this was her fault. It was mine."

"I thought about killing you, too. About killing the both of us."

"I'd be willing to believe murder from you, Robi. But never suicide."

"No." Again that raspy laugh. "No, never suicide. But I thought about it. If it would be best for both of us."

He stepped closer to her, amazed to find his hand reaching out, cupping her chin. She looked just as shocked, and for a moment so terrifyingly *young*, young as she had been when they met.

"T…Thomas?"

"I should have let you go." Admitting it was like pushing rocks off his chest. His breathing eased. "But I never loved Madeline half as much as you, Robi. Now it's too late."

"It…" She was looking into his eyes, almost black, yellowing with age and whatever was chewing him up inside. "I can save you." It came out like blood from a wound.

"Nothing can, Robi."

"*I* can." Her voice got stronger as she found words somewhere. "You have a son. Does he have children?"

"A son as well." Thomas' eyes narrowed.

"With the girls… there would be enough. I'd have to give up some, but… do you remember? The nights in the hospital? I asked you what you wanted? Why you were… why we were there? Why you helped me? I asked you."

"I didn't have an answer." His eyes were clouding up as the memory came to him. "The world didn't make sense anymore. I needed just one thing…"

"Yes." She nodded, stepped closer. Put her hands on him and oh *God* it was still there, everything she'd felt and feared and couldn't do, the rush of it, like being in that bed again too weak and sick and stained to ever be a child again but alive, she'd been alive and she was alive now. He'd asked her for nothing. She'd wanted to… "I can *make* it make sense. Thomas. I can *force* it. I can save you. We can… we can live forever. You and I. Here, or somewhere else, it doesn't matter, just needs to be near water, brackish is best, mix of sea and fresh, tamed and untamed."

"I don't understand, Robi, what…"

"I waited." She felt like she was going to unspool. Raifa wouldn't talk to her anymore, would only come out when the children or the children's children were there. She lived for that. But Robi… she'd been the one who suffered, the one who paid the costs. She *wanted*. He was old and sick and dying and his body was ravaged, she could see the seams on his face, the withering flesh. Death's hand was in him. And she could *fix* him. It was so perfect, so very perfect it was…

"I'm sorry, but there's no more *time*." He leaned himself against the wall. "It's why I wrote, why I left you the box, the money. It's all I have left to give."

"Can you call your son? Get him to come here?"

"I could. But why?"

"Someone has to die, Thomas. But it doesn't have to be *you*."

*

"That's where it stops."

"Then you don't actually *know* she…" Thea exhaled. She felt light-headed, dazed, her face flushing and then cold. She was staring out the window, putting everything they knew together in her head. The woman in her vision. The woman in *his*. The marriages. The children. It all lined up, but it didn't, couldn't make any sense. "Okay. Okay, she was never… I mean, when I was six my mom would try and take me to see her and she'd *cackle*, she was awful but, nobody liked her but this is…"

"All I know is there's something there. On the farm. Something in that collapsed lodge." Thomas was looking at his hands, remembering exploring the tumbled ruin as a child. The rats in the walls, the floors. The sound of them, scurrying. The vision had him nervous. He didn't want to know what happened after, but knew he needed to.

"Thomas." Thea's voice sounded harsh and he snapped his head to look at her. Her eyes were huge, staring in the dim as sunset approached. "I think I've handled this all very well so far."

"You have."

"But this is… she's my *grandmother.*" She took a long breath. "Your grandmother isn't supposed to try and kill you."

"I never really knew mine."

"They're supposed to bake cookies and get you things for Christmas and your birthday and I was okay with none of that, I was okay with her being a weird old crone that we all avoided, but now… did she kill my mom? Is she why my mom's *ghost* is… did my fucking *Nana Rafiela* kill my uncle, too? How many of them has she killed? We tell *jokes* about all her dead husbands, it's supposed to be this family thing, it's not…" She gritted her teeth and grunted, pushing air past her teeth to stop from talking. He reached out his arm and slid it around her shoulders and she let herself lean on him, the warmth of his skin through his shirt.

"I'm sorry." He whispered. "If it helps I'm goddamn terrified."

"The bit about..." She swallowed. "Do you think she meant it? About him..."

"I think whoever her eldest children were they were probably his, yeah." Thomas made a sound like a laugh if you crossed it with a grunt. "Grandpa Willrew was always such a bloodless man, I had no idea."

"Eldest. Well, then, that's good at least?" She smiled thinly. "My mom and uncle Paolo were her youngest."

He clearly didn't understand and she *did* laugh.

"We're not related, dummy."

"Oh." He looked up at the hood of the car. "Right. That actually didn't matter to me."

"Really?"

"If I found out we were cousins? No, I wouldn't have cared. Not at this point." He smirked at her. "Very hard to try and transition to 'Hey, cos' after I've orgasmed so hard that I may have dented the hood of my car with you."

Thea tittered, and then *he* giggled at her, and from there it was the two of them laughing, nearly frantic, convulsive laughter that did its best to clear the atmosphere of the car. A thunderstorm after too many searing days. It took at least four minutes before they were anywhere near able to talk again, him wiping at his eyes, her shaking in her seat.

"I don't think there's anything... I love you." He was turned in his seat to face her. "I fell for you the night we met. I don't care if you're my fucking sister at this point."

"If I was, I would be." She chuckled again. "I've never... this is my first real love thing. The odds are that it won't work out. I mean, my grandmother might kill us both for starters."

"Yeah. I get it."

"Then how come you're still... I mean..." She wanted to slap herself but kept talking. "I love you, and I hate myself for saying it, and I hate myself worse because I don't want you to go away but *fuck* you should. You should toss my ass to the curb and run. I don't like that it scares me that you will. I never cared before, it was just me and my dad and my cousins, and then it was just me and them. Why are you still here?"

"It's my car." He almost laughed at the look on her face, but knew she was being serious. "Thea, I was ready to kill myself in a stupid ritual I knew wouldn't work. You're asking me why I'm still here? You're not my reason for living, but you make living *worth* something. You make it interesting, you make it…" He stopped. "Whatever is happening, whatever she is, whatever she *did*, I'm not running."

The light of the setting sun played over them, a red sliver in the sky just over the horizon. Through Thea's window the bay was visible, with the island limned with fire.

"I still feel like I want to freak out really bad."

"I do too."

"So let's not." She stretched. "We should get back."

"Yes." He swallowed, his throat dry. She reached out and touched his face, smiled when he turned.

"You want to find out the rest. That's why we're out there."

"It's a reason. Not the only one."

"Then we will. Now drive, Willrew. I want to take a nap." She arched slightly, enjoyed the reality of his eyes on her. "Someone tired me out."

He laughed, a clean, clear sound. She smiled, and closed her eyes, let him worry for a bit about where they were going. When it was her turn she'd take it up again.

Chapter Thirteen

Twisting

Joe was relieved when the car finally came into sight about a quarter mile down the dirt (now snow, mostly) road. Seri had been spending the day talking with the kid, who was starting to respond with *noises*, much like a newborn might. It was disturbing to see a kid well past the toddler stage acting like a baby. Those black marks on his... aura? Soul? Joe had no idea what to call it, but they'd receded and he looked much like any other kid his age might.

Well, except for the blue eyes and dark brown hair. The *hair* didn't quite match up, it wasn't the same color as he and Seri and Thea's was, but the eyes were. Joe was getting used to being able to *see* things, but the *knowing*, the certainty that just came to him was still disconcerting. He turned to look at the collapsed houses again, the weird stone lodges, and he shuddered.

It was like a black sunset over there, but not black, not the absence of *light*. The absence was nothing so simple as light. It made his eyes hurt to look at it. He'd been concerned from the moment they'd arrived, but didn't know Thomas well enough to say anything.

The guy could be a creep, a maniac, maybe he brought us here to kill us.

Well, no. The guy helped save him. He'd be dead if not for him and Thea, for the way that they felt about each other. He didn't think Thea had ever felt that way before, he couldn't piss on that. But he was still nervous. Things were so different now. Being able to see, to understand things that were impossible, it was clawing at his self control. And he'd missed a week of school, even with the lackadaisical theatre program at WBC that was going to make for problems.

He walked over to the front door and opened it, leaning on

the jamb.

The car pulled up and Joe watched them get out, seeing the glowing filaments that constantly extended between them. He didn't know if he and Bishop would ever get those, didn't know if he even wanted them. He closed his eyes and concentrated, filtering things out.

"Joe, shut the freaking door. It's freezing out."

"One you two get inside, sure." True to his word, he waited for them to be inside before closing it up. The round kitchen table was free, so Thea went and sat down there, leaving him looking up at her... boyfriend? Lover? Eventual person Joe made awkward small talk with at every Thanksgiving?

Remember that time I died?

"We're going to try something tonight." That deep voice made the room shake, just a little. "If it works maybe everyone can get back to normal soon. Almost normal, anyway."

"That'd be nice."

"Did you want to be there? I doubt Seri would want to be." Thea had shrugged her borrowed jacket off and was rubbing her arms. "Man, I hate cold."

"The biggest blizzard of the century hit the year you were born."

"Maybe that's why."

"We can hold off if..."

"No, fuck that. You probably won't sleep tonight if we don't get it done." He'd walked close to her, sat down near the weird hutch thing they had in the kitchen. The house was half modernized – a pretty nice shower, good water pressure considering it drew from a well, a modern set of kitchen appliances – and half stuck in the past, pre 1930's lighting fixtures and windows. Joe didn't know the story and didn't much care. "Should we tell them?"

"Probably. But let's get Seri in here, if we're going to tell it I don't want to have to tell it over and over again."

"Tell us what?"

"We think we know who's trying to kill us." Thea's voice was unusually solemn, and Joe felt clammy realizing it. "Based on my vision, and his."

"When you jumpstarted me back to life, you mean."

"Yes." She put her hands on the kitchen table. "Do you need to talk about that? I know we haven't."

"I'm not sure there's anything to say. I'd rather be alive than dead. And people get... remember that kid we knew, Aaron Coltes? The one who drowned? They got him going again."

"True." Thea nodded. The big man didn't say anything, just looked at him with those green eyes. He wasn't Joe's type, exactly, but the eyes were nice. He remembered waking up next to Bishop, wished the man was still there.

"I'm not saying it doesn't bother me. Or that it does. I just..." He sat down himself. "I haven't really thought much about it. Tried not to at all."

"Well, if you want to talk I'm here."

"Is... Seri keeps pretending she's normal. She called David, by the way. I guess they're still a whatever."

"Good." Thea seemed to mean that.

"She's not, though, is she?"

"None of us are. But she doesn't really want it. So she likely can keep not knowing and she'll be fine. If we can I'd like to keep her as far away from it as possible." Thea looked away from Joe, out the window. "But I don't want to lie, so..."

"That implies I want this." Joe fought to keep from turning it back on. "That scares me, a little. What about you?" He turned to Thomas. "What's *your* deal? You're not a relative."

"Thankfully." Joe raised an eyebrow at that. "At this point we're all going to have to compare notes. Is Seri still with... the boy? Who I really wish had a name."

"She was out back with him. He's walking now."

"I'll go get her." Thea stood up. "You two stay here. Joe, stop being so *you* about everything."

"What's *that* supposed to mean?"

"It means you're standing *in loco parentis* and it's not working." She kissed him on the cheek on her way by. "I'm really sorry you two are in this, but you were anyway, you know. Trust me.

As soon as we're all here we'll start talking."

The two men watched her leave. Joe looked back first and saw the expression on Thomas' face, the *awe*. It was hard to hate a dude who loved your baby sister that much, and that's how Joe saw Thea.

"Okay. She's right, I'm not being very grateful."

"Why should you be grateful?" Thomas stood up, walked to the fridge. Looked at the beer in there for a moment before taking out a soda. "If I ended up crashing in the middle of nowhere because of shit like what happened to you, I wouldn't be."

"She's really important to Seri and me. She's all the family we have left, really."

"I get that."

"I guess there's Nana, but…" Joe saw the look crawl across his face. "Is something wrong with my grandmother now?"

"I wouldn't worry about her." Thomas said, the look on his face like someone chewing his own tongue to keep from speaking. "So, Bishop's coming back tomorrow night."

"That's the plan. Assuming whatever mysterious thing you do tonight doesn't have us all home by then."

"Probably not that fast." He swigged his soda. "Bishop's a good guy."

"So far that has been my assessment."

"His last real serious relationship wasn't… it didn't end well."

"I'd gathered." Joe narrowed his eyebrows. "Wait. Are *you* giving *me* the talk?"

"Not exactly?"

"You *are*." Joe actually hooted. "You're nailing my little cousin…"

"She's *nineteen*."

"And how old are *you*?"

"I'm twenty."

"Really? Huh." Joe was surprised. "I figured you for like twenty five."

"My birthday's this month, I'll be twenty one."

"You're over a year younger than I am. That's depressing."

"Why?"

"Because you're a fucking *giant*."

"Bishop's taller than I am."

"He's also a year *older* than you are."

"I think we're all past puberty at this point so it doesn't really matter."

"He's also barely taller than you are. Maybe an inch, if that." Joe couldn't keep from grinning. "Okay, tell you what. I won't get too 'older brother' about you and Thea, and you don't try and probe me for my intentions regarding Bishop. Deal?"

"Deal." There was a bit of sagging in relief as the two men shook hands on it.

"Grab me a soda." As Thomas did this, Joe sat back down. "Sorry Bishop left the beer there."

"I'm being obvious?"

"You have the look of someone who really doesn't want it around."

"After my parents... I may have overindulged." He sat down, his fingers utterly obscuring the red can, and took a swig. "I'm having trouble remembering what they looked like."

"I remember my dad pretty well. Take me, but taller and with more muscles. He worked in landscaping. My mom... harder to remember there."

Seria, Thea and the boy came tromping in, snow blowing in behind them. Thomas took a moment to realize the kid was wearing his old jacket, pants and boots, from when he was around the same age. He looked disturbingly familiar like that, if not for the blue eyes. He could see the resemblance to Thea's and her family, but there was...

"Thea."

"Hmm? Just give me a second, we need to get his boots off..."

"Look at his face. Closely."

"We said in the car..."

"Look again. Stop looking for your features."

"What's he on about?" Seri asked. Thea was busy looking, at

the set of the boy's jaw. There was a broadness there, a sign of a jaw and chin that were going to get wide and jut forth in a visible sign of stubbornness. He met her gaze with no guile, just a curiosity that was as appealing as it was frightening, a sign of what had been stripped from him. She turned back to Thomas, looked at his face.

"Wow. How did we not see that?"

"We weren't looking."

"Does someone want to explain this to me?" Seri snorted.

"I don't want to, no. But you have to know." She indicated the table once they'd gotten their charge out of his boots and jacket. Seri handed the boy over to Joe as she sat down.

"Wait, why am I..."

"Because I've been doing it all day, you can handle a shift."

"We don't even know this kid."

"I'm pretty sure he's our cousin." Thea sat down next to Thomas. "And if we're right, he's Thomas' cousin too."

"I don't understand." Seri was leaning forward, letting herself relax, her posture like a marionette longing for its strings to break. "I'm getting used to not understanding."

Thea told them about her vision, then about Thomas'. They took it in, Joe's eyes narrowing as he balanced the boy on his knee, checking so often to make sure the black marks on the boy hadn't returned. When Thea was finally done talking they were both unsure of what to say.

"Nana?"

"I mean, okay, she was a terrible person, but..." Joe stopped. He'd been forced to visit his Nana Rafiela a few times over the years, had always hated it. He remembered being six and trapped in her kitchen while she and his father screamed at each other, couldn't remember what. His mother had always hated her. "I mean, *killing* us?"

"I don't think she actually wants us dead. She wants something else from us. She wants Thomas dead, though."

"You think your Grandfather and our Grandmother..." Seri looked aghast. "But not us, right?"

"I think whoever those two men who attacked were, and

this kid. They have a little of my grandfather in them, the color of the hair, the look of their faces." Thomas considered. "Well, mostly this kid, I can't say I ever actually saw those two."

"You didn't miss much." Joe was leaning back in his chair, stunned. "Thea, are you sure about what you saw?"

"I'm sure." Thea didn't cry or break down very often and she wasn't now, but she was doing what she usually did instead, which was to get a grim, hard cast to her face. "And it matches what Thomas saw. We've gone over it, his description... you know that weird scar she has on her arm? He knew about it before I mentioned it."

"So what the hell are we going to do? Do we go whack our grandmother?" Seri's voice was a trifle shrill. But they all felt a little tense, so no one felt like making an issue of it.

"Confronting her blind is not a good idea." Thomas was looking at a faded photograph of a man and woman, flanked by two older sets of men and women, hanging on the wall. Two of the men looked very similar, and Thomas had much of their faces, but his build clearly came from the woman and *her* two parents, much taller, larger. "Whatever she did here, we need to know it. We need to know how bad this can get."

"How do we do that?"

"My vision cuts out in front of the old stone lodges across the field there." He sighed. "They were intact. I think she did something that made them not be intact any more. So I think we go and find out what she did."

*

Jimmy Williams coughed into his hand. "It's like twenty-six degrees out."

"So keep your clothes on and you should be fine." Morgan was watching out the window of the GTO. They'd left the truck in the salvage yard. It's not like switching cars was an automatic win for them, but it wasn't like it hurt to not be as easily recognized. Enough people had seen the salvage truck.

"So why are we here?"

"First off, this is where Cousin Joe goes to school." Morgan said Cousin Joe like it burned his mouth. "He works over in that bagel shop."

"Well, shit, let's go…"

"He's not there, numbnuts. Two weird magic monsters attacked him in one fucking day, how goddamn stupid do you think he is?"

"So if he's not here, why are we?"

Morgan bit back a retort, because the answer was *I'm out of ideas*. They'd driven to the house Thomas and Thea had been sharing, no luck there, and the wards were active. Same for Thea's family home. No one had returned to Seria and Joe's duplex. And Seria's boyfriend had gone straight home from the hospital and hadn't left his house in days. That part made Morgan smile.

Because I'm tapped out. I don't know where they are. I don't know how to find them. I don't know if finding them is going to help us kill her. I'm done, you whining pissbag. I haven't got anything left.

He was about to blurt out another insult when he saw the woman walking.

It was seven PM, so the sun had been gone for hours. She had long brown hair, pale skin. She was what Morgan would have called 'a piece' and both Williams brothers were immediately revolted by her.

"Shit." Jimmy reached under his seat, but Morgan stopped him.

"Wait."

"One of those freaks? You know the old woman…"

"Exactly." Morgan was smiling now. "I do know the old woman. Come on."

They got out of the car. Jimmy immediately regretting he hadn't brought gloves. Morgan handed him a pair. He begrudgingly put them on, pissed that Morgan had assumed he'd need them, but aware that he did. They started walking in the same direction as the woman, past the post office, towards an old bookstore. She tried the door, opened it, stepped inside.

"Do we follow?"

Morgan considered it. Neither he or Jimmy were big readers, or looked it. Hell, they both had nasty brown and purple bruises on their faces, a legacy of the previous weekend. But they couldn't hear anything out there. He nodded, and they walked inside, Morgan holding the door open for Jimmy.

Inside they just caught the brown haired thing chatting up the cashier. Now she actually was attractive, Morgan though. None of that 'fresh from Hell' shit sticking to her like she'd just walked out of a latrine. He liked the red in her hair. He gestured to Jimmy to hold back, and his brother busied himself in the magazine rack looking at a rather impressive selection of very old car magazines. If you liked that kind of thing, anyway.

Morgan walked up to the counter. He hadn't actually worked in a few days, so his daily shower had been enough to keep him looking presentable. No grime under his nails. The cashier fixed him a look that said *oh God what do you want*.

"Sorry to bother you."

"Not at all, sir, how can I help you?" *Well, she's got fake sincerity down.*

"That woman who just walked in, do you know her?"

"No?" She immediately got wary. "Why do you ask?"

Morgan was sizing her up and knew she was sizing him up. Ordinarily, he'd try bullshit, but he didn't think he could float it past the alert suspicion on her face. He decided to go for a version of the truth.

"My name's Morgan Williams." He held out his hand. She took it, clearly not sure about the handshake. It was a nice firm grip. "So, me and my brother over there are looking for some long lost family? Cousins, same grandmother. We never actually knew them, big family, lots of cousins, but we really need to find them now. And we think she might know something about them."

"Now I'm going to have to ask you why again. Who *is* she?"

"I have no idea, but I heard her asking questions about them too." That was grade A bullshit, but he felt like he'd laid on enough technically true statements to cover it. "It's all really complicated and I don't want to waste your time with it. Just can you tell me if she asked about them, or anything?"

"She just asked to see my boss. She didn't mention anyone else. You're not looking for *Stuart*, are you? The guy who owns this store?"

"No." Morgan put his hand over his face, tried to think. The bagel shop was literally their last stop for any information about any of the Rafiela/Mendel family. He decided to throw a Hail Mary. "Maybe you've heard of them? Do the names Seria Rafiela, or Joseph Rafiela..."

"Uh, yeah. Weird. I was just talking to Joe's cousin Thea today." The girl looked down at her fingers for some reason. "She, ah, came in with an old friend of mine."

"Really large fellow?" Morgan put his hand up above his head approximating where Thomas' head would be. "Bit of a beard?"

"Full on beard now. Yeah, that's him." Morgan assumed no one had said anything to this girl about two men trying to come in swinging at their house and failing miserably. That was a bit of a relief. She looked less suspicious now.

Evvie, however, was a lot more suspicious at that moment. There was something really off-putting about this guy, something that said *You don't want to be talking to him* to Evvie. She'd been strangely attracted and repulsed to the woman who'd come in earlier, the one in the back with Stuart, but this guy just screamed *creep* to her. She wanted to get rid of him as badly as she possibly could.

She was starting to seriously regret Tom's visit. He and his weird girlfriend (*she wasn't weird at all, she was actually kind of nice*) were trailing shit behind them and now it was up in her face. Evvie had moved from New York to go to school in Bristol, Rhode Island precisely to avoid having this kind of thing happen to her.

Jimmy had run out of old car magazines and decided to head up to the counter. Morgan was chatting up a girl with a very nice look to her, Jimmy had always liked the pierced and colored look... and there was a couple of tattoos visible through the shirt. Daddy issues. Jimmy loved daddy issues. She looked a little upscale for him, but that wasn't usually a problem.

"What're we doing?" He said to Morgan.

"She's in back." Morgan looked from Jimmy to the cashier. "I'm going to go see what's what."

The look Morgan was giving clearly said *don't do anything stupid*, and that only made Jimmy the more determined to do something fun. They were both going to end up dead anyway once the old woman caught up to them. Why not?

"Fine by me. I'll stay out here." Every inch of exposed skin on Evvie, which wasn't much in her work clothes considering it was *December* started to crawl. The first guy had creeped her out. This guy *skeeved* her out. He looked at her like she wasn't even there, blatantly trying to check her out in a way that felt completely dehumanizing, like he didn't have to care what she thought about it. Evvie liked to think she was an okay looking person – she'd dated, she'd go out sometimes and go dance in clubs in Providence or even up to Boston for a weekend with friends if she was feeling it – but this was just repulsive, a naked *I'm trying to decide if you're worth fucking* that didn't bother with niceties like looking at her face. She was about to open her mouth to say something, ask him to back up so she could work, and so she didn't see him do something with his left hand.

The room shivered. The glass of the windows expanded just slightly as Jimmy Williams did the only trick he knew, the sum total of his ability to imagine and experiment over the past decade of his life. Evvie Fraser didn't even see it settle in around her, subtly playing with her perceptions.

"So," Jimmy said, what looked to Evvie like a pleasant smile on his face. Anyone else seeing it would have thought otherwise. "You from around here?"

*

Morgan got as close to the back as he felt comfortable, then chanted softly to himself. *Athene noctua*, he thought again and again, barely breathing the words. His face and hands tingled. This was always the part he hated, reaching into himself like this. The old woman had berated him for it so many times, for how clumsy he was. *I should geld you, maybe that would help*. But he knew she didn't *want* him to be proficient. *Athene noctua, owl's eyes, owl's ears, show me.*

It felt almost like an orgasm being cut off when it happened, his whole world going dark, leaning against the wall. His vision shifting, twisting. He saw the inside of a tight little room. Inside, two monsters wearing human form, their voices distant and tinny but audible.

*

"So." Stuart was *very* uncomfortable with Mercy's presence in his store. "What do you want?"

"You're not happy to see me."

"I'm generally not happy to see *anyone*, Miss Brown." She laughed at that. It was a beautiful laugh. Stuart couldn't stand the way it still affected him. He remembered seeing her across the quad, the sun lighting the edge of the sky like it was trying to backlight her in fire.

"I like that. Miss Brown. It makes me sound like a schoolteacher."

"Please," he sighed.

"You know, if you don't want any of us coming in here, then operating a store was a huge mistake."

"Why?"

"A store invites people in." Mercy's face wasn't ravishing or alluring, but there was a beauty about it even death hadn't fundamentally changed. She'd look good on the cover of an L.M. Montgomery book. "It says *everyone can come inside*. Buy a house. Houses say *knock first*."

"I'll keep that in mind. Houses aren't cheap."

"You've owned this store for four decades and you spend no money on anything else." She managed to look sad. "Why not come back with me? You don't have to stay here. Mother loves you."

"I'm not terribly fond of *her*."

"Poor Stuart." Mercy sat on the edge of his desk. "You could have been great. Now you're just this."

Stuart gave up talking and just stared at her, waiting. Mercy was older, but he still had decades of experience in doing not much at all, and she broke first.

"Mother wants to know if you've seen a few people."

"How would I? I don't *go* anywhere."

"Ah, but you *talk* to quite a few, don't you? Between your strange diet... I mean, really, love, pigs... and your 'collection' here, a lot of students, eccentrics and others converse with you." She sniffed. Mercy found the idea of animal blood extremely distasteful, from experience. She was as old school as someone could get when they were only brought over a century or so before. "Mother would simply like to know what *you* know."

"So far you haven't told me what you actually want to know, so I can't answer."

"Here." She pulled a slip of paper out of her jacket, put it down on the desk. He looked down at it. The first three names meant nothing to him. The last he knew. He kept looking at it, thinking.

"I'll need to make some phone calls."

"Go right ahead."

"I can't make them at night, Mercy. People sleep."

"It's what, seven thirty?"

"Believe it or not, some of the people I know are old, Mercy."

"I don't really have much difficulty believing that." She stood up gracefully, put her arm on his shoulder in what she seemed to think was a comforting gesture. It wasn't. It brought back a rush of memory – her face inches from his, the sounds of a party just out of sight, the two of them outside in the dark, talking. He remembered telling her about his brother, about how he didn't know how to measure up to a dead war hero.

You can exceed him in every way.

He'd loved her for saying that. Even now the memory of the emotion made him stand a little taller.

"You know I liked you." She whispered it. It was easy for them to whisper. They often forgot to breathe. "I would have just eaten you if I didn't like you."

"You should have."

"If you really want to die, watch a sunrise." She smiled sadly at him. "I miss sunrise, myself. Oh, I can go out if it's overcast enough, but it's not the same."

"I tried, once."

"Did you?"

"When you actually catch on fire, the wisdom of it gets swallowed up in *oh fuck me I'm fucking on fire aaaah fuck fuck*. I ended up jumping down a well and spending a pretty shitty day regrowing my face." They were close enough to kiss now, and her remembered doing just that, how cold she'd felt then. She wouldn't feel cold now.

"You know, I've fed recently."

"I can smell it."

"I could share." She arched her neck. "Have you had it real recently?"

"Not since 1972."

"What happened in 1972?"

"Mercy." His voice sounded ragged to his own ears. "Please put your neck away."

She gave him a very long measuring look and he hated it and wanted it. The fact that he still felt these things around Mercy, probably always would, it was something he couldn't give up. It was good to feel. And for her part she didn't push it too far, didn't use it to extort his obedience. She didn't have to. She stepped back, pulled the collar of her coat up.

"What frustrates me is that you want to."

"More than anything I want to."

"We could be great together."

"I'll make those phone calls." He was looking down because he didn't want to see the sadness. If she'd been angry at him, or contemptuous of him, that he could have taken. But she was just sad, sorry for him, for his weakness. "Are you still…"

"We're at the house." She smiled. "I talked mother into a computer."

"Does anyone know how to use it?"

"It's not *that* hard, Stuart." She smiled again. "You should come by."

"Someday I probably will." He admitted. Eventually he'd break and go to her, or walk out into a bright beautiful morning. Those were his options.

"But not tonight?"

"Not tonight."

"Well, then." She walked around the desk, away from him. Looked around the room again. "I'll come by again tomorrow."

He didn't say anything, just waited for her to leave. Sat down at his desk, looking at the paper. He didn't owe Willrew anything. They barely liked each other. And the kid didn't seem helpless to him – if Mercy's mother wanted to go toe to toe with a guy who glowed like that, maybe she'd get herself turned to a cloud of ash and solve one of Stuart's problems.

And maybe she'll take Mercy with her.

The past decades he had a particular dream. It wasn't an actual dream, because he didn't sleep, or rest in a coffin, or whatever you were supposed to do when it was daylight out. Unless you counted his office. But in the dream, or daydream, or whatever, he and Mercy spent the day out in the sun, saw the world. He wanted that. He needed it. The idea of never getting it…

The paper sat there on his desk, laughing at him.

*

Mercy saw him immediately upon leaving Stuart's office.

Maybe to make hunting easier, or because they fed on life itself, people have a kind of sheen to them. Mercy could tell by looking if someone was sick or healthy, fit or exhausted and worn out. Some preferred to feed on those who were weakened by disease or ravaged by age, but Mercy had inherited her mother's proclivities. She liked health. Stuart had been *very* healthy then. She still remembered the gorgeous burst of him running down her throat, how giddy she'd felt as she slit her own chest open to let him drink from her. Bringing him over. She shook her head at his foolishness now.

But the man outside Stuart's office was a paradox. He was physically healthy enough, not spectacularly so, but strong from a life of toil. That was all fine. But the unnatural clung to him, and she could see it, like a weak echo of the horrible old bitch, the bonfire of her. This one was like a fire that someone hadn't quite extinguished properly, cherry red and threatening to burst out into actual flames.

"Howdy." He held up a hand. "I think you and I should talk."

"You are?"

"Name's Morgan. I ran into a couple of yours back when I was working for my grandmother. I've recently decided to go into business for myself." He made a face that a shark might have mistaken for a smile. Mercy wondered if he was insane. With the old bitch for a grandmother that seemed likely. "Which means I need to negotiate my severance."

"I'm not much for innuendo. You want to kill the old bitch."

"Ah, you've met her?"

"I have."

"So *you* must want to kill her, too."

"I wouldn't be sad about her death." Mercy knew better than to commit to anything. When she spoke, she was speaking as her mother's agent in the world. At present her mother had arranged a détente with that woman, and Mercy wasn't going to violate it. Neither was she going to pass up a chance to benefit her mother, if it presented itself. "Why don't you do something for me, as a show of good faith? Since you clearly want something from me."

"Depends on what it is."

"I've already eaten."

"Good, that makes this less tense." Morgan relaxed, slightly. The old woman hadn't taught him much, and he wasn't at all confident in his ability against something like her. "Walk?"

There was another slightly unusual human at the front of the store, chatting with the cashier. The girl had all the symptoms of being enthralled – pulse sped up, a slightly dazed expression on her face, a slight slurring of her speech. The kicker was the way her attention was zeroed in on him.

"So how about you give me your number..."

"Jimmy." The one named Morgan said, clearly displeased. Mercy filed this away. Mother liked details. It had occurred to Mercy many times over the years that her feelings for Mother could be just as artificial, for Mother was ancient and her power was great. But it didn't matter. They were there. Worrying about *why* she felt them seemed pointless.

"Oh, come on."

"We're leaving."

"Just five minutes..."

"She works for a fucking vampire.s you goddamn idiot. For all you know you're poaching his favorite blood bag." Mercy was surprised he'd made that assumption. He hadn't even seen Stuart. Had he somehow eavesdropped on them? She would have heard his heart if he'd been close. Her estimation of his cleverness rose.

"How the hell should I have..."

"Huh?" Evvie shook her head, feeling strange. Jimmy almost swore out loud. Morgan had distracted him. "Who's a vampire?"

"Bela Lugosi." Morgan actually grabbed Jimmy's arm. "Sorry to bother you. Let's *go.*" Jimmy let himself be dragged out, since it suited him to not have to have the girl asking *him* all sorts of questions about why she'd thought he was cool and funny and charming not a minute ago. The woman in the long coat smiled pleasantly and Evvie shuddered again at how it felt like she was a mouse being condescended to by a cat.

She felt very odd. It was hard to remember why she'd talked for so long with that guy, what they'd even talked *about*. He'd asked her a lot of questions. He'd asked her for her number, and she'd been about to give it to him. Why? He didn't...

"Evvie." She looked up. Stuart was dressed in his 'going out' coat. Christ, the guy was pale. Most people she saw in Bristol were pale compared to her but holy *shit* Stuart was pale. His weird visitor lady was pale, too. Why was it so hard to think? Why did the word *vampire* keep coming up? *Don't be crazy, why are you suddenly thinking Stuart's a vampire?*

"Yeah?"

"Gonna close up early tonight."

"Oh, I'm not done with the register, just…"

"I'll take care of it tomorrow. In fact, take the day off."

"Say what?" Stuart had never done this in four years. "Are you… is everything okay?"

"Nope." Without touching her he ushered her over to her coat. "I may have to go out of town for a few days. Family emergency."

"Oh." Evvie hadn't been aware Stuart *had* family. "Anything I can do?"

"Actually…" He stopped at the door. "Two things. One, go back to the counter. Everyone's paychecks for the week are there. Take yours, drop everyone else's in the mail. Here." He handed her a twenty. "Keep the change."

"Uh… sure." It was weird, but Stuart was a weird guy, so she didn't push. "Anything else?"

"Willrew. You still have his phone number?"

"I have the old one. I don't know if he still…"

"Give it to me."

Chapter Fourteen

Yule

The phone rang. This surprised everyone in the house.

The farm had a land line, and an old rotary phone actually hanging on the wall, an orange plastic thing. After their talk the four of them had gone about preparing dinner, Thea and Seria surprised to find themselves sitting as Joe and Thomas did most of the work.

"Did you know Joe could cook?"

"Did *you* know you'd managed to land a man who cooks?" Seri actually looked a little excited by this.

"Down, girl."

"Oh, I'm not interested that way." She smiled back at Thea, a trifle arch. "I'm just thrilled that someone will know how to make the food hot for my eventual nieces."

"Woman, you *know* I know how to cook."

"I see so little evidence."

"I'm going to slap your sister, Joe."

"I wouldn't."

"Right in the mouth."

"I sincerely don't recommend it."

"She wouldn't slap me. She loves me." Seri reached out and pushed a strand of hair out of Thea's face. "I like the short do."

"You did it."

"I do good work." She came in a little closer, spoke softly. "You look... I kind of feel like I'm falling apart, but you look good. I'm a little envious."

"It's weird for me too, love." Thea didn't often see Seri admit to uncertainty, it rattled her. She pulled a little closer. "But I feel like I've been waiting for something ever since mom died, and now... it's happening. Even when it's scary and awful it's real."

"Nana Rafiela, though."

"Maybe I'm just an awful person but I'm relieved." Joe came to the table with two large bowls full of pasta and red sauce. They'd found some hot sausage in the freezer and made use of that, along with garlic and some peppers from the garden Thomas' father had started. "Eat, *mangia*, that's all the Italian I know."

Thomas was still at the counter cleaning up a little, rinsing the cutting board and putting the knives in to soak when the phone rang. Everyone in the room turned to stare at it.

"I didn't know that thing actually worked."

"It doesn't quite." Thomas walked over and answered it. "Hello." He said *hello* the way other people say *I will fucking kill you*.

"Willrew."

"Stuart. How did you get my phone number?"

"I could have dialed information..."

"No, you couldn't have." His voice was getting deep. Despite herself, Thea felt a bit of a tingle. She loved Thomas' growly voice.

"I got it from Evvie."

"When you say..."

"I didn't do anything to her. Just listen to me for a minute, okay? You can do whatever you want after."

"All right. Listening."

"There's a woman I know. She's like me. She's *why* I'm like me. She came by today, she had a list with four names on it. One of them is you."

"What are the other three names?"

"Joseph Rafiela, Seria Rafiela, Thea Mendel." The plastic of the handset creaked in Thomas' hand as he clenched it. He had to stop himself from crushing it. "Look, it's none of my business, but you pissed off someone very bad, if whoever it is can get these people asking about you."

"So why warn me?"

"Because... look, I don't want to be involved in this."

"Calling me is a spectacularly bad way to be uninvolved." Thomas considered this. "But thank you."

"The woman in question. Her name's Mercy. It would be a

nice way to repay me if you didn't make her explode or whatever it is you can do. The rest of them I don't care about."

"I will consider this." He looked over at Thea. "I'm not promising you anything."

"Look, they're expecting an answer from me tomorrow."

"So answer them."

"What?"

"What do you actually *know*, Stuart? I used to work for you, I'm not normal and you're a little afraid of me. Tell her that. Give her my address in Cranston if you want. My last check went there, it should be in your files. They're going to find out more than that sooner or later, I don't mind you giving it to them."

"I..."

"You don't want to get involved. Don't try and lie. Just tell them enough to get them off your back. I gotta go."

"Sure. Okay. Hey, before I do, you might want to check on Evvie. There were these two weirdoes in her tonight, I watched them leave, one of them... well, she was acting weird."

"Describe them."

"One of them had long brown hair, the other was either really pale blond or white. Both looked like they'd gotten tuned up recently."

"Thanks." Thomas hung up the phone, working his jaw, trying not to growl.

"So, not good news."

"Your grandmother seems to be reaching out." Joe was filling a bowl for himself, walked it over to the table and sat down. "After you guys eat, we should get on with things."

"You're not going to eat?"

"I don't think..."

"You helped *cook*. You have to eat it. If the cook doesn't eat, that's just weird."

"Joe, I know you don't know me very well..."

"It's the principle of the thing." He stood up and walked back over, ladled food into a bowl. "I got a lot of sausage in this one. You strike me as a meat guy."

"Oh my God so many dirty ways to take that." Seri snorted.

"He's offering my boyfriend extra sausage." Thea snickered.

"He wants your boyfriend to be a meat guy."

"I'm dying."

"If I eat this will you two stop this?"

"Never."

"Never *ever*."

Thomas took the bowl from Joe and sat down with as much wounded dignity as an ancient prelate might in a rude animal skin yurt. It didn't help them stop laughing any.

*

Seri hated winter.

She liked certain aspects of it. She liked snow when she didn't have to be out in it, for example. She was a big fan of white Christmases and being inside with some hot chocolate while the world got quiet and peaceful under a white blanket. She hated shoveling, cleaning off her car, having to wear huge clunky snow boots. She hated how they dumped salt and sand on the roads so her car, already exposed to seawater, got pitted and rotted out. She hated *driving* in it.

And she especially hated standing outside in it watching her cousin and her cousin's boyfriend doing... whatever the hell they were doing. She'd hated the last time they'd done this, the frantic, desperate attempt to save Joe. She wasn't liking the slower, more methodical digging of weird symbols into the snow.

"We don't really know what we're doing." Thea walked over to where Joe and Seri were waiting, near the stone wall. Thomas was in the middle of the field between the wall and the stone lodges, still working on what looked like the most complicated snow angel in existence.

"Please pretend you do next time." Joe deadpanned.

"Well, we have some books."

"Fantastic, you have some books. Every time I realize I should be dead except that Thea's read some books, I feel really great about everything."

"You get very cranky when you're cold."

"And when you dabble in powers beyond our ken, I also get cranky then."

"Did you rhyme that on purpose?"

"Kinda wish I did, but no." Joe shivered in his coat, not sure if he was cold or just scared. "So what are you doing?"

"Thomas is using planetary alchemical symbols. The one on the left there is Mars, *Avtotar*. He who listens." Thea pointed out the strange mark Thomas had shaped in the snow. "Over there, I put in *Liiansa*. He who is first in truth. That squiggle with the line over it is the alchemical symbol for amalgamation."

To Seri, it all sounded like gibberish that made her head hurt. Joe could see lines, patterns appearing over the symbols, connecting and linking them.

"What's that thing that looks like a TIE fighter?"

"It means *spirit*." Thea laughed, delight in her voice. "It *does* look like a TIE fighter. Maybe we can get Darth Vader to help us."

"I'm ready." Thomas said, peeling off his jacket and shirt.

"Aren't you cold?" Seri said to distract herself. She was really missing David after a week.

"I'm about to channel a lot of power." They were equally surprised to see Thea stripping down as well, although she left her shirt on. Seri watched Thomas turn to her cousin, the look they exchanged. It carried meaning she didn't really understand. *I've never felt that way.* It was a sad thing to realize.

"I'm good when you're good." Thea said, bracing herself.

"Okay." They'd spent the past half hour before coming out here making out in the bedroom, deliberately not getting further than third base. The feeling of it burned up and down his spine. He honestly might not have needed the jacket right now even *without* what was coming. She gave him a little seraphic grin, a shared moment between them. He dropped to one knee and finished the mark for eye, *ooanoa* in Dee's likely wholly imaginary Enochian language. It didn't matter if it was real. It was a bridge between concepts.

The surge hit him and leapt to Thea, linking them. They both inhaled sharply, holding the air for a moment, the sensation of being both at once so strong, sensual in the best way. She could feel his fingers moving, his skin beading up with sweat. He knew how it felt to ache in a place he didn't have, could see that one of her eyes saw more color than the other. The distance between them, a few feet, it felt so trivial.

The part that was Thea pushed, wanting to see what had been. The part that was Thomas was bound to the land. He had grown here, bled here, *shed* blood here. The year a drunken hunter mistook him for a deer and put an arrow in his leg, the summers in the slaughterhouse, a young child falling out of a tree. The island knew him.

Together they felt it regard them. The houses, the trees, the grass and snow. Deer in the woods around them. Birds on trees, foxes in dens. A long abandoned feral dog lifted its head on Pine Hill, the largest predator on the whole of the island. To the south the less than a hundred people who made it their yearlong home, their cats and dogs and other pets. Seagulls.

Thea felt the unease at that. The gulls were wrong. Not all, but some.

Thomas was gripped in the regard of the rock and soil. The things that crawled or tunneled through it, lived on it, or above it. It wasn't *alive*, it had no mind. But it had a will. It had existed, it wanted to exist. And here, on this spot, it had been wounded terribly, so terribly that it sought to swallow what had happened.

Tell me. He sent out. *Show me*.

In a house in Little Compton, a woman who'd once called herself Robia bolted upright from a nap she'd been taking in her chair. She felt it, surging, a call from the eyes she'd set loose. She could feel the wound she'd made to the world as it wailed, so long buried, seeking the air.

She couldn't escape the memory of it. His face, shocked, as she'd called it up. The *Beharion*, the broken *thing*, the mockery of earth she'd called. It wrenched itself out of the ground, made of soil and mud and shards of buried schist left behind by glaciers before man had walked the continent. She saw it again, and she knew someone *else* could see it. Someone else knew that he'd collapsed. Someone else knew that she'd killed him, that her anger had... that she'd left him gasping, crawling away from the thing she'd pulled to the surface, she'd stood there and watched him crawl off to die.

Someone knew.

Someone knew.

This time when she shrieked, the birds bound to her will shrieked. Her home swayed. The garden out behind it convulsed, the plants waving. Her fury was unending. It threatened to pour out of her and into the world like Pompeii, a cloud of ash that consumed all it touched. But she was also smiling.

I have you now, boy.

What she saw and what Thomas saw were different. She *knew* what she'd done. She didn't have to linger. She didn't see the rotten, corrupt thing rising up out of the ground, how it carried pieces of bone, decomposing flesh, the remains of the few hardy settlers who tried to make a home on the windswept northern cove, before abandoning it. The animals that had died there. What she'd done had called corruption forth, from worms tunneling through flesh to the lingering traces of death, and had made it stand. Walk.

His grandfather had seen death. He'd been a doctor in a time of war. It had broken him. Robia had been the one success, the one who'd survived. Proof that you could live through it. It wasn't the monstrosity that she'd summoned that had caused him to collapse. It was seeing her, knowing that *this* impossible thing had come, somehow, from her. That she'd been forced to endure this to survive.

His heart had broken for her. Thomas could *feel* his grandfather, in that place, at that time. Could feel him crawling back to the house, weeping, his chest on fire. She'd put the monster back, but not properly. The magic was twisted up, leeched into the soil, the houses had collapsed in ruin from it.

Thea realized it first. Felt it, felt the eyes upon them. The seagulls were staring. Crying out as they whirled in the air above them, as the ground around them convulsed. Felt everything going to hell. Her thoughts were full of images of domes, walls, shields, and the idea took the initial impact of rage like black lightning, ground it.

But that wasn't safe either. The ground here was soaked, permeated in blood and death, and she'd already called it up once. This time it shrieked. Joe shrieked along with it, nearly blinded by what he was seeing, and Seria caught him as he fell.

"What's happening?"

"Bad shit." Thea grunted. "Nana found us."

Thomas heard the baying, his fingers sunk through the snow and into the soil, which shivered and trembled. It was almost liquefied by what was passing through it, and as they all watched the ruined lodges fell into themselves, the last remaining pillars of stone collapsing into clouds of dust and powdered snow. Behind them the trees shook.

"Thea." Thomas grunted. "I need time."

"I'm on it." She saw the trees part. A huge form, massive, easily ten feet tall came striding out. It was wearing furs, rude ones, almost just hides torn from prey. Massive antlers jutted from his head. Thea had seen antlers like those. They looked like the ones on the reindeer she'd seen when she was eight and her mother took her to Christmas Village. His eyes were huge, black of iris, and his mouth split his face with jagged teeth. He bellowed and green flames loped out of the woods, lolling from black, canine jaws like the tongues of fire that they were.

"Holy God." Seri moaned in disbelief. They were a little more than two hundred yards away and moving quickly. The monster-man with the antlers hefted a spear and bellowed again, pointing at them. *Oh, Nana, you hideous bitch*.

"What the fuck are we..."

"Quiet." Thea dropped down onto her knees to get at the snow. She didn't have time to make much of a symbol, but what she wanted was the snow itself. The cold of it. The idea it created. She imagined it quickly, concisely, and wished for it as hard as she could, holding onto that memory of her mother's voice.

Look, Thea. There he is!

Both her hands went into the snow now. *There he is*, she thought. *Merry Christmas.*

The huntsman was charging now, loping at them, when the sound of bells filled the air. It turned, sniffing for a scent, a creature of pure predation. It didn't look up fast enough.

Joe was still moaning, holding his hands over his eyes. Thea's eyes were closed, her whole being concentrated in what she was doing. Thomas was doing something else. So it was Seri who saw it.

The sleigh came out of the air.

It was being pulled.

By reindeer.

Eight of them. No, nine. There was a ninth reindeer in the lead, with a splash of what looked like blood on its muzzle, but glowing, gleaming. Their antlers were similar to the ones on the huntsman's head, huge curving things that looked almost black in the moonlight. The sleigh was massive, piled with a huge sack filled with boxes, the sack almost obscenely full, and it crashed down right where the huntsman had been standing, crushing the ground. Had he not leapt aside it was impossible *not* to imagine him being crushed by the weight of the sleigh.

"Thea?"

"Is it there?" Her cousin hissed. "Kind of hard to watch and do this."

"Is... that..."

A man with a long white beard and pointed ears, dressed in exquisitely trimmed red furs (fox? Deer? What animal could they come from?) leapt from the sleigh and swept a colossal gloved hand in a blow that barely missed the huntsman's face, then leapt back to avoid a strike from the spear that would have gutted him. The reindeer snorted and pawed the earth, released from the sleigh, driving the wolves back to keep them from their master's side.

"Well, okay then." Joe was sitting up now, blinking.

The wolves were snarling, snapping at the reindeer for a few moments. Seria started to think *okay, maybe we're going to be all right* when the wolves turned, staring at where the four of them stood, defenseless. Then they started to run again, right at them.

The flames of their tongues were also visible in their eyes as well, flickering green light bleeding out across the snow.

"Uh, Thea?"

"Seri, I'm kinda busy here..."

"The wolf monster things. They're not, Santa isn't stopping them." She swallowed back some hot acid spit. "I think we're in trouble."

"Thomas?"

"Almost.. got... it." For his part, Thomas hand was nearly frozen now, the pain incredible. He welcomed it. When working together with Thea, he could channel pleasure, but alone like this pain was more familiar, easier. He'd recognized the Wild Hunt as soon as he'd seen it, known what the old woman had done. He'd been amazed at Thea's riposte, his lips curled up in something very much like delight, but he'd kept working himself. The wolves were now less than a hundred feet away from him as let the cold set his hand on fire.

What could stop a pack of demon wolves?

The king of wolves. Maimer of Tyr. Killer of the Grey One.

The wolves were almost upon him when he howled, the shape of a great wolf in his shadow. One leapt, the tongue of fire lolling from slavering jaws, only for Thomas to burst from his kneeling position, his hand a claw to rip a throat out in a bound, slamming the creature hard against the ground. Its spine shattered from the impact, but he didn't release it. Behind him, the whirling spear of the huntsman slashed at the red-clad man, sinking into his shoulder. Thea grunted, but kept her eyes shut, forcing everything she had into keeping herself focused.

Thomas hurled the body of the wolf in his hand into the onrushing pack, followed it snarling. One of the wolves leapt onto his back, another tried to bite his throat. He felt no pain at all, only a soaring, frenzied rage born of loss and fear, unwilling to suffer again. Teeth bit into his shoulder and neck, he reached up and crushed the monster beast's head with his hands, tore it free from himself and channeled the injury, the blood, into what he had become. His shadow was enormous, spread out over the snow, a black muzzle with frothing fangs. The river monster, sun-eater, killer of the god.

The huntsman's wolves were as nothing to him. He snapped, tore, crushed them. The last one died against the rocks of the old wall, hurled aside after he'd snapped its neck in his hands. He turned to face the huntsman and his foe, barely able to distinguish between them.

He charged, the wounds on his neck and sides and back streaming blood even while they closed. The huntsman had at last backed his enemy up and was preparing to hurl his spear when the black shadow of the wolf-god came over him. He turned, knowing his killer had come.

Thomas, barely himself, saw the spear shifted, knew it would come at him.

So distracted the huntsman did not see the reindeer, driven by their master, as they charged. How had he gotten back on the sleigh? No one saw. What they *did* see was the spear go wide, twirling into the air, as the nine reindeer drove his rude furs into the snowy earth, followed by the massive sleigh crushing him wholly under its runners. What was left of it began to dissipate in a cloud, black steam, even before Thomas managed to drop to all fours as the last essence of the wolf god left him. There were a few marks on his neck and shoulder, but nothing like the gaping gashes he'd suffered.

He struggled to his feet, panting. By the time he'd gained them, the sleigh and the reindeer were gone. He could hear the others, turned to find Thea walking to him, exhausted and laughing.

"Did you see that?"

"I did." He was grinning at her. "*Santa*?"

"Tell me it didn't work."

"Oh, it worked. It was perfect. I would never have thought of that." She was in his arms now, feeling warm and he delighted in every place they touched.

"I liked your giant wolf thing. What was that?"

"Fenrir. Norse myth. Killed Odin. Odin's sometimes seen as the head of the Wild Hunt."

"Was the dude with antlers supposed to be Odin?"

"Myths get messed up." He kissed her then, hard, and she wrapped both hands around his head, holding him tightly against her. They stayed like that for a while. "I want you so fucking bad. I want you forever."

"If my cousins weren't watching we could..." She left that unfinished. "Did you see, before she..."

"Yes." He sighed. "I did."

"We still don't know what she's planning." They were walking back, her arm around his waist. He bent to kiss her again as they walked. It made it harder to get anywhere, but she didn't want to stop. Eventually they were back to where the ritual had started.

"So, nothing?"

"Something." Thomas said. "She told him she'd make him new. That was the last thing I heard before..."

"Okay. How's that help us?"

"I think that's what she wants you all for. To make her new."

*

The morning came sluggishly.

"I guess I'm less scared?" Seri was looking out the window in the living room, a cramped room mostly built around a big fireplace. Thomas had gone out chopping wood for them, and both Seri and Thea had watched him, fascinated for different reasons. "Can I confess something, Joey?"

"Always."

"I just don't want Thea to freak out."

"Okay. What's up?"

"I'm *really*... I'm missing David. A lot more than I thought I would. But..." She blushed, covered her face in her hair for a moment. "I miss the sex, but I don't miss him."

"What the hell else does he have to miss?"

"That's not really fair."

"Yeah, I'm the older brother. I don't do fair."

"You're younger than I am!"

"That's never been proven. Why would it freak Thea out?

She's not exactly number one on the 'Yay David' email list."

"She might get all…" Seri gestured. "I'm not going to just dump David."

"Uh… why not?"

"Well, for starters, I really miss the sex."

"There are other people who will have sex with you." Joe said. "I remember getting in quite a few fights with people over this."

"You did?"

"You were very popular before you hooked up with that human air hockey table."

"Joey!"

"Look, Seri, I tried to like the guy. And he's not a monster or anything. He's just a self centered idiot who coasts and lets the world work itself out around himself. Without really caring what happens to anyone else. I could handle the former but the latter…" He shrugged, looked out the window at the cove. Thought about Bishop, an actual trust fund baby who didn't even bother to get a job. *He called. David doesn't. Seri always calls him.*

Seri was looking at her hands. "It's just hard. To end six years. To say 'It's not working out' or whatever. There's a lot of memories there. Rocky Point. My first time. He took me to the planetarium for my birthday a couple of years ago, it was really sweet, there was a horse drawn carriage ride in Providence and everything."

"Horses," the boy said.

"That's really great, Seri, but…" Joe stopped. Turned his head and looked at the boy.

"Did he just…" Seri was standing up now.

"Horses," the boy said again. "Clip clop."

"Seriously, this day." Joe pointed up to the ceiling. "Do we go get them, or…"

The sound of faint creaking and the occasional moan had been a fairly incessant one the entire time the two of them had been in the living room. You couldn't make out much in the way of details – the house was amazingly well put together considering it was originally at least three hundred years old – but you could definitely tell that the wild rumpus was yet to abate.

"I'm going to say we wait a little." Seri sat down on the couch next to the boy. "Can you tell me your name?"

"No." The boy giggled.

"Well, crap. He's learned no." Joe scratched his head. "Do we have any developmental psych books around?"

"I forgot to pack mine."

*

Upstairs, they were in a gentle, post-coital phase, lying on their sides and touching each other. Thea had her legs wrapped around him, keeping him inside her.

"We should get up." He groaned.

"Why? You don't want to. I don't want to." She nuzzled in, feeling the heat of his skin, the flush of their recent exertion. "Oh, Tommy."

"You only call me Tommy after this."

"I only like it after this." She purred, bit his earlobe gently. "When you're my Tommy."

He rolled and she ended up on top of him, both of them grinning.

"I want to say something awesome but my brain's all scrambled." He openly looked at her, admiring her naked, and she let him. It wasn't that she was shy about her body, but she'd never felt quite this... adored? She was looking at him, at the slope of his hips, the muscles of his flanks. "You're so beautiful you make me feel like I'm going to bite my tongue trying to talk to you."

"That's okay. I can always..." She let herself move forward to rest on him. "...come up with a better use for your tongue."

After a while she finally slid off of him.

"Sorry, bathroom calls."

"Okay." He smiled. "I gotta take off the glove anyway. Need to stand up if I don't want to make a mess."

She walked across the hall. The upstairs 'bathroom' was

really just a toilet and a sink in an uncomfortably small room, but it meant not having to risk going downstairs. Seri and Joe were probably still up and for once, she didn't want to be teased about anything. She loved them both, but after what they'd just done, she was feeling raw and vulnerable and desperately aroused.

Tommy will be up for it soon.

She used the bathroom on autopilot, thinking about what they'd done. How well they'd done it. If the old woman tried again, there was nothing for her to draw on, no long-buried mass of emotional muck to stab with black lightning. She'd have to come at them with something new. And Thea was so keyed up, so achingly hot, she almost wanted it to happen.

Bring it, old woman. He's mine.

When she got back from the bathroom he was lying in bed, looking out the small window. These rooms were originally an attic – sometimes Thomas would bash his head hard standing up, because the edges of the room sloped upward to the roof. She took a moment to admire him. Before Thomas she'd always dated men like Karl, men shorter than her, slighter. She'd thought her type was beautiful boys, but Thomas wasn't that, and it worked for her. She slid into the bed, into the covers and against his side.

"She returns."

"And is cold." She bit gently at his neck. "If we stayed here we'd need to invest in better insulation."

"Would you want to?" He rolled to face her, pressing up close. Despite the look on his face, the stirring between his legs got her attention.

"Not forever. But it would be a nice place to spend a weekend from time to time." She slid her hand down his abdomen, loving the little pants he let out. Wrapped her fingers gently around him. "Especially without all the other people."

"Yes." His hands were around her now, cupping her. His fingers were starting to play, and she hissed in pleasure as one started to find her clit, the other sliding around her asshole.

"Don't stop doing that." She moaned into his neck. "Oh, wow, I didn't know I liked that. Do *you* like that?"

"Never tried it."

"Want to?"

"I'm willing to experiment." He looked serious and yet amused, but behind all that was the lazy, almost gentle heat of someone so aroused he'd lost the ability to protest. "Anything you want to try."

She kept one hand on his cock, kept it stimulated, while her mouth went to his navel, gently licking, biting. The other hand slid between his ass cheeks, found the spot and gently pressed on it. Felt him convulse in her hands and grinned.

"I think you do."

"I think I like anything you do." He was full on groaning now, his head back. "I love everything you are."

"My Tommy." She slid down slightly, still gently playing with the bud, a knuckle inside him. Ran her tongue up the side of his cock. Felt him twitching, his hips rocking forward. Swirled herself around the head, then pushed forward, bathing the tip with her tongue. Loved his moans, loved knowing he was hers. She could do anything she wanted. Pulled herself off of him. "I love you. It scares me every time I say it, but I do. I love you. I want you. Can I have you? Please?"

"Yes. God, yes. I'm yours. Anything you want." He felt like metal about to snap. And then she started again, and he lost the ability to think about how he felt at all, lost it in a slow, sweet build of anticipation, a symphony conducted by her.

After she was finished with him, and he recovered, he returned the favor, exploring her. It was slow, and gentle, and then it wasn't, based on her cries and a few barked commands that made him grin even as he obeyed them. He found that even when his tongue was tired he could slide it along her folds and recover while using his hands to make up for it, feeling her buck against his fingers. She pinned his face down with both legs against his ears, panting and moaning and begging.

"Please. Please please *please*."

"Please what?" His face was wet, her right leg folded up against the back of his neck.

"Make me come you bastard make me come I'm so *close*." He slid a finger up into her, felt her clench around him. "Ohmygod *yes*."

He took a second to look at her body as she writhed, to watch it flex and move. She had a gorgeous little mole under her left breast, usually hidden by the breast itself. The way the light from the moon and the stars played over her, left pools of darkness and peaks of light, he felt a little awestruck.

When she came she bit down on a pillow to keep from shrieking, her hips bucking. She nearly broke his nose, he barely managed to keep it out of the way. Finally she collapsed, and he slid up to kiss her, tasting himself on her.

They didn't say anything, both breathing hard, just lying together finally spent. It felt so good to be sated, to rest in each other for a while. Eventually thoughts began to rear their ugly head, but she wasn't sure how long it had been. The moon wasn't visible anymore, but the light was still coming in, so not morning yet.

"What do we do about her?"

"I'm not sure."

"Can we..." She swallowed. "Can we stop her without killing her?"

He lay there, feeling her head resting against him, wanting to say yes but having no idea if it was the case. He never wanted to lie to Thea.

"I don't even know if we can stop her at all."

"Note to self, my lover is terrible at comforting lies." She shifted, but didn't pull away. "I'm going to sleep like this now."

He didn't say anything, because he was afraid to say what he was thinking. That she was his forever person. That he'd never love anyone like this again, even if she left him tomorrow he was hers, forever. She could keep him or throw him away and it didn't matter. He would do anything for her.

He would even live for her.

Chapter Fifteen

Finale of Seem

Mercy hadn't been to a restaurant in a couple of years. Back when she'd hunted more for her own food, they'd been rare. Usually part of a family owned business. Mercy had seen the gradual transformation of the state, had watched the Great War (comfortably detached from it, but she'd been aware it was happening) and the excess of the Jazz Age. She'd been there when the Biltmore had opened, in an elegant little flapper's dress. It hadn't really suited her.

Sometimes she wondered about the girl they'd put in her crypt. The one who'd been exhumed. She'd been dead, of course. Mercy had lived with her name for many years, until just about anyone who knew who she was had died themselves.

Would Sarah have gone to this garishly lit ice cream shop with these two boys? Mercy didn't think so. She watched them drink their very large shakes, surprised that they were so eager to act like children.

"How old are you?"

"I'm twenty-four. Jimmy's twenty-two." Morgan wiped at his lip. "Look, you come here, you get an Awful Awful. It's just what you *do*."

"I was nineteen." She smiled. "But when I was nineteen this place wasn't even here." They'd driven up to Barrington from Bristol to go to the Newport Creamery, mainly because Morgan had talked Mercy into paying. She'd looked on it as an investment.

Jimmy couldn't help but stare at her. She wasn't *model* hot, but she was pretty and if you didn't look at the squiggles she had a killer body, and she *acted* like she was friendly and outgoing. He knew she'd probably kill him if he tried anything but he couldn't help it. Every time she noticed him doing it she gave him this look, not a come hither look, just a *I see you doing that* that was equal parts amused and smug. It was Morgan she was interacting with.

Morgan was keenly aware he was talking to a dead thing. He knew he couldn't do anything that would really *hurt* her, but he'd built up an incantation in his head anyway about Phaethon and Helios. Maybe it would work.

"And that's all you know about her?"

"Lady, that's more than anyone else knows about her." Morgan scowled. "I wasn't around when she came to this country, no idea why she did. All I know is what I've seen and that's plenty."

"Hmm." Mercy turned this idea over in her head. The boys *had* witnessed a lot, but were rarely informed of the *why* of their actions. Still, she now knew that the old woman had sent them to kill the boy Willrew and his parents, and that the other names on her list were other grandchildren, like these two. That she had many more, in a book on her property, and she kept track of them through various means. "She never told you exactly why she's so interested in these particular cousins?"

"They're girls."

"And that's important?"

"Yeah. I don't know why. They're also the youngest. If she could she'd crank out more kids now, get a *really* young one." Morgan considered. "And everyone in the family dies young."

Mercy arched an eyebrow at that.

"Our parents went out in a plane crash." Jimmy spoke up. "Left us the sal... the family business and Byron. She really didn't like Byron."

"Why?"

"She was mad he was a boy, because he's young. He's like ten now." Jimmy scowled. "Why do you care about all this?"

"Mother wants to know why she wants these people found." Mercy smiled at him, and he couldn't figure out why he was scared of such a friendly smile. "And what mother wants, I provide."

"Okay, well, that's it. That's what we know." Morgan said, grabbing hold of the conversation away from Jimmy. "Now it's your turn."

"Right now I don't know much to *tell* you."

"I'm not looking for information. I know who she wants just fine. What I want is to set up a relationship. No, I'm not trying to get in your pants, I'm not Jimmy stupid."

Mercy laughed at that.

"No interest at all?"

"You look at me like I look at a basket of hot fries."

Privately, Mercy had actually upgraded Morgan. *Jimmy* she'd eat with minimal regret, he was a clod who used coercion like a poor carpenter using a hammer for every problem. But Morgan had potential. He was rough around the edges, untutored, but there was a core there she could work with. He understood family and responsibility. The things *he* could do weren't the same as mother's gift, but he was aware of the world in a way most weren't when mother brought them across.

But she knew better than to say any of this yet.

"To what end, this relationship."

"She's crazy and whatever she's going to do, I'm going to end up dead. Unless she goes down first."

"And you expect what, help?"

"Not directly. Just… stay out of the way. Let us get this done."

"The two of you? By yourselves?"

"Maybe. Maybe not. That list of yours… the enemy of my enemy doesn't have to be my friend, but it can still hurt my enemy." He took another sip of his giant shake. "She used to say that."

"I'll think about it." She stood up, pulling several twenties out of her wallet. "This should more than cover it. Get some real food. You're both too thin."

"Thanks?"

"Consider it me fattening you up for later if it makes you more comfortable." She loved the way Jimmy *flinched* when she smiled at him. Turned and left the store, walked to her car, checked the time. 9 pm. Plenty of time to…

The cell phone in her pocket rang. She was surprised. No one from home would call yet. Too early. She didn't recognize the number. Answered it on the third ring.

"Mercy."

"It's me."

"Stuart." She purred as she put the car in reverse, backed away from the restaurant. "I wasn't expecting a call so soon. How'd you get the number?"

"I called home."

"*Did* you? Did you talk to mother?"

"No." He sounded terse. Of course he'd never been very comfortable around mother. She was, after all, the perfect vampire. "She's got company from what Sevvy said."

"She was upset recently. She needs to work it out of her system."

"Look, I have some information for you. I've decided to just give it to you instead of trying to play both ends against the middle. You ready?"

"I'm always ready, Stuart."

"So, you probably know I recognized one of the names on the list."

"I was curious why you pretended you wouldn't call people late at seven pm, yes."

"The Willrew kid. Mercy, I *really* don't think you should get involved here."

"Oh?"

"He's... not normal."

"Well, that's a very broad category." She drove the car around a hole in the road, deciding to go north, drive through Providence. "Don't tell me we have poachers? No one's come in to challenge us in *years*."

"He's not a bloodsucker."

"What, then?"

"I don't fucking know, I'm not an expert, I just know he hurts my eyes to look at. He used to work for me, in the store. Back then he was normal. Then his parents died and he got fucking weird and now he's like a fucking house fire, threatening to burn everything in sight. He's dating a woman, didn't get her name, she's just as bad. They're *dangerous*, Mercy."

Mercy considered the story the Williams boys had told her about how Thomas Willrew's parents died, about how he'd failed to join them.

"Why are you telling me this? You've never cared what happens..."

"I don't care what happens to *them*." He made a gurgling sound. She realized he was probably drinking his pig blood to try and keep the rage from turning into bloodlust. "I care what happens to *you*."

"I could stop by."

"Please don't."

"You're a maddening boy, Stuart. You call me, tell me that, and then ask me to stay away." She clucked her tongue at him. "I could come anyway. Take you away from all this."

"You did that once and it didn't work out."

"Maybe I didn't try hard enough." She thought about it. "But I won't. I don't want you to be unhappy. More unhappy? If you want me to stay away I will."

"It's not..." Another gurgle. Pig blood was so *unsatisfying*. She'd never told him, but she'd tried it for a while after she'd first died. It never really cut the craving for her. "I don't want to be this."

"I know."

"Just stay away from him. Please."

"I will consider your warning. Do you know how I could get in touch with him?"

"I've got a phone number he'll probably change soon and an address I'm sure he's not using."

"Do you have email yet?"

"Ugh."

"Is that a no?"

"I use a computer at the library sometimes."

"Stuart."

"It's *weird*."

"Get a computer." She sighed. "Give me the contact information now, I'll just have to *remember* it."

He did. She would remember it, of course. Mercy

remembered everything.

*

Bishop had surprised everyone by showing up at the crack of dawn, except Thomas, who was already up taking care of the animals. He strode into the house with several boxes of donuts and a four pack of coffee. By the time the smell had everyone up he was puttering around the kitchen. Joe was the first to rise, and thus the first to see it.

"You brought donuts."

"And coffee. There's a few crullers in there somewhere. I remembered you saying." Bishop had his hair tied back, his beard trimmed down to a Van Dyke. He looked *good*, Joe thought as he sat down at the table and began rummaging through the boxes.

"Wow, it's even honey dip."

"Baked goods, man. You should never skint on them."

"So, how were things back at the homestead?"

"My parents continue to disapprove." Bishop's smile never wavered. "They're not really sure what they disapprove of, nowadays. Just a kind of low level disapproval."

"Ah." Joe didn't really know what that was like. Uncle Greg had been fairly supportive. He hadn't really understood about Joe being gay, but he hadn't felt like it was that big a concern either. *Be safe and be happy, and if you find love, hold on.* The man had always looked so sad when he said that.

"So I couldn't help but notice there's a big hole where there used to be a bunch of buildings over to the north pasture."

"Right." Joe took a sip of coffee.

"No chance I could get that explained?"

"Santa Claus beat up a man with antlers and no pants."

"So I probably *shouldn't* have it explained."

"There's a lot more details, but it boils down to we figured out who's after us." Bishop stopped messing around with the stove long enough to look over at Joe expectantly. "Turns out my grandmother killed Thomas' grandfather, sort of. They were... I'm not sure if they were doing it or not, really."

"Wait, what? Your..."

"Yeah. My Nana sent monsters after us." Joe smiled like he'd just bitten into a rancid plum. "The door's over there if you need to run away screaming."

"I'll admit I'd prefer it if there *weren't* monsters."

"Monsters!" The boy walked into the room. Bishop immediately noticed he was talking. And thank *God* he was finally wearing clothes.

"Oh, yeah, and he can talk now."

"Do we know your name yet?"

"No!"

"Ask a silly question..." Bishop turned the heat on the pan of eggs he was making down and dropped to his knees to face the boy. "Any chance you feel like telling us your name?"

"No." The kid got solemn on him. "No name. Took my name out."

"What?" Thea walked down the stairs in one of Thomas' T-shirts. It fit her like a dress, and that wasn't a small feat — Bishop hadn't really checked out Thea before, but she was a tall girl, with long legs. Anyone else's shirt wouldn't have managed to cover below the hips. "Whassat he just said? When did he start saying things?"

"Last night." Joe took another bite of cruller. "You sounded occupied."

"Uhn." She blinked, obviously barely awake. "Yah. Tired. Good tired." She looked at the boy. "Who took your name?"

"She did." His lip was quivering. Bishop saw it and acted.

"Y'all can play twenty questions with him later. Go sit down, have a coffee. There's donuts." He winked at the boy, went back to making eggs. Some of the kid's playful demeanor came back, if not all.

"Coffee." Thea staggered over. Lifted a cup, sniffed it. "Oh thank you for the black coffee I hate junk in my coffee."

"I always just get black and let people add what they want."

"You're dating the right guy then." Thea took a long drink.

"None of us like junk in our coffee."

"Huh, really?"

"My slovenly cousin is correct." Joe was by now mostly done with his. "Sometimes Seri puts milk in hers, mostly just to annoy me."

"And because I want to keep my stomach lining." Seri had actually bothered to get dressed, which put her one up on Joe in his boxers and T-shirt and Thea in her borrowed shirt and panties. "Hello, Bishop. Glad you got down here okay."

"Was just a ferry ride, no big deal."

"Okay." Seria didn't say *you caught the very first ferry down here* or *you brought enough baked goods to feed an army and now you're making breakfast* or *just take my brother in the back already* but she thought all these things. She didn't really know Bishop that well yet, but she was willing to wait and see if he made her brother happy. Instead she sat down at the table and drank coffee. "So, what was the name of that girl you wanted to check up on?"

"Whassat?" Thea was still blinking. "Oh don't *talk* to me yet."

"Did you two sleep at all last night?"

"In bursts." Thea was looking at the cup in her hand disappointedly, feeling its emptiness. "Mostly we had sex and talked about if we were going to have to kill Nana or not."

"Kill Nana!" The little boy chimed in. Four sets of eyes turned to him.

"I really wish he'd tell us his name."

"No name anymore." He shook his head sadly. "Not Byron anymore."

"Your name is.. *was* Byron?" Joe asked, gently as he could. The boy nodded. "Why isn't it anymore?"

"She took it. Pulled it out. 'Useless, useless.' Put something else inside. Wasn't me anymore." He looked so lost in that moment that Seri pulled him up onto her lap. He wasn't crying, but he leaned against her and made a little gasping sound. "She took my mom."

Nobody really had much to say to that. Seria held on to the kid as he fought his way through to sobbing. Bishop busied himself on the eggs. Joe *looked* at the kid. Most of what had been done to him had healed, he didn't see any of the awful shit from before, the antithesis of light that had been wound around him. But anything that awful left scars. He'd have them for years.

What the hell do we do with him? Take him to a shrink? 'Hey, my witch of a grandmother literally ripped this kid's soul in half and jammed monster ghosts in him, help him out with that?' He's probably a relative, we can't just dump him.

Eventually he calmed down, looking around the table curiously. He was acting more like a child, but still not one his actual age. Of course they were *guessing* on that one. Somewhere between eight and ten, Joe thought.

"You want a donut?"

"Okay." Joe opened the box and after a few seconds he grabbed out a chocolate donut and started happily eating it.

"I'm gonna go put on some pants." Thea stood up. "Seri, you down for going into town today?"

"Yes. How are we getting there?"

"Thomas wants to go to his house. Get some things. I figure we'll hitch a ride. My car's parked at the house, we can use that after."

"I'm surprised the two of you can bear to be apart."

"Don't do that." Thea shook her head. "I haven't done that about David."

"You used to." Seri put Byron, or not-Byron, on her chair as she stood up. "But I'll be the bigger person and cut you some slack."

"You two going to be all right here by yourselves?"

"We'll think of something to do."

"You'll have to watch him, you know."

"Yes, I was aware of that, thank you." Joe waved a hand. Bishop brought a rather neat looking omelet over and put it in front of Byron's chair. The kid looked up at him quizzically.

"They're eggs."

"I know."

"You should eat them."

"Why?"

"You're still growing and you need the protein." He considered this.

"Okay." He reached for the eggs and Bishop made a snorting sound. "What's wrong?"

"Let me get you a fork. You'll make a mess eating that with your hands." He headed over to do just that. Byron considered this.

"Oh. Okay." He waited for the fork and then set to eating. Bishop had no idea if that was normal. He had no idea what normal really meant anymore. He looked across at Joe, who was looking at him.

"This isn't how I expected our next date to go."

"Me neither." Joe smiled. "So this is a date?"

"It has certain date-like qualities."

"It's date-adjacent?"

"Date-esque." Bishop found himself smiling. "So what was Seri talking about?"

"Oh, some vampire called last night. Apparently..."

"Wait, back up. A *vampire* called?"

*

Thea had brushed her hair in a hurry, glad that it was shorter now, and she and Seri were outside. It was a warmer day, slightly above freezing, the sun felt stronger somehow. Like the previous night had ripped a haze away from the place.

Thomas was near the barn, one of the big horses with its head on his shoulder. He was patting its neck, talking softly to it. It was chewing on something, and Thomas handed it another bite. Thea was in awe of just how big the horses were, huge white things with grey underneath. Thomas called them 'dappled' and she didn't really know what that meant. She was a suburban girl to the bone. She could get used to the horses, though.

"Hi there." He didn't turn around. "Ramses here just decided he wanted some attention. And carrots. Mostly the carrots."

"Where'd you get carrots?"

"They're in the garden over there. I guess Paul's been

keeping it."

"How much do you pay that guy?" Seri asked.

"My grandfather arranged it. Bank pays him. I have no idea how much."

"Whatever it is it's not enough."

"Can I..." Thea half extended her hand, then stopped, not sure if the horse would let her. He was so big he made Thomas look like a child.

"Sure. He's a goon. Pat him right there. Here." Thomas handed her a carrot, and the big horse's eyes trailed it with honest avarice. "Give him that. He'll love you forever."

"One carrot?"

"He's easy. John's even easier. Give him an apple, you'll be his best friend for life." Thea offered the carrot to the horse, who made a sound like a soft snickering laugh and then the carrot was gone and he was pushing his nose into her hand. He was very warm to the touch.

"I'm amazed last night didn't freak them out."

"They're descended from old war horses. Not much freaks these two out." He laughed as Ramses settled in for his proper adoration, letting Thea gently touch his neck. "My dad sold all the other horses but kept them."

"So, we're hitching a ride into town."

"All right. Let me make sure this beast has enough hay for later and we can get going." He patted Ramses again, then walked into the barn. The horse followed after a moment. Patting was nice, but there was *food* in the barn. The two women stood side by side watching, looking more like sisters than ever.

"I really can't figure you two out."

"Neither can I. Don't need to."

"The closest ex of yours is Shannon."

"Shannon and I were just friends."

"Thea, I caught you two naked."

"There may have been some benefits. But we were just friends. She was hung up on Roxy."

"Wait, Roxanne Caldarello? The sausage girl?"

"She wasn't a sausage girl, she just had the same name. My *God*, Seri."

"Hey, I like their sausage."

"You're five sometimes, I swear." Thea broke out in a smile. It was good to see the part of Seri that would tell awful jokes.

"Speaking of sausage, the two of you leave that bed intact?"

"Were we being noisy?"

"Just a bit."

"Good."

"And that takes care of Ramses. He'll have his head jammed into that feed bag all day." Both women burst out laughing, leaving Thomas standing there looking a little bemused.

"Sorry. Bad timing."

"As my cousin reminds me, I am often five."

"That's okay." He and Thea kissed, a pleasant thing with only a hint of the frenzied heat of the previous night. He'd enjoyed that. He enjoyed this, too, the feeling of comfort in touch. "So what's the plan?"

Chapter Sixteen

Salvage

Evvie Fraser wasn't awake yet when the knocking on her door forced her to bolt upright.

Her apartment was the top floor of a converted old whaler's house, with a view of the bay. The ceiling sloped sharply leaving half of the room really only useful for furniture. Trying to stand would mean taking a forehead blow to the dome. She'd come home from work, her head still muzzy, unable to stop thinking the strangest things about Stuart. A wild night of dreams of him sporting fangs and attacking her had left her jumpy and irritable and unable to settle into real sleep.

She certainly hadn't expected knocking at her door.

She pulled herself off of the couch. *Why'd I crash on the couch? I have a bed.* She was wearing most of her work outfit, jeans, a white t-shirt. She preferred to dress down even though Stuart (*fangs sliding out of his jaw, slick, oily smell, teeth in her neck*) never really leered.

Maybe a little.

She pressed her hand to her neck and was relieved to find no marks. Do they leave marks?

Your boss is not a vampire why are you even thinking this?
The knocking on the door again.

"Just a second!" She yelled. She wasn't feeling guests. Who the hell would even visit? Carrie and Esme had both moved away after graduating, she'd *seen* Tommy her one visit of the year this week, Bishop... well, he may have been a lot of things but he wasn't a stalker, when she'd cut it off he'd left it alone.

Honestly, I almost wouldn't mind seeing him at this point. Just to talk to someone.

She staggered to the door and opened it, immediately

surprised to see the two dark haired girls. The one with the shorter hair she recognized immediately, but the one next to her looked enough like her that for a second she wondered if she was seeing things. There were some differences – she was a little thinner and a little shorter, still a couple of inches taller than Evvie, and her eyes were a different shade of blue. Still, she was *very* hot. Evvie felt a momentary twinge of admiration.

"Uh... hi?"

"Hey." Thea looked in the room. "You alone?"

"Yeah, I may have just woke up."

"Can we come in? This is my cousin Seri. Seri, this is Evvie. We met yesterday at that bookstore."

"Right." Seri looked her over, like she was putting a puzzle together, and her eyes narrowed. "You don't look good. You okay?"

"I... feel kind of dizzy." Before Evvie realized it Seri was next to her, supporting her weight, helping her back to her couch. "It's so weird. It's like I got drunk last night but I didn't..."

"Just hang on a second, I'll get you a water." Seri put her hand on Thea's arm, walked her to the sink. "Okay, what's up with that sparkly shit around her? Can you see that?"

"Can *you*?" Thea could indeed see it. "You didn't see much of anything before."

"Maybe the constant crazy bullshit's worn me down." She found a glass in a dish drying rack, filled it with water from the tap. "What the hell do you think happened to her?"

"No idea yet." They walked back over together and Seri handed her the glass. She took it in shaky fingers, swallowed half of it quickly. "Thanks, I was just..."

"It's okay. Look, this is complicated but your boss called our house last night and warned us about some people."

"Stuart's a vampire?"

"I...didn't *say* that, no."

"Sorry, I just can't... it's so *weird*. These two guys came in to the store last night and they were *creepy*, one of them was way too focused and affable, he felt completely fake, and the other... well, it's just that I initially felt like, he was..." She looked down at her shirt. "You know?"

"He was groping you with his eyes?" Seria asked.

"Yeah! But then he started talking to me, and… I don't know, it's after that it gets hard to focus. Someone said something about Stuart being a vampire, or Bela Lugosi. How could Stuart be Bela Lugosi? He doesn't look anything like Bela Lugosi. Then he gave me the day off…"

"Hold on a second." Thea sat down next to her, took her hand. "You've already had a really rough day, so just try and relax. Take a few deep breaths." Evvie did so, immediately. Thea watched the sparkling lights around her. "I'm going to ask you some questions. Just answer them, please?"

"I'll answer them." Seri frowned and bent to whisper in Thea's ear.

"Is she…"

"Shh." Thea turned back to Evvie. "Would you take your clothes off if I asked you to?"

"Yes." She blinked. "Why…"

"Just answer for now." Thea was full on frowning now. "Do you remember clearly what happened yesterday? If I ask you to detail it, would you?"

"Yes and yes."

"Please do. Be completely honest. Everything after the creepy people came in the store."

They listened as Evvie related the visit. How Morgan Williams had asked about them, called them distant cousins. How Jimmy Williams (he'd told her his name) had told her to be trusting, and accepting, and listen to orders. To be obedient. He'd been just about to get her number when he'd been interrupted, so he'd left without *ending* what he'd done. Leaving Evvie groggy, disoriented, and easy prey for anyone who discovered her condition.

"That *motherfucker*." Seri growled. "Can you fix her?"

"I think so." Thea was looking very closely at the magic around her. "Jesus, he's weak *and* stupid. I could do better than this my first day."

"Which was what, a month or so ago?"

"And yet." Thea reached out, her will, her perception, and settled it around Evvie. The magic itself was very simple in some ways, almost banal. If you knew about magic at all it wouldn't work, you'd realize the spell was working on you and resist it. She remembered a passage from her old copy of the *Encyclopedia of Occultism*, closed her eyes and concentrated on the idea of magnetism and twisted her hand into a fist, and *pulled*.

The glow around Evvie tore off of her and gathered in Thea's fist, as if she'd yanked a spider web off of the girl. She hissed in air as her thoughts cleared.

"What the fuck just happened to me?" She was blinking and staring at the glass of water in her hand. "What did you just do?"

"I undid. Someone else did." Thea kept the magic tight in her fist. Evvie couldn't see it, but Seri could, a series of small points of light orbiting her cousin's hand. She wanted not to be able to, but she could, and she couldn't deny that she could. She realized that she just couldn't bring herself to disbelieve. Evvie was blinking, clearly trying to grasp what was happening. "The one that did this. You said his name was Jimmy?"

"He said it was. While he was..." She went pale. "He wanted my phone number. He'd have..."

"Yeah, you'd have given it to him. Did you tell him your address?"

"I don't remember."

"We can't leave her here." Seri spoke up. "He might be able to find her even if she didn't."

"Christ." Thea looked down at her fist. "Wait."

"Wait, wait for what, what's going on? How did he..."

"Short version. Magic is real. I can do things. So could the guy you ran into last night." Thea dropped to her knees so that she was eye to eye with Evvie. "You don't know me, but right now I'm your best shot at keeping this fucker far away from you. Okay?" She very deliberately didn't will the girl to believe her. She just met her gaze and waited. Let her work through what had happened, cursing herself the whole time, and cursing Seri a little for being right. They *couldn't* just leave her.

"What did he *do*?" It came out a whisper.

"Messed with your head. Paracelsus used to do something like it. I bet he has a magnet he carries around on him. It's not... the important thing is, Seri's right. He could find you now. But it works both ways."

Evvie's head was pounding, her heart not far behind it. She was so scared she was fighting the shakes, because she *believed* it. She'd felt what he'd done to her. Behind the fear was a terrible, blinding, white hot rage. She'd moved away from Red Hook to get away from this kind of shit, from her wretch of a stepfather and his hands in places they weren't wanted. She'd fought him off for six years before finally getting a scholarship, taking the first one that got her out of that house. And now someone just waved his fucking fingers around and tried to put her right back there.

"What do I have to do?"

Thea fought back a smile. She'd worried that Evvie would be too freaked out or scared to help. But anger was useful now. Anger she could do something with.

"We go track him down."

*

The CRX wasn't made for three people, even three relatively slim people.

"Sorry about the accommodations."

"It's fine." Evvie was using her old dance class to control her breathing. They'd driven up to 195 and into Providence, Thea in the passenger seat, Seri driving. Evvie still felt like a fuse had been lit somewhere inside her, sparks making their way down to an explosion. "What are we doing, exactly?"

"Ever heard of dowsing?"

"Vaguely."

"Well, we're doing something like that." Looking at Evvie, Thea couldn't see even a little bit of the potential. Seri had it, she could see it by looking at her, but Evvie absolutely didn't. So she wasn't sure how much detail to use. "When he put this on you, he created a link between you and him. I pulled it off you, but the resonance is still on you."

"Resonance?"

"Yeah, I don't know how to really explain it. It's like the idea of what he did is still there." Thea frowned. "You're not controlled or susceptible now, but you *were*, and it's affected you. Everything we do in life or have done to us affects us, leaves marks on us."

"Great." Evvie felt that fuse get shorter.

"I'm using that to help me narrow his location down."

"Are we sure we want to do this?" Seri said. "It's just the two of us, should we call…"

"Please." Evvie spoke up from the back seat. "I really don't want anyone else to know about this."

There was nothing else to say to that, so Seri stopped talking and drove.

"Let me know when to turn, at least."

"Head to Kennedy Plaza. We'll navigate from there." Thea could feel an itching where the magic in her fist tugged. She turned in her seat. "You okay?"

"Kind of."

"We won't tell anyone you don't want told."

"Appreciate it." Evvie finally had to ask. "So is this what you do?"

"It's the first time I've had to do this particular thing."

"But you're a… what do I even call you? A witch?"

"Eeeeeh, maybe? I don't know. I'm not really into Wicca or anything." Thea smiled, and Evvie had to admit it was a nice smile. "Sometimes I *rhyme* with witch."

"This is where you laugh politely." Seri turned the car off of the freeway and into downtown Providence, driving past the Biltmore. "You got anything for me, Magellan?"

"Head south."

"I'm used to people being shits." Evvie screwed up her face. "But this is way over my head."

"Hey. Listen." Thea found herself reaching over the seat, touching Evvie's arm. "We'll take care of it. It's okay to be freaked out right now. I was freaked out the first time I had to deal with shit like this."

"Yeah? What happened to you?"

"My mom's ghost." Seri nearly jerked the wheel in surprise. Thea realized she hadn't actually explained that one to Seri yet. "It's a big story, but just trust me, I get it."

"Yeah. Ghosts. Ghosts are a thing. Totally not about to lose control and start shrieking now. Thanks."

"Thea's not one for easing people into things."

"I'm pretty sure we should be on Westminster heading towards Hartford." Thea said, concentrating. "That's where this thing is trying to go."

"How do you know that?"

"I can visualize a map of the city."

"She's always been good like that." Seri was dutifully taking the car onto Westminster. "Thea only has to go someplace once to know how to get there again."

"Jesus, I could have used *that* when I moved here." Evvie shifted, uncomfortable wedged in the back as she was. They'd folded down the divider between the hatchback to give her a ledge, but it still wasn't designed for a passenger. "It took me two years to be able to find the train station."

"Providence can be a pain in the ass to navigate." Thea nodded. The pulsing in her hand got more rhythmic, suggesting they were closing in. They passed under Route 10, the sensation getting stronger, more insistent. "We used to come up all the time once Seri got her driver's license."

"Uncle Greg would let me borrow his truck."

"Remember that place out in East Providence?"

"Riverside. The carousel in Riverside."

"Riverside, East Providence, same difference."

"Amazingly not so." Seri snorted. "Yes, I remember. We'd hang out with that girl you knew, the one who was into tattoos and piercings. At fifteen."

"Marci was ahead of her time." Thea smiled remembering her. "She got into Brown."

"That girl? Really?" Seri frowned. "Now I feel like an underachiever."

"Nothing wrong with URI."

"I have to call my advisor, I have three exams I need to get done."

"This is the thing where you two talk a lot to distract me?"

"See, you're getting to know us." Thea looked back over her seat. "I take it you're not distracted?"

"I'm not screaming or shaking, maybe I'm a little distracted." Evvie rubbed her hand over her face.

"Okay." Thea felt the change in the raw magic in her hand. "We're here. Look around."

Seri pulled over and the three of them got out of the car. There were various neighborhood stores – a blue and orange Cumberland Farms that had seen better days was kitty-corner to a mom and pop store just named *Jole's* with a sign indicating fresh chourico.

Thea walked past them, Seri flanking her and Evvie hesitantly making up the rear. They came to a stop near a chain link fence. A sign that was nearly as run down as the Cumberland Farms said *Morgan Williams Salvage*, and Thea studied it.

"That's the name you said?"

"Yeah. The blond one. Or white hair, honestly not sure which. He said his name was Morgan." She wanted to spit.

"So what now?" Seri was looking around. "We could just hop the fence..."

"No. There's a door there. It's not chained." She pointed to the entrance, to the smaller chain-link door set into the fence. "We'll just walk in."

*

Thomas Willrew was going through everything he'd been afraid to go through before.

He'd torn his parents' room apart, searching under the bed, looking through boxes of their old papers. The majority of it was useless. Pictures of Thomas and Elspeth Willrew at a gun range, or out bow hunting. How his mother and father had met was still a mystery to him. He'd loved his mother, but she'd never particularly wanted to talk much about herself or her life.

She'd been less than fond of her father in law, he knew that much. Considering what he'd seen of the man's life and the way he'd treated his wife and son, he could understand that.

He eventually ended up in the basement. It was getting dark out, sunset coming right around 4 pm. He wondered what Thea and Seri were up to. For the first time in his life he wished he had a cell phone. He dug through boxes looking for something, anything that could tell him if his grandfather had left some clue behind. Ignored the two golden urns on the pool table, the ritual he'd left set up around them. He stopped to rub at his forehead.

That's when he saw the flashlight through the small storm window. For a moment he was awash in light, his eyes going almost blind from the change. All he could see were those urns, gleaming and reflecting, and then the light faded as whoever it was kept walking around the outside of his house.

It's not the Whatleys. They wouldn't use flashlights.

He touched his hand to the sigils on the pool table and let himself flow out into the web of sigils and wards he'd laid around the house. Immediately he knew that they were human, but tainted, twisted. His wards would repel but not destroy them. They could enter, if they were willing to take pain.

He stood up. There was an old cricket bat down there, one of the things his grandfather had brought back from Europe. He wrapped his hand around the handle and walked to the bulkhead, with the ancient dresser jammed in the doorway.

He reached out and shoved it aside. It scraped against the concrete, but all three hundred pounds of it shifted. Thomas rarely showed off, and usually when he did, it was something otherworldly, something to reinforce belief. He wasn't doing that now.

He flung the bulkhead open and walked out as the metal door slammed into the concrete with a rattling bang, catching the three men with flashlights off guard. He regarded them, at the strange swirling motes in the air around them, like dust in a sunbeam. There was no sunbeam and barely enough moonlight, he could mostly see them by the motes and their flashlights.

"Can I help you?" He asked, the cricket bat up on his shoulder. "You're in my yard."

They had their flashlights pointed at him. It was impossible to see their faces, but their body language was readable. They were sizing him up. He remembered his mother taking him out shooting once.

If anyone is ever in a position to threaten you, never let them go first.

"Yeah, sorry about that," the closest one said. "We didn't…"

Thomas had closed the gap between them while they'd looked around, and now he moved, smashing the first one in the chest with the bat hard enough to break his collarbone. Unlike Thea, he didn't have formal training. What he had was mass, and his mother's lessons. He was already smashing the second one's flashlight out of his hands while the third one was reaching behind himself for something. He lashed out, driving the end of the bat into his crotch and following it with an elbow to the face that sent teeth flying.

They were all in crepuscular darkness now, the red fire of a fading sun just along the edge of the sky. Thomas could see them more clearly now without the flashlights, see them purely by whatever they'd done to themselves. He could tell that broken bones and crushed gonads weren't going to stop them, could see those strange dark motes in the air flowing around them where he'd hit them. The one with the shattered jaw and lost teeth was convulsing as his body changed, new teeth sliding into position.

The first one leapt at him, clearing the distance faster than he should have been able to. Thomas took a blow to the chest that nearly cost him his footing, managed to avoid a headbutt. His assailant reeked, his breath coming out like the worst case of halitosis ever mixed the decay of offal. He used the bat to take a kick and then brought it down while using his shoulder as a fulcrum, smashing the knee hard and driving him into the ground.

The other two were coming in on him. He whirled the bat around and caught the closer of the two in the face, smashing him down but leaving himself open for the one who'd lost half his teeth. His *new* teeth were jagged, awful things and Thomas barely managed to avoid a bite from them, unable to avoid getting bowled over by a charge. The stench was even worse from this one.

The first one was getting up, and Thomas wrenched himself upright, bearing his attacker up into the air and throwing him into the ground head first. He was breathing heavy but not particularly hurt aside from a trickle of blood from the side of his face where he'd hit the ground – the one he'd just bodyslammed was staying down for the moment. He circled to the left.

"That's enough."

He looked up, blinking. This one was impossible to miss. If Stuart was awful to look at, she was at once worse and yet much more *interesting*, seething rot wrapped up in scintillant red. She stopped a few feet away from the three he'd been fighting, all of which were deliberately standing between him and her.

"Mister Willrew."

"That's my name."

"You're not very friendly."

"You don't respect people's property very well."

"I don't suppose we could talk about this inside?"

"There's absolutely no way I will ever invite you into my house." His eyes had adjusted enough to the fading light that he could see her face. She reminded him of the *Little House on the Prairie* books his mom had collected. She laughed at his bland hostility.

"I suppose I wouldn't either." She snapped her fingers and her three… thugs? Thomas didn't know what they were. He watched them retreat behind her, walking down his lawn towards the street. "Believe it or not, we didn't know for sure if you were home."

"I believe it." He'd deliberately parked his car down the road in front of old man Harris' house, just in case. "If you'd known I wasn't, you'd have broken in. If you had known I was…"

"Well." She was looking very carefully at him. She understood now why Stuart had been so ill at ease. Something about him was easy to miss but impossible to ignore. "What do we do now?"

"Now? You get away from my house."

"There's a slight problem. The person I report to owes someone a debt, and she wants you. If I leave now I'll have to report where I found you."

"Go ahead. I'm not going to be here, and by now she knows where to find me anyway." He leaned on the cricket bat, using it to draw a moon and a ram's head in the dirt.

"Perhaps we could help each other."

"I don't see how that's possible. You're not going to do anything directly against her." He finished the ram's head and started drawing a series of small towers, like rooks on a chessboard. Once he had four drawn, he circled the third. It was all crude but good enough.

"There's things I would like to know. In return, I could tell you what *I* know."

"You first, then."

"All right. Your enemy has press-ganged several of her own grandsons into service. I met two recently."

"I knew she had two goons." He felt the sigils on the ground, drew up the power inherent in the idea. Held it leashed around himself. "What else?"

"I'd like to see some of *yours* now, before I show you any of mine."

"Are you sure?" He shifted and for a moment flaming wings curled around him. Surprised, she took a step back. "Let's make this simple. I know she wants to kill me. She tried. Twice now. That's something you can take back with you, right? Your turn."

"I know she's been around for a while. Since the fifties."

"You're older, of course."

"Of course." She looked back over her shoulder at her goons

getting into a van. "Whatever she's doing, she's worked with us for years. There are things we can do better than the breathers…"

"Breathers?"

"We have slang for you. Well, not you. I have no idea what *you* are, you're like her." He fought to not bristle. "But there's the whole bag of rules. And they're inconsistent. Sunlight, for instance. When I was younger that wasn't nearly so bad. We didn't *like* it, but…"

"It's what people generally believe."

"Yes, but that's because of the movies, when I was…"

"No, you're not following me. The reason the sunlight is so bad for you now is because people *believe* that it is." He let the wings flare forth, light the back yard for a moment. The Whatleys could probably see, but he didn't much care if they did. "Get back to her. I'm aware you're trying to draw me out."

"She did jobs for us. Things we couldn't do as easily. In return we did things for her. This meeting is because she wanted us to find you, but she asked in a way that annoyed us. So we wanted to know why she wanted it."

"You know enough." It was getting harder and harder to keep from letting himself burn, a blinding light, a flaming sword.

"You're not going to ask…"

"I know where she is." He walked over to the bulkhead and closed it, and then concentrated on it, watched as it began to glow cherry red as he bled off the stored power of the angel of the third tower in heat that fused the metal together. It would never open again. That was fine by him. He turned to her, seeing her watch him avidly, trying to understand.

"So what now?"

"Now you can please get off of my property, which you are forever *not* invited onto or into." He made several new symbols in the hot metal with his finger, letting the angel's fire crawl out over his skin. Anyone who tried to touch that would feel an utter sense of revulsion. "Also, you should probably stop letting those guys drink your blood or whatever it is you do to them, it's messing them up pretty bad."

"Always more where they come from."

"Well, *that's* gross." He straightened up. If she stayed he was going to incinerate her and the hell with whatever her people would do in response, if he had to he'd hunt them all down, he was *tired* of her. But she was already backing off, moving away to a parked car. He watched and waited to be sure they were gone before he discharged the power of the angel, releasing it in a crack of fire and lightning that sounded like thunder across a cloudless sky.

He walked around to his back door, holding the cricket bat and watching the deepening shadows carefully as the sky went fully dark. Inside the house he grabbed up the phone and dialed.

It rang three times.

"Jesus, whaaaaaat?" Bishop's voice, panting.

"That's how you answer my phone? You had no idea who was even calling."

"I knew it had to be you because we just got the kid to go take a nap and I was *finally* about to get laid."

"Sorry to interrupt."

"Yeah, yeah, what is it?"

"Thea and Seria back yet?"

"No, because if they were back *they* could have fucking answered this."

"Shit."

"Why shit?"

"I just got jumped by three goons outside the house in Cranston. They were working for a vampire."

"Okay, seriously now, there are *vampires*? I thought they were kidding about that."

"Nope. Vampires. As real as Shoggoths."

"What the hell is a Shoggoth?"

"You saw me blow one up..."

"I didn't know what it was *named*, how do *you* know what it's named?"

"I read a lot."

"I'm positive that's not a comforting answer."

"Look, I'm going to try and find them. Remind me to buy a

cell phone."

"You want a cell phone?"

"I'd like to be able to reach her…"

"Any doubts I had about you and this girl just died." Bishop snorted. "Look, I left Joe all sorts of warmed up, and he's a thinker, I don't want him to get distracted so…"

"Yes, go, have your wicked way with him."

"Thanks. Bye. If the girls call I'll tell them you were looking for them."

He checked the clock. 5 pm. He was cutting it close on the last ferry over to Wolfshead. Wondered if maybe they were already there. But after the walking dead and her marching band had made a move on him, he was in the mood to check up on things. So he started digging out his sketchpad.

*

Jimmy Williams was, by nature, a lazy man.

He'd learned a long time before his parents had died that Morgan would always do the lion's share of the work in any join endeavour. Morgan couldn't abide slipshod work, it was against his nature. He wasn't particularly neat or organized but once he started a job, he finished it.

Jimmy walked the fence, his spine ice, watching the birds watch him.

Morgan took care of the books for the salvage yard. He had ever since he'd taken over for their father, Morgan Senior, who'd made the terrible mistake of falling in love with Maria Mancini. Maria had three siblings (a twin sister, Claudia, and two brothers, Marco and Stephan – Jimmy had never met any of them save for his aunt Claudia, who'd died before his mother and father did) and a host of half-siblings. There were a lot of different last names involved. He didn't much care, really. But Morgan Sr. had married her, they'd had children together, had seemed happy as far as Jimmy knew.

Then they died. Plane crash. Maria had a strange thing about flying, she and Morgan were taking lessons. She liked flying over the bay, the small islands between Warwick and Bristol. One day they went up into a clear sky and came down upside down into the bay and that was that. Morgan had been seventeen, Jimmy fifteen.

He felt the seagulls watching him and shivered. *Horrible little shit machines.* He wanted very much to poison them, just poison them all right there. Or get a .22 and pick them off, one at a time. But he didn't dare.

He walked into the office. Morgan was out tinkering with the truck, replacing the radiator hoses, when he wasn't tinkering. Morgan was mechanical by nature. Jimmy wasn't. If it weren't for Morgan's insistence that he help out with the business... but then again, what else did he have to do with his life?

He regretted yet again that Morgan had pulled him out of the bookstore so soon. The cashier had been on the hook, all he'd needed to do was reel her in, and Morgan gets all huffy about what some freaking jumped up dead mosquito man would think. It wouldn't have mattered, if Jimmy had gotten her phone number. He could have called, had her give him the address, head over and spent a few days distracting himself in a place the birds wouldn't have known to look.

The phone rang. He reached over and answered it.

"Williams Salvage."

"There you are." He didn't drop the phone. He didn't scream or shit himself. He felt very calm at the voice at the other end of the phone, surprisingly calm. If he was being honest, terrifyingly calm. "Imagine my surprise."

"Sorry." He licked his lips, everything dry. "He's in the garage."

"I didn't call to talk to him." Jimmy hated the very idea of her calling to talk to him. "Morgan has his virtues – he's ruthless and more intelligent than you are – but he lacks your finely honed gift for self-serving rationalization."

He fought to keep from nodding.

"You're going to do something for me."

"I'm not..."

"Oh, you will." Her voice cracked. "You'll do it because I won't just kill you if you don't. I'll do things. I'll play with you. Like I did your little brother. You remember? The way he screamed?" Now her voice was silk, smooth, just a hint of an accent. "I actually found him charming. I don't find you charming."

He couldn't keep from remembering it. He'd decided a long time ago he'd do anything to avoid being the one making those sounds.

"Here's what you have to do." She told him. He actually *nodded* because he couldn't speak. She didn't seem to care that he didn't respond. "I'll be in touch." The phone went dead in his hand.

He stood there, realizing what he was going to do. Knowing that Morgan would never do it to *him*. Morgan would take the bullet first. He'd never really understood why. They couldn't stand each other, but…

The bell over the door rang. He looked up to see three women walking into the room, and recognized all three. His already dry throat made a squealing sound.

He moved as fast as he could to grab the bat from under the desk and the slightly shorter one with the longer hair (the hotter one in his opinion, although it was hard to think that way now that he knew who she was) reached over and smashed him face first into the desk. He staggered away and she swung a fist into his abdomen, knocking the air out of him, then grabbing the arm he held out to ward her off and wrenched it into a choke hold. He was taller than her but not by much and she had the leverage, she forced his face into the wall with almost no effort.

"Christ!" There was blood dribbling down his face and he was pretty sure she'd broken his nose.

"Keep struggling and I'll smash you into something else."

"I told you, cop over lawyer."

"Not *now,* Thea."

Jimmy was blinking, his whole face hurting. He'd look like a raccoon in a few minutes, he could feel it, two black eyes. The other one, the one with the boobs, walked over so that he could see her. It wasn't easy with the other one pinning his cheek to the wall.

"So you're an idiot." He wanted to call her names, quite a few of them, but he couldn't see that working out well for him. "I brought you something."

He opened his mouth to tell her to fuck off. She opened her hand and he saw it, tangled up in her hand, the thing he'd spent time learning how to weave together. The thing he'd last seen on the one in the back with the hair red around the edges.

Her smile was that of a cat about to jump on a squirrel and break its neck.

"Now let's talk."

*

Morgan was bent over the truck, working on the engine. Half of the hoses in the damn thing were shot and he couldn't keep relying on fucking electrical tape to keep them going, so he'd replaced just about all of them. It took his mind off of what was going to happen.

He'd been preparing for her as well as he was able ever since the Thanksgiving fuckup, but he had no illusions. She'd blow through his defences and kill him. He was a stumbling, barely trained, barely skilled amateur and she'd been at it for decades. She'd killed his parents and no one even *noticed*. Hell, he hadn't either until that night in the dark when she'd told him.

His chest itched, remembering that night. Remembering her fingers slowly parting the skin over his heart. Unable to scream, he'd thrashed, but it had been her who'd decided his fate that night. Not him. He hadn't been in charge of his own life in years.

He heard the buzzer that told him the gate was opening. That wasn't uncommon. People came in to dicker over selling a junker, or buying an old alternator for a model they don't make parts for anymore, they had fairly steady foot traffic. Jimmy was the personable one of the two of them, usually Morgan let him handle it. He looked up, seeing some legs just on the edge of the lights from the office, and realized it was already past sunset.

Fucking December.

He went back to working. Minutes passed and he'd almost forgotten that someone had come in. He closed the hood of the truck, wiping sweat off with the back of his hand. Sweating when it was cold out was the worst, your clothes turned into clammy messes and the oil and grease and other residue on his hands was now on his face. If there was anything he hated about the salvage yard, it was everything, but that was the most awful part.

He was walking out of the garage when it rolled across his spine.

He'd put wards up. He'd gone and bought several books he could barely understand, one by a guy named Buckland, another called *Devil Worship in France* and none of it made any goddamn sense to him, but he'd done his best. The one ward he'd felt pretty confident on was the one that had just gone off. Someone had just done something somewhere close.

He turned and ran back into the garage, pulled the tarp off of the thing he'd been welding together when he wasn't working. It was a patchwork mess of car parts, the body of an old Packard (since the damn thing was built like a tank) and a set of welded together legs, two per wheel well. He'd carved shapes and sigils into it, crap he barely understood, swirls and teeth and jagged lines. The engine compartment was where he'd taken to killing rats, the only reliable form of sacrifice he had.

Their blood had pooled and dried inside it. It reeked. He didn't care. He picked up a ball-peen hammer from the bench and rapped it hard on a set of interlocking triangles up front.

"Abra fucking cadabra."

It lurched. Watching metal twitch and heave itself up on a bad approximation of insect legs would normally have made him very uncomfortable. At the moment all he could think about was if she was there. He'd spent the past week elbow deep in grease, oil and rat blood making this fucking thing and now he was going to see what he'd done.

"Find anyone who's not me or my brother and fucking kill him or her or *it*." He felt like he was going to vomit watching it skitter off, wished he'd thought to give it claws or something. *It can*

crush her with those fucking legs or drop itself on her just kill her.
He knew he was kidding himself.

*

The pen moved without him thinking. He was never a particularly good artist, but he liked to draw, liked to unfocus and let the pen or pencil move. The sketchpad was full of juvenilia – sketches of comic book characters, robots, big swords and the other refuges he'd always sought from life as a runty bookworm in a small place. Cranston didn't really count as a small town, but somehow, all of the state felt like it.

Ten times bigger than Andorra, though. That made him snort remembering Delphy's outrage. She'd gone off on a ten minute tirade about how provincial he was and he'd pointed out that Rhode Island was bigger *and* more densely populated than the entirety of her country.

He'd sketched a series of swirling shapes, like a trefoil, but sharper. He'd gotten the original image from a book on the runic alphabet, one he'd found in his father's possessions. He was starting to wonder how much of his dad's weird obsessions went back to that night in his vision, how much his grandfather had told him. He'd probably never know.

I took them up screaming.

"I always liked that one."

The bat was up and in his hand instantly. He turned, but didn't swing.

There was a man with a close cropped beard in his house. He looked mid-fifties. Thomas felt an intense state of déjà vu looking at him.

"Nine nights, myself to myself. You only did seven, right? You got off light."

"Who are you?" Thomas had the cricket bat in a firm grip, ready to swing it.

"Many names have I/ lost and remembered/ for I am the king of foolish causes/ I am the nameless one." He smiled, and it felt to Thomas like sitting in a classroom all over again, listening to his teachers pontificate. "You can call me whatever you like."

Thomas considered this. Looked down at the sketch, the wheel with the three interlocking horns, the wheel of runes.

"I called you here."

"Got it in one! Nice job. I thought you were going to attack me."

"I'm not a thug."

"No, you aren't. That's always surprising. I've known many thugs in my time."

"I was trying to find Thea."

"She's fine. Headstrong, but fine."

"Why headstrong?"

"I assume her upbringing…"

"Why did you *say* headstrong?"

"Oh, she went to pick a fight with those Williams boys. The ones the vampire told you about. Now *those* two are thugs. Not that being a thug is always bad." He walked over to the fridge, opened it, peered inside. "No alcohol. Huh."

"I stopped drinking."

"Don't need it anymore. I got you." He took out a bottle of Coke. "Of course, you keep the liquid stimulant around."

"Thea likes it."

"I bet she does." Thomas involuntarily growled at that. "Easy, boy. I'm not disparaging her. You're both very gifted. I'm lucky to find two with such potential in one generation."

"What the hell *are* you?"

"That depends. I might just be an aspect of yourself, your inner *gnosis*. I might be a figure out of ancient myth, the dweller on the threshold, the guardian between forevers. I might be a delusion." He sipped at the cola. "Defining myself ruins everything, though. You'll figure that out."

"Running out of patience."

"Thomas, you need to calm down. Thea's fine. She's gotten herself into trouble, yes. But she'll get herself out long before you can get to her."

"Where *is* she?"

"Oh, a junkyard in Providence. That's not important right now." He tipped back the last of his soda. "What *is* important is that you let the vampire go."

"Yes. And?"

"Well, she told you why she was here." He put the bottle down on the counter. "Now, you've got this place impressively warded up, but it's not perfect, and you *do* need to leave. When you do..."

There's a sound that large animals make when they move. Thomas had grown up around draft horses and cattle, he knew that sound, the way their feet make echoes when they step. He could hear it now, just outside his back door, prowling in the darkness of his back yard.

"They told her where I am."

"And that you're here alone, yep." He laughed. "So, off with you then."

"What?"

"Get out there and kill it, that's a good lad."

"Get out... what the hell *is* it?"

"Oh, it's a horrible thing. Huge and ravenous. A monster out of nightmare itself. I'm sure it'll be quite the fight. If you survive I'll be impressed. Well, more impressed. The trick the other day was pretty impressive, the whole bull slaying/life like fire from heaven bit. Very nice."

"Why shouldn't I just wait in here? It can't get in..." He thought about that.

"Yes, there's a good lad, *thinking* again. Don't do it too much, though. Everyone would have been better off if Hamlet had killed his uncle in Act 1." He walked to the back door, opened it, and stepped outside. It closed behind him, clicked shut. And Thomas was alone.

He looked over at the symbol he'd drawn, the runes he'd chosen.

Amid the chaos the sky will open and Muspell shall ride upon it.

He couldn't leave it out there. Thea would finish up with whatever she was doing, she'd come here to find him, and she'd walk right into it. *He* was forewarned.

The house shook slightly as it grew restless in the dark.

He closed his eyes and opened the door.

It was a truly massive thing. His yard was big – it wrapped not just behind the house but took up a large chunk of land to the side, with a tall fence. Almost another house lot. There were high bushes between his yard and the Whatley's yard, but those were gone now, trampled.

In the dark he could see it lined with red light, as if it glowed. Its fur was tawny, a reddish gold, with a long mane of red hair. Its head was easily eight feet off of the ground. In its jaws a dog hung limply, dead in one bite. To call the creature a lion seemed insufficient. He wondered if the Whatley's had gone down its gullet as well, or just their viciously abused snarling victim of a dog. His father's voice in his ears.

Never known a mean dog who didn't have shitty people involved somewhere.

It chewed the dog up in front of him. Three bites to crush its bones and swallow the rest, and Thomas made himself watch it. Felt the lines of a poem in his head.

With the scourge of branches,/ The sun of the battle-gods shone from his sword;/ The crags are sundered.

It wheeled and leapt, so impossibly huge, as big as two horses. The cricket bat in his hands trembled violently and then it wasn't anymore. What he held was pure brilliance, a light so bright and intense it was as if he held daylight in his fingers, a piece of noon in the shape of a blade. He rolled, ducking under the creature and swelling as it crashed into the garage, crushing it flat and spinning to loom over him.

But it couldn't.

His skin, his hair were like molten metal. He knew that his neighbors *must* be able to see this, and yet he didn't worry at all. None of them would want to. He was twelve feet tall if he was a foot, and the glowing, gleaming sword of pure blood red light made his hand ache.

He held up his other hand and gestured with two fingers. It was horribly cheesy, he'd seen it in a kung fu movie.

The Lion leapt.

*

Seri was, by and large, a phlegmatic person. Sure, she'd freaked out when two armed men invaded her house and hurt her boyfriend, and then there was a Crown Royal bag with a monster in it and Joe had died and, really, she didn't think you could blame her for getting a bit freaked out.

She certainly wasn't going to let herself freak out again.

So when the thing that looked like a spider made out of old junk welded together smashed in the *wall*, she didn't panic. She simply tightened her grip on Jimmy Williams' neck and spun him between herself and it, keeping his arm pinned behind his back.

"Call it off!"

"How? Fuck! You can break my arm if you want, I don't know what the fuck that even is!"

Now *Evvie* was freaking out, and Seri felt bad for her. Things were getting entirely too real in their unrealness, and the three of them had come in here without a plan besides Thea's *'trust me'*.

The segmented metal legs skittered, if you could call it that when the thing skittering probably weighed at least two tons. It was hard not to think of the headlights as eyes.

"Here's what's going to happen." The other Williams brother yelled from outside. "You're going to send my brother out to me, right fucking now."

"Or?" Thea yelled back. Then she turned to Seri. The cousins exchanged an entire conversation in a look.

"Or? Did you miss the part where I have a fucking metal monster in there with you? I fucking tell it to kill you, that's what *or.*"

"Considering I have your weasel of a brother in a choke hold, it's going to be pretty hard for your... what the fuck is this thing?"

"It's an old Packard."

"Pretty sure those came with tires."

"I was inspired."

"Why not make like six smaller things instead of this thing?" Thea gave a grim little chuckle as she studied the metal, unraveling the meaning behind the symbols and sigils he'd scratched into it. It was *very* crude, and powered by death. Many small deaths. She wrinkled her nose in disgust. She had the other brother's inept little magic curled up in her fist, began using it up, kindling to spare herself supplying her own fire.

"Because this is what I *made*!" He sounded completely exasperated. Not that Seri could see him, but she knew the type. "I got the idea and I made it happen, I'm sorry that the first fucking time I tried it you're not satisfied with how I'm going to kill you."

"It's just a bit much."

"You know what? I don't even like Jimmy all that much. Maybe I'll just kill the three of you and take my chances that he gets it too."

"You could have done that already." Seri yelled. She tightened her grip. "Tell your brother I think he's bluffing."

"Hard to… talk… when… you're choking me."

"Jimmy here says you're bluffing."

"Hey, scrapheap! Kill one of the ones *not* holding Jimmy!"

From outside, clutching the hammer in his hand, Morgan watched the old Packard jam its way into the office through the smashed in door. He waited to hear screams.

Inside, Thea had almost pulled it apart when he told it to kill someone. She didn't have time to be subtle, so instead she reached out for the spiritual energy *powering* the thing. Dozens of dead rats.

People are so weird about rats. She groaned as the binding magic, sloppy and unsubtle but strong for that, tried to hold their spirits in place. She got a quick flash of dozens of little eyes looking at her, grounded in the memory of their last moment. Thea had never had a pet herself, but Karl had a rat, a little white thing he'd adopted because it reminded him of himself. It had been much less of a dick than he was, she'd always liked the little girl. She thought hard about cooing at it, letting it walk on her arm, the day they'd had to bury the little thing. That was the last time she'd ever seen Karl express an emotion that wasn't rage.

You can go home. Thea strained as the thing crab walked at her, wrenching itself through the ruined doorway. *I can show you.*

Dozens of little eyes followed her as her head began to pound, the metal skin began to shake.

Morgan was getting ready to hear screams. He was tired of people shitting on him. Jimmy. The old crone. Now *these* bitches. Someone was going to pay for it. Someone was going to die for it.

Then a white hot pain rocketed up his arm, making him drop the hammer he'd used to wake the thing. He clutched at his wrist, openly weeping from pain and shock. It hurt worse than when he'd dropped a 77 Delta 88 on his foot while trying to change the tires.

"Now. My turn." He managed to lift his head from his hand to see two of the women come out. They both looked enough like *her*, now that he could see it, that it was a struggle to keep from pissing himself. The slightly taller one in the tank top had the steering wheel from the Packard in her hand. "Rats? Really? You know they're really smart. They make great pets."

He could just make out dozens of tiny eyes in the dark behind them.

"Take what you can get." He gritted his teeth. He didn't think he could get his hand to work well enough to pick up the hammer before she could get to him, and he remembered how poorly he'd done fighting her last time. "Get it over with."

"Oh for fuck's sake." She walked up and hit him in the face with the steering wheel, knocking him prone on his back. "Look, you stupid stupid asshole, if I wanted you dead I would have just brought this whole goddamn place down around you and buried you in your trash collection."

"I wouldn't have minded that," Evvie said. She was fighting very hard not to shake herself into tiny pieces. "There really was a metal spider thing? I did see that?"

"You did." Seri tossed Jimmy so that he landed in front of his brother. "We want two things. You need to keep this little shithead of yours on a better leash. And we want to know what you know about her."

"You mean our grandmother." Morgan had gotten to his feet. He was rubbing his face, welted from where Thea had smacked him.

"Yes. *Our* grandmother." Thea looked back at the ruined office. "No more weird things crawling out of the woodwork?"

"That was the first time I ever tried anything like that."

"Should have tried harder."

"You know what? I got enough shit about not being good at this crap from her. What, you bucking to take her place as monster bitch of Rhode Island?" He let himself sneer at her.

"Poor baby. If you want, I could..."

"Thea." Seri cut in. "Let me."

"You want to talk to this asshole, go for it."

"You two are *dog vomit*," Seri turned to face the Williams brother.

"This is your version of good cop?" Morgan replied.

"The question is, do you want to stay dog vomit? Do you want to run around carrying out errands for... for someone who kills our parents." This was the first time Seri had really admitted it to herself, that her mother and father were dead because of all this. That it wasn't that people died young in their family. They didn't. Not naturally, and not because of misfortune or happenstance. It was because of her. She did it. "I don't care about you. I don't even know you. The first time I met you my door came off the hinges and you attacked us. So fuck you. Whatever. Keep being shit if you want. But goddamn it, don't you want... she *killed our parents!*"

"Oh, fuck this horseshit."

"Jimmy..." Morgan started, but Jimmy wasn't in the mood.

"No! These two come stalking in the door, beat the shit out of me, and now it's violins about our dead parents? You know what? She's going to kill *us*. She said..." He shut his mouth but everyone around him had picked up on it.

"She said what?" Morgan stepped a little closer. "Since when does she talk to *you*?"

"She doesn't. I meant when she told us to go grab them."

"You weren't even *there*. I told *you* about that." He got very calm, which was somehow worse. "When did she talk to you?"

"She'll *kill us*, Morg. Or worse. You want to end up like Byron? We don't have fucking vaginas, Morg!"

"Wait." Thea spoke up. "Not that I'm not curious about when your date rapist of a brother talked to her, but what does having a vagina have to do with anything?"

"She calls you 'girl children'." Morgan was still staring at Jimmy. "She wanted you two alive. She was eager to get you before you started doing any of the really weird shit."

"That ship has sailed." Seria deadpanned.

"Yeah, well, this was back at Thanksgiving, okay?"

"Byron's your brother?"

"Yeah."

"He's okay." Thea put it out there. "He's talking."

It was in that moment that the Williams boys finally showed themselves. Jimmy didn't even react, busy glaring at Morgan for all he was worth. Morgan, however, turned his head to take the two of them in, gauge their sincerity.

"What's he saying?"

"Nothing too profound. How old is he?"

"He's... ten? Yeah, ten this year."

"How old was he when..."

"He was fucking six." Jimmy said. "And that was after four years of threatening. She was so pissed he was a boy."

"And we're back to that." Thea gestured and the swarm of rat ghosts pooled around her feet, terrifyingly silent. "Thomas is a man and he does this stuff fine."

"She didn't tell us. She just was really focused on your two. Wanted you alive and intact. Especially didn't want your faces marred."

"*Christ*, Morg."

Morgan lashed out and slapped Jimmy in the face, fairly hard, harder than either Seria or Thea had expected. Behind them Evvie smiled a bit, still just barely holding on to sanity.

"*Wake up.*" Morgan was back in Jimmy's face. "Whatever she

told you during your little chat was bullshit. Get that through that stupid skull of yours." Jimmy was cradling his face, shocked. Morgan had rarely gotten angry enough to hit him. "You've been sloppy and stupid for *years* and I've covered for it. You're an anchor around my fucking neck at this point, these three wouldn't even be here if you could keep it in your pants, and if you think you can make a deal with her behind my back and get away with it I'll kill you myself. Are we clear on that, little brother?"

Jimmy just nodded, his eyes wide. His usual defiance had gone up in the shock of that slap, the sight of his brother with froth in the corner of his mouth.

Morgan turned back to Thea and Seria.

"We don't know what's special about women. We just know she hated us for being men. Especially Byron. His being a boy drove her fucking *insane*. I guess he's the youngest grandchild she has, and she was sure he was going to be a girl." He shrugged. "Is he..."

"You're awfully concerned for someone who used him as a battering ram."

"Yeah, what did you call me? Dog vomit? I'm not pretending." He shrugged. "Ever since she showed up I've been trying to keep the three of us alive. And here we are." He gestured at the ruined office. "My kingdom of broken shit. You want to take her on? Be my guest. You know her address?"

"I've been there... twice?"

"Yeah." Seri nodded. "About that."

"What are you going to do with him?"

"We hadn't really decided." Seri took a step closer. "We're taking care of him for now."

"He's a good kid. He's not like us."

"Were you, before her? What *were* you two like?" Seri held up a hand. "I'm not your shrink. Like I said, don't really care, I have enough problems. But you don't have to be this. Even *he* doesn't have to be this."

"He was always an asshole." Morgan grunted. "So was I, probably. But Byron was just a kid. He deserved better." He turned. "Do whatever you're going to do. I think it's time I get the fuck out of here."

"She told me…" Jimmy swallowed. "She'd do us both like Byron for this."

"Yeah, well, tough shit for you, huh?" Morgan shoved his brother out of the way. "Because the truck's in my name, and I'm taking it and getting as far away from this fucking place as I can get. She can come find me if she wants me."

The women watched him leave, watched Jimmy standing there looking like he was in shock. It was hard to feel much pity for him. After a while he looked up, saw them, twisted up his face in what might have been rage but looked mostly like petulance.

He especially glared at Evvie, who was on the verge of walking over and punching him in the face.

"Shoulda got your number, huh?"

"Don't." Thea said to Evvie, put her hand on the girl's shoulder. "Let's just get out of here."

"Oh, you're too good to kick me now that I'm down, bitch?"

"Pretty much, yeah."

"Yeah, well, she's fucking killing that boyfriend of yours *right now*." He spat that out, his eyes wide, his black eyes and broken lip adding to the expression of dementia. "She fucking told me *that*, too. Told me you'd come sniffing around, that I should keep you here long enough. He's probably already fucking *dead*. So how you feel about me now, cunt? Huh?"

Thea's face went hot, and her fingers twitched. The swarm of rat ghosts around her moved, preparing to enact her will as soon as she went from shock to fury. The air seemed to build up static.

Seri kicked him in the balls before Thea could lash out. It was such a sudden move that both Evvie and Thea were taken aback. Seri grabbed him by the back of the head as he collapsed, twisted so he could hear her as she whispered.

"I just saved your life, idiot. She'd have killed you for that. She still may. You'd better hope he's alive." She dropped him in the dirt, stood up brushing off her hands. "Let's go. We left him at the house."

"I'll drive…"

"Thea, you're going to be busy doing that shit you do. I'll drive. Let's go."

*

They'd ended up in the pool.

It was just a frozen hole in the ground now, of course. He hadn't drained it or put in a new liner, and neither of his parents had for the year before, so consecutive winters had combined with the neglect to create a giant pit in his backyard. The Lion had leapt and caught him in the chest and together they'd tumbled into it.

They slammed into the bottom of the frozen dirt and ice as the Lion snapped those jaws shut inches from his face. He managed to get the shining sword up. The Lion assumed itself invulnerable to the blade, and the angle was terrible, but he managed to drag the edge across its belly and it roared, leaping away from him in surprise.

He held up the sword, the slayer of Beli's Bane. His shoulders and neck bore deep slashes from its claws, but pure flame leaked out instead of blood. They circled each other in the ruined pool, a poor substitute for an arena, barely large enough to hold the two of them.

He knew somewhere the old woman could see this, was watching. His fingers wrapped around the hilt of the sword, his breathing even. Let her watch, then.

The Lion bounded again, managing to duck under a swing that left him overextended and lashing out with a great clawed paw across his face. More jagged tears, more leaking fire, and the impact threw him back against the crumbling walls of the pool. Outside, the concrete surrounding it buckled and heaved upwards, the diving board toppled. He could hear the dirt hissing as he melted the ice from it.

It came in again, going for his neck. It was what a Lion would do with prey. This time it was his turn to move too fast for it, slashing with the sword in his hand. It checked itself, but not quite fast enough – all that bulk doesn't stop easily, and it was easily twice the size of a normal lion. The searing, glowing tip of the shining blade slashed through its muzzle and across one of its eyes.

In a way he felt bad for it, even though he knew it was just a sending, animated by her will.

Then he considered what that meant.

"Robia." He said out loud, his voice booming, like Surtsey erupting. "I know what you did."

The Lion was already backing away from him. The sides of the pit were steep, there was only one slope, the former shallow end of the pool before the collapse. It snarled, blood dripping down its muzzle from its ruined eye. He couldn't tell if it was listening.

"We can stop this right now."

It snarled again and leapt, but not at him, bouncing itself off of the concrete lip around the edge of the pool and going for his back. He managed to roll forward but the Lion's claws still ripped across his back, pain rocketing up the spine it had just attempted to sever. He came to his feet, met a charge with a whirling sweep of the sword that didn't connect.

His foot, however, caught it on the blind side, smashing it up into the wall.

The difference between a summoning and embodying what you call is that it doesn't hurt you personally when your summoning gets kicked four meters into a wall. On the other hand, there's no concentration needed to embody. He *was* the killer of Freyr, volcano lord, harbinger of hero wine spilled on sand. He could outlast her, if need be.

The Lion pulled itself from the wall and leapt for the edge again. He grabbed its leg as it cleared his head, wrenched hard, and smashed it back first into the frozen dirt so hard that the entire yard shook. Everywhere it had slashed at him burned, molten fire leaking from him. Bleeding would sap his strength, had already done so. It roared, furious, trying to tear at him with all four of its legs, fighting from its back. He closed his hand around its throat and took a kick to his stomach from its back leg that would have killed a mortal man in a second.

"I wish you would stop this." His voice rasped out, stones

sliding into molten rock.

The sword, bright as a sunset, flashed up in his hand. Another paw ripped across his shoulder, down his chest, leaving glowing furrows.

Then he slammed the blade down into its chest and wrenched, a strike that would have left a real animal torn in half. But this was no animal. The power she'd sent at him unraveled, an old tapestry shredded by uncaring hands. He could see the threads of it fray apart, hear a storm of dissonance as it was unmade. It couldn't *die*, not so long as the legend endured, but it was gone.

He knew that Dassalia was probably in agony. What she did meant that the fight had been painless for her and agonizing for him, but now that he'd won, she had *all* the pain at once. It must have been awful. He dragged himself up the side of the pool, heaved himself out. The sword in his hand flickered, diminished, and sputtered out, no longer a blade of pure light the color of heroic blood, now just a cricket bat again.

He directed the last of the power into himself, closed up as much as he could. Focused on his stomach and chest, so he wouldn't bleed to death. He fell onto his side, panting, ice cold. Realized he wasn't going to be able to get up.

Well, shit.

His hands were trembling, his clothes ruined. It was likely none of his neighbors would intervene, or even want to look in the direction of the house until morning had come. No one wanted to believe in things like this.

I'm going to freeze to death in my backyard. Ten feet from my house.

He tried again to get up but it wasn't possible. Everything worked but there wasn't anything left to push with. He'd closed up the wounds but they'd still bled.

He lost consciousness trying to roll over onto his back.

Chapter Seventeen

The Benefit of Hindsight

"Can you drive faster?"

"Thea, it's your car, and it normally seats two, what do *you* think?"

Thea wasn't panicking. They were already almost to the house, and she was spending most of her time coming up with a *you don't notice us* sigil and working it, keeping the car essentially invisible to any police that might notice a speeding CRX with three women in it.

"I'm sure Tom is fine." Evvie completely lacked conviction. Thea didn't even bother to snap at the woman. She was probably just trying to convince *herself* everything was fine.

Seri turned down Pontiac. They were close now. Thea tried again to reach out to him, the little rat ghost in her lap. The others had all gone when she'd shown them the way, drifting off to whatever little rat afterlife there was. Perhaps a giant landfill with no one to bother them, or a cage with all the water and pellets you could ever want and a really nice wheel. But this one hadn't gone. She didn't know why, but those tiny little red eyes and the silvery fur was comforting, so she let it stay for now.

"I can't... I'm not even sure how I would talk to him, we've never done anything like that."

"It was worth a try." Seri said, turning onto Colonial. "You can work out something later."

"Cell phones are cheap and you don't have to chant or wave your fingers around to use one." Evvie said. Seri groaned internally but Thea appeared to be paying almost no attention. Seri had in fact tried to get Thea to buy a cell several times, but she'd always refused.

They pulled into the driveway and the headlights immediately showed that garage was crushed. It looked like a tree had fallen on it.

Thea was out of the car so fast that Seri hadn't even had time to put it in park. She ran up to the garage, looked inside it, her hand glowing.

"He's not in here!"

"There's a lot of shit, maybe he's under…"

"He'd glow." She swept her hand around, looking at the ruin of the backyard – the toppled diving board, cracked concrete – and indeed, there he was, faintly glowing a soft green color when the golden light from her hand touched him. She made a noise and ran over to him, Seri and Evvie trailing.

"Thomas. Thomas, it's me." She bent her head, heard him inhale. "He's breathing." She put her hand to his face, saw the slashes. "Jesus he's all cut up. Seri, he's all cut up."

"I know." She took stock, her first aid training kicking in. "We can't leave him out here. He'll get hypothermia."

"Should we move him?" Evvie was wishing she had even the slightest idea what to do.

Thea had already drawn a caduceus in the snow next to him, and before either Seri or Evvie could debate any further, she bit her own lip hard enough to draw blood. It brought tears to her eyes. She'd never done that on purpose before, it was very hard to do, and she bent over him and kissed him with the bloody lip while pressing her hand into the mark on the ground.

Light flared up around them and he gasped, his eyes opening. Even having seen all the other shit Evvie felt the skin on her arms start crawling at the sight.

"Thomas?" Thea's voice. "Are you…"

"Cold." His teeth chattered.

"Can you stand?" Seria asked.

"Maybe." He wasn't sure, but he grunted and heaved, and then Thea was under his arm and amazingly, together they got him up. She hissed as she saw his back. He wondered what it looked like. He felt better, whatever she'd done helping. Together they tottered to the back door and then they were inside the house, and she helped him to the couch. She looked around briefly at the kitchen that she'd started to think of as hers before checking him over.

"How bad?"

"I'll live." He shuddered again.

"Seri, there are blankets in the room down the hallway, next to the bathroom. Get them."

"On it."

The next half hour was spent making sure he wasn't wearing anything wet, getting him bundled up. Thea knew the magic she'd cast had been a quick and dirty thing, just enough to get him up, so she let Seri take charge. She knew first aid. She *wanted* to take him to the hospital, but he was phobic ever since his coma, and she didn't want to freak him out.

The little rat ghost scampered around, seemingly perfectly content to orbit her.

"I gotta call Bishop and Joe," Seri said after checking Thomas' temperature for the sixth time. "We missed the last boat over."

"Tell them we're staying here overnight."

"Is that a good idea? I mean..."

"It'll be fine." Thomas spoke up from the couch. "I killed her sending. Right now she's worse off than I am."

"Do you think..." Thea hesitated. On the one hand, it was her grandmother she was talking about. On the other hand, she'd almost killed him. She'd *tried* to kill him. "Maybe it killed her? She's old."

"I wouldn't count on it." He still looked drained. "But if she can do anything more strenuous than lighting a candle right now I'd be surprised."

"I'll reinforce the wards anyway." Thea turned to Seri. "Go ahead and make that call."

Evvie found herself sitting in a kitchen she'd only been in once before, watching two women she didn't really know as they took over the place, while her ex huddled under blankets near the heating vent, and she could *see* the cuts and slashes on him closing up. They wouldn't even be there by the morning.

She walked over and sat down across from him. He looked up, surprised.

"Evvie?"

"Hi. Guess you didn't notice me before."

"No." He blinked. "It's been a day."

"For all of us, really." She turned her head. Seri was on the phone, and Thea was moving around doing *something*, Evvie had no idea what. "So, this is all real."

"Yes."

"Has it... was this *always* you? Did I miss this?"

"It's been a part of my life for years, but I didn't really twig to it until the accident." He exhaled, inhaled slowly, letting his chest expand. "I wasn't running around fighting giant monster lions when we were dating, no."

"Is that what..."

"After the vampire showed up, yeah."

"*After* the vampire." She nodded. "Well, yeah, wouldn't want to double book that." A thought occurred to her. "Is Stuart a vampire?"

"Yep."

"Did you know?"

"Just found out."

"Is that why you got weird? Told me to take a sabbatical? Because that was weird."

"Well, you should do that anyway. But yeah. I didn't want to say 'quit your job because Stuart's a vampire and he *probably* won't hurt you but I'm not big on taking the chance.' I didn't think you'd go for it."

She considered this.

"I guess I... probably wouldn't have? I woke up this morning with a weird hangover and a strange desire to do whatever someone told me to do and I end up in my ex's house watching his girlfriend and her cousin deal with... a monster cat?"

"The Nemean Lion."

"What, the *actual* Nemean Lion? That's a thing?"

"It was a summoning. She called it up, *made* it real. Then I killed it, so it went back to being an idea again." He sighed, shuddered again. "Oh, thank God I'm starting to get warm."

"I'm done." Thea dropped down next to him on the couch. "I'm sorry, I didn't..."

"We can argue later."

"We're going to argue?"

"I'm pretty pissed off that you went off after the Williams boys without telling me."

"It just sort of happened."

"There's a phone right there." He pointed to where Seri was still talking. "Takes ten seconds to call."

"I didn't know I needed permission."

"You don't need permission. I can't tell you what to do." He hissed as one of the deeper slashes, the one on his stomach, closed up. "Letting me know isn't the same as getting my approval."

"I... yeah. Okay. I should have told you what we were doing." She shot a look over at Evvie. "Do you mind..."

"Oh, I have *zero* desire to be around for this." She stood up. "Tommy, I'm glad you're alright, and you are fucking weird now."

"I always was, Ev." He waited for her to walk into the kitchen. "I'm not *super* angry or anything. It's the kind of shit I'd probably do, so..."

"I left you alone and she went after you."

"She's come after me a few times. You, too." She felt so off balance, angry and embarrassed and hurt and *scared*. Not for herself, but for him. What if they'd been a few minutes later? Would she have found him dead on the ground?

"Everyone I ever... my mom, my dad, my uncle Paolo... they're all dead." He didn't say anything, just looked at her with those huge green eyes of his and she kept going. "And they're all dead because of *her*. She killed them. Directly or indirectly."

"Know the feeling."

"I want to kill her for this. For doing this, tonight, for making me... for *scaring* me. For putting this fear in me that I'll..." She took a breath, looked down at her hands. "I figured I'd never, couldn't ever feel this way about anybody. Nobody seemed *real*, you know? I always wondered how they could care about the things they did, trivial shit, trivial to *me* anyway. I'd get mad because they'd bitch that their mom didn't buy them this or that and I'd be like *my mom hung herself in my fucking basement so you enjoy that goddamn red Honda you got for your sweet sixteen.*"

She looked at him, saw that he was listening, and kept going.

"I don't want to hurt like that again."

"I don't blame you." He was bracing himself, she could see it. She reached out and touched his face, where the scratches had been.

"I'm not dumping you."

"Good." He shuddered again. "It's already been a bad day."

"I'm not used to worrying about other people."

"I'm pretty awful at being worried about." He smiled, and turned to brush his lips against her hand. "When I found out you went after them by yourself I almost ripped the kitchen apart."

"How *did* you find that out?"

"Magic." They both smiled at that.

"I guess I should have guessed."

"I was thinking we should get cell phones."

"Evvie suggested that in the car."

"How the hell did *that* happen?"

"After that vampire called I felt like someone should check up on her. And no offense, but if I was having problems the last person I'd want to see would be my ex who I cheated on."

"You know about that?"

"Bishop has a terrible poker face." She slid her hand down to feel at the marks on his chest. "Looks like it's all healing up."

"You hurt yourself."

"I bit my lip, I didn't open a vein." She slid closer to him, lay her head on his shoulder. "Is this okay?"

"Yeah, I feel mostly fine now." He adjusted himself. "I don't want to lose you either, you know."

"I do. Sometimes it scares me, I'm going to disappoint you, or just…" She hissed. "I feel like you're this small glass thing I'm going to break. Not always, but…"

"I just got into a fight with a lion the size of a freaking dinosaur. I'm not fragile."

"I'm jealous. All I got was an old car turned into a robot spider." The rat ghost ran up the side of the couch and looked down on the two of them, rubbing its face with its little hand-paws. "Oh, and I got this."

"Is that a..."

"It's a rat ghost, yeah. The older Williams was using a bunch of them to power his spider-robot-monster thing."

"What, like a golem?"

"Kinda? He doesn't really know what the fuck he's doing."

"What the hell..." He watched the rat run around on the couch. "What do we *do* with it?"

"It's not hurting anything. I want to keep it. I've never had a pet before."

He watched it a little longer.

"Ah, fuck it. If I really have a problem I'll get over it. What's one more weird fucking thing?"

"Exactly." She fought to keep her voice even. She was afraid, angry, anxious, her emotional state was made up of words starting with A. *Anguish, that's a good one, that starts with A.* They'd met the last day of October. It was the middle of December.

She loved him.

And everyone she had ever loved died.

Joe hasn't died. Seri hasn't.

She closed her eyes and breathed and let herself listen to him breathe, and tried not to be terrified.

*

Joe hung up the phone and turned to Bishop, who was sitting at the table watching Byron eat.

"So my sister says they're all staying hunkered down over there tonight and coming back tomorrow."

"Okay." Bishop watched the kid eat another recently reheated dinosaur shaped chicken nugget. It seemed weird to eat pre-processed food considering they had livestock and a chicken coop, but there was no freaking way Bishop was going to go out there and kill a chicken. He'd stopped at the grocery store before riding his car across the ferry. "Am I going to want to know how eventful?"

"I didn't get a lot of specifics. Said she'd tell me when she saw us."

Bishop nodded, because he had no idea what else to do. He and Joe had spent the day trying to make sure the kid didn't drink bleach or eat a rock – he was acting more and more like a typical kid, he'd even gotten somewhat verbal with them. But neither of them had any experience with a kid around ten, or however old he was. Considering what they knew it was hard to blame him for not being normal.

"It's boring here," Byron said.

"Yeah, but we think your crazy grandmother will stay away from us," Bishop said. "That's a selling point."

"She hurt me."

"Yes."

"She hurt you, too." Byron pointed at Joe. "I can see it."

"Can you?" Joe sat down across from him. "What can you see?"

"You have a mark, here." He touched Joe's neck, where the Hound had bitten him. "You were cut off. Your thread was severed. That's what she showed me. Threads."

"Yeah. I can see them too."

"Oh good, we're talking about this." Bishop got up from the table. "I'm getting a soda. Either of you want one?"

"No."

"None for me," Joe said, then turned back to Byron. "I only met her a few times."

"She came after our mom and dad died. She was mad at me." The boy ducked his head, looked down at the table. "She wanted me to be more like her. But I *am*. She didn't see it but I am."

Joe frowned.

"Like her how?"

"I am." He was crying, shaking his head. "She was so mad. *Filthy, worthless, I needed a girl child, more girl children to be my dressing gowns*." His voice changed, a rather frighteningly good impersonation, and Joe wondered at it, at the way the boy had flared up in that strange other-sight of his. There was something off about Byron, even after he'd healed from the marks the spiritual parasites had left on him. Not *wrong*, but not what he expected. "I tried to tell her but she didn't listen."

"Tried to tell her what, exactly?" Joe reached out, touched hands. A slow sense of comprehension was beginning to dawn on him. "You're not a boy, are you?"

A shake of a small dirty blond head. Tears refusing to be shed, crying that refused to happen again.

"I told her. She didn't listen."

"I'm *lost*." Bishop said. Joe gave him a look that said *just be quiet* and that's what he did.

"Well, I'm sorry. She's not a very good person."

"She's not. She's mean and she's scary and I hate her and I'm *not*. I'm like her but I'm *not*."

"I'm like her, too. And I'm not. You know Thea and Seri, right?" The little girl Joe had suddenly discovered he was in charge of nodded her head. "I'll explain what you told me and we'll figure out what you need, okay?"

She nodded again.

"What… do you mind being called Byron?"

"No." She sniffled. "Morgan called me Bry. He used to take me to the park, we'd play ball. Sometimes he'd get me a doll. He didn't understand why, but 'It's no skin off my ass if you like Barbie. Just don't tell Jimmy, or mom. Especially not mom.'" Again that terrifyingly accurate impression. Joe thought that Bry was actually changing her throat in some way to do it. "You can call me Bry if you want."

"I will." He nodded and stood up. "Now I'm going to take Bishop in the other room and talk about you behind your back." She frowned at him. "Sometimes adults need things explained a few times before they understand them, okay?"

She shrugged. Went back to eating her dinosaur chicken. Joe put his hand on Bishop's arm and practically dragged him into the living room.

"What the hell…"

"Shhh."

"Look, not to perv out here, but I lifted that kid's naked body out of the mud and snow, so I'm pretty sure I got a decent idea of what the block and tackle looked like."

"First off, don't be disgusting. Second, just… it's not a super common thing but it does happen, okay? Dr. Gonzales covered it in *Developmental Identity*."

"That sounds like a made up class."

"It was my psychology elective."

Bry tuned the rest of it out. She was hungry and there wasn't any point to listening to Joe explain it to Bishop. There was going to be a lot of explaining. Her mother had never really gotten it, had tried to toughen her 'son' up, dressed Bry in boy clothes and bought trucks and robots. She'd liked the robots, but that didn't make her a boy. She wasn't one. She'd always known that. She didn't need Joe's class for that.

She bit the head off of another dinosaur and wished it was her grandmother. Her awful grandmother. Memories were too easy. Bry would have loved to forget what had been done, what she'd experienced. The monster she'd been. Even now she felt like if she lost focus she'd be something, someone else, it was hard to stay the same from day to day.

She ate another dinosaur and focused on that. Let Joe worry about telling people things.

*

This time she didn't scream or thrash around her house.

She was sitting in an old chair, gasping, pallid as a fish on a dock. Almost as damp, her sweat soaking her old black dress and blouse. She'd set the house to watching, so no one could disturb her, and then as soon as she'd gotten the phone call she'd completed the rite and sent it after him. His house had been warded but that was fine. She was patient. She'd set up everything in advance.

But it hadn't worked, and now she was realizing how *tired* she was.

She couldn't stand. Could just barely feel her heart hammering away in her chest. Every part of her hurt. To call it pain was to mock the severity of it, and yet, her heart continued to beat. She lived. That might have been the worst part, that she survived to feel it.

You could just let me go.

"But I won't, ever," she whispered. "I still have a chance. Two of them close enough, I can still force them into it."

At least one of them is awake. You'll have to...

"I know what I'll have to do. She'll have to allow it. I know her weak point now. I'll press it."

Robi...

"If I do what you want, it was all for nothing. You. Him. The children. All I've done..." She couldn't even weep. There wasn't even enough left for *that*. If they came upon her now, once they got past the garden she'd be helpless. She sat there and sweated and wore pain with resentful familiarity.

It was the middle of December.

One way or another it would all end soon. She knew it. She forced her hand to move, grunting with each twitch of the fingers.

"I will have them both, and I'll start over. Maybe..."

Robi, don't do this.

"If you won't help me then be silent! Why should she have what I never had? What I *wanted*? What you kept me from having?"

I never stopped you. You wouldn't let yourself. You could have asked him.

"He'd have never left her." Her head bowed under the weight of it, the past rushing up to crush her. She rocked forward and back, trying to stand. "I *will* live. If that's all that's left me, fine, but I will have it."

There was no reply.

She let the pain be all she was, let herself drown in it. It was preferable to nothing.

Book Three

The Bleak December

Chapter Eighteen

Unwanted Company

James Williams had recently decided not to go by Jimmy anymore.

He made this decision after finishing off his third bottle of Jack Daniels. Technically they were called *fifths*, as in *a fifth of Jack Daniels* but saying he'd drunk three fifths felt too much like math to him.

Morgan had driven the truck to the house, emptied it out of everything he considered his (it wasn't a lot of stuff) and taken the fuck off. This left James in a quandary. Technically the salvage yard was in Morgan's name, as was the house. At any moment either could go up for sale. This would leave James with no income to speak of, and no place to live. Considering he had dropped out of high school at fifteen to work in the salvage yard, that left him with few skills as such.

James had no idea if there was any money left or not. If *he* was Morgan... well, if he was Morgan he would have kicked his own ass out of the house years ago. But if he was Morgan right at this moment, he would have driven to the bank first thing and emptied out the salvage yard's account before Jimmy... before *James* could beat him to it. That left James with the money he had in his wallet, minus the five bottles of Jack he'd picked up on his way back to the house.

They lived close to City Liquors, at least.

The house was a few blocks from the yard, but Jimmy... *James* had been a trifle battered and wobbly walking home, and so he hadn't seen any sign of Morgan. Byron's room was untouched, all those weird stuffed dolls he had liked before. James had never really understood Byron, he was an *extremely* sissy little boy back before the woman had gotten her claws into them all.

And so he'd drunk.

He drank the first bottle and went up to sleep. The next day, when he'd woken up and everything still sucked, he drank the second and passed right out again. The third bottle actually took him two days to finish, and that's about when he decided he needed a more adult sounding name if he was going to be in charge of the salvage yard until Morgan came back.

There were several problems with this idea. The first was, he wasn't good with tools or anything mechanical. Never had been. The second was that the office was destroyed and he'd left it sitting there for the past three days. By now it had probably been ransacked by neighborhood kids. Morgan had driven off with the torches and a complete tool set in the truck, but the stuff in the garage was likely gone as well. Even if he'd remembered to lock it up, three days was plenty of time.

None of this was the *big* problem. It just helped keep his mind off of that one.

He checked his wallet, saw that he was down to a hundred bucks, and decided to get it over with. Headed down to City Liquors and bought another five bottles of Jack, his best smile plastered on his face. He was legal, but they'd refused to sell to him before when he walked in drunk. So now the chore was to be drunk, but not *seem* so. James was good at presenting himself as something he wasn't. It was his only real skill.

The woman behind the cash register at City was in her twenties, plain, maybe even homely with a weak chin and lank hair, watery blue-green eyes. He smiled and laughed and flirted with her and she melted, and he left the store with seven bottles of Jack Daniels 'for a party' as well as her phone number. He loved girls who knew they weren't very hot. The less hot a girl was, the more likely she was to put out. Or put up with his shit.

It occurred to him that if he played it cool, he could end up crashing at her place. A few crumbs of affection would be enough. He'd never tried that before, but desperate times.

He arrived back at the house as the day was already fading

into night. It was December 10 or 11, he wasn't sure. Middle of December for sure. Days getting shorter. Might as well stay in and get drunk and wait for the lights to get turned off.

He was half-way through the second bottle and considering finishing it when the doorbell rang.

The walls kept trying to hit him. But he managed to get to the front door and look out the glass. He considered trying to run, but with the floor and walls being dicks, that didn't seem like a plan.

He opened the door.

"I am amazed to find you here."

"Nowhere else to go." He stepped back to let her come in. Wasn't much point in trying to stop her, after all. She closed the door behind her and looked around at trash strewn everywhere, looked into the kitchen. They rarely ate anything that needed cooking so it was actually fairly okay, in comparison to the living room.

"I don't seem able to find Morgan."

"He left."

"Yes." She looked at Jim…*James*. "Do you know where?"

"If I knew where I'd have mailed it to you in a letter and ran my white ass off in the other direction."

"Indeed." She brushed a bag of store brand Nacho Chips off of the couch and sat down. James took the moment to really *look* at her, his horrible old hag of a grandmother. You could tell she used to be hot – the cheekbones, the broad forehead, the long hair a mix of black and silver, those terrifying blue eyes. She was tall for an old woman, as tall as Jimmy, and she held herself with a completely ramrod straight posture that told everyone who looked at her she wasn't someone to fuck with. "I admit, I'm surprised. I always assumed *you* would be the one to abandon him."

"He found out you'd called."

"Ah. When the ladies came calling?" He was too tired and too drunk to freak out but she laughed, so he figured it still showed on his face. "Such troublesome children. I should have taken them in hand, but I thought *you* two would be the harder to control."

"Yeah, turns out they're both chips off the old bi… block." He wasn't sure why he caught himself. She was going to kill him anyway. Eventually.

"So here you stand. Your brother gone. Waiting for the inevitable." He swayed on his feet.

"Sure."

"No defiance?"

"I'm tired, I have twelve dollars left, and my only prospect is a liquor store clerk who'd probably faint dead away if anyone said two kind words to her in a row. I'm not sober enough for hope."

"Fortunately for you, I find myself disadvantaged."

He waited for that to make sense. She sighed.

"Clean this shithole up. I want it to look like humans once lived in it. Then I will provide you with a list of things I require. Feel free to take whatever of your possessions are available to the nearest pawnshop and procure funding for said items."

"I don't..."

"Nor are you required to." She turned those terrifying eyes on him and he felt the alcohol in his system burn away, like it had never been there. "All you need to do is obey. Do that, and I may let you continue living just a little bit longer."

He was about to say something, ask a question, and then she made a fist and he collapsed to the floor, his entire abdomen on fire. He convulsed and barely managed to keep from biting the tip off of his own tongue before she relaxed her hand and allowed him to stand back up.

"I can do that to you anywhere. Do as I say."

He moved off. He'd have been sullen about it – it was an old habit – but he knew she'd kill him for it. And as shitty as his life might have been at that moment he wasn't done with it yet.

*

Thea had driven. Thomas still hated to do it, and she already knew the way.

She didn't know what she'd expected to find at her grandmother's shitty little house in Little Compton. A dirt road up to the place? Check. Snow everywhere? Double check, it had been a cold month and there wasn't much sign of it changing any time soon. The house itself was unimpressive. She'd expected it to be foreboding, looming, menacing now that she knew what she knew about it. But it wasn't. It was just *there,* a little cottage with a garden in the back. She remembered the last time she'd visited it, five years before – the woman couldn't even remember her name, calling her *Dara* over and over again.

Had that been an act? She didn't know.

"We don't have to…"

"Yeah we do." Thea shut the car down, pocketed the keys. "She'll just keep coming unless we find her."

The car door squealed as they got out. Thomas made a note to check that. They'd been driving the car more than it was used to in winter. It had spent a year in a garage when he left the country, there was likely some wear and tear built up. It was a little amazing to him that he could make himself think about that.

"It looks really boring." Thea said as they walked up the stairs. She tried the door, but it was locked. "Do you see any…"

"No." He dropped to one knee and lifted the mat in front of the door. It was just a mat, it didn't say *welcome* or anything. Sure enough there was a key under it.

"Jesus, she could have at least hidden it under a flower pot. Or in one."

"This place feels dead." He put the key in the door, opened the lock. It swung open, a clear sign of a house not built properly level. They both peered inside and then at each other.

"Not it," Thea said, smiling at him.

"Why do I always have to go face first into the awful places?"

"You're the big strong man."

"This is a double standard." He groused but stepped inside. They both knew he wouldn't want to let her do it if she'd insisted. Nothing happened when his feet hit the floor. She followed him in a moment later.

"This is bizarre."

"It looks very ordinary." Thomas looked around the kitchen,

the room they'd stepped into. A small bathroom just off to the left, the toilet visible through the open door. To their right, a small living room, with a noticeable lack of anything but an old couch. Thea frowned, remembering the huge old cabinet TV she'd had for years.

"I guess we snoop?"

"I guess we do."

There weren't close neighbors and Thea *was* her granddaughter, so they weren't that afraid that anyone would come find them essentially ransacking the place. Plus, there really wasn't much of anything to ransack. They ended up in her bedroom, which smelled like mothballs and rubbing alcohol, and found nothing much in there. Not even old notebooks full of spells or something.

"I expected wards, like at your place."

"Not so much." Thea could see that Thomas was freaked out by how sterile the place was. "The air here feels wrong. I know it's winter, but it just feels so utterly *dead*."

Thea ran her finger along the edge of the dresser. There wasn't any dust.

"She hasn't been gone long."

"Where the hell is she?"

"Fucked if I know. I have uncles and aunts I've never met, she had like ten kids and at least four of them moved out of state."

"Five sets of twins." Thomas leaned against the bed. "How is that even possible? One set of twins, maybe. Two, feasible. But she gets pregnant five times and they're *all* twins?" In his frustration his hand jerked to the left and knocked over an ashtray full of coins on her nightstand, sending the coins spilling. The cascade of coins on the older wooden floor sounded like a wind chime breaking down. "Shit!"

"It's okay. Not like anyone is here to..." Thea stopped talking. "Uh. Okay."

"What?"

"Take a look at the coins."

He did, not really understanding why. But he soon figured it out.

They'd all come up heads.

"Do you have any change on you?" Thea was patting herself down. "I just have my wallet and some paper money."

"Hold on." He fished around in his pockets, produced a quarter. Handed it to her. "I knocked over the others, let's see if it carries over."

She tossed the coin up into the air and let it bounce and ring off of the wooden planks of the floor. After four bounces it rattled to a stop, head up. She reached down and picked it up.

"You try."

He did. Same result. Same number of bounces, even, and a head up result.

Thea tried again. Same.

Thomas tried again. Same.

"Okay. This is weird. Was she involved in an extremely competitive coin toss league, or…"

"I think this answers my question." Thomas scooped the coins up off of the floor, held them in his hands for a moment, and then just tossed them all up into the air. Some hit the bed, bounced off of it, others just fell to the floor. All bounced four times. All came up heads.

"How the hell would she even do this?"

"I'm not sure this is the cause or the effect." They walked out of the bedroom together. "Maybe the five sets of twins were a consequence, not what she was going for. And maybe the bedroom is fucked up because she spent time there, not because of anything she deliberately did."

"She fucks around with luck just by staying in a place?"

"Luck. Probability. I'm not sure." He shrugged. "Now I'm wondering if *we* do that."

"Oooh that's weird. I don't even want to think about having twins."

"I wasn't…" He sputtered and she laughed and touched his arm.

"I know, it's okay."

After they were sure she'd left nothing useful behind they left the house. Thea didn't bother to lock it – for one thing, she didn't feel particularly motivated to protect the woman's property and for another if any of her neighbors decided to break into the place, more power to them.

"What the hell do we do now?"

"I wish I could figure out what she wants. We have pieces..." Thomas sighed as they got back into the car. "After what Joe told us about Bry, I started wondering about her obsession with girl offspring. She killed your mother, why keep *you* alive? Why Seri? Why was she so upset about Bry?"

"Hell, *I* didn't know you could be a girl in a boy's body, I doubt my grandmother is up on it."

"It's an alchemical idea. The Rebis." He was rubbing his head now. "She should have been *thrilled*. The Divine Hermaphrodite."

"Bry's not..."

"Male and female in one body? In a way, she is. It carries a lot of symbolic weight. But she *wasn't* happy. The more I learn, the less I understand."

"Love." Thea reached out and put her hand on his face, waited for him to face her. "This isn't all up to you to figure out."

"I know, but..."

"You're freaking out a little."

"I'm freaking out a *lot*." He exhaled. "What you said... she killed my mom and dad and my grandfather before that. Maybe not on purpose with him, I honestly couldn't tell you. But it makes me... I have to *stop* this."

"I get it." She started the car. "I'm saying there's a bunch of us in this now."

"I know. I'm sorry."

"Nothing to be sorry about." She backed the car around, pointed it down the dirt road, and watched the house gradually disappear in the rear view mirror. "I was thinking of a different way to do this."

"Like what?"

"We know someone who knows someone who knows something about her." Thea was still smiling but it was a slightly sinister smile now. "So I think we should ask for some help."

*

Keeping the store closed over December would have been like stabbing himself in the eye, so Stuart had reopened it. He'd also gone to a realtor's office and started the process of buying a house, because Mercy had been right. He needed a place he could secure in case Akivasha sent anyone.

Evvie had called in and quit via the phone. She hadn't said why. He couldn't pretend he was surprised by it. Right now Miki was handling the register while he tried to do the work she'd done, getting all the pre-orders and rush orders straightened out. Stuart felt a lot of pressure from big chain stores, even in Rhode Island it was there and it was only going to get worse. For all he knew people would start buying books in some new way and cut him and his store out entirely. He'd adapt, of course. That was what he did.

Once the sun was well on its way to setting he went up to the front and checked on Miki. She wasn't as experienced as Evvie was, so he wanted to make sure she was okay. Indeed, she looked frazzled.

"Problems?"

"Some woman just tried to get me to sell her that wizard book you got from England. I explained it was a special order, we were getting it in special, and she lost it at me."

"You can always call me when that happens."

"Usually Evvie would handle it." Miki gave him a suspicious look. "Why'd she quit?"

"She didn't say. Probably she's thinking of moving away. She's from New York and she graduated this year." She narrowed her eyes at him but said nothing. *She quit because I'm a bloodsucker and her ex likely told her to, okay?* He could weather Miki's disapproval. She would likely be quitting herself in a few weeks. It would be a pain to replace her, but he'd live with it.

"We need to hire at least two people to do all she did."

"That's probably true." Stuart was terrible with people. He had no real idea how to mollify Miki. He could tell that agreeing with her was just annoying her, but he didn't know what *wouldn't* annoy her. He was about to try just walking away with the bell over the door rang.

Evvie Fraser walked in, wearing a pair of sunglasses (at dusk no less) and looking like she was getting ready for a fight. Stuart hadn't expected that.

"Hey!" Miki sounded excited. "I didn't think I'd get to see you again."

"Hey, Miki." Evvie had a mild smile on when she talked to the younger girl. It went away when she looked to Stuart. "You and I need to talk."

He gestured towards his office and she strode past him, brisk as an autumn morning.

Last time you saw one of those you had to dive into a well.

He followed, waiting. If he had nothing else he had patience.

Once they were inside his office she wheeled on him.

"You almost got Tom killed."

"He told me to tell her."

"Yeah, because he's an idiot." She'd dyed her hair a dark auburn color, from roots to tip. It looked good on her. Stuart frowned, wondering if he was being creepy by noticing that. "You know these... people?.. better than any of us do. You know how they think."

"I'm actually the worst person to try and tell you how they think."

"Why's that?"

"No offense, but why are you here, grilling me in my office?"

"Because someone nearly turned me into a bobblehead doll nodding yes like a grinning idiot and I hate owing people." She shuddered, cold even in the office. "Look, you need me to work here."

"I've kept this place running for years before I met you."

"Yeah, and in four years of working here I took more than half the load off of you and you *know* it."

"You did." He sat down at his desk. "You don't want to be mixed up with Mercy. I don't, either, but I don't have a choice."

"So you talk to her for us."

"Oh my God, that's a *terrible* idea." He looked up at Evvie, confused, curious. He wasn't used to either. "Seriously, are you still into this guy or something, because…"

She laughed. It shivered with tension, piano wire about to snap.

"In the past week I have learned that he and I were never any damn thing at all but friends. That's the thing. I like it better as friends. And I want to help my friend because he's in fucking deep with some crazy bullshit. You know? Friends?"

"I don't really, no."

"What, you never had any?"

"I had a few, before. I had to let them go." He shrugged. "They're almost all dead now. That's what happens."

"So make new ones."

"Sure. You want to be my friend?" He smiled and let the teeth slide out, let her see them.

"Stuart, don't even fucking try. I saw… Christ, I don't even know what I saw. It was like a spider and a car had babies and it was *walking*."

"Seriously?"

"You like weird shit so much, you should hang out with them." She rubbed at her face with a hand. "Do you actually want friends?"

"I… haven't really considered it."

"Well, friends help each other out." She leaned her hands on the desk. "You know what? Fuck bravado. I'm really goddamn scared and I want my old life back, the one where I worked at a bookstore and my boss was creepy because he stared at my breasts too much. Where Miki had a little crush on me she was never going to act on and I didn't know things that don't make any sense. Where you weren't a vampire and now every time I think back on the past four years I wonder if you were thinking about killing me."

"I wasn't. I was checking out your breasts."

She laughed.

"How does that work? Aren't you, like, dead?"

"I still like to look. It's complicated." He spread his hands out. "Having you work here isn't a problem for me, but it would probably be smarter if you ran and didn't look back."

"I still need you to talk to your friends."

"They're not my friends. They're... we all come from the same place. Mercy made me. Someone else made her. Akivasha, the Mother. I can go and ask but there's no guarantee they'll tell me anything."

"Can you make an introduction?"

"There is no way I'm introducing you to..."

"Not me." He chewed on that idea for a while.

Akivasha might want to meet them, or she might get angry at the idea of it. He normally didn't care if he pissed her off, but he wasn't eager to die, and pushing her too far was a good way to end up dead. On the other hand, he'd felt what Willrew was, him and his weird girlfriend.

What really decided it was simple, though. Evvie knew what he was and she was there, in his office, asking him. That was something he'd never really had, someone who knew. Someone he might be able to talk to about it. Could he trust her?

Do you want friends?

"I'll talk to them. See if I can set it up." There was always that sensation when he spoke, of having to take in air so he could form words with it, forcing his useless lungs to do something. It imagined it was something like a phantom limb might feel, but he didn't really know. The one time he'd lost an arm, it had grown back.

"I'll tell Tom."

"Tell him he may not be happy with what he gets."

*

"Come along." She didn't bother to knock on his door; she just strode into his room, naked. She spent a lot of time around the house naked since she'd moved in. The worst part was how little she cared what he thought about it. Or if he was dressed. Which he wasn't.

"Where are we…"

"We are in the shabby house your father left behind." She sniffed at him. Stared at him, unblinking. It was strange how she was *clearly* old, seventy or eighty years old and yet it was hard to tell by looking at her, exactly. Not a lot of wrinkles or sagging on her.

You are staring at your naked grandmother.

James forced himself up out of bed and pulled clothing on. He was getting used to being her errand boy. It turned out that Morgan had left about half of the money in the account, a last act of, what? Kindness? Something, anyway. It meant that he hadn't pawned anything yet. He had no illusions on that score.

Eventually she'd take everything from him. When he turned around she was sitting on the edge of his bed, still naked, looking up at the ceiling.

"If we're going somewhere, shouldn't you put on clothes?"

"I'm skyclad." She snickered. "That's what they call it now. We didn't, we were just naked and we knew it, it was easier naked." She exhaled, her face sagging, looking impossibly old compared to her bizarrely ageless body. "We'll take my car."

He didn't bother to point out that he didn't have a car.

She got dressed while he was loading the car with all the weird shit she'd made him buy. He'd expected it to all be witchy shit, and there was some of that – she'd had him find an old herb store and get belladonna (the clerk had insisted on calling it Deadly Nightshade) but she'd also had him get a bunch of roses, a whole lot of freaky looking roots, and a *lot* of pot. James wasn't against marijuana. It wasn't his high, but he was totally okay with it. She'd also had him get amber, frankincense, and something actually called Dragon's Blood. It had taken him most of two days to pick it all up.

He didn't know what she did with most of it, but she definitely baked the pot into a tray of brownies and ate them. She'd even given him one. When he stared at her she just laughed at him.

"I'm old and everything hurts. You have no idea what it is like when your body starts to stop working, and you're inside it, feeling it. No escape from it."

After a week of her mercurial moods and strange behavior

James was numb to it all. Now they were driving somewhere, him doing the driving. She would tell him to turn, but otherwise sat quietly in the passenger's seat, looking up at the sky. At the seagulls circling overhead, really. Eventually they ended up on Cranston Street, and that's when he realized where they were going.

"We're going to St. Anne's?"

"I'm surprised. Yes."

"If you told me that I could have just driven straight here."

"Giving you boys latitude hasn't worked out for me so far." She burst out in a laugh that made the skin on his face want to shudder itself off and run away. "I keep forgetting your name. What's your name again?"

"James."

"You were Maria's son." She got solemn. "My poor daughters. Born to the wrong woman." He knew a lot better than to interrupt her when she was on a tear, driving up Church Street in silence. "I didn't know it would kill them. But I didn't stop once I found out, either. I'll kill you, eventually."

"I figured."

"It doesn't have to be soon." She lay a hand on his face, brushed the hair out of it. If she'd been someone else, an actual grandmother, it might have been comforting and not the cause of a liquid panic in his gut that made him clench very hard for fear of ruining his pants. "I don't *have* to hurt you. I can make it quick and painless. Perhaps even like drifting off into a pleasant dream. But you have to stop disappointing me."

The steering wheel felt like he might crush it. Thankfully she stopped touching him.

When they got to the cemetery his first thought was to how clean and perfect it looked, lines of headstones or markers cradled in white that glowed softly in the light leaking through the clouds, trails stretching off towards Dyer Pond. She made him take a plastic kitchen container of red stuff out of the back of the car and follow her. She'd done a lot of stuff in the kitchen, which he'd been happy to let be her business. He sure as hell didn't want any part of it.

Not that she cared what he wanted.

They were halfway to the lake when they stopped. The Mancinis had a family plot, with five headstones. Maria, Claudia, Marco and Stephan, plus a Stephan Sr. - James guessed that was his grandfather, the hapless first husband of the woman standing next to him. It was off the path a bit, and with the cold and the snow there weren't any people around. Not a lot of foot traffic for a cemetery in the middle of December. People didn't like to be reminded of death during the holiday.

"Hello." She spoke to the stones. "I'm afraid I have need of you."

She held out her hand and James handed her the plastic container. She took the reddish glop inside of it out, marked each stone in turn, then put a little on herself, on her face under her right eye. She produced a knife out of her coat and inclined her head to regard him.

"Come here." He hesitated, his eyes on the blade, a wide, broad thing vaguely leaf shaped. She snickered, her strange accent flattening out. "Boy, if I meant to kill you with the knife I'd have stabbed you as soon as we got here."

He stepped closer. She took his arm, turned it so his palm was upright, grazed the blade against it.

"You remind me of your grandfather. Oh, you lack his strength of will, his morality. But a little of his eyes, his jaw, you have those." She grew thoughtful, looking again at the graves. "Now? Where were you a day ago, Raifa? Yes. *Yes*."

He was holding his breath. Finally he had to breathe again. She stood there staring at the ground holding his hand, sliding the knife against it. He was afraid someone would come and force her hand, or ask what they were doing.

"I should have taught you. Taught everyone. I wanted ignorance, and then I got ignorance. What right do I have to complain that my tools are poor when I refused to spend the effort to get good ones?" She blinked several times, lost in her own thoughts. "I just wanted it to link us. Fate is an old bitch who spins a web and traps us all in it."

She released his hand, took a piece of knotted cord out of

her pocket. It had ten knots in it. Slowly, she undid four, her long white fingers working steadily. He wondered how she could bear the cold. He was in his twenties and his hands ached, but there she was, deftly untying the cord knot by knot with those long thin hands of hers, the fingers almost crawling to their task. When she was done she rubbed the cord in the red from the container, placed it back in her pocket. Turned to him with avid eyes.

"Power comes from many things. But I have no access to the sea, and no time to call it from the air or earth. Here is your choice. It's time for you to make it."

"What choice? What are you talking about you..." He managed to stop but she just laughed at him.

"Either you take off your shirt and kneel down here and I bleed you... not enough to kill you, I still need you for a while yet, but I will hurt you because your pain is what I need, or... well, we don't have to use pain." Her smile was a horrible thing to him, amused and tolerant in a way that said clearly that she could not care even slightly less what he chose.

"What, *here*?" He looked around at the snowy graveyard. There were a few black dots off in the distance, milling around graves. In the distance he could see the church where they'd had his parents' funeral. It had been raining that day, because of course it was, and he remembered the soggy walk to the graves. He always wondered why his father had been buried alone. Now he knew why, because *she* couldn't have cared less about the man. Her children were what mattered.

"Would location matter to you?" She reached up and undid the knot of hair that held her long grey-black tresses in check, let it fall down. She was pulling her coat off.

He swallowed. James Williams *hated* pain. Hated the very idea of it. When that bitch had kicked him in the side and he'd collapsed he'd honestly wished he could stab her in the heart for it, and when the other one broke his nose... he swallowed, looked at her as she was pulling her dress off in complete defiance of the cold, her weirdly smooth but terrifyingly thin body.

"I'll take the knife." His voice was shrill and hollow in his ears. She nodded, because it truly hadn't mattered to her at all, either way.

"Take off your shirt, then."

She spent several minutes cutting things into his back while he bit down on his wallet. He felt it squeal, left teeth marks in the leather. She made small cooing sounds and flicked the blade onto the graves every time she needed to clear it of his blood, worked something that felt like he was melting into the wounds. He would have shrieked but the feel of her cool hand in his hair and the cold wind that would occasionally blow over him somehow made it bearable.

"That's good." She cooed in his ear. "You're doing much better than I expected."

When she was done she let him slump over, his hands in the snow. She wiped at his back with something, he couldn't tell what, and then brought it to the graves. She was speaking but all he could hear or feel was his back, what felt like a wheel of scar tissue she must have given him.

"Roll over into the snow."

He did it and he *did* scream, managed to get to his feet as the cold and the pain combined into something so awful he didn't think it was possible. She let loose another of those cackles of hers as she pulled her clothing back on.

"What the fuck…"

"I just wanted to see if you'd do it."

She walked over, dressed again, and helped him get dressed.

"Why aren't I…"

"I made sure you wouldn't bleed too much. I still need you." Her hand in his hair again. "You did so well. You did very well, James."

He felt himself smile and loathed that he did it.

"What happens now?"

"We have other stops to make." She moved down the path. "The Rafiela plot is this way."

*

"I'm so much more comfortable here." Joe was lying in his own bed, back in his own rented house, after a day spent at school catching up on everything he'd missed. He was looking at Bishop, admiring him, really. "I mean, I appreciate Thomas letting us stay there…"

"You can hate being stuck in the middle of fucking nowhere, I won't mind."

"What gets me is it's not even that *far*. It's closer to here than Bristol is."

"Sure, if you have a boat or a plane or something. Otherwise it's *drive to Bristol, get on a ferry, ride to the Island*. And then you're suddenly in a place with one fucking store that charges you double for every fucking thing imaginable." Bishop had a lean but muscular build. Joe loved looking at it, at the golden hair dotting his shoulders and chest, the tawny patch just above his cock. He slid into the bed and pressed his ice-cold feet against Joe's legs and grinned when he yelped.

"Christ it's like cuddling up with the Snow Miser."

"Not all of me is." Joe was always amazed at how good Bishop was at kissing. He always felt like a slow, clumsy thing, but Bishop tilted his head back slightly and then made Joe's head spin and his lips almost burn, grazing the skin of his lower lip with his teeth. He felt Bishop's much warmer hand drifting down his stomach just as the phone started to ring.

"Should I stop?"

"Seri's here, she can get it, maybe it's David." Joe panted. "*Please* don't stop."

That got him one of Bishop's fantastic smiles. *Christ you're beautiful. You could do so much better than me. Why are you even here?* He tried to ignore that voice as Bishop's hand began drifting down again, felt it leaving a warm trail across the skin of his stomach, anticipation sending blood to harden him.

"*WHAT!?!?*"

Seri's voice, a full fledged shriek. Since she so rarely shrieked, Joe bolted up.

"Okay, *now* I'm stopping." Bishop sounded both concerned and frustrated at once. Joe could relate. He managed to pull a pair of underwear on before Seri started knocking on the door to his room.

"Joe?"

"Yeah. I'm decent." He looked over at Bishop, wrestling on a pair of jeans. He nodded. "Come on in."

Seri was crying. By itself that was unusual. Seri didn't cry often.

"What the hell happened? Who was that on the phone?"

"It was the police." She sat down on the edge of his bed, in her bathrobe and slippers. "They... I guess there were some vandals at the graveyard, St. Anne's."

Joe had heard the expression *his blood ran cold* a few times. Now he knew how that felt. It was as if he'd been dunked in a tank of water and then thrown onto a snowbank.

"Vandals?"

"Dad's grave, and aunt Paola's." She was dialing the phone in her hand. "I have to call Thea."

Inside the house in Cranston, two people were enjoying their alone time. Thomas hadn't minded having Thea's cousins in the house, really, nor had either of them really let it inhibit them much, but it was still always easier when there wasn't anyone around to worry about overhearing you.

Thea was at that exact moment engaged in very similar behavior to what Bishop had been, trailing little kisses down Thomas's neck and chest. He was panting.

"You make the best noises." She smiled, bit him very slightly. He was rasping now.

"You are *killing* me."

"Oh no. No, that won't do." The new cell phone on the table next to the bed began beeping at them. Thea frowned.

"Go ahead." Thomas was counting in his head, trying to remain calm. She slid across him, maintaining just enough physical contact to make him moan.

"That was fast, we just got me this thing. What's up?"

Thomas watched as her face went from smiling to frowning to scowling, completely changing everything. She pulled away and he tried very hard to focus and ignore the throbbing in his testicles. "Did they say when? No. No, I'll... we'll come over. We can all go up together. Yeah. No, thanks for calling, love. I'll be right there." She hung up the phone, put it down while staring at it.

"Thea?"

"Sorry. I, ah..." She twisted up her face for a moment. "My mom's grave. Something happened. Cops called Seri."

"What happened?"

"It's gone."

They got dressed without any further words. Thomas wanted to offer sympathy and Thea knew he did, but she couldn't take it at the moment and was grateful that he could tell that and didn't offer it. They drove the CRX south to Warwick, arriving at Joe and Seri's house not long after the call. It was getting darker out, heading towards nine PM.

Chapter Nineteen

Vandali

Seri opened the door and Thea hugged her, both of them fighting back tears. They locked arms together and walked inside, followed by Thomas, who closed the door behind them. He could see some signs that Joe had been practising warding around the house, a few alchemical symbols in the corners faintly glowing. He saw Bishop drinking a beer in the kitchen and nodded to him, got a nod back.

"So what did they tell you?" Joe was sitting on the couch and Seri sat down next to him, with Thea on the other side, still with her arm around Seri and Seri's around her.

"I guess some other graves got the same treatment. Six in all. A family plot, the Mancinis? He asked if I knew them, I said it sounded familiar."

"Shit, it does." Joe was scratching the back of his head. "Where do I know that name from?"

"The graveyard's closed now, right?"

"Yeah, why?"

"Because I want to see it." Thea had a look on her face Joe had seen a few times, the same look she'd gotten back when her mother had died and everyone had tried to keep her from looking inside the casket. She'd done it anyway, looking at the ligature marks that even the undertaker couldn't quite hide. "I want to see what happened."

"We could go up anyway." Thomas said. She looked up at him. "I'm sure we could get in pretty easily."

"They'll have more security..." Seri started.

"I'm not going to hop the fence." Thomas replied, trying to be gentle.

"We don't actually have to go there at all for that, do we?" Joe said. "I mean, the three of us, can't we just…" He wiggled his fingers and despite herself Thea laughed.

"Yeah, we'll play piano. That'll get it done."

"You know what I mean."

"It's probably a better idea than going up and doing something flashy." Thomas inclined his head. It was his general tendency to want to do something big, like the rite in front of the collapsed lodges, something huge and showy.

"Why is everybody here?" They all looked up to see Bry coming down the stairs. Seri had taken the girl in – she didn't know of any other family for her besides her awful brothers, and of course their evil grandmother. She was currently sleeping on a futon in Seri's room until they had a better plan. There was a storage room up there she wanted to convert. Thomas still found it a little weird to see the child dressed up in a pink jumper and pajama pants. "Why are you crying?"

"Something bad happened, little girl." Seri patted the couch and Bry came over and climbed into her arms, nestling in. "My daddy's grave… some bad people did something to it."

"I'm sorry."

"Thank you."

"I'm going to lose my mind trying to remember where I've heard the name Mancini before."

"My uncle Marco?" Bry looked over at Joe, clearly confused. "He's gone. Like mom and dad. How do you know uncle Marco? Or do you mean uncle Stephan?"

"What?" Joe was now focused fully on Bry. "What do you mean?"

"My mom had a sister, aunt Claudia. And then there was uncle Marco and uncle Stephan. They all died. I remember." Bry nodded while ticking this all off on her hand. "Uncle Marco always said 'I put the Man in Mancini' and then he'd laugh but no one else did. I tried to laugh just so he wouldn't feel bad, but… it wasn't funny, really."

"That's where I remember the name from." Joe was rubbing

his five o'clock shadow, which was on its way to a beard. "That ridiculous family reunion back in 88."

"Christ, that was awkward." Thea said, reaching over to rub Bry's hair. "Thank you, honey. You helped us figure something out."

"What did I say? Is this about uncle Marco?"

"It probably is." Seri bent down to kiss Bry's head. "I'll talk to you more tomorrow, but can you go back up? Try and get to sleep?"

"Yeah, but I gotta use the bathroom first."

"Go ahead and use the one down here, then come back. I'll take you up."

"Maybe a story?"

"Sure." Seri smiled. It seemed to be a good enough smile for Bry, who smiled back and went off to use the bathroom. "I can't tell if she's super well-adjusted or not, honestly."

"She's got you." Joe shrugged. "She's got us all, really."

"We have to look into getting her into school. DCYF is going to want to know how she ended up here, why her brothers aren't taking care of her, there's going to be…"

"One crisis at a time, Seri." Thea patted her cousin's back. "We'll cheat if we have to."

"I'm not sure we should. I'm not sure what the right thing to do is."

"Well, I'm a product of the idle rich, so, I can offer money for a lawyer but I'm useless when it comes to knowing how to keep a kid from being fucked up." Bishop came fully into the living room. "I can take her upstairs if you want to be down here."

"Come up with us. She likes you."

"And it gets me out of the way for the weird shit, so I am absolutely sold on this idea." As soon as Bry came out Seri took her hand and the three of them went upstairs, leaving Joe, Thomas and Thea in the living room.

"So how do we do this?"

"Got a map?" Thomas suggested. "I've done some map work before."

"When?" Thea looked surprised.

"When I was trying to find who killed my parents. In

retrospect I get why I couldn't, but at the time it was driving me crazy."

"I have a road guide out in my car." Joe stood up. "I'll be right back."

*

They'd sat in her Impala watching the house. James was driving. She seemed to like it when he drove instead of her. The way she held herself it was hard to tell what she was thinking. She made a sound when she saw Willrew and her granddaughter come out of the house, get into a small car and drive off.

"She looks like Raifa." He had no idea who Raifa was. So he didn't interject. He was learning not to do that. His back still throbbed from when she'd cut him up. It had all closed up – that glop she'd put on it, maybe – and he felt strange, almost like when he'd gotten a contact high back in high school.

They waited a few minutes after the CRX drove away. James cleared his throat.

"Are we going to do anything?"

"No. Well, yes, but no. You're going to do something, and then I'm going to do something separately." She opened the door and stepped out into the night, as always seemingly unmoved by the cold. He followed, and they walked up towards the house. Her eyes widened as they walked up the driveway.

"My word."

"Sorry?"

"You can see it, yes?" She gestured to the house. There was a wide concrete slab with a lot of junk at the end of the driveway, and that caught James' eyes first. There was a tool set and a workbench and a whole lot of other gear, he realized it looked like there had been a garage on that spot and now it was ruined, like a giant foot had stepped on the roof. Someone had clearly worked to clean it up, and just as clearly hadn't figured out what to do with the remains yet. But he eventually turned and looked at the house.

"You mean the squiggles?" She gave him a look, equal parts

exasperation and pity.

"I knew he had wards. I felt them, when I sent the Lion. But this! Oh, I sense our girl's hand in this, they've been reinforced. Several times." Her lips curled up in a smile. "She reminds me of me."

That ain't a good thing, James was more than aware he shouldn't say. Still, a little tremor of pity for the giant went through him. *Maybe he's lucky the old bitch is like to kill him first.*

"So what's the plan, then? Morg and I..."

"You'll be able to go inside." She smiled. "What I did today will make sure of that."

He gave her a look, but her expression was at once imperious and affable, and he knew he didn't have a choice. He walked up, tried the door, wasn't surprised it was locked. Luckily, working in salvage over the years had taught him a few things, like how to use the set of bump keys he had on him. He checked the door's lock – it looked old, at least no newer than the 40s. After trying two of the ten he had, the third on the ring slid in and he bumped it open in two tries. If they'd been *home* they'd have heard him, but they weren't.

The door swung open and he took a breath and stepped over the threshold.

His back caught on something, like a web he couldn't see, and then the marks on his back began to scream at him. He barely realized it was happening before he seized up, knocked to his knees by pain.

Then there was a sound like a car backfire and the first mark exploded, blood staining his shirt. He shrieked, weeping and terrified as the next one went up as well, the rest of them now so horribly hot that he was afraid his clothing would burn off of him.

She swept past him. Didn't even bother to look down to determine if he was all right. Just walked into the house, looked around. Stood in the kitchen for a moment, sniffing the air. As long as the sigils she'd carved into James held, the wards would think they were still unbroken. She had time.

Well, unless he died. But she was willing to take that risk.

She walked around. There were books everywhere, some she'd read, others mass market things that she wouldn't have bothered with. Some were completely unrelated as far as she could tell. But she knew well enough that there was a mythology to the state, to its people, and so she noted them as she moved on.

Thomas' son's son, and my daughter's daughter. How you mock back, Atropos. I made sport with your rules, and you laugh at all my efforts in return. She found herself wondering what it was like for them. Robia Dassalia enjoyed her body so much that the idea of leaving it horrified her, and she wondered if her granddaughter was the same. She walked into the room they were clearly sharing, smelled the air. It didn't reek, but the sheets were scattered and there were condoms.

More books. A few old notebooks, mostly about plants. It seemed Thomas' son had been terrified of what his father had told him, had prepared for worse to come. *If only he'd listened and let me kill you then.*

Eventually she went upstairs, turning to see James now lying on his side staring blankly at the ceiling, gasping. Another sigil had erupted, but there were three left, and they seemed to be holding for now. She was impressed at his fortitude. Then again, he shared blood with the Willrew boy, and that helped him. Some of the wards were confused by that. She expected the ones Thea had set up were the ones that weren't – a woman who loves someone knows that person in a way he or she does not.

The upstairs was fairly deserted. There was a bedroom, not currently in use with a stripped down bed and piles of books. Most of them mass market trash. Some of them were interesting for all that. When she first moved to Rhode Island Robia had found the state's native mythology fascinating, both the myths it told about itself and the ones written by and about it. One writer in particular, a Providence native, had concocted a large shared myth with others all over the country, and even beyond it. Robia was fairly well read, and the stories themselves were at best potboilers, written for lurid thrills (although she enjoyed *The Vengeance of Nitocris,* perhaps because it contained the germ of its author's future works) and simply not to her taste. She'd seen enough real horror to realize that the mind could absorb much and retain itself.

Clearly the boy had read the books. Even more clearly, one story in particular was highlighted and annotated. He'd circled a pair of incantations – *could it work? Must find out what essential salts are* – and she flipped through the story. It matched her own interests, and she smiled at the irony of it.

We're not so different.

She was still planning to kill him, of course.

It was as if they'd abandoned the use of these rooms. The next room was even more deserted, it lacked even furniture. It wasn't a work room of any kind – no sort of preparations or protections, it was simply a deserted room. There was a taste of fear in it. She turned away and walked down the stairs.

James had pulled himself to a standing position and was leaning against the counter in the kitchen, his shirt ruined by blood. His eyes were hollow with pain, but she saw no sign that he'd lost another sigil. She smiled and walked down the stairs to the basement.

Here she found a treasure.

She could actually see it before she finished descending the steps. It writhed and pulsed, alive with will and purpose, a grand and laborious construction of runes and sigils and alchemical symbols and even things she didn't recognize. In that moment she felt wonder and even admiration for her enemy. The boy had clearly dedicated much of his time and effort to this.

She ran a finger along the path of symbols, studying the aethyrs involved. He'd read Dee's system, probably in one of those mass market books upstairs. When *she* had started trying to understand what she'd become there had been fewer options. In those days she'd made use of libraries, the Athenaeum, used bookstores, and of course she'd had her connections after she'd made contact with them.

Kids today, she thought, and smiled to herself.

After studying the handiwork for a few more minutes, she realized why he'd never tried to do it. The amount of resistance to what he was trying to accomplish was staggering, and he'd accounted for it, worked it into his plan. This incantation would almost certainly kill him. It was *designed* to kill whoever used it, to channel their life into the working. But that wouldn't be enough.

No, not enough at all.

She reached out her hands and took the two urns. As the focus point of the rite, they'd been suffused in it for months, were inextricably linked to it. She could make use of them. She wrapped them in a shirt hanging in the laundry room, took another she thought might fit James as she headed upstairs.

When she came up the stairs James was on his knees, gasping. Two of the sigils on his back had given way, leaving him broken, in so much pain he couldn't see. There was blood on his face, running down from his mouth – he'd convulsed and chewed holes in his tongue and cheeks. She walked past him, placed the urns in the car, and then walked back inside.

There was a small cat watching her. She saw it, but it offered her no hostility so she let it be. She didn't inflict pain merely for her own amusement. She did it because it got her what she wanted. Taking the urns would do that more effectively than anything else.

"James. Stand, please."

He did it, but only because she tapped into her will and forced his muscles to move. She didn't resent him for it – she doubted he could hear her. Using that will she walked him outside and let him collapse into the snow, this time on purpose to cool his ruined back and dissipate the power the wards had set into his flesh. She worked quickly to peel his ruined shirt off of him and check the markings. Amazingly, they weren't deep wounds, just damage to the surface, the skin. Bloody but not nearly as bad as they could have been.

"Can you hear me?"

He moaned but nodded. She bent and kissed him, cradled his face in her hands. He kissed back, not really cognizant of what she was doing, just feeling his ravaged flesh closing up as she pulled his pain out of him, stored it away. Her hair grew darker, her face smoothed out.

She had his blood on her lips when she pulled away.

"Stand for me now."

This time he did it himself, on legs that threatened to melt away and pitch him to the ground. She helped him dress in the black T-shirt she'd retrieved from the basement. It was huge on him. He felt like he'd aged ten years, his throat hoarse from screaming, and she let him slide into the passenger seat, still smiling faintly. He'd proved so useful.

I should have taken a more direct hand with the boys years ago.

Across two streets and up a small embankment there was a park consisting of three baseball diamonds, bordered by a public swimming pool and a bit of forest around an old pond. On the ledge of that embankment, a white-haired man was watching Robia Dassalia through a scope. The scope was attached to an old Remington .308 that had been in the closet for years, a rifle Morgan Williams Sr. had almost forgotten he had when he died.

The scope was lined up perfectly, as she walked around the car, stopped to check on whatever she'd stowed in the trunk. He could put a bullet right in her back. His finger started to squeeze.

And if it doesn't work?

He didn't have an answer for that one. He'd never tried to shoot her. Of course he hadn't. Before last Christmas he'd never tried to kill *anyone*. He'd kept his monster of a brother fed and out of sight, kept his other monster of a brother occupied, kept her at arm's length with groveling obedience. The crosshairs were lined up on the middle of her spine. He kept squeezing.

He imagined the gunshot, the echo of the shot as it bounced off of nearby houses. The whine of the bullet in the air.

Imagined it not working.

There were so many ways it might not work. Maybe she didn't count as alive, and so the bullet would just pass through and blow some dust out. Maybe it would just go wide because she told it to, or the gun would explode in his hand. He still remembered seeing Jimmy nearly lose his hand because that woman – Thea, her name was Thea – simply wanted it to. What would happen to him if a rifle blew up in his hands? Or maybe the bullet would get all the way there, turn around mid flight, and come back to shoot *him*.

His finger felt like it was pulling a car up a hill, not squeezing down on a small metal trigger.

It's not going to work and worse it'll give away where I am.

He took a breath, steadied himself.

She got into the car, started it, backed out of the driveway. He watched through the scope, watched them both drive off. Jimmy looked like shit. He had no idea what they'd done inside the house, hell, he didn't even know how they'd gotten in. It looked like Jimmy had paid the price for it. He stood up, shouldered the rifle and walked to his truck. He knew where they were staying, he didn't have to follow them.

It's your fault. He slid the rifle behind the seat and started the engine, thought about it. He'd left Jimmy, driven off, gone to a hotel. Stewed. By the time he'd decided that idiot or not Jimmy was his brother, she'd already moved into his house. *His* house. His name on the fucking deed. They'd left everything to him, it was his, and she was in there using it and he couldn't get her out.

He picked up the cell phone and dialed a number he'd gotten on a trip to Newport Creamery.

"Hello?"

"This Mercy Brown?"

"Indeed I am. Who might... oh, I think I remember your voice. It's very distinctive. Morgan, was it?"

"Yeah."

"Well, what can I do for you?"

"I know where she is." His voice echoed off of the roof of the cab, the windows fogging up from his breath and body heat. "Just spent the day following her around."

"And what did you see her doing?"

"Why don't we meet up? There's stuff I want from you, too."

"How do I know what you know is worth my time?"

"Because otherwise I wouldn't be putting myself in biting range of you." She chuckled.

"You're an interesting boy, aren't you, Morgan?"

"I'm twenty-four."

"It's all relative, I suppose. Where are you now?" He gave her the address in Cranston. "Why don't we meet at the Baskin Robbins up Reservoir Ave? I adore ice cream."

"You can eat?"

"Not productively, but I can still taste things." She seemed amused, and he wasn't sure if he should be offended or not. "I'll see you soon, Morgan."

He hung up and put the truck in drive. There was a sinking sensation in the pit of his stomach, because he knew he was in too deep and he likely wasn't coming out of this one. But it was late, and the sun was gone from the sky, and he had to pick which devil he hated more.

Chapter Twenty

Monsters

Thea didn't want to see it, but she ended up seeing it anyway.

She hated to admit it but she'd been in shock after her father died. She could see that now. At the time she'd been *I'm fine, everything is fine, I saw it coming* but looking at the graves had brought it home – she *wasn't* fine.

They'd sat around the kitchen table with the map book open to Cranston and they'd focused on the idea of the place. They hadn't linked hands. Thea didn't always mind that, but it kind of made things feel like playing with an Ouija board and she hated that crap, always had. Blame it on actually seeing ghosts for years. When the image appeared over the table she'd been surprised at the fidelity of it. It was like looking through a window, except the window was above a table.

Her father's stone was pushed over, as was her aunt Meredith's, Paolo's wife. She didn't remember the woman very well, aside from her being very huggy. She'd always had some small piece of candy on her, possibly a habit learned from trying to wrangle her twins, and she always cooed and liked to brush Thea's hair out of her eyes. *You look just like Seri did at that age*. She'd said that a lot.

Her eyes watered up and she grimaced remembering it.

Seri had made the arrangements for Gregory Mendel. Thea hadn't realized she'd made sure he was buried next to her mother. She felt the urge to go hug her, thank her for it, but she didn't. She focused on what she was seeing. Two gravestones pushed over, that could have been the work of random vandals.

The two graves that were ripped open, with mounds of displaced dirt and shattered caskets, that seemed less like vandalism. She was breathing through her nose, trying not to let emotion overwhelm her. Her mother's body. Her uncle's, too. She had no doubt what they'd see if they switched to view the Mancini's graves. More empty graves.

She stood and walked away, looking out the window into the back yard. It was still somewhat torn up from when she'd helped bring Joe back. She couldn't see much, though, with the image of an open grave floating in front of her eyes.

Eventually she looked over to see Thomas was still looking at the image, studying it. A flare went up her back at that. *What the fuck is he looking at? It's just a mess. Just the people I loved torn out of the ground. Just everything awful shoved in our faces, everything that bitch took from us.*

She walked over to stand next to him, tried to sound calm.

"See anything you like?"

"What?" He pulled his attention back. Joe hissed and let go and the image faded out.

"You were looking at it. What was so interesting?"

"There were flecks of something orange-red on the gravestones." He frowned, half of his attention on what he had seen, half on the slowly dawning awareness that something was wrong. "I was trying…"

"Yeah. I guess it's easy when it's not the people you cared about." *What the hell are you doing? Why are you mad at him, he didn't…* "Let me know if you Encyclopedia Brown anything useful. I'm going out back."

She turned and walked away before she said anything else. She wasn't even sure why she was so pissed at him. Why *would* it affect him like it did her? It wasn't *his* family. She slammed the door despite not particularly wanting to, walked around in the snow for a few minutes regretting not having grabbed a coat.

I wasn't ready for you to die. Not any of you. I wasn't ready.

It hurt and she didn't know what to do with it. She'd been so sure she was over it, that her father's death had just been the end of an awful chapter, but seeing his grave again for the first time since his funeral had proved her a liar. He'd only been dead five months. There was an urge to scream *it's not fair* and she knew that was stupid and childish and weak and she hated it the more because it wouldn't go away.

He met her. Fell in love with her. She loved him back. And then they both died and it's over, it's over and that fucking old thing won't even let them be dead together. They can't even have that.

"Hey."

She looked up to see Seri coming outside. Seri, as the smart cousin, had put on a jacket.

"Oh. Hey. I was just…"

"I heard the door slam." She came closer. "You want to talk about it?"

"No. God no, I don't. I don't want to talk about it because I don't want it to be real, not any of this, I don't want to mourn anyone anymore. I'm so fucking *tired* of it, Seri." She fought to keep her voice level. "She took my mom and your dad."

"You know it was her?"

"In my gut I do." She sighed, let a little of it out like steam from a radiator. "She's not going to stop taking things from us."

"See, I don't *get* it." Seri walked closer, standing an arm's length away from Thea. "She wasn't *always* awful. I remember visits where she'd smile and she had these weird licorice tasting candy things and… am I crazy? Do I just have delusions about this?"

"I remember one time." Thea was looking down into the snow. "She came to the house. She was all smiles. Mom was confused. They seemed to have a nice talk, but near the end she got weird and abstract and she left suddenly." She remembered the woman in her vision, the one at the carousel. How much she looked like Seri, or even her mother, or… "I don't know what it means. I don't know what she is."

"She's not…" Seri put her hands to her forehead and stared intently, then made a sound that resembled a bad impression of fireworks. "Y'know, a wizard or whatever?"

"I think she was." Thea laughed. "You missed your calling as a charades player."

"I do my best."

They stayed there for a little bit longer, Thea wrapping her arm around Seri's shoulder.

"I may have been a bit of a bitch in there."

"You were upset." Seri kissed her forehead. "You're passionate about things."

"This all sounds like shorthand for 'we all knew you were a bitch already' Seri."

"Well, I wouldn't exactly say we were *ignorant* of it…" Thea hip-bumped her and she laughed. "It's fine. Let's go inside. I'm freaking cold and I have a jacket on."

"I keep wondering if I should just bind a fire elemental to myself so I'm always warm."

"Can you do that?"

"*We* could do it."

"Oh, leave me out of that shit. I don't even like that I can see it now."

Thea didn't say *Seri, I'd feel better if I knew you could defend yourself from this shit* because it wouldn't do anything but push a guilt trip. Seri didn't want it, and it was all about wanting. No matter how weird and awful it got, deep down Thea had *always* wanted it, and just hadn't known what it was. Her phone buzzed inside her pocket, she fished it out.

"Talk fast, I'm cold."

"Hey, uh, Thea? It's me, Evvie, you gave me this number."

"I do remember that, yes. What can I do for you, please say nothing, it's been a hell of a night."

"Well, you remember that thing we talked about? Uh… I'm not sure how much to say on the phone…"

"Go ahead and tell me about the vampires." Thea leaned against the house, nodded to Seri, who walked inside with a concerned look on her face. "If someone's tapping the call then let them know up front that I'm a crazy person. What news?"

"Well, I talked to him, and he just called me back. He got in touch with his contact, and she'll meet with you two. Tonight if you can swing it."

"Sure." She looked inside. Thomas was sitting with his hand

on his chin, playing absently with his beard the way he did when he was tense. "Where and when?"

Inside the house, Seri checked in on Joe, who looked pale and frail and older.

"Bad?"

"So bad." She put her arm around his shoulder, and he reached up and touched her hand with his. "They... dad and Aunt Paola are *gone*. Mom's grave, and uncle Greg's, they..." He stopped talking because he'd started retching into his mouth, fought it back. "Why the hell would she do this?"

"I don't know." Seri hugged him, and he squeezed her hand in return. "Why don't you go up? Bishop and Bry are watching *The Land Before Time*."

"Well, shit, why not, I haven't wept openly yet today." He stood up, turned to look at Thomas who was still in full brood. "Hey, about before..."

"It's okay. I'm fine."

"I just wanted to say I know you weren't being flip about it."

"Thanks." Thomas turned his attention to Joe and Seri, both of whom were staring at him. "I'm not going to just run off into the night because she got sharp with me."

"Good."

"Very much so because she does it a *lot*."

"It's kind of her thing." Joe saw Thea finally walk back inside. "And on that note I'm outta here before she realizes I was badmouthing her."

"I just assume you always are."

"Safe bet, really." He kissed Thea's cheek, held her gaze for a moment. "We're around if you need."

"Same." She sat down in the chair he'd vacated. "So, Evvie just called. We've got a meetup with the Kolchaks if we want it."

"Kolchak?"

"You know, the Night Stalker?"

"Yeah, *I* know it, I'm just wondering how *you* do, that show's 20 years before your time."

"You're what, less than two years older than me? It's before your time too." She let herself smile. "My dad and I used to stay up late and watch reruns on Channel 12."

"Huh. I used to do that too." He leaned back in the chair. "Where and when?"

"Tonight. I got a phone number we can call, set it up. I'm a little nervous about leaving everyone alone here, though."

"You think she might come here?"

"I don't even know. I'd like to try and ward the place up."

"Makes..." Thomas had been about to say *sense*. Instead, he grunted, his face twisted up. Thea felt a weird flush, like a sudden rush of warm air, and then icy coldness in her hands. She looked over at him, confused.

"Was that..."

"The wards." He stood up suddenly, almost knocking the chair over. "I have to..."

"*We* have to."

"We shouldn't leave everyone here alone."

"We already did this dance once. She doesn't want *us* dead." Thea turned to Seri. "Go upstairs. Joe's been studying, tell him to ward this place up like fucking Fort Knox. Stay near a phone. If we have to I'll have a dragon fly us back or something."

"You can do that?"

"I *will* do it." She kissed her cousin and grabbed her jacket from the table. "Let's go."

The walk to the car was quiet. Thea fought with herself up until they were both in and the engine was started, waited for them to be on the road. Thomas was driving which meant he was distracted by what was happening.

"Anything on the wards?"

"They're still up." He was staring straight ahead, driving. "I don't know what that was."

"Look... I shouldn't have, before, I was upset." Her hands were balled up into fists.

"It's okay."

"Is it?"

"I saw what you saw. I'd have been just as upset." He rolled his window down to get cold air blowing in. "Although the Encyclopedia Brown crack was harsh."

"I liked him as a kid. I guess I've always had a thing for nerdy boys." He laughed a little. "Thomas, you don't think..."

"I do, honest. All the time. Too much, maybe."

"Maybe she did all that just to get us out of the house?"

"No. It was... there was a rite performed there. She did something. I don't know what, but something. That doesn't mean she didn't take advantage of us leaving. But the wards are still up." He went through the various sigils he'd worked into the house, the star with the burning eye in the center, the peacock tail, the wheels on fire. The stylized bat symbol, the orphan who seeks justice. He could feel them, but he'd felt them shudder, like they'd discharged. If they'd discharged why were they still up? "Christ, you're right, I really *am* up my own asshole."

"Hey, I didn't say that. I don't *think* that." She wanted to reach out to him but his body language said not to, the way his shoulders were tensed. He was keyed up.

It took about twenty minutes to get from Joe and Seri's place to his. They pulled into the driveway and immediately saw the stain on the ground near the back door, the scrap of ruined cloth. The back door was open. Jericho Whatley was laying on his back in front of the door.

"That's who triggered the ward." Thomas said as he walked over and picked Jer up by his collar. His voice was that thick bass growl, the one he used when he was on the verge of an explosion. "Thea, please go check inside?"

"On it." The wards knew her, let her pass right through. Thomas stayed outside, questioning his neighbor's eldest in a low tone. She immediately saw more blood, a bloody handprint on the counter, stains on the floor. She took stock.

The door to the basement was open.

"Oh fuck no. No no no." She ran down the stairs, terrified of what she'd find.

The urns were gone. The rite, so long left charged, ready to go was now dead with the focal items removed. The sigils, runes, symbols of Thomas' year of isolation and madness were still there, but the urns were gone.

She'd taken his parents too.

Her gut lurched and she forced herself to not get sick as she realized she now had to go upstairs and tell him. It was as if each step increased her weight twice over, by the time she'd reached the top step dread was actively trying to push her back down the stairs. She saw him outside shoving Jer Whatley back towards his house, and she didn't even bother to register the ratlike face of the boy as he tried to subtly gawk at her.

He took one look at her face and stepped into the room, clearly concerned.

"What is it? You look…"

"Thomas, I'm so sorry." She wished so badly that she hadn't snapped at him before. It was minor, really. But now it felt huge. "The urns… they're gone. She took them."

He didn't scream or throw a fit. He stood there, his face utter confusion.

"Why?" He closed the back door and looked at the blood in his kitchen. "This doesn't make sense, if the wards discharged…"

He sat down on one of the kitchen chairs, looking at the blood. Then he looked up to her.

"She's out-thinking us. She's out there somewhere and she's doing shit that I don't understand. I don't know what the rules are." He sounded young and so very tired. She sat down next to him. "I don't get the *point*."

"Maybe there is no point. Maybe she's just crazy."

"Maybe. But I don't think so. What she said to my grandfather… 'Someone has to die. But it doesn't have to be you.' I don't know. I don't *know*." His breathing was ragged and the sound of it hurt because it reminded her of standing out in Joe and Seri's backyard, feeling helpless. "Your mom, Joe and Seri's dad, the Mancini's, those are her people. It's creepy and sick, sure, but… hell, my parents made me get them cremated, there's no *bodies* anymore, I needed a transmutation spell just to cope with that, I can't…"

"It's okay." She put her hand on his face, wanting to comfort, and then when his hand came up to touch her side she started to shake. "I'm here. You're here."

"I'm sorry, that I wasn't... I just wanted to fix it, somehow. But it's not fixable." He put his head to hers. "I'm sorry, Thea."

"You didn't do it." She wanted to scream, to smash things, to find that old crone and rip her withered guts out, spread them out across a field and let crows eat them. She wanted comfort, and to offer it. "We didn't do this. It's not our fault."

"I wonder what would have happened if I'd stayed over there. If they'd be alive now, or if they'd have died and I'd have had to come home and..." He looked at her and she felt very much like hiding her face, almost wished her hair was long again so she could cover up behind it. "And we would never have met, maybe, and I can't want that. If someone told me I could undo everything that's happened, and the cost was you..." He shook his head.

"Jesus, Tommy. Getting real on me here."

"It's what it is." He didn't shrug or look away. She worked her dry mouth, trying to get it moist enough to talk. Looked again at the handprint on the counter.

"I'm scared. I hate that I'm scared. That she scares me, that this... I want to be brave all the time, I want to never feel afraid or small, never want to go hide. But I do. And I can't. And..." The sound of the bracelet on her arm tapping against the counter, dim light from outside playing over her shoulder, casting a shadow in the kitchen. "I think of this place as our place."

"I do too."

"I think of you as... I'm not even twenty yet. Less than a decade ago I was still playing with an EZ Bake Oven. I think my Big Wheel is still in storage at the house. Now I'm an orphan and I have a house to get rid of and I need a job and I love a man and... just so much *shit* out of nowhere and I just have to deal with it. Monsters and blood and death. Graves being ripped open. I'm scared, and I know you're scared too, I can see it, I want to tell you things will be all right when I don't even believe it myself."

"We're quite a pair." He was smiling, that faint smile she'd gotten familiar with in so short a period of time. "You're right. I'm frigging terrified. Mostly by all the shit I don't understand."

"It's *all* shit I don't understand. I have to pay taxes now." She laughed at the look on his face. "Didn't occur to you?"

"No, I have a big tax bill for that floating farm. Trust pays it, but I still had to look at it. It was… yeah." He laughed. "Eventually I gotta sell *something* and get a real job."

"After we deal with… this." She gestured at the blood stain.

"After that." He nodded, stood up. She decided to say the last thing she'd been holding back.

"Tommy?"

"Yeah."

"I really do love you. A lot." She was blinking a little. "It would hurt if you were… you know what I mean. Right?"

"I do." He took her hand and they stayed like that for a little while. Then she stood up and kissed him, like she was afraid to pop him and be alone, a gentle thing brushing across his skin. His return kiss wasn't so gentle, and she let herself focus on that, on the reality of it and him and her, the tangible warmth and scent of their bodies together.

"Okay," she breathed when they stopped. "As good as this is, and as much as my lower regions are getting ideas, I think we have to deal with how the fuck she got in." She tried very hard not to notice his erection, tried not to roll her hips against it. His groan told her she hadn't quite succeeded.

"Yeah. Yeah." He backed away. Took a moment to inhale, exhale, stare at the handprint on the counter. Thought about things for a while. Snapped his fingers as it came to him.

"I got it."

"Got what?"

"The blood. It's not her blood." He walked over to the ward for the flaming wheel he'd put up. "This one is keyed to me. Me and anyone I tell it to let in. That's how you and Seri and Joe and Bish can get in, and that's how *you* brought Evvie in."

"Makes sense so far."

"The ward thought it was me."

"And how did she do that?"

"She brought in *almost* me." He pointed to the blood. "Someone close enough to me to fool the ward, someone whose blood goes back to the same source. We know she had kids with my grandfather. We know she desecrated *two* sets of graves today."

"So, what, did she send one of *them* in?"

"No. I think Bry and her brothers are my cousins." He was pacing now. She'd seen it before, when they'd discussed how to improve the resurrection rite. "There were two sets of Mancini twins. But I think one of those sets, the one with Bry's mom, they were actually Willrews by blood. My half-aunts. So any children of theirs..."

"And she did what? Close to you isn't *actually* you. And *I* did some of these wards..."

"And he'd be *your* cousin too."

"So she what, made a skeleton key to our wards out of..." She paused, considering it. It made a certain kind of sense. If you squinted. She could see the old woman doing it. "So the blood is because she took this poor bastard and used him like a piece of aluminum foil to bridge a dead fuse?"

"Yeah, exactly." He nodded. His smile was back. "So it's got to be one of the two brothers helping her."

"Well, it's probably not the blond. He was *pissed*."

"What about the other one?"

"He was pretty terrible." She considered it. "Not too smart. I laid him out with his own stupid spell. I could have made him dip his junk in honey and wave it in a bear's face if I wanted." She snorted. "But that's the thing. He learned one spell and he used it to talk women out of their pants. She'd terrify him." She rubbed her arms, cold even though the room was warm. "She terrifies *me* and I have a backbone and a moral compass."

"Table it for now." He started digging around under the sink. "I'm going to clean this shit up. You should call our new vampire friends and set up the meeting."

"Great."

"If you want, I can call them and..."

"Oh fuck no, I'm down with you cleaning up the blood. That shit's nasty." She took her cell phone out, dialing the number from memory. Thea had a very good memory. "Of course, we could just invite them over and they'd…"

"No." He pulled out a bottle of Pine Sol.

*

Morgan Williams watched in utter fascination as Mercy Brown ate an ice-cream cone.

"Something wrong?"

"Depends on your definition of wrong."

"Oh, you're being male." She smirked, let her tongue slide up the side of the chocolate ice cream. "Would you really want to experience that with someone like me?"

"You're a hard person to get a bead on." He considered it. "Up until you used me as a snack I probably would be happy with it."

"Aren't you a flatterer?"

"I'm a dude in his twenties who just lost his job, I'm not kidding myself about how attractive *any* woman is going to find me." He considered his work pants and t-shirt.

"This is nice. I should get out more."

"Yeah, I'm sure this is going to go swimmingly."

"Swimmingly?" She laughed again. "So she didn't see you, did she?"

"If she did she didn't act like it."

Mercy licked her ice cream cone again and considered it. Being dead had its problems – for one thing, eating did absolutely nothing for her. She didn't even pass things she ate, they just seemed to disintegrate inside her, perhaps utterly destroyed by whatever made her what she was. But she could still *taste*. And she loved to taste things, loved to wallow in sensation. It was the best lie ever, she thought, her dead body pretending to be alive.

She looked over at Morgan again. He wasn't like Stuart. Stuart had been shy and unsure of himself and timid and yet, idealistic and hopeful. Death had changed him, but his core remained, stubbornly refusing to become the kind of monster she was. Mercy liked that about him. She was fond of Stuart. She didn't think she'd ever be fond of Morgan that way, but he'd make an *excellent* vampire. Strong willed, family minded, willing and capable of violence, and not deluded about his own ability. And underneath the caked on dirt and terrible sense of style, really not bad looking.

She gave the ice cream cone another lick just to watch his blood move around. Mercy had been born and had died in rural Exeter a century earlier. She'd died without really getting to know many men. Maybe that was why she liked playing with them so much. Even sex, which was so much *work* when you were dead – so much easier and more pleasant to just feed, ultimately, but Mercy still liked it. Liked feeling their orgasm.

"So what now?" Morgan was watching the door.

"She said they'd be here in a few minutes."

"Last time I saw her it didn't go well."

"But you're *family*." She snickered at the look on his face. "The more I learn about this twisted clan of yours the better I feel about mine, and mine's all walking corpses who drink people's blood."

"Yeah, great." He stiffened seeing the Camaro pull into the parking lot. The giant got out first. *Jesus, he's almost as big as Byron was. Maybe not as tall, but...* He hadn't even seen the guy in action, but the fact that he was alive after going toe to toe with Byron, *and* that he'd somehow shrunk him down to normal again, that was intimidating. Thea got out next, and she was both less frightening and *more* frightening, because he'd seen her in action and knew she was the real deal. The two of them were holding hands. It would have been cute if not for the looks on their faces.

I gotta get laid.

Mercy kept merrily eating her ice cream cone. Morgan admired her ability to just not give a shit about anything, he wished he had it. Maybe being dead wasn't so bad if nothing scared you anymore. He was beyond fucking tired of being scared all the time.

Mercy didn't look up until they were inside and sitting down at the booth.

"Well hello again."

"You're aware that I know you told her where to find me last time."

"I told you why I was looking for you." She licked her cone. "And this must be Thea? You're quite lovely. I can see the family resemblance."

"Up front, the best way to get on my good side is *not* to remind me of that fact." Thea didn't even try to hide the bristling. "Also your taste in company is interesting."

"Right, you and Morgan have met already. Well, I shan't waste time on introductions, then." She suddenly took a large bite of the cone, taking most of the ice cream in one go. Morgan winced a little. "Stuart tells me you want to know where to find her. Morgan here has been following her around."

They both turned to stare at Morgan.

"Right. So by now you've noticed she was in your house."

"Along with your brother." Morgan wished he could *not* be intimidated by how deep the guy's voice was, how it seemed to come from a giant bass speaker inside his chest.

"Yeah." Morgan nodded. "She's been dragging him around with her ever since she moved into my house."

"You *live* with her?" Thea didn't like Morgan, but she wouldn't wish that on anyone, not him, not even his brother.

"No. Fuck no. You kidding me? I'd be dead by now. Jimmy's got a finely honed sense of survival." He snorted, took a sip of the soda Mercy'd bought for him. "I don't know what's going on in there, but he was always good at making himself useful."

They exchanged looks but didn't say anything to that. The big dude spoke, still like a subwoofer on steroids. Hell, maybe *he* took steroids.

"Where's your house?"

"Here." Morgan handed over his driver's license. "You can write it down or whatever."

Thea had produced a pen and a small notebook from inside her pants pocket and did exactly that, then they handed the license back.

"So, uh… how'd *you* know about Jimmy? Some kind of weird magic thing?"

"He bled all over my kitchen." It was a very flat delivery, neither gleeful nor angry, just like he was telling someone about bad traffic conditions or tomorrow's weather. "Not enough to kill him, but a decent amount."

"Right." Morgan was shocked to find himself caring. Jimmy was an asshole. He never stopped talking back, he'd taken up with *her*, he was constantly getting Morgan in trouble. But he was still his brother, and he was his responsibility, and he'd walked away and now she was living in his house doing God knew what to him. He took another sip to compose himself. "I saw him come out. He was still breathing then."

"How'd you see any of it?"

"You know that park near your place? The one slightly uphill? I was over there. Saw it all."

Thomas merely nodded. He did know that park, and it would work well enough for that. He'd used to hide on the lip of the grass and watch the cars drive by his house. You could see right up his driveway from there. Something to consider.

"So, are we all happy, then?" Mercy chirped up. "I could spring for ice cream."

"What?" Thea furrowed her forehead. "Are you for real?"

"Of course not. I'm over a hundred years old, I know how ridiculous this is. But it doesn't benefit us any to get too deeply involved in your little Witch Spat or whatever it is you're doing." She finished off her ice cream cone, sighing as the last of the cold and the waffle cone vanished. "Eventually we'll have to deal with the winner, yes? But right now it benefits us most to stay out of the way and let you get on with killing each other."

"I could just take you out right now."

"Indeed you could. All sorts of inventive threats. Your, ah, whatever should we call her? Opponent? She made similar threats." Mercy met Thea's eyes. "My family has been in this state since the 1890s and we haven't swarmed the place with monstrosities. We want what you want. Peace. Order. A place to raise our children. We made a deal with *her* because it suited us both. It could benefit you just as much."

"If we win."

"Of course. We're hardly going to pick sides and risk pissing off the victor. We told her where to find you. Now we tell you where to find her. Everybody is equally offended and equally in our debt." She let the mask of affability drop, just a little. "Also, we're not all Stuart. You'd find I can put up significantly more of a fight than he can."

"Thea." Thomas put his hand on her shoulder, not restraining her, just letting her know he was there. She nodded slightly to him, leaned back a little in her chair. "So what now?"

"I was serious about the ice cream." Mercy let herself relax. She *could* fight, but really didn't want to. Not here, anyway, it was one of her favorite places. "You know, we *could* all end up fast friends. I'm told I'm quite engaging."

"By who?"

"By the other bloodsucking night monsters I spend most of my time with. Who else?" Thea couldn't help it, she snorted a laugh. Mercy inclined her head in recognition of it. "So, any takers?"

"I think we're going to have to pass." Thea stood up. "Places to see. People to go."

Thomas slid upwards and they turned to leave, but then he stopped and turned back.

"Bry is doing well. We're all trying to make sure... well. She said you were the only one who tried to treat her the way she wanted."

"Uh. Oh. Yeah, the girl thing." He shrugged. "I didn't get it, but whatever, sometimes being a dude sucks ass. All that matters is being the fuck away from us."

"I haven't forgotten about my parents." Morgan went pale at that. "But I don't think crushing your head over it would make me feel any better." The look on the man's face was almost bleak, like letting go of a dream. It made Morgan feel worse than spitting and screaming would have. "It's like hating a knife because someone stabbed you with it, instead of the person who did it."

Morgan watched them link hands and walk out, Thea murmuring something to him. He nodded, his shaggy head moving in the light so that the hair looked almost wine-red. Then they were outside, and gone, and he relaxed just a little before remembering he was sitting at a table with a monster.

"So what was that little exchange about?"

"She... *I* killed his parents. On her orders. Really, I just set Byron loose on them. Pushed their car right off the road and into a guardrail." Morgan hadn't felt guilty about it then, just relieved. He hadn't hated those people, or wanted them dead, but he sure as fuck didn't want to end up dead himself, or worse. And Byron had been living proof of worse. He'd never even considered another option.

"I'm surprised. He seems the vengeful type."

"I think he is." He licked his lips. "But I guess he hates her worse than me."

"Like I said, the more I see *your* family..."

"Thanks. You'd make an excellent grief counselor."

"I've done it before. It's not easy to come across, you know. Not everyone handles it well." She was dabbing at the corner of her mouth with a napkin. "So. I suppose I'll take my leave as well. Mother will be interested in an update." She took some money out of her pocket – a *lot* of money, a few hundred dollars – and left it on the table.

"What..."

"It's only money, Morgan. We have lots." She smiled at him. "Go buy some clothes. Next time we do this I'd like you cleaned up."

"Next time?"

"Our second date, of course. I've decided I need to socialize more." She laughed at his expression as she pulled her completely unnecessary jacket on.

"You still want to, after what I just said?"

"Morgan, you know what I am. I've killed a lot of people." Her laugh was the delight of a small child at the look on his face. "Oh, don't fret so much. When I ask a man out for dinner, I really mean dinner. I won't kill you until after the sex."

He sat there and considered what the hell *that* meant as she left.

Chapter Twenty One

And Take My Waking Slow

She stepped out of the bath and donned a robe. Ordinarily she'd force James to attend her. It amused her to watch him flush and stare anywhere except at her body, to find himself torn between disgust, confusion and admiration. Every so often he'd remember she was his grandmother and it would all get worse for him, and that was delicious to her.

But Raifa stayed silent.

She'd done things that should have had her howling, and nothing. That was terrifying. *Why* wasn't she speaking? In the past the two of them would contend for control, and usually Robia would win, but the struggle left her disoriented, weak and confused. Sometimes she'd let Raifa have it, let her play with the children. When they'd been conceived Robia was usually in charge, but she'd gladly let Raifa deliver them. It had worked for both of them. Who could say which of them was the mother? It was the same body now, and they were twins. Did it matter?

It matters because she found a way to love them and you never could.

So she had expected Raifa to protest. Instead silence.

Talk to me! Curse me, beg me to stop, but talk to me!

Nothing came of it.

She got dressed and looked in the mirror. Already her hair was darker, less gray. It was temporary, of course. She'd pulled on the web she'd created, abused those trapped in it, and so the original plan was utterly unworkable now.

But she could start over again.

She only had two choices now. One was to stop. The choice that wasn't a choice at all, the surrender. This she was utterly unwilling to do. The other… it would require leverage. Enough force brought to bear to move the immovable. Then two would become three, and…

I have a hard enough time keeping Raifa in check.

She pushed that thought away and went to check on James.

Of all her grandchildren, she'd probably thought the least of James, but he was surprising her. He hadn't whined. She'd always believed him a sniveler, but there he was, laying feverish in bed with his back ruined (she'd taken most of his pain, but enough remained that his sleep was fitful) and he hadn't complained. There had been tears, but she'd been married three times, she'd seen men cry.

He'd proved useful. That was probably the closest she could come to actually *liking* someone.

She worried that Raifa was influencing her somehow. Maybe she should kill him now, just to be safe. But he'd proved tractable, and she was going to need someone to help her once she had the new form, someone to help rebuild the web. Atropos laughed, but she would laugh last. She doubted James would balk at the task she would ask him to perform.

If I could do it without Thomas' other grandson knowing, I could use him instead.

That had appeal. It would be more difficult, but…

The doorbell rang. James was clearly in no shape to answer it for her. She's warded the house, a gorgon's head, the lion headed god, the serpent shrouded one. It would serve.

She walked down the stairs to the front door.

*

"So, I just want to make sure we're all on the same page." The sun had come up an hour ago, and both Thea and Thomas were feeling gritty and exhausted. Seri was sitting in the backseat, and they both envied her the ability to stretch out. "We're *sure* this is where she's staying?"

"That would be correct."

"And you're planning on doing, what, exactly? Storming in?

Unleashing the Easter Bunny on her?"

"Don't be ridiculous." Thea sipped at a coffee from the local McD's. They'd picked up a couple of big breakfasts for Thomas and a hash brown for Thea. Seri hadn't wanted to eat. Didn't think she could. She wished she had a gun. "I was thinking Uncle Sam himself. Top hat, the whole enchilada."

"Enchilada?"

"Please don't start with that again."

"She's right." Thomas had just finished drinking his orange juice. "If we go in there…"

"If?" Thea tried to sound calm and placid about it. "There's an if to this?"

"*If* we go in there, what are we going in there to do? Are we going in there to…" He swallowed. "Are we willing to walk in and murder an old woman?"

"I don't see it as murder."

"Cops likely will." Seri could imagine gruff old Sergeant, her faculty advisor, the one who'd pointed her at Criminal Justice as a major. He'd definitely see it as murder.

"Cops? So far the cops are less than useless when it comes to this shit, because no one *believes* in it." Thea drained the rest of her coffee.

"I'm not saying it's right or wrong." Thomas said, rubbing his forehead. "I'm just saying, once we do this we're committed to it. We go in there to kill her, we have to be willing, *ready* to do it."

Thea was holding her empty cup, staring into it. Was she ready for that? She'd taken out the Hound, but that was a monster, it wasn't a person. As horrible as the old crone was, as much as she'd hurt Thea and the people she cared about, it was still a big deal to do that.

"What are our options? Just keep staking the place out?" Seri had insisted they bring her. Now she wished she hadn't. If weird shit happened, and weird shit *kept* happening, what was she going to do? Jab it with her keys? Think really hard at it?

"I have an idea." Thomas sounded like he already knew they'd hate it, which meant that they likely would.

"And that would be, love of my life?"

"I'm being obvious?"

"Like a thirty foot high sign with flaming letters."

"We could try talking to her."

Both women just stared at him. Thea realized her mouth was open, closed it. Tried to get her brain to make words.

"You are aware she's tried to kill you several times?" Seri was just as agog, but quicker to come back to speech. "The last time you looked like frozen hamburger when we found you."

"I'm not saying we walk in defenseless. For starters, you stay out here and get ready to take off. It would be Thea and me. I'd prefer it was just me…"

"Not happening."

"…but I am a realist." He smiled. Seri had been around Thomas enough by now to understand that smile, how it hid a lot. "I already have a very large rite all set to go. If she tries anything…"

"Okay, so we go in ready to fight and don't? That's the plan?"

"If she attacks us it's self defense. If not, maybe we can learn something."

"Or maybe she learns something about us."

"That's the risk." He nodded. "I'm not saying I like this idea. But it's not just marching up to the door, smashing it in and trying to seek and destroy your grandmother." He looked down at the dashboard. "I'm not… I've killed things, but never a person. I don't want to if I can avoid it."

Thomas turned so he could look at both of them. Two sets of those eyes in one car, it was hard not to feel like he was being dissected. They looked at each other and then back to him, a conversation of expressions playing out between them.

"Give me the keys." Seri sighed. "I'll wait out here. If I see a dragon come out of that place I'm definitely leaving."

"Please do." Thea said softly. "You have your phone? If shit gets real I want Joe warned."

"I have it." They embraced. "I really, really, *really* hate this."

"Yeah." They broke the hug and then Thea nodded to him

and got out, so he handed the keys over to Seri and stepped out himself. They were parked on Eldridge, just up the block from the house, he'd been there a few times. He'd been interested in a girl who'd lived not too far from there, had been to a party at her house once. At this hour of the morning people were on their way to work, he saw a minivan pass them with a family in it.

Not likely to ever be you, Willrew.

"Hey." He turned as Thea approached. "Before we do this. If we *have* to…"

"If we have to it's because she makes us." He reached out and took her hand. She squeezed.

"This has really been the strangest year."

"For me too." He laughed. "I'm glad… well, for you, really. Not much else."

"Too bad we can't just run away." She squeezed again. "For God's sake, Tommy, kiss me already so we can go do this."

He did, marveling that she still made him feel gooseflesh, still made his stomach flutter. There was almost a sense of gravity pulling on him when he kissed Thea, like he wasn't fully in control of himself anymore. Her mouth became the focus of his whole world, the feel of her lips gliding across his, the occasional sharpness of her teeth grazing him. Her hand in his hair, the insistence of her. As frightened as he was, there was a solidity in her that steadied him. He hoped he could give her something like it.

"Okay. Before we start giving the neighborhood a show." She breathed against his face. "Let's get this over with."

"You want to get married?" He blinked. He hadn't expected that to come out of his mouth.

"What?"

"I, uh, well, I don't mean right now…"

"What." She started laughing. "You ask me now? Seriously? We're about to… Jesus, I don't even know what we're about to do and you ask me that now? Tommy, sometimes, I really wonder about you."

"Not actually hearing a no."

"Not actually *saying* a no." She was leaning against the car, his old school jacket wrapped around her. "I can come up with a whole lot of reasons why it would be a terrible idea, but... ask me again after all this. Okay?"

"Yeah. I'm not sure why I did that."

"Broke the tension." She laughed again. "I love you, Tommy."

"I love you too, Mendel." He reached out and she took his hand. "Now let's go meet the dragon."

*

The Lion-Headed God flared as she opened the door.

She hated to admit that she could still be surprised, but there she was, with the door open and her errant granddaughter standing there, cool as the morning itself. She had true youth, not the stolen version Robia was making use of, born of pain and blood and fear. Robia felt a stab of envy and then her eyes tracked the giant man next to her. His father's face, his mother in his build. She knew both now.

She had of course prepared for them, even if she hadn't expected a polite ringing of the bell. A moment's thought and the Lion-Headed God would...

No.

She'd been alarmed at Raifa's silence. But her voice was the more alarming, because it came at the head of a tidal wave that swamped her. Raifa had been biding her time, waiting for this one moment when she was at a low ebb, distracted, and now she surged forward and demanded the body. Robia clawed at blankness, screamed.

Not now! Not now you can't have it now!

But Raifa's timing was perfect. Robia was dragged down into the dark place where time wasn't, the waiting place inside concepts grinding against each other, tectonic thoughts. And Raifa rose in her place, settled into the fleshly existence. It took a moment.

From outside Thea saw the woman's features shift. Thomas was on a hair trigger, he'd *felt* her do something and almost completed his own incantation, but she managed to stop him with a hand on his arm. The face looking at her was the same as it had been when the door opened, but what lay behind it... she recognized it.

"You found me, little girl." Raifa moved out of the door, waved her hand and dismissed the Lion-Headed God. "Well, I should say you found us."

Thea stepped in, gestured to Thomas who followed, still ready.

"You were in my dream. But you're trying to... you said us." Thea looked around the house at the network of power that had been thrown around it, the crescent moon, the severed head symbol on the far wall. They glowed with stored power. "Who are you?"

"Robi is sleeping. For now. She's very angry and I won't have long." She sat down on a ragged couch in the middle of the room. "Please. Have a seat. And you, of course."

"Robi is you." Thomas rumbled. "I *saw* you, and my grandfather..."

"Just the body." She looked sad. "She didn't want to hurt Thomas. She loved him, even if she couldn't admit it. Her great love. He and I never... I didn't want to get in the way." She ran a trembling hand down the side of her face. "She's changed us again. I never know what I'll wake up to."

"If you're not her, who *are* you?"

"I'm Raifa. Raifa Dassalia. The person you're trying to stop is Robia. My sister. We're twins." Her smile was genuine but a little wan. It was costing her. "The body is, well, it's both of us. We're your grandmother."

"What *happened*?"

"Bad things." The smile was gone now. For Thomas, seeing someone who looked a great deal like Thea might someday sitting there wasn't quite what he'd expected. There were differences, things that Thea undoubtedly got from her grandfather and father, but the eyes and hair were *very* close, and the structure of the face... she was what his mother called *handsome*, severe but not unlovely. "We don't really have time."

"What *do* we have time for? What's she doing?"

"She didn't want me to know, just as I didn't want *her* to know that I was planning this. I was going to call you, actually. On the phone." She was looking at her hands now, at the wrinkles and spots on them. "I couldn't find your number. She knows about the island. I've seen it when she thought I wasn't looking."

"Assuming I believe this..."

"It's her, Tommy." Thea looked over at him. "From the vision. At the carousel."

"She could be..."

"She's not, I know it's her." Thea leaned on him with her eyes and he backed off. Then she turned back to the woman on the couch. "What's her plan?"

"She wants to make the best of the bad. She was making a web. The first one to die was Claudia, an accident. It wasn't supposed to happen that way." She shifted in her seat, looking around the room, then back to Thea. "Before then I hadn't objected to the rites, the binding. She wanted to keep tabs on our children, I thought. I was never... she's the wonder worker. I'm merely the first attempt."

"Did she kill her... your... husbands?"

"Not exactly. Not that she would have balked at it." Raifa sighed. "She did something in the house, she wanted twins. Just twins. She wanted *girl* twins, but she didn't always get that. Marco and Stephan were boys, and then she had Paolo and Paola later on. The middle girls – Serena, Eva, Joann and Margret – all moved out of state, went to college as far away as possible. Too much of Robia being out, not enough of me. But they were all bonded, too." She started to sob quietly.

Thea had no idea what to do. She wanted to reassure her, but she didn't want to *touch* her. Thomas was even more uncomfortable.

"I'm sorry. I always took the body when it was time to deliver." She sniffled. "So I always felt like they were more *my* babies. She got to make them, but I had to bear them."

"You said something about a web." Thomas tried to be

gentle about it.

"The web. We lost our family. Robia didn't accept it. Couldn't. So she made the web, and I thought it was to... protect them. So we'd always know where they were. But it wasn't. She told me, once it started going wrong. It was meant to connect them, all to all. The way she and I are, but in separate bodies. All her daughters would be *her*, and all their daughters as well. One mind, many bodies, one will. And it would keep going. We'd live forever through our children and their children. But then they started dying. Accidents. Sicknesses. Depression. The drain on them... she pulled on the weave of things and it got tangled and threads broke too soon. But she didn't stop."

"Why not?"

"Because in death they fed her. She decided she could use that, keep the next generation ignorant, pick one of you and start over. She was so excited when Byron was born, because it was a young grandchild and it was *his* grandchild and she'd get to live in that body, but then Byron was a boy. So she was stuck with your two, and you're not... you're too willful, the two of you, you always were. Gio's children's children." She laughed again. "I liked Gio best of her men. I even got to..." She actually blushed. "I often wondered if he knew."

Thomas felt like he was standing exposed on an open field with an archer in the brush, just waiting to get hit. It wasn't a good feeling. In a way it was useful, though, because it was adding to the stress and tension he was under, the heightened emotional state he'd been forced to live in for the past month. It felt like his spine was being twisted.

"So what now?" Thea's voice was hushed. The Dassalia woman, whoever she was, turned her attention full on her.

"You should kill me while you..." Raifa twitched. "Oh. No."

Thea bolted up and away from her. Raifa lost the body with a shudder, the flesh on her face actually writhing as Robia clawed her way free and screamed, tearing at the weave of power around them and hurling it at Thomas. Thea watched it happen in a second, her guts heaving in shock at how *fast* it was. A form with wings and a lion's head, two snakes wrapped around it, hands like claws slashing for his throat.

Thomas had been ready for it.

His scream was impossibly loud, a long low roar that dragged on and on and on, shaking everything around him. Thea could see an after image as Dassalia's Lion-Headed God slashed claws at him that struck something *around* him, and then Thomas simply stepped on it, smashing it to the floor with one foot. He was *much* taller, almost twice his normal height, hunched slightly and his back through the ceiling. Dassalia was backing away, alarmed.

His mouth opened and blue light crackled up and down his back.

Then he looked down and spit a stream of blinding white light and flames onto the Lion-Headed God. Dassalia was already heading up the stairs. Thea didn't know for sure if Thomas was in control of himself, or if the house would survive this, but she knew they couldn't let the woman leave.

She bolted after her.

Upstairs, James Williams came to consciousness when that horrible long scream shook his house. James had loved movies as a child. He'd especially loved Channel 25 in Boston because they'd shown all sorts of bad movies on their overnight programming. Giant ants, sasquatches, stuff from Hong Kong and Japan. One of the movies he'd especially loved was *Destroy All Monsters*, which had led to a general love of films where people in elaborate rubber suits walked over model buildings and pretended to be fighting. But then he'd seen the first such movie, and that had been genuine in a way most of them weren't. It had stuck with him.

Now that sound, the roar of the monster as it came out of the water, was echoing through his house. He dragged himself to his feet, hearing it in his teeth. He staggered out into the hallway, saw his grandmother running up the stairs. For a moment he was surprised – her hair was much darker than it had been, she looked younger. Then he saw another woman chasing after her.

He reacted without thinking, throwing himself at Thea, who didn't see him until he managed to tackle her and drag her to the floor. Dassalia just kept running, went right past him into the room she'd been sleeping in, Morgan's old room (and their parents before him) and slammed the door. He looked up, confused.

Thea crashed her elbow into his face and twisted, her hand now on the back of his head, and drove his face into the floor. Barely conscious to begin with, he slumped off of her and Thea stood up, her back hurting from being tackled into wood.

"Motherfucker, you have no goddamn sense." Gritting her teeth she charged the door, slamming her shoulder into it once, twice, again, and on the fourth teeth-rattling impact it popped open.

The room was pretty big, with a small balcony and large windows that opened onto it. Dassalia was standing there, holding the two urns, doing something on the ground with something orange. She had a container of the stuff open at her feet. She turned and looked at Thea, and the look was unreadable, no emotion Thea had ever seen in her life.

"You'll do. When the time comes. I've made my choice."

"I'm going to kill you, old woman."

"You should have done it when Raifa took the body. Soft. Not a mistake I'd make." She put one of her bare feet down on the orange circle and black erupted from it, not light, it made Thea's eyes burn. She called up memories of a trip to Block Island her father had taken them all on, the plane ride, a rainbow they'd all seen out the window. The room flared with the light as Thea released it.

A creature with bat wings made of nightmares had leathery arms and legs wrapped around Dassalia, was hauling her up into the air. She cackled as Thea cleared the room, already twenty feet away and moving too fast for her to try and grab her.

Stupid! Why weren't you ready for that?

Snarling she turned and ran out of the room. Williams was trying to get to his feet, and Thea could see the hamburger of his back, the emaciation of his limbs. Dassalia had been killing him slowly and he didn't even see it. Another long screeching scream rocked the house from below. She had no idea how much longer the building had.

She got her arm under Williams' shoulder and yanked him to his feet. He didn't resist. She wasn't even sure he was conscious at this point, but she dragged him down the stairs anyway.

The living room was gone. There were huge holes in the floor, the retaining wall into the kitchen was also gone. Thomas inside the flickering image of a vaguely reptilian shape was simply destroying everything in sight while fighting Dassalia's creation. Luckily there was still a path out the front door, and she took it, dragging Williams onto his lawn. Seria saw them come out and came running over from the car.

"What..."

"The car, get him inside it."

"What are you..."

"I gotta get Thomas, take him!" She shoved Williams at Seri, then turned and ran back inside the house, completely swamped by fear and anger at herself. *Why didn't I kill her when she was helpless? Anything she does now is on me, I could have...*

Thomas was smashing his feet repeatedly into the summoning, grinding it apart. It was clearly no longer a threat but she wasn't sure if he could tell or not.

"Hey! *Hey!*" She screamed so loud she was afraid she might rupture something. "Stop playing with that fucking thing, we have to go now! Like *right now!*"

She was afraid he'd ignore her, but he didn't. Instead he kicked one last time, smashing it half through the kitchen floor, and then turned to run, scooping her up on the way by and shrinking with her in his arms. He cleared the entire living room and was out the door in one jump, and made it to the car in another, letting her out of his grip at the driver's side door.

"You drive." His voice sounded like someone scraping the string on a bass guitar. "I gotta concentrate."

She let him clamber into the back seat of the Camaro, then got in herself. She discharged the last bit of power, what she'd used the call the rainbow, on twisting the car's image so that anyone looking outside their window at all that noise wouldn't know what they saw. She hoped it would work.

The car rolled forward, Seri sitting up front with her, staring out the window.

"What happened?"

"Nana Rafiela says hi." Thea kept her eyes straight ahead, driving just fast enough, trying not to look like she was fleeing the scene. "Apparently she wants to move into one of our bodies."

"She…"

"Thomas?"

"I'm here." He sounded more himself now. He was looking over James Williams. "Jesus, what did she *do* to this guy?"

"The face bruises are me." She gripped the steering wheel tighter. "I was right on her and he tackled me to save her."

"He…" Thomas was looking over the man's back, which was a mass of welts and scabs. "Why the hell would he help her?"

"Because he's a crazy asshole, or because she messed with his head, or who the fuck knows?" Thea was so angry she could barely keep her voice level. "I was in the fucking room with her and she summoned a fucking gargoyle or something to fly her off and I didn't *have* anything, I called a *rainbow.*"

"There was a lot going on."

"You had something!"

"And it nearly brought the house down on top of us." Thomas' voice was especially deep, likely because he was still shrugging off what he'd called up. "You were shaken up."

"I don't get what happened…" Seri said, looking from Thea to Thomas. "Can someone tell me what's going on?"

"Back at the house." Thomas replied. Thea nodded, her eyes still on the road. She finally relaxed, let the mask she'd put around the car slide off. It wasn't a long drive back. She took Pontiac and let herself just go by memory.

Chapter Twenty Two

Wild Water

Bishop and Joe were making out.

They'd gotten Bry to watch TV, even though it meant going to Sears at the Rhode Island Mall first and *buying* her a TV to watch, and now they were sitting in the kitchen having a sloppy make out session while she watched *Power Rangers*. She seemed to like it well enough.

"We..." Bishop brushed Joe's face with his hand, enjoying the sensation of his stubble, the firmness of his lips. "Should have gotten her a VCR."

"DVDs are the thing now."

"What, I'm made of money now?"

"I'm pretty sure..." Joe then moved in and took charge for a few minutes, and all they exchanged in that time was heavy breathing and their bodies pressed up against each other, their tongues and mouths coupled. Joe felt Bishop's erection and giggled.

"What?"

"I'm sorry, it always feels funny poking me in the stomach."

"There's absolutely nothing I like better than my boyfriend laughing at my cock."

"Oh, I'm not laughing at your best feature, believe me."

"I'm hungry." Bry called from the living room. "Can we eat something?" Joe muttered under his breath but turned to speak to the girl.

"Sure, any ideas on what you want?"

"Food?"

"Going to need more specifics."

"Tasty food?" She turned and grinned at them. It was a heck of a grin and it was hard to resent her for interrupting them, considering they'd spent thirty minutes getting to second base.

"All right, let me look around. Thea probably keeps the place stocked."

"You think?" Bishop let him go and they started checking cupboards. "Tommy could barely manage to keep ramen in here."

"My cousin's essentially taken the kitchen over. Trust me. She and Seri used to have wars over kitchen control." He opened the fridge. "See?"

"Well I'll be dipped."

"One of Thea's delinquents had a dad who was a chef, taught his son, son taught Thea. She's kept up on it since. Don't tell Seri, but Thea's a better cook..."

The door opened before Joe could finish, and Thomas walked in carrying someone in his arms like a small child. It took Joe a second to recognize one of the men who'd come in his house the day his life changed, the one who threw the bundle on the ground. He looked like a badly tenderized steak. Seri and Thea followed him in. Bry jumped up, shocked.

"Jimmy!" She ran over. "What happened to Jimmy? Jimmy, it's me! It's me!"

"Our grandmother happened to him." Seri intercepted Bry before she could get in the way. "Honey, please. He's not conscious right now. We're going to help him but you need to give them some space, okay?"

"What did she..." Bry's lip was trembling. "Like me? Like she did to me?"

"We don't know." Thomas was already descending the stairs to the basement. Thea looked back, met Bry's eyes for a moment, then closed the door. "But we'll do what we can."

Thomas walked James' body to the pool table, took a moment to look at the space where the urns had been, and then placed him on it. He didn't even react when his back contacted the felt.

"Is he..."

"He's breathing." He shook his head. "We're going to have to wiggle our fingers."

"I don't…" Thea sat down against the wall, leaned her head back. "I could do it for you because… because I *love* you, I want you to be… but him? I don't give a shit what happens to him."

"Yeah, me neither." Thomas was looking up at the ceiling. "But I love you, and he might know something that we can use to keep everybody safe."

"Knowing that and feeling it are two different things." She looked up at him. "He helped her get in here. He helped her steal the urns, probably helped her… my mom, my uncle…"

"You're right." He dropped down to sit next to her. "You're absolutely right."

They sat there watching him breathe.

"I let her get away. With your parents' urns. Why does she want them so bad?"

"I spent a year fucking around with that ritual. They were the center." He sighed, ran his hand through his hair. Leaned back and thunked his head against the wall. "I guess, anyway. Maybe she just likes pissing me off."

"We talked about it, about going in ready to… and I wasn't ready to."

"Hard thing to do. Especially after…" He sighed. "I could have killed her, and I didn't."

"I…" She looked at him. "I wasn't sure you were in control there."

"I was. I was furiously angry, but I was." He was looking back at her. "I just couldn't knowing that there was someone innocent inside her, and maybe that's what she's counting on. I'm in way over my head here."

"She… she said we should. *'You should kill me while you…'* I froze up when she said it, and then… a fucking rainbow. That's all I had in the tank."

"We can sit here and beat ourselves up all night." He laughed, not very convincingly. "Maybe if we have Bry come down here, she can…"

"No." The voice came from the table. They both stood up, shocked that he could speak. He looked worse than he had when

Thea had bounced his face off of the floor, *much* worse. "Leave Byron alone."

"You're going to die if we don't…"

"Then let it happen. It's what Morgan always said would happen." His laugh was a creaky screen door. "It's what I knew would happen the second she showed up on my doorstep."

"Then why'd you *help* her?"

"Why not? Wasn't all bad." He coughed. "I got to see my mom again. Briefly. She wasn't looking too good."

Thea felt rage claw at her, like a wild thing using her spine as a ladder, ascending vertebrae by vertebrae. He couldn't be this deluded, he couldn't be.

"Without Bry or someone else who cares about you, I don't know if we can save you." Thomas' voice echoed in the room, bouncing off of the fake wood paneling on the concrete.

"So don't."

"You want to die?"

"No." He gasped. "Fuck no. But why would you want to save me? I came at you with a gun and a monster in a bag, sicced my freak brother on you, tried to…" He suddenly lurched into a sitting position as he coughed. Thomas took the opportunity to look at his back, shot a look to Thea. She walked around and looked, and hissed.

"They're still…"

"Yeah. Still active, still working. Part of whatever she did."

"I'm going to go get Joe." Thea headed for the stairs. "Can you…"

"He'll still be alive when you get back down here."

Thomas didn't look to see her go, just listened to her feet on the stairs. He managed to pull up enough will to pin the man in place, keep him from sinking, but he couldn't tell what the marks on his back were or what they were doing to him. He didn't want to get too fancy with him.

"So you're the one she wants dead."

"Right now that might be both of us."

"She had plenty of time to kill me." He coughed again.

"Although who knows with her? Maybe she likes it slow."

"Maybe." Thomas had no idea what to say to the man. *Hey, by the way, we're related* didn't seem like a good idea. He didn't see any reason to admit that. He certainly didn't feel any family bond, considering he'd helped kill both of Thomas' parents, and almost killed Thomas. Sure, the old woman told them to do it, and sure, saying no probably wasn't an option. It didn't make him like them any better. He felt the pull on the man increase, and it was difficult to find enough will in himself to stop it, enough reason to care if he died. He liked Bry – she was a good kid, and you couldn't hold her responsible for what she'd been turned into, what she'd been forced to do – but he didn't know if he could keep her brother alive on just that.

"Hey." Joe and Thea came down the stairs. Joe hissed. "Jesus, his back."

"I think she's killing him long distance." Thomas grunted. "Feels like it."

"Thea, can you help him? I need to look at this." Joe knew less than Thomas, but he could see more clearly than either of them – his actual magic gifts were lacking, he couldn't work his will with anything like the power and focus Thea or Thomas could, but his vision was clear and precise. He let himself focus on the marks, on the filaments of power he could see woven into them. "It almost looks like needlepoint. Like she stitched power into him. The ones that are bleeding…"

"Yeah." Thea had cheated – she didn't care at all about James Williams, but she loved Thomas, and so she was lending her strength to *him* instead of the injured man. It was so much easier. They always seemed to fit together so well, she could taste his moods and feel him, almost hear his thoughts. Right now he was bearing down, just trying to keep Williams from being ripped out of his body. "The question is, what do we do about it?"

"Could go with my suggestion." James sounded like he had a leak.

"Don't tempt me." She growled at him. "Look, if nothing else Bry would…"

"Oh fuck off with that shit." He groaned as Thomas lost grip for a second and a bit more of his life wrenched out of his back.

"Thea." Thomas' voice was deeper than ever, a sign of him being truly angry. Thea knew it wasn't at her. She knew exactly how he felt in that moment. "Go upstairs. Outside. Look for a pickup truck."

"You think…"

"He's been following them. He may have been there this morning. It's our only shot."

She kissed him, a quick thing, and released the link between them with a little regret. She ran up the stairs and saw Seri and Bry sitting in the living room, the little girl clearly agitated.

"What's up?" Bishop was the one who spoke up.

"I'll be right back, I hope. Joe's helping Thomas with him."

"I thought…" Bry almost screamed, then managed to quiet herself. "I thought you were going to help Jimmy."

"We're trying. We just need some help. I promise I'll try and be right back." She was out the door without her jacket, because looking at the kid's face was too much, equal parts fear and love and rage, it reminded her too much of how she'd felt at twelve. She looked around the side streets as she walked up the driveway, looked for the embankment he'd mentioned before. If he wasn't here…

But there it was, less than a block away down where Colonial turned into Aqueduct. It had been painted, a cheap matte black color. He was sitting in the cab, watching the house through binoculars, and he clearly saw her standing there staring at him. She was afraid he'd start up the truck and take off, but he didn't as she stalked at him. He got out before she got there.

"Look, I saw you leave the house…"

"Come on. Don't ask me questions, just follow me." She turned on her heel and stalked back to the house, making sure to tell the wards not to fry Morgan. The house was starting to get confused with all the people coming and going, she could feel it, tried to reassure the spirits that made it up.

When they were inside Bry was up and on Morgan before

anyone could respond, throwing herself into his arms. He stooped to catch her.

"Jimmy's *hurt* she hurt Jimmy he's downstairs I don't know what to *do* Morgan where have you been I haven't seen you and she hurt Jimmy and everyone's nice did you know we had other family I didn't know and I think she did something to me and I think I hurt people like she hurts people and I'm *scared*."

"Hey. Hey." Morgan rubbed his hand up and down Bry's back. "Hey, shh. It's okay, kiddo. It's okay." He squeezed his eyes shut as hard as he could, tried to breathe evenly. "You look good, kid. Are you... they're treating you okay?"

"Seri's nice, and Thea showed me how to do eye makeup, and I got to ride Thomas' horses. Joe can't play checkers as well as you can, though."

"He probably doesn't cheat." Morgan gave his confusing brother (or sister, or whatever, it didn't matter to him) a squeeze, straightened up. "I gotta go down and see Jimmy now, okay? You stay up here and be good. Do what they tell you."

"You gotta help him."

"I'll do what I can, squirt." He smiled, hoped it was a good one. "You just hold tight."

He managed to gently disentangle her arms from around him, handed her back to Seri. She nodded, like she had at the salvage yard. Then he turned and followed Thea, feeling the eyes of the dude in the kitchen, the one he'd coldcocked, on his back.

"Thanks."

"I haven't done anything for you." Thea replied.

Morgan had told himself he was done with his snotty, sarcastic little weasel of a brother. He'd honestly had no idea of what he was about to see until he rounded the corner of the staircase and saw the three men, two standing, one slumped sitting on the pool table. He honestly didn't recognize his brother for a moment, the sunken, hollow faced, ashen *thing* sitting there with his back in ruins.

"What..."

"Hey Morg." James Williams laughed, or perhaps barked. It

certainly wasn't a sound with humor in it. "Looks like you're in time to watch."

"She did this? You *let* her?"

"I didn't like Door #2."

Morgan looked to the giant, whose hand was sparking. He was doing something, it was hard to tell what, but Bry said that *she'd* done it, and Jimmy had basically confirmed it.

"She put marks on his back. Linked herself into him, used him to get inside here. Also used him as an anchor, the pain it caused him, she channeled it as power." Thomas flexed his hand, and Morgan swallowed watching that massive arm work. "She's still doing it."

Morgan nodded because he had no idea what the fuck to say to that.

"I'm a battery." His brother barked again. "Stick me on your tongue and I'll make your mouth tingle."

"Christ, Jimmy."

"It's *James*. Jimmy sounds like a kid. A man should die with a man's name. I'm Jaaaaames." His head dropped to his chest. "Morg make them stop please. Just let me go, I'm gone already."

"We can save him." Thea spoke up. "There's just one problem."

"What?"

"Frankly I think he's a piece of shit and I can't work up the emotion needed to do it." She turned to face Morgan. "I think you're a piece of shit too, just so we're clear."

"Yeah, I got it."

"I might have put it differently," The giant rumbled. "But I'm basically in the same boat. Everyone here has reason to dislike you both. Intellectually I know we need everything he knows, but..." He let himself trail off as his arm corded up, obviously trying to fight to keep Jimmy in place.

James. He wants to be called James, and he's dying, give him what he wants.

"So what did you bring me down here for?"

"He's your brother." Thea shrugged. "You might care more

than we do."

*

Upstairs, Bry was frantic.

She knew her brothers had done bad things. She wasn't stupid, was getting less stupid every day as what her grandmother did to her faded. She knew she was different now, of course. She'd gone into the bathroom and practiced, making her hair change color, her eyes, growing a few inches or shrinking a few. One time she'd stripped naked and made herself look more like Seri did. But she didn't know what Thea or Seri looked like naked, was far too embarrassed to ask.

Going back to like she was now was hard. She'd almost forgotten what she looked like. In the end she'd copied Seri's eyes, was pretty close to the right height. She was afraid to talk about it, even though she knew they could all do things, too.

They can help Jimmy. She had to believe that.

She didn't always like Jimmy very much. He could be kind of an asshole, if she was being completely honest – he'd hold her down and laugh as she panicked and tried to get up. She remembered being six or seven, just before the old woman came and hurt her, Jimmy had stolen all of her dolls and hid them somewhere to *'toughen him up'* and Morgan had found out and slapped him a few times.

Oh, we're toughening people up around here? You first.

He was still her brother, though. They were her brothers. She was scared for them, for herself. Everybody had been nice, had taken care of her, she appreciated it but they weren't her brothers.

"Seri?"

"Yeah?" Seri was sitting on the couch with her. They'd turned the TV off because Bry didn't want it on anymore, didn't care about it.

"Is it my fault?"

"How could it be your fault? No, no honey it's all on her. It's nothing you did." Seri very rarely indulged in anger. She felt it, of course, everybody got angry, but she didn't let it run her, didn't let it make decisions for her. Right now that was *very* hard. Seeing her parent's graves despoiled, seeing aunt Paola's and uncle Greg's, that had hit her so hard she was still wincing. Aunt Paola had been her second mother, taken from her too soon after her first had died, and for years she'd resented her for it despite trying so hard not to. Knowing now that it was *her*, the witch that was her grandmother, that Paola *hadn't*...

"It's because I wasn't born right."

"It's because she's a monster, and nothing to do with you. Nothing." Seri swallowed. "She killed my mom and my dad and that's on *her*, it's on her what she does. Not us. Don't ever think that. Don't give her that. Don't let her into your head like that, okay? She doesn't deserve to be in there."

Downstairs, Morgan had taken off his shirt. He was actually in better shape than Joe had expected. Thin, but looked like he exerted himself regularly. Sometimes Joe wondered why he needed to check out every single man he saw, even guys he felt zero attraction to.

"So what do I do?"

"You should be touching him." Thea indicated James, who was sitting up staring ahead, barely responsive. Morgan took his brother's hand, felt how cold and slack it was. He was neither participating nor resisting. "Thomas?"

"You'd better do it soon." He sounded like a bear, his voice scraping the floor and ceiling.

"What now?" Morgan sounded terrified to himself.

"You need to be the center. Just concentrate on him, memories of him, whatever you have." She reached inside herself for the image of the staff of Asclepius, and beyond that to the serpent itself shedding its skin, the symbol of regeneration, imagined it climbing up the side of a tree topped by a nest and in that nest an egg that smoldered, surrounded by flames and ash. She bore down on the image, imagining now the egg splintering from within, cracking open, flaming wings burst forth to scream at the sky, a firebird, a phoenix born from its own ashes.

Thomas let go, let the concepts carved into Williams' back try and draw from him again, saw them grow taut as they sensed new life to steal. In his mind he was a shrieking thing, with talons like razors. A bird that took elephants. The killer eagle. As James Williams groaned and began to die he swept his hand in an arc and sheared through the filaments hooked into him as Thea's rite smashed into his broken body, guided by his brother.

Morgan had been remembering the last good day, before the end of everything. He'd been about to graduate high school, Jimmy was fourteen or fifteen, and Bry was a kid, barely five. Morgan had never asked his father why they suddenly decided to have another kid – it wasn't the kind of thing you asked. Because Bry was so young, it was just easier to act adult with him. Jimmy was always a bit of a shit to Bry, but that day, they'd all gone out on the bay on an old boat one of their dad's friends let them use. Dad had drunk a few beers, mom had fished, Jimmy spent the time staring at girls in bikini's who'd sail by or even swim, they were in a cove near some island. Mom had insisted they go there.

It's pretty, isn't it? She'd said, her voice sad, haunted by something. *I don't know why but I always love coming here. I'd like to move here.*

It's in the middle of nowhere, Mar. His dad scoffed, but gently. *Hard to run a salvage yard from out here.*

You could switch to boats.

He didn't know why he was thinking about his mom instead of Jimmy until he realized that Jimmy and Bry were the last family he had, and they hadn't always been what *she'd* made them. And maybe that was on him. He hadn't been strong enough to protect them, or brave enough to stand up to her, and now…

I left him and she did this to him. If he dies it's on me.

His mom and dad would have expected him to do better.

He still could.

The pain hit as soon as Thea started working, his hand on fire where it was touching James. *He's James now. Look at him. He earned it.* His brother was clutching his hand, his wrist, his face naked misery.

"Morgan. Morgan, *please.*"

"Just fucking hold on. Hold *on,* goddamn it." There was blood leaking from Morgan's palm where his nails were digging in, he almost collapsed from it. Slapped his left hand, bloody palm down, on the pool table to hold himself up. His right locked around James' hand.

Thomas swung his talons, tore another set of filaments loose. Thea held the channel in place, the snake ascending, the firebird spreading its wings. Life. The idea of the glowing lantern from the original rite on this very table came to her and she smiled, remembering her and Thomas linked in the backyard.

Then to bring power.

The last set of filaments tore apart as Thomas' hand passed through them and James Williams couldn't even scream as the air was forced out of his lungs, the power flowing into him now *staying* in him. If not for Morgan's hand on his he would have thrashed, slammed his back onto the table. He almost yanked Morgan over as he twitched.

"What's happening?"

"Just hold him!" Thea screamed. "Thomas!"

"He's cut loose." Thomas didn't have to yell. His voice carried, a bird's call that could echo across miles. He held out his hand to Thea. "Here."

She took it and they were together again, like that time in the yard, linked. She drew from him. He let her. Now it was so much easier to guide the fire, the green flame of power and make it dance, make it sing, make it work for her. She didn't need to care about James Williams anymore, someone else was doing that. All she needed to do was burn.

The marks on his back scarred over, closed up. His ravaged face eased, lines and creases wiped away. He sagged, passing out and Morgan caught him before he toppled off of the table.

Joe had been watching, of course, covering in case their grandmother sensed what they were doing and tried something. But nothing had come. He watched as Thea and Thomas came back to themselves, let go of each other, let their glances linger before turning to the table.

"Is he…"

"He's not dead. Shouldn't be dying." Thea felt stiff all over. "Should be in better shape than he was before all this, really. But I doubt he'll wake up soon."

"We need him awake." Thomas grunted.

"We should let him sleep for at least a couple of hours, and you know it." She shook her head. "He won't be any use to us without some rest."

*

She hated boats.

She'd felt James growing weaker. It hadn't pleased her. She'd intended to keep him for a while longer, perhaps even past the point of success when it came. But as he faltered she grew stronger, her skin smoother. She could be mistaken for a woman in her thirties.

She didn't have much time now.

The creature had dropped her off in Bristol. It was the middle of the day, two days to Christmas, and the last day ferries would be running between the island and the mainland. That would give her some time. But even as she paid for a ticket and endured the stare of the young boy who handed her change back (she knew she was a striking woman again, her skin nearly flawless, her eye almost glacial, and it pleased her to be so for a time) her thoughts were elsewhere. Once she truly began, they would come.

She was seated atop the ferry watching the water and waiting for it to pull from the dock when the pain hit her. She'd felt the Lion-Headed God die, of course, but that had been tied up in the wards she'd laid days earlier, she hadn't felt it keenly. But she'd personally marked James, personally laid in the connection that was feeding her his pain, his death. There had been a slowing, something holding her off, but that hadn't concerned her. Slowing it down didn't bother her, in a way the struggle made it better.

But when the first connection was severed she felt her

whole body convulse and knew what was coming. The second and third sheared apart and left her sweating, trying to hold on. If she hadn't stolen so much of him already the cost would have been more severe, but to a woman in the prime of youth it wasn't so terrible. December all around her quickly worked to convince her body to stop sweating.

By the time the boat's engine kicked up and they pulled away from the dock, she was again fine. It was possible they'd saved James, but unlikely, especially if the younger Thomas knew that James had helped him become an orphan. It was more likely they'd sought to cripple her again.

She was so angry at Raifa that it was hard to think calmly. She inhaled cool air, watched the seagulls wheel over the boat as it chugged forward. A few of them were hers, she'd fed so many seagulls over the years that there were almost always a few of hers aloft at any given moment. She reached out, ordered them to fly ahead. Give her an idea of how many people would be on the island over the next two or three days. How many she had to work with.

Why did you do it?

They were our children. She blinked, surprised that Raifa was talking to her again.

"You know I didn't..."

You didn't stop once it started. You kept going.

We couldn't stop! It would be for nothing if we stopped.

It always was, Robi. Raifa sounded tired. Despite everything she wanted to reach out, to say something, but her own grief and anger choked her. A few more seconds and they might have...

So you'd let them kill me?

Kill us. Yes. It's time. Well past time. She looked so much like Paola, how do you not see that? How do you not care?

"The web, we'd all be one person, it's *better* than being apart. Better than being alone. Then, you die and you're gone forever. With the web they're always with us. It's better." She was sputtering, trying to find words to convince Raifa.

The web didn't work.

"They weren't strong enough. These two, though. They're

finally strong enough." She wiped at her face. "Raifa, please, it's for you too, so you'll always be here."

I died in 1942. Robia jerked at that. *You just won't let me rest, that's all.*

No. No no no I saved you, I saved us both, you...

I'm tired, Robi. Please stop. Please stop dragging me along.

She felt Raifa sink into the nothing place. She spent longer and longer there now, only coming forth to criticize her. The brackish water swirled as the boat's propellers churned it, and Robia Dassalia sat there, not quite weeping.

"You'll see, Raifa. You'll see. Everything will be... I'll *make* it be right. You. Me. I'll even get him back. It'll be perfect. I'll make it perfect."

The gulls overhead kept flying.

Thirty minutes later the boat eased up to the dock. She watched the crew jump across the gap, throwing ropes back over to the boat to tie off. There was a small store and a gas station there, both of which vastly overcharged because everything was brought in across the water. She had no need for either, of course. It would be a bit of a walk to get to the farm, especially with it being cold out, but she knew she wouldn't need to walk it.

She watched the gulls. Several of them landed near the dock, waiting for her. She walked to them, spoke briefly. There were less than a hundred people on the island, less than usual, for some were off having Christmas in other places. Still, it would serve.

"Hey, miss?"

She turned her head and saw a man nearly as old as she truly was walking her way, his red baseball cap in his hands.

"I thought I recognized you. You were one of the girls that came down here with Little Tom? I'm sorry, I know he introduced us... Seri? That was your name?"

She smiled, pleased with her snarling of skeins.

"You can call me that." She reached out a hand, let him take it. He did so deferentially, a man from another time. "I know Tom, yes."

"I remembered you and your cousin both looked close." He

let her hand go, looking a little abashed. "I'm sorry to say I couldn't remember if you were the young lady he was seeing or not."

"I'm told we all look much alike. Family resemblance."

"That's for sure. You, your cousin, and your brother all like peas in a pod." He smiled. "I'm Paul, if you're as bad with names as I am."

"Paul. Yes. Thank you." She kept the smile on her face.

"So, are you heading back up to Little Tom's place? It's a bit of a walk this time of year."

"Yes, I suppose it is."

"Well, I have to go up anyway, check on everything. I could give you a ride if you like."

"Thank you, Paul." Her smile became more genuine. "I appreciate it."

*

Thomas ended up carrying James up the stairs while the rest of them followed, Thea last so she could keep an eye on Morgan. They put him on the couch in the carpeted room that was probably the living room. Thea could never tell what the room adjacent to the kitchen was, if it was the den or dining room or what. There were couches and a TV in it, so maybe a den?

"You watch him?" Thea turned to Joe.

"Sure. If he sprouts wings or whatever I'll shriek really loud." He gave her a grin, bumped her head with his. "You go deal with things."

As soon as Morgan was in sight Bry was all over him, wanting to talk. He let her drag him over to the couch and fielded her many rapid fire questions as best he could. That left Thomas and Thea to talk with Seri and Bishop.

"So we seriously saved that asshole now?"

"We need what he knows, Bish."

"Dude, I know the hired help when I see it."

"You should, you've gone through enough of it in your life."

"Low blow. My point is, if she told him anything of substance

I'll be fucking amazed."

"It's not just about what she told him." Thea was leaning against the counter. "It's about what he saw, what she made him do, any fucking clue we can get."

"What are we going to do with the two of them?" Seri was watching Bry talk to Morgan. "She really loves them. Even the asshole on the couch. I don't know… do we just let them take her?"

"You're assuming that's what they want." Thomas cracked his neck. It occurred to everyone standing around him that if he chose the man could be terrifying. "Blondie there deliberately left her with us. They might both be utter fucking assholes but he seems to genuinely care about her. Hell, he even genuinely cares about the other one, and that guy would have been better off a stain on the inside of his father's underwear."

Thea whistled. "That's a very specific way to put that."

"I get mad too." The grin he gave her was wolfish. She found herself giving it back, moving closer to him. "So what do we do until he wakes up?"

"I'll head over there." Bishop walked around the counter. "Just in case they get any ideas."

"You sure? The last time…" Thea gestured to her forehead.

"He caught me off guard." Bishop's smile was beatific, suspiciously so. But they all let him head over, watched him sit across from Bry and her brother.

"Hey." Bishop said.

"Bishop this is Morgan." Bry nodded to him. "Morgan, Bishop bought me this TV."

"We've met." Bishop said. Morgan looked him over. He didn't seem ready to start shit, but he was a big guy and Morgan didn't have a baseball bat on him this time. "Morgan's got a heck of a swing."

"Yeah." Morgan replied. "Thanks for helping Bry out."

"She's a good kid." Morgan just nodded. Truth be told, he didn't feel all that bad for cracking a rich boy in the skull, but he wasn't going to make an issue out of it, either. "How's your brother?"

"He's... breathing."

"You said he was going to be okay!"

"Bry..." Morgan shook his head. "I said he wasn't going to die. I don't know how he'll be when he wakes up. I don't know what she did to him."

"What..." Bry was in that stage between crying and shouting. "What did she do to *me*? Why can't I... everything hurts when I try and remember and I'm older now, and I keep... nothing is *right*, Morgan. I'm not right, I'm not..."

"She hurt you really bad, Bry." He swallowed a lump. "I didn't think we'd ever get you back. It made James and me scared. That's why she did it, to scare us."

"I didn't do anything to her."

"People aren't... they're not *people* to her." Morgan looked up to see Bishop watching him. *Yes, Rich Boy, I get the irony.* "Just things for her to use. I'm sorry I didn't keep her away from you."

"I don't like her."

"Yeah, me neither." He chuckled in her ear. It was getting easier to think of Bry as a girl for him, maybe because she was free to act like one. He made himself not cry. Crying was bullshit. He could feel the rich pretty boy watching him and he really didn't feel like showing the asshole anything.

*

The horses had fled the barn as soon as she'd come near it. They'd kicked the stalls open and forced their way through the sliding door and were gone. It was no matter to her.

Thomas' son had done a lot of work on the property, intending to settle it. The house in particular told her in no uncertain terms that it would not allow her to enter. Older and wiser than the house in the city, it was not fooled by her. She could try and force her way in, but in the end it wouldn't benefit her to do so. She didn't need what was inside the house.

They'd dissipated the cracked shells she'd called up. She walked the property, especially the collapsed lodges. She could feel the traces of what they'd done, and part of her was impressed. At Thea's age she wouldn't have been able to do this.

I kept Raifa alive when I was younger than she is now.

She wondered if that mattered.

"How many people do you think are here for the holiday, Paul?"

"Maybe a hundred." He sounded distant. She wondered what he thought was happening. After all, his entire life consisted of moments and none of them were like this. He followed her as obediently as a loyal hound, his steps matched to hers. He'd resisted, of course, and she'd been impressed again by how hard he'd fought.

"And there are no more ferries?"

"Not until after Christmas."

"Very good." She smiled. "Why don't you drive me down to your house?" It wasn't a request and they walked to his truck. She needed rest and time to prepare. A hundred people would be enough to start.

*

"Christ." James Williams was extremely uncomfortable. For one thing, he was still insanely sore, his entire body felt like he'd gotten the shit kicked out of him. For the other, he was shirtless in front of two women who he knew from experience would beat the shit out of him themselves. Morgan was also there, not saying much of anything. There was an old church organ in the living room. Where the fuck did they get a church organ? "Look, I told you, she didn't confide in me."

"What did she do with..." Seri took a breath. "Where's my dad's body?"

"Gone." He made himself look her in the eyes. "Same as my mom, my aunt and my uncles."

"What did she *do*?" This time it was Thea, who's stripped down to a tank top and a pair of jeans with blown knees. Her arms were tensed, and he half expected a broken nose or a busted lip, but she didn't actually threaten him.

"She dragged me out to the cemetery, carved my back up like a goddamn turkey, and..." He swallowed, remembering the way she'd cooed in his ear, her hands on him. "We visited two sets of graves, did it twice. She had a whole bucket of gunk she was using, she had me get the ingredients. Bunch of stores. And yeah, Morgan, I just did what she told me to do."

"I didn't say anything."

"You still have a face."

"Hey." Thea's voice cut between them. "Forget him. Answer *me*. What happened next?"

"We went back to the house. When it got darker..." He felt sick remembering it. "They came to the door."

"They?"

"My mom's fucking rotten corpse. All of them. Dead, decomposing, what do you want to hear? Dead people knocked on my door." He was shaking now. "She'd made me drive her here first, so I guess they were walking over there the whole time. I was pretty out of it by then."

"You helped her get in."

"Yeah, and? You want me to apologize? She almost killed me. I didn't know what she was doing until it happened." He felt hot all over. "We got back to the house, she made me walk... my legs moving by themselves. I was checked out. She plopped me on the couch and..." He stopped talking, remembering what she'd done next.

"And?"

"You don't need to know that part." He met Thea's eyes. "You can kill me if you want."

Both Thea and Seri narrowed their eyes. Thea was used to reading people, and Seri had a lot of psych classes under her belt. Both were unhappy with what they suspected had happened. Morgan spoke up.

"You want to tell me?"

"Fuck no." He looked over at his brother. "You already think I'm a shithead. Let it go."

"Fine, forget it." Thea stepped closer. "You were telling us about our parents."

"Six of them shambled in. I didn't recognize any of them. Hard to without faces." He shivered. "But my mom had a ring, blue stone. I recognized it. That was the last thing I remember seeing until I tried to tackle you in the hallway."

"Were they still in the house?"

"Shit, do we have to go *back*?" Seri looked alarmed at this idea.

"They're not there." Morgan replied. "I went back in before I came here. Wanted to see what was what. Cops showed up and I told them I was ripping the place down. Since it's my house…" He cut off, realizing that his mother's body was gone and he had no idea where it was.

"Shit." Thea snorted. She still didn't much care for James Williams, but getting angry at him wasn't going to fix anything now. "You, stay here and try not to *do* anything. You." She pointed at Morgan. "You might as well stay in here too."

"Yes ma'am." Morgan drawled, and once the two women had left the room he sat down next to James, who was staring at the floor.

"You sure you don't want to talk about it?"

"I don't even know what the hell to say." He looked from the floor to the ceiling. "Guess I got mine."

"Don't."

"How many times did you tell me not to fuck around?"

"She's a scary old bitch who pushes people around because she can, she ain't karma come to bite you in the ass." Morgan looked around the room. "Whatever we did, we didn't have *that* coming. Nobody has that coming."

"Sure." James just stared at the ceiling, remembering.

Thomas had come in from the back yard and Thea walked up to him.

"Sleeping Beauty's up."

"Anything useful."

"Aside from finding out she's even creepier than I thought?

Not really." She pressed up against him, laid her head on his chest. He brushed his hand through her hair. "Can we go be alone? I'd really like to be alone with you."

"I would like that." He breathed in the smell of her hair. Neither of them had showered yet. He liked it.

"Hey, Seri." Thea looked over at her cousin, who was digging through the fridge.

"I overheard. Joe and I'll watch them. Bishop's got Bry in hand for the moment." She frowned at a packet of yogurt. Thea kept buying it and then never eating it. "We need to figure out what to do with them."

"Later." She had Thomas' hand and pulled him to the room they shared, closed the door behind them. "I, ah…"

"It's fine. I'm tired too." He sat down on the bed.

"It's not that I don't want to…"

"Thea. It's fine." He stretched out, lying sideways across the mattress. "You're a beautiful woman and you turn me on like you wouldn't believe but right now I'm tense and exhausted. If you feel anything like I do…"

"I'm so fucking angry I feel like I'm going to pop." She lay down lengthwise, resting her head against his legs. "*Breathing* pisses me off right now."

"I'm thinking about the visions."

"Yeah? What about them?" She let his arm wrap around his leg, just held on, listened to his voice. Tried to relax, let the anger die down so that she could rest.

"You told me you were at a carousel. Since everything we do relates to symbols, that seems like a big one. The idea of going around and around, the colored horses, people riding them."

"I get you." She closed her eyes. "You smell good."

"I thought you didn't…"

"You still smell good." She smiled and let herself drift. "I get your point about the vision. And it's where I saw… Raifa. And she's real. So that's important."

"My vision was more literal. It showed us things that happened."

"Yeah, and she tried to kill us when we…" She opened her eyes. "Wait. *Was* she trying to kill us?"

"I guess?" Thomas sat up so he could look at her. "I mean, it seemed pretty unambiguous."

"Every other time she seems to go after *you*. The Lion was after you. Not *us*." Thea's brain was whirling in her head now. "Like you said, like Raifa said, she wants Seri and me. One of us, anyway."

"Maybe a giant dump truck could just fall on her." He stretched. "That would be nice. Just *whoomp* and we wouldn't have to deal with it anymore."

"From where, a passing airplane?"

"Sure, why not?"

"If we're getting silly, maybe a giant red tyrannosaur could just eat her." She reached up and tweaked his nose, feeling how warm he was.

He yawned.

"You falling asleep?"

"Yeah. I know it's still early but…"

"Been a day, yeah." She stretched out, letting her arm lie across his chest. "Like I wouldn't believe?"

"If I felt like I could move I'd show you." He yawned while talking that time. "You're so beautiful sometimes I feel like I have no business being with you."

"Dating me, it's not a job, it's an adventure." She snorted, broke into giggles. "Oh I *am* tired."

"Go to sleep."

"*You* go to sleep."

"That is the plan, yes."

"Now I'm getting a little…" She arched to rub her head against him. "Way too tired, but kinda."

"We'll both be here in the morning." His voice was slurring. "Love you."

"Love you too."

"I meant the thing before. You know that?"

"I do." She nodded, turned her head to the side. "Gonna use you as a pillow now."

She let it happen, still angry, but less seething about it. She liked how solid he was, how surrounded she felt in that moment. Free to leave, or to stay. To choose.

She smiled and pulled up her legs, curling up against him. *My Tommy. You poor thing, not letting you go now. No matter what.*

Seri poked her head in twenty minutes later, saw them sleeping, and closed the door as quietly as she'd opened it.

*

She had Paul drive her to the cove in the morning.

He was openly shaking now from the strain. He wasn't a young man. She watched him do it. Occasionally his face would twitch. The idea that it might kill him was there, but she simply didn't care one way or another. He was neither important enough for her to need him nor someone she particularly despised, he was just there. A person. The truck had an automatic transmission, she knew how to drive those, and she was *young* for a while longer.

She left him sitting in the cab with the engine idling and walked down to the dock. If not for the snow everywhere she'd have sat down. If it were warm she'd have put her feet in the water. When she'd been a child she'd loved the sea, remembered a trip the family had taken to the Adriatic coast. She'd been a child, then, her and Raifa running along the shore.

Those days gone, all she could do now is wait.

It took them longer than she expected. She was beginning to wonder if they'd been lost somehow when the first of them walked out of the water and onto the snow, waterlogged and mostly skeletal now. The decay was increasing. Still, they'd last long enough for her purposes. She was lucky anything was left of them really. One after another the bodies walked ashore, remarkably normal gaits.

These are the bodies of our children. Raifa's voice. *Please, please Robi. Let them rest, let us rest. When is it enough?*

She didn't have an answer for that. Likely it would never be.

She walked to where they were approaching her, gestured

and walked back to the truck. Paul's eyes conveyed horror at what he was seeing, at the wet, rotten things standing behind her, reeking of brackish water and their own decay.

"Get in the back." They did, climbing up into the pickup truck. She turned to Paul.

"Do you know how to put up posts?"

"Yes."

"Good. You'll supervise." She slid into the passenger seat. She wondered how long it would take them to put up a hundred stakes.

*

Thea blinked awake to the smell of coffee.

"Thought that might get you." Thomas was sitting on the edge of the bed. He'd lost his shirt somewhere along the way, so she took the moment to stare. She'd been attracted to people before, but with Thomas there was always an element of knowing just how strong he was, of feeling like she was in control of that much physical power. He could likely pick her up with one hand.

Next to him on the bed was a tray with coffee, a small plate with two English muffins (buttered, no jam, the way she liked them) and a larger plate with hash browns and bacon.

"We're out of eggs. Sorry."

"Are you kidding?" She sat up. "What did I do to get this?"

"Yesterday was…" He gestured. "I figured it couldn't hurt."

"It doesn't." She gave him a smile, her canines showing. "Gimme food."

He sat there and watched her eat. He wasn't feeling very hungry, at least not right at that moment. Watching her eat felt normal and real and he could just sit there and do that. He'd watched her sleep, only getting up when his body demanded it, and then he'd decided to make her food before the extended horde of guests in his house woke up. Bishop and Joe had spent yesterday getting the upstairs habitable, they were likely in his parents' old bed right now. Seri was on the couch in the living room, while Bry was using his old room. He didn't know where they'd stashed the Williams brothers, perhaps the basement. Maybe they'd left for all he cared.

Thea, though... he'd known he was in love with her a month before. What he was starting to realize was that he didn't think he could live without her, or at least that he didn't want to. It was terrifying, but he couldn't make himself turn away from it.

"Did I get food on my face?"

"No, it's called adoration." He smirked at her. "It's what makes new couples so disgusting to all their friends."

"We're not bad, though." She ate a piece of bacon, looked up at him. "I mean, I guess we're touchy feely with each other, but I try really hard not to name drop you every 20 seconds or call you 'Widdums'."

"For which I fervently thank you."

"I do call you Tommy a lot more." She looked down at her plate and he saw that her cheeks were flushed. "It's just what I think of you as."

"I don't mind, if that's the problem."

"Well, I wouldn't if I thought you hated it." She sipped her coffee. "But it's more... okay, this is going to sound maybe weird?"

"Weird for us, or..."

"Not *weird* weird, just... last night, when we were talking and I was leaning on you, I was so tired and angry and being with you made it bother me less. You make things better. You don't fix all my problems, but they don't seem as awful when I know I can count on you." He nodded.

"I've felt that way. With you. I trust you."

"Sometimes I feel like I should be warning you not to do that."

"Why?" She looked up in surprise, took a long look at his face. He'd look great in twenty years. She felt a little spasm at the idea of Thomas in his forties, wanting to see that. He didn't seem to be kidding.

"Her. You know... I mean, I'm not, there's a lot of stuff that I do that isn't great, I'm selfish, I'm a bit of a slob about food, I've dated around a bit, and…" She took a breath, let it out. "What if I'm like her?"

"You're not."

"But really, what if I am? I mean, whatever happened to her, we don't know what we'd be like if we went through that." It was like the words had started off small, a rock rolling down a hill, and now there were so many of them crashing down, jostling each other to get out. "You try and look hard, and part of you is, but you're in danger because you love me. You shouldn't have to be. And if I am like her, you deserve so much better than that, you deserve…"

"We're not them. You're not her, I'm not him." He moved closer so he could touch her hand, did so. She closed her fingers around his. "Of all the things I worry about, I have never once worried that you're like her. You're not. You're strong, and you're much kinder than you think you are, and I love you for it."

"We *are* disgusting." She pushed the tray away. "I never get to say I love you first."

"I'm sure you'll get it one of these days."

"Do you ever feel possessive?"

"Are you serious?" He laughed this time. "Remember the time in the kitchen?"

"Oh, right, David. You're not still…"

"Of him? No. Hell, I think he and Seri are done and they just haven't admitted it yet."

"Yeah, I think so too. I probably shouldn't be glad about it."

"He was a fucking tool."

"Not that your biased."

"Yeah, I get possessive all the time."

"Well, good, kind of. As long as you keep it under control. Because I do."

"You keep it under control or you get possessive?"

"Both, I hope." She patted the bed near her. "Come here."

He slid himself across, causing the mattress to deform under him. She ended up falling forward and laying on top of him.

"I keep forgetting you have a gravity well." She brushed her hands across his chest, toying with his nipples. He made a little noise. "I love playing with you."

"I love being played with." His voice quivered. "How much time do you think we have before we have to deal with..."

"Enough." She slid forward, brought her mouth down on his. The kiss was slow. She wanted to take her time, explore. She shifted to straddle him, felt him getting hard. She broke the kiss to look in his eyes.

"I love you, Tommy."

"See? You got it first." His hands were on her back. She closed her eyes and just felt his fingers moving along her skin, his erection trapped under her hips. "I love you too."

"Prove it." She lowered herself back down. "Slowly."

*

"Okay, they're going to be in there for a while." Seri was leaning against the kitchen counter, looking at her phone. "I suppose I'm going to go ask the downstairs boys if they want food."

"We're going to *feed* them now?" Bishop was chewing on a piece of toast.

"Look, you tell me what the right thing to do is." Seri straightened up, blew some hair out of her face. "Yeah, they're assholes. They *attacked* us. I don't... but they're Bry's brothers and they had to live with her directly pushing them around. How much better would Joe or Thea or I have done if Uncle Greg hadn't been there? Maybe I'd have ended up worse."

"Are you hearing this?" Bishop turned to Joe, who was studiously working on a bowl of cereal.

"Do not drag me into your argument with her. Nobody can actually *win* an argument with Seri."

"Christ. Well, *I'm* not related to them."

"Lucky you." Joe drawled before going back to his cereal.

"Just be cool." Seri walked around the counter. She stopped at her purse and pulled out a can of mace.

"Okay, if I'm being cool, why are you bringing mace with you?"

"Because I don't trust them." She opened the basement door and walked downstairs. Morgan had cleared the battered old couch down there, and James was sleeping on it. Morgan was slumped in a chair, and she couldn't tell if he'd slept or not. He started as she came into view.

"Oh." He opened and closed his eyes. "Uh… hey."

"I just… you hungry?"

"Me? No." She could tell he was lying by the way he licked his lips at the question. "I can go a while without eating."

"You look like you have already."

"I'm always skinny."

"What about him?" She inclined her head at James, who was still unconscious even while the two of them whispered at each other.

"You want to feed *him*?"

"Want to? No. Feel obliged to? Yeah."

"You don't owe us anything." Morgan stood up. "I'll go…"

"Look, can we just stop?" She fought the urge to put her hand in her pocket. "Yeah, I get it. We don't like each other, and we may never like each other. Great. But you know, we are related, and just because *she's* a horrible shitstain doesn't mean we have to keep treating each other like… this."

"You'd be an idiot to trust us. I'd look *down* on you for trusting us."

"Then today's your lucky day." She produced the can, showed it to him. "I don't."

They stood there for a moment.

"You look a lot like her." Morgan's voice cracked. "It freaks me out every time I look at you."

"Well, I'm not her. You know, you don't look all that different, except the hair." She tapped the side of her head. "You got the eyes."

"Don't remind me." He sat down again. "Were you at that family reunion? The one… back in 88? All her kids, I think the last one they ever did."

"Probably." Seri tried to remember. "I think I was eleven. My mom and dad died the next year."

"Same."

"She didn't seem…"

"Just old and bitchy." He looked at her, really *at* her and not seeing someone else. "I've been piss scared for the past decade. I… fuck, I can't make myself apologize. I'm actually trying to do it and I can't, I can't fucking do it, I know what I did. Can't."

"I didn't ask."

"Why the fuck not?"

"Because I don't need one? Shit, I don't know. Some of the shit you did you *can't* apologize for. How old are you?"

"Twenty five."

"So you were fifteen when she came around. I can barely handle it *now*." She took a step closer. "For now, I won't feel sorry for you and you won't apologize and you can come upstairs and eat some food, and bring something down for him. I wouldn't let that woman get her hands on a sewer rat that bit me, much less you."

She held out her hand to him. Inside she felt like pissing herself. She was close enough that he could grab her and the mace would be very hard to get him with. It was easy to talk big about it, but this? Her insides felt like they wanted to jump out of her.

He looked at her hand for a moment, then took it. Let her help him up.

"You still freak me out."

"Well, *I* never broke into anyone's house, so…" Once he was up she let go of his hand and turned. "Come on. We don't have a ton of options, but we can make some oatmeal for him, and you can have whatever we can dig up."

*

Thea enjoyed the boneless feeling.

Thomas was half-asleep. They'd knocked the tray with her mostly-eaten breakfast onto the floor. Luckily nothing was broken. She'd have hated to have to pick mug fragments out of the rug. She watched his chest rise and fall, looked for the scars she knew were gone now. It was always strange to look for marks you'd seen, to know they'd been healed.

"Do you think we could get tattoos?"

"Sure? Why wouldn't we be able to?"

"Well, your scars got healed." She ran her hand along his ribcage. "You had a mark right here."

"Yeah, but that was from the night with Joe."

"Okay." She leaned in and smelled him. "I was thinking we could get some when we got married."

He raised an eyebrow and she slid up and kissed his forehead above his eye.

"You did ask me."

"Yeah, and you said we'd talk about it."

"So let's." She supported herself on her elbows above his head. "When?"

"After her..."

"That goes without saying. How much longer?"

"As soon as you're comfortable with?" He was blinking, the light coming in the window playing over them both as the sun rose. "I've never been engaged, I don't know how long you're supposed to wait."

"You have to go back to school first."

"I do?"

"Evvie told me you had like a semester to go."

"Christ, you're *talking* with her?"

"Yes."

"No guy likes it when his ex talks to his current girlfriend."

"Fiancée." She poked him. "Get used to that. You have to go finish school so I can go."

"Why can't we go at the same time?"

"With what money? I don't even know how we're going to pay for me to go at all. I mean, hopefully the house in Warwick will sell, but still. It ain't cheap." She brushed her hand through his chest hair. "So you go to school, finish up, then get a job. I go after. Maybe we get married after you graduate?"

"If that's what you want to do." He took a breath. "I don't

want to rush you."

"We'll see. Maybe I'll just want to be engaged forever." She dropped herself onto him, loving how he didn't even grunt when her full weight landed on his torso. "Besides, you have to get me a ring."

"I actually have a ring."

"What, really?"

"My grandmother Willrew left it to me." He gestured towards the bookcase. "It's over there."

"Break that bad boy out!" She rolled off of him. "Come on, do the whole thing. You know, the thing."

"Okay, calm your jets."

"My jets are entirely agitated, hurry up." She was sitting up on the edge of the bed watching as he walked over, opened the top drawer and took a small box out. "Oh my *God* you actually do have a ring."

"I just told you that."

"Yeah, but that was just mouth noises." He walked back and dropped to one knee. "Don't be ironic about this."

"I'm *not.*"

"You're smirking."

"I'm a little amused but I'm entirely serious." He opened the box and took out a silver band. "This is the engagement ring. There's a wedding ring, too, if you want it, or I can buy you another one."

"Come on, hurry up, ring me, I want to go show Seri, it's crucial to the whole process."

"'*Ring me.*'" He laughed, slid the ring on her finger. She looked at it more closely, saw there were small gemstones set in the band, some blue, some clear.

"It's really pretty." She held it up to the light. "Now I feel like a jerk. I don't deserve it."

"It's the ring I have, Thea." He was smiling gently. "As far as I'm concerned you can have everything."

She bent down and kissed him hard, nearly knocking him over. Her eyes matched the ring. He wasn't sure that was a lucky accident.

"Come on. I have to tell Seri." She grabbed his hand and yanked, knowing that she couldn't possibly move him if he wouldn't come and knowing he would. He let her drag him out of the room and into the hallway, and so they saw Joe and Bishop sitting in the living room staring into the kitchen, while Seri and Morgan Williams were apparently... *talking*?

To each other?

"Uh...hi?" Thea said, not sure what else to say at this development.

"Hey, welcome to the waking world." Seri stood up. "He's telling me what he knows about her. General stuff. Then he's going to take some food downstairs."

"I should probably do that now." He stood up, grabbed the bowl of oatmeal, and nodded to Seri. She nodded back. Then he went down as fast as he could without looking like he was scurrying away, which he absolutely was. Seri closed the door behind him.

"What the hell did I just see?"

"Either we're going to work with them or we're not." Seri looked Thea up and down. "You're wearing an engagement ring."

"You did *not* just ruin my big reveal."

"You were going to waste time asking me about feeding and treating them like people, we all know we're going to be better than she is, so I moved it along." She took Thea's hand gently, pulled her over to the kitchen and sat her down gently. "Christ, that's a nice ring." A smile quirked Seri's lip. "You got engaged before me. My baby cousin. Congratulations, you horrible woman."

"You'll do the whole..." Thea bit her lip, feeling unusually nervous. "You know, maid of honor thing?"

"Of course. Who else? Shut up Joe."

"I wasn't going to... you shut up." Joe got up and walked over, hugging Thea. "Congratulations, brat. You both have awful timing."

Bishop looked over at Thomas, gave him the standard *are you sure* head tilt, and Thomas nodded. That settled, he went back to watching the three of them get excited about the ring and making plans for the future.

Thomas wanted to take part in it, but he couldn't. Something was tickling at the back of his skull. Something he couldn't quite sense, couldn't quite feel but knew was happening. He shook his head, feeling like he was going to charge something.

"Tommy?" Thea had noticed. That made him smile, that she could pick up on it. "You okay?"

"Yeah, I'm okay. I'm going to go for a walk around back." He stepped to her, kissed her just to let himself feel something comforting, lingered as her hand brushed across his cheek. "You three go ahead and make ridiculously elaborate plans."

"I can do that." He could see concern on her face, in the set of those lovely eyes. He wished he knew what he was feeling, where it was coming from. He pulled on his boots and threw on his jacket and went outside, looking at the ruins of his backyard, the collapsed garage, the destroyed pool. He might as well just fill it in. The concrete was buckled in several places.

He saw Denny Whatley peering over the fence into his yard. That made him low level irritated, since he knew the Whatleys had made several trips into the ruined garage to steal things. He found himself walking counter-clockwise around the pool, trying to unfocus and let whatever was bothering him come up.

"That's unlucky."

"Be more specific." He'd known who it was when he didn't hear anyone get anywhere near him, looked up to see the close cropped beard and glasses. "I definitely didn't call you this time."

"Maybe I stay called. Or…"

"Maybe you're just in my head." Thomas sighed. "I really hate the cryptic bit."

"Was I really all that cryptic? It's possible I don't know either. You could try and have some sympathy for me." He had a smile that completely undercut his words. "Anyway, what's bothering you?"

"I don't know. It's like an itch. The feeling of *wrong.*"

"It's possible you're just now realizing that if anything happens to her…"

"That's not new. I've been aware of that for a while." He

looked up at the grey sky. "Maybe since I saw her at the party."

"Ah, love at first sight."

"If you're just here to bag on her…"

"I told you before, I think she's excellent." The smile this time was much less acidic. "I'm just trying to move your thoughts along. If it's not about her, what *is* it about?"

"It's about Dassalia." They were still walking around the pool. Thomas looked inside at the collapsed diving board. "I need a way to find her. I feel like I should already know where she is."

"It's a shame you don't have a place with resonance. You know, a place where she did a working." The bearded man stopped walking at one of the buckled concrete slabs, put his hand into the snow and pulled a chunk of broken dirt out of the ground, held it. "All things connect to all other things, after all."

Thomas stared at him for a moment.

"I'm a motherfucking assclown."

"Well, *that's* colorful."

"She tried to kill me right here."

"Indeed."

"She dropped a magic fucking Lion on me right goddamn *here*."

"This is the crux of what I was saying."

Thomas ignored that, turned and walked to where he'd been standing when he'd finally killed the damn thing, the place he collapsed. Where Thea had found him. There were still scorch marks on the concrete, he could see them under the dusting of snow. The mark where she'd healed him. Near that, he walked until he found the exact spot it had died, the claw marks torn into concrete.

He drew a poor peacock in the snow, and a worse rooster, wishing he had a way to color it gold. *You could go in and get Thea, maybe Joe, they could help.*

He thought about that. He really didn't want to involve them. What if she was ready for this? What if she could somehow attack them through it? But he remembered the night it had happened, how she'd gone off without him and he'd been angry, they'd argued. Now he was going to do that? With her less than twenty yards away?

Finally he walked over, opened the door, looked inside. Thea and Seri were still talking at the counter. He watched Thea's head move to the side, her hand outstretched, that strange little rat ghost floating around her arm and her stroking behind what would be its head, if it wasn't a ghost. She fit his life so well, made it feel like a life, he didn't know what he'd do without her. She looked up as the door opened, smiling.

"Hey, there you are. I was just starting to worry you fell in that giant hole."

"Can you come out?"

"Sure. What's up?"

"I think I can find her." That hung there for a moment. He could see the rat ghost dance around, watched Balthazar stalking it. The cat had tried several times to catch it already. Thea pushed away from the counter.

"You want me to come out too?" Joe spoke up from the den. Thomas turned his head, looked at him and Bishop sitting on the couch.

"Someone needs to stay in here." He didn't say *I don't want to leave those two assholes alone in my house*, he didn't have to say it. Seri spoke up.

"Bish and I can handle them. You three go play Magical Nancy Drew and the Hardy Wizards."

And so the three of them ended up outside, with Thomas explaining his basic idea.

"Like the map viewing we did." Joe was biting his fingernails. It was a nervous habit, Thomas was starting to recognize it. "The symbols?"

"The peacock for Argus." Thea said. "I'm not sure what the chicken is for."

"It's a rooster. Associated with Heimdall. Sentinel of Bifrost. It's a Norse thing."

"We need to broaden our tastes." Thea half-smiled. "I bet there's an awesome Japanese god of watching things we could have used here."

"So how do we help you?" Joe said.

"I'm going to focus on the symbols, try and let them work on my subconscious. I'm the one she tried to hit, so I can exploit that. Thea and I can link pretty well by now, so she'll tether me. You watch for a backlash."

"You think she can hit back?"

"It can't hurt to be ready just in case." Joe just nodded at that. Thomas looked to Thea, who stepped behind him, put her hands on his shoulders.

"You ready?"

"The sooner we get it done the better." She bent down and whispered in his ear. "I'll be right here if she does anything."

He sat down in the snow, crossed his legs beneath him. It took him several minutes to get his thoughts to settle, to focus upon the idea of watching, the *panoptes*, keen-eyed and seeking. His legs were starting to cramp up from the cold when the sensation worrying at the back of his thoughts merged with the all-seeing force he was directing, and he lurched as the claw marks in the ground flared in hot white light.

He saw the horses eating in a field far from the barn. They wouldn't go back. Ramses looked up as his attention passed over them, but he went back to cropping grass. The big Percheron knew the farm, knew the land around it. It was wrong now.

He frowned. Why wouldn't Paul have...

His vision lurched again and he saw Paul, standing in a field, sweating in the cold. His lips were bitten, his eyes wide and staring as he directed shapes. He let his focus switch from Paul to the shapes and nearly recoiled. They were corpses, ice crystals forming in their dead flesh as they worked. Much of them was exposed bone. He'd seen dead things before but not like this, not such utter mockeries of what life was, what they were supposed to be. Worse, inside them he could feel the pulsating void, the cracked shells of the Beharion.

They were erecting posts. There was a small forest of them, filling up the former north pasture, where the stone lodges had collapsed into the ground. He didn't know how many.

Thomas was trembling, but no longer cold, burning up as he forced himself to keep seeing. He knew that through the link Thea could see everything, could feel her practically holding him in place, keeping him from losing his focus.

The old house welcomed him. Viewed like this it was almost a person. It assured him it had not let her in, that it would sooner collapse in flames than do so. It very much wanted him to know it was a good, faithful house. It had enjoyed their stay, enjoyed being used for its purpose again. It was an old house, and many had lived within it – it cared for its purpose. It would not let her in.

He coughed. Put both of his hands flat in the snow and heaved himself upright, feeling himself here in the back yard, and also there, where his family had set themselves into the soil. Where he'd bled and shed blood, where he'd run in the woods and slept under the stars and watched bonfires. Thea's hands felt like banked coals through his shirt, so hot they almost burned him. He welcomed it, the heat of them, the counter-pull they exerted.

The chicken coop was empty. She'd have killed the horses if she could have caught them, but she couldn't, so the chickens, and a fox that got too close had ended up chopped. Their blood had filled two buckets, and she'd drawn a large shape in the snow. A twisted, gnarled version of a star, with a burning eye in the center, roughly twenty feet across. It was right there in front of the forest of stakes.

He saw cars driving up the road. One after another. The drivers gripped in panic, each wondering why they had no choice but to drive north to the old Willrew place. Faces twisted in confusion and fear, compelled. Waiting for them, she scattered the rest of the blood along the edges of the old lodges, the heaped soil where they'd been swallowed, humming to herself.

He let go, sweat in his eyes, running down his face.

Thea was supporting him physically, which he knew must have been an effort for her. She didn't show it, though, helping him walk over to the house and inside the kitchen. She guided him to the counter, sat him down on one of the stools.

"That was a weird thing to watch." Joe said as he walked inside. "I didn't see any sign that she was doing anything back."

"She's busy." Thomas said thickly, trying to shake himself back to normal.

"That's one way to put it." He looked up at Thea's voice, saw the disgust on her face. "But we know where she is now." Her hands were still on him, and he reached up to cup one, clasp it to himself. She brushed his hair out of his face. "She's on the farm."

*

It was approaching night by the time the last ropes were tied.

There ended up only being 84 people to restrain. Lastly she ordered Paul against one of the stakes, had him tied in his turn, and finally released him. He sagged in relief, while his face twisted in horror at the sight of her, or what she brought with her.

"You're... not..."

"No. I'm not." She tried to smile but the look of it only frightened him. There were voices all around them raised in outrage, fear, outright disgust if they could see her shambling children. She ignored them. Each of the stakes had been marked, the sign carved in turn. She walked away from the stakes. It was possible some of them could work their way free after a few hours.

They didn't have a few hours.

She walked past the boat up on a trailer, parked near the barn. She wished she'd managed to get the horses. She probably could have held them all insensate indefinitely with that much life. The darkness was coming on fast, it wasn't even five pm yet and she could see lights in the cove.

She stopped walking.

Why were there lights in the cove?

She walked towards the stone wall around the old house, peered over it into the darkness. There was a large, expensive looking boat pulling up to the dock. The lights cut out suddenly, sooner than she'd expect. Wouldn't they want to tie off? With the lights gone she couldn't see much of anything from that distance. She turned to the rotten prisons of her children's souls.

"Go kill those."

Chapter Twenty Three

Who Are Like God

"So how do we get down there? The ferry service is stopped until the 27th." Joe was pacing.

"Well, first off, *we* don't all have to go there." Thea replied. Behind the couch Morgan Williams was pacing, while Bry followed him, perhaps unconsciously imitating him. The little girl's unconditional love had been earned with a few simple gestures back before Dassalia had happened, and she didn't seem inclined to abandon it. "Thomas and I can…"

"Letting the two of you go in without backup is a great way for us all to end up dead." Morgan replied, and Thea fought the urge to tell him to go fuck himself.

"You're a hero now?"

"No, but I know a little something about all this shit, and even if you have the jolly green giant over there you're going to need some backup." He stopped pacing. "And if I get taken out, who cares?"

Bry was staring at him as if what was actually happening was finally occurring to her, she was finally getting what Morgan was saying. She didn't say anything, but her blue eyes were huge.

Thomas stood up and walked over to Williams, stared at him for a moment. Williams met those green eyes stare for stare, even though the bigger man could likely break his neck in a single shot without even doing anything magical. Then Thomas turned to Thea.

"He's right."

"I must admit I didn't expect *you* of all people to back him up."

"I don't have to like him to know he's right. If the two of us go in alone, especially once we've used magic to get there…"

"Why would you use magic to get there?" Bishop spoke up from the couch.

"Because the only boat I have access to is on that island right now?"

"What kind of boat do you want to use?" He was looking at his watch. "Ten minute drive to my house and I can have the keys to a yacht, a nice Boston Whaler or a sailboat. I think my dad took the sailboat to Saint Barts, but at least two of the boats will still be there."

"You have three boats?" Morgan said. He looked utterly nonplussed.

"I'm the designated disappointment to two very wealthy people." Bishop stood up. "Why don't we all go for a ride? Even if we don't all get on the boat..."

He stopped talking when James Williams came up out of the basement, wearing clothes. They wouldn't have fit him a week before, because they were Thomas' old pre-growth spurt jeans, but now they fit him and that was pretty terrifying. He looked like a vengeful scarecrow.

"What the hell are you doing up here?"

"Turns out the floor's not real insulated." He looked at the assembled group. "If you're going after her, I'm coming."

"I barely trust *him*." Thea hooked a thumb at Morgan. "Why in God's name would I trust you?"

"Because she pinned me down on a couch and..." He stopped, looked down at Bry. Looked back up, his eyes wild, wet things, equal parts rage and self loathing. "Don't bring me and I'll figure out how to steal a boat from somebody and get there myself."

"For Christ's sake, Jimm... *James*, look at yourself." Morgan stepped closer. "You're a walking corpse."

"That makes me even with mom then." He met his brother's eyes. "Don't play big brother now. We've never been good at it. I'm *going*."

"Let him." Joe spoke up. Even Seria, who usually backed up Joe when he put himself forward, didn't believe this one. He looked at the pairs of eyes staring at him and nodded at James. "He's got as much right to face her as any of us, and it might be the only way he ever becomes something more than a worthless sack of shit."

"Thanks."

"Don't thank me. I figure you're an extra target." Joe walked over and pulled on a coat. "Let's go for that drive and we can argue more once we actually have a boat."

*

Shambling corpses can't actually see any better in the dark than living things. They're just not particularly put off by that fact. They only moved through Dassalia's intervention – the animating force was supplied by the long imprisoned spirits of her dead children, pulled from life too soon by the force of the web she'd attempted to knit between them, but they had very little in the way of minds.

They usually didn't need to be able to think particularly clearly.

They were at the bottom of the hill and on the snow-covered path to the dock when the first person stepped into their view. He was carrying a large hammer, a sledge. He was large himself, imposing. This of course meant little to them.

They were capable of moving quickly, despite much of their flesh being missing or frozen from their walk along the bottom of the bay. They did so, bounding through the snow at him.

"I'm sorry."

He smashed the handle of the sledgehammer into the ground and a sound like thunder pealed, the snow blasted away from him by the impact. The corpse that was closest to him was also blasted away. It was much stronger than human, powered by Dassalia's rite. It pried itself up from the snow. The rest of them circled him, their crude minds unable to understand what he'd done.

He held the hammer above his head. The sky closed up, the moon and stars vanishing behind clouds. The rumbling began in earnest.

Atop the hill, Dassalia raised an eyebrow in surprise at how blatant it was. He wasn't trying to sneak up on her. He was openly, *brazenly* calling on power. Well, two could do that. And she had many, many more sources of pain and fear and rage to draw on than he did. She dropped on her haunches in the snow, ignoring the cold as it washed through her dress into her legs. She completed the mark of Yig, then the four triangles of the Enochian Aethyrs, and finally the three-lobed burning eye. Each of the stakes flared as her guests writhed, their emotions fed into the marks she'd prepared with sacrificed blood.

In her mind she called on the watcher. No mere hound, not even a lion, she called upon the triple maw, the eater of the dead, that which chased after Hades' prisoners. It shimmered like a heat mirage over snowy fields, made itself real. She exulted, so much power available to her she didn't even have to concentrate.

The air seemed to tear apart like a caul as the three headed beast slavered from three maws, shaking its heads, towering fifteen feet from the ground. Its saliva hissed as it hit the snow. Six eyes turned to her, waiting.

"Down the hill. He shakes the Earth and the Sky. Bring him to me, alive if possible. Intact if not."

It bounded, larger than an elephant, much faster. She had elsewhere to be. The cairn of stones, where he'd been laid to rest.

She picked up the two urns and made her way there, her shoes almost useless in the snow.

Thea was leading the others up the hill while Thomas played distraction. Both of the Williams boys had guns – Jimmy was carrying a pistol Morgan had handed him from inside his truck, while Morgan had a rifle slung over his shoulder. Nobody was particularly sanguine about them working. Bishop had stayed on the boat, moved it away from the dock and back out into the bay proper. None of them had any idea what he could do if they failed but somebody had to escape. That left Thea, Joe and Seri to count on each other, and Thea's own ability to work magic.

She felt cold in a way the winter night could never match, moved beyond fear by what she could see. They'd watched the corpses march down the hill, known who they were, and nobody had argued when Thomas had said he'd deal with them. They weren't *his* parents.

But when the giant three-headed monster dog leapt over the hill and bounded down towards the dock, they'd all stopped moving for a moment. Thea barely managed to keep from completing what she'd called up, let it rush past them.

"It's heading right for…"

"He'll be fine." She didn't believe it herself but she had to say it. Thomas was good at the fighting, she'd seen him in action. She had to trust him now, and do her part of the plan. Such as it was. She gestured and they started walking again, Joe and Thea scanning for any surprises along the way.

"She doesn't look to have prepared for us."

"Why would she? No ferry, no reason for us to even know what she's doing." Joe said.

"Do we?" They were all whispering, not seeing her anywhere. To the north the forest of stakes, each visible if you could see the lines and sparks of magic, a hideous dull red color that sucked greedily at the poor bastards tied in place. There were men and women and even a few children. They didn't see any infants. Thea felt a wave of nausea at that idea.

"Can we go cut them down?"

"There's like ninety people over there." Morgan hissed. "It'll take a while and I'm positive she'll notice."

"Maybe that's how we get her to come back over." Seri turned to face him. "You have a better idea?"

"It'll kill them." Thea said.

"You're sure?"

"If I were doing a big ritual like this? She's drawing on their pain for power. As long as they are alive and suffering they're a renewable resource. But if she's going to lose one anyway…"

"They might as well die and give her a burst." James finished for her. He knew better than anyone how their grandmother prolonged things, and why.

They walked around the stone wall and onto the property,

scanning for her. It was Seri who pointed at the snow.

"Hey, not that weirdo magic vision isn't great, but there's footprints there."

"Sure. Use *eyes*." James laughed, fought back a cough. The edge of his voice suggested he was on the verge of open panic. "Looks like she went around between that house and the barn there."

"Come on." Thea tried to sound like she had any idea what she was doing. "Let's see if we can surprise Nana."

Down the hill, he'd been about ready to consider himself victorious.

The corpses were strong, fast, and there were six of them. However, they fought like the mindless dead things they were. The hammer weighed nothing in his hand, he could swing it like a child's prop weapon, but it crashed into them like the wrath of heaven. He spun and twirled and smashed and the peals of thunder echoed as he struck.

"I'm sorry." He said as he crushed what he thought was a woman's body. Perhaps Thea's mother, or the Williams brothers'. It was hard to feel triumphant seeing this evidence of what she'd done. He hoped that destroying the bodies bought them some kind of freedom, but he had no idea. He just knew it had to happen. He imagined Thea having to do this instead of him and grew so angry he could hear his pulse hammering...

Why would my pulse be getting louder?

He turned in time to see it leap over a large drift, charging right at him. Three heads, each trailing froth as it beat the ground with huge black paws. It made a bear look like a kitten. He threw the hammer, sending it arcing through the last of the shambling bodies and sending bone and gristle flying, then leapt as Cerberus (because what else could it be, with three heads and a freaking snake-head on its tail) crashed down where he was standing. He barely managed to clear it, several snake heads hidden under its shaggy fur lashing out to try and bite him.

He caught the hammer in his hand and let it pull him. He wasn't limited – the thunder god had modern four color myths, and he was as free to borrow from Simonson as he was Sturluson. He came to earth some sixty yards away from it, while it snapped at the air and ripped the ground with its claws, confused by how he got away from it. He spun the hammer, wishing he'd thought to attach a thong, and smashed the ground in front of him to set off a peal of thunder and keep the hound from focusing on something else.

Something or someone.

It barked, each head in turn, ringing out across the island. He could see the mane of snakes now, risen from its fur, their tongues flicking in the air. It leapt forward, and he felt the drop of fear in the base of his guts, the urge to run clawing at him. *You can't stand against that.*

But the thunder god of the Norse would stand against a serpent as big as the world. The dog was big, but it wasn't *that* big. He whirled with the hammer in his hands and smashed the leftmost head, which was on his right, as they came in to try and tear him apart. The burst of thunder blew the snow away, sent Cerberus reeling to the side. He held the hammer aloft, called on the sky to answer him.

Lightning crackled. Ordinarily he'd be in a hurry to get past this, get to *her*. But his role now was to keep her attention, make her think this was where the fight was. He didn't have to rush. As long as he trusted Thea, he could keep his pace, let the monster make mistakes.

It howled in pain as it righted itself only to taste lightning. The three headed hound of Hades was a child of Typhon, the fearsome many headed volcano beast, enemy of Zeus. Lightning was not its friend. It glared at him with five eyes now, the leftmost eye crushed by the hammer. Blood trailed down its muzzle, lapped at by the snakes in its mane.

He tapped the ground with the hammer again. Above him, the sky was now boiling, clouds thick and dark crashing against one another, a great wind blowing in from the west. He wanted the farm downwind so the hound couldn't smell them, wanted constant thunder to keep it from hearing them.

It charged again, and he followed suit, hurling the hammer

into the teeth of the middle head, hearing its jaw crack from the impact, the head snapped back. The lightning ripped the air apart as it came down, seeking and finding the hammer lodged in the dog's broken jaw.

He was amazed to see it still moving, still stalking around him. The middle head looked ravaged, but it still snarled defiance. He held out his hand and the hammer tore free and flew to him. The sound of many snakes hissing, the snow actually catching fire from its blood. And the longer it kept him there...

Don't panic. Trust her. She can do this.

Up the hill they heard the snarls, the barks, and the thunder as lightning tore down, felt the wind as the clouds warred in the sky above them.

"Jesus." James whispered. "He's not subtle."

Thea just smiled. They rounded the corner and saw her past the barn, sitting at the base of a stone cairn, placing the urns. She didn't seem to have noticed them. Both of the Williams boys froze in place, conditioned to fear her. Seri, who hadn't seen her yet since this all started, turned to Thea.

"Is that her? She's got black hair."

"It's her." Now that they were there, Thea had no idea how to proceed. Was it okay to just kill her with her back turned? She'd hesitated before and now they were there and people were writhing on stakes over in the north pasture. *You have to do this.*

Joe was watching what she was doing. It was clearly magic, and it just as clearly pulled hard on the people she'd confined to stakes. He turned to his cousins, fighting to keep his voice down.

"We have to do something now, like right now."

"Do you?" She spoke, clearly audible from at least forty yards away and they all jerked. Thea almost bit her own *tongue* for not having just attacked her on sight. "Oh, I knew you were coming. I knew he'd come down alone if you let him, but I also knew you'd never let him."

"Fuck this." James said, stepping around Thea and firing, emptying the pistol.

She stood there, smiling at him. His hand was trembling now, the gun still held out in front of him.

"Transmutation spell." She indicated the urns. "A strong one, too. A talented boy you've chosen. Almost as talented as you, perhaps." She turned to face James. "I'm not angry."

His knuckles were as white as his lips. Morgan had his rifle down off of his shoulder but wasn't bothering to point it at her.

"All my grandchildren in one place. Thank you. It saves me time finding you. I was going to have to, after." Above her, points of light began to shimmer. "And here are your parents, and your aunts and uncles. A pity that the bodies were destroyed. But I'll have your bodies to use, I suppose."

"You could just stop this." Thea said, her hair whipping in the storm blowing up the hill. Even in the jacket and gloves and boots she'd worn the cold sliced into her. "Let them all go, walk away. You're young again, that's what you wanted."

"Oh, no, this is already running away from me." She shook her head. "I would need to keep them all like that indefinitely and they'll die in a day or two, exposed as they are. No, there's no going back."

"We're seriously trying to reason with her?" Morgan grunted. "There's no option b?"

"Please." Seri was standing next to Thea. "You *can't* be this bad. Nobody could be this bad. You have to see that. Even the people you want to keep didn't want what you offered them, it was that wrong. Everything you're doing... even your *sister*."

Seri had the uncomfortable experience of seeing her own face twist in fury at her.

"Don't mention Raifa to me. She's the one who wept over you all. She chose you squirming bundles of shit over her own sister. From the same womb and she picks you." She grunted. "No more of this."

"I asked nicely." Thea said. She could feel the old woman doing something else, and so she thought back to the discussion the night before, after she and Thomas had finished tasting and teasing and touching one another and lay spent, bodies entwined. The discussion of what they'd wished would happen.

Dassalia lashed out, calling on the leather winged nightmare monsters, calling forth one for each of her wayward grandchildren. Her intention was to see the children all safely bound, bundled into the air to watch helplessly. The monsters wheeled into view, screeching from the storm clouds above.

What she hadn't expected was the bright red maw that closed on the first one, crushing it with teeth the size of small swords. The feet, with enormous claws that crushed two as they tried to land. Shocked, she turned to see Thea smiling, walking at her.

"Remember, you picked door number two." Thea felt sick, but she forced the smile. Belief was a big part of it. Dassalia had all those people to use. She had to be kept off balance. "Turns out it's got dinosaurs behind it."

She turned to Seri, a half step behind her. "The four of you can't help me. Take them. Try and get those people out." Then she turned her attention back to her wicked grandmother, who was balling up her fists next to the stone cairn that lay atop Thomas' grandfather. "Nana and I need to have a chat."

*

Thomas' jacket was shredded from a near-miss, the serpent that was the monster's tail having ripped across his back as he avoided those massive yellow fangs. Its breath was astonishing, a reek that made anything he'd ever smelled pale in comparison, and he'd worked on a farm in high summer.

His arms and legs were starting to get tired. He could only hold the god in his flesh for so long, he wasn't meant to *be* a god. Dassalia's sending had been pulled forth with many sacrificial victims, it would outlast him and for a giant three headed dog it didn't seem to be making mistakes. It was circling him now, looking for a way past the hammer and the thunder it unleashed. He was starting to feel dizzy with it constantly pathing to its left...

He stopped trying to keep it from getting around him, instead dropping to place the head of the hammer on the ground.

He bent his head and concentrated on the slight dizziness, the turning and turning. He heard it make a sound, opened his eyes. It was staring at him, the leftmost head whimpering from its shattered eye socket, the middle head grinding that broken jaw.

It waited, trying to understand. Not able to see it yet. Around them the wind was picking up. Thomas finally stood, holding the hammer up above his head, calling to the sky. Cerberus was a hound of the deep earth, the Hadean depths, a chthonic being. It didn't understand wind.

The dog of hell tired of waiting and leapt for him.

He waited until it was almost on top of him before crashing the hammer down into the ground, sending another wave of force at it, knocking it prone for a moment. Only a moment. Barely a heartbeat before it righted itself, snarling from three heads at his trick.

The wind was now shrieking at them.

The hound only realized what was happening when the snow around them began to rise into the air in great streams, reverse snow showers as small wind devils formed.

They were harbingers.

The funnel that touched down around them was as wide as a football field and it tore at the earth, at the snow and ice, and at the two of them. Thomas merely held onto the hammer and rose in the heart of the cyclone, watching it spin around him. Driven by his will.

The guardian of the underworld had no idea what was happening. A tornado was utterly beyond its understanding. It was ripped from the ground by 300 mile an hour winds, hit with swirling shards of ice and even rocks and broken wood as the dock was torn up into fragments, howling in confusion.

Thomas guided the wind out into the cove, himself at its heart. He was glad Bishop had moved the boat away. The tornado became a waterspout, water mist mixing with the ice and wreckage. He made it spin faster, feeling himself stretching thin, but battering the dog monster the harder.

Then he simply let the tornado stop spinning. A natural one couldn't have done it, but this wasn't natural, and it fell apart and dumped the monster dog into the water. It thrashed, having no experience of anything like this – there was no myth of Cerebus swimming, or being dropped from a height into a half-iced brackish cove.

Thomas angled himself and dropped from the sky, throwing the hammer as he fell. He crashed into a snow bank. The fall likely would have killed him had he been himself, but he wasn't. He struggled to his feet, saw the blast of yellow-white light as the hammer crashed into the open mouth of the thrashing, struggling beast. Like lightning from heaven the hammer fell and the monster with it, and Thomas knew he was finally just himself again.

He knew this because everything hurt as he dragged himself free from the snowbank, his whole body threatening to start shuddering in the cold. He forced himself onto the road, packed down by the treads of many more cars than it was used to, and headed north.

Five minutes of fighting the wind he'd called up, slow to dissipate, and he was cresting the hill and on the farm. *His* farm. He could see the magic in the field of posts and it made his stomach flip. If he'd recently eaten he might have been sick. He could also see Joe and Seri and the two Williams brothers, on the edge of the posts arguing back and forth.

And he could see a T-Rex fighting monster bats...*were* those bats... past the barn.

He headed that way.

"Here." Joe was pointing at the blood mark on the stone wall around the north pasture. "Look at this."

"What *about* it?" Seri replied. "It hurts my head to look at it, so what?"

"It anchors this." Joe pointed to the stakes. "See the mark on the base of each stake?"

"It looks familiar..."

"I've seen it before." Morgan said. He hooked a thumb towards his brother. "It's on his back."

They all got quiet for a second, thinking about what that meant.

"If she put it on you…"

"She was marking me. Saying she owned me." James had put the gun away. "It was the one that *didn't* blow up when the others did. So it was how she was… when she was getting younger and I was dying, that's how she did it." All four of them could see things, of course, but Joe was the best at it. James dropped to his knees to stare at it, shivering. "Christ, I'm cold."

"You shouldn't be here at all." Seri tried not to sound unkind about it.

"Yeah." He pointed at the swirl of symbols, at one in particular. It was a larger circle, with a smaller inside it, and six jagged bolts linking the two. "This is the one she's using the most."

"So we can get them off the stakes if we get rid of this…" Seri looked around.

"Not that easy." Joe said. "Tampering with this is going to set it off. It'll kill them instantly."

"Not if I do it." James stood up.

"What? No offense, but why would you be able to?"

"She marked me. And the mark is still there, on my back." He swallowed, remembering. "She used me to get into that house, but she had to invest in me to do it. I can do this."

"We'll have to do them one at a time." Morgan swallowed. "She's going to notice once you start getting them out."

"Then we'd better get started." Seri looked James in the eye. "You up for this?"

"No." He spit into the snow. "But I'll be dipped in pig shit if I let her get away with a goddamn thing. Let's do this."

"Give me that pistol." Morgan held out his hand. James handed it to him. He popped the magazine and looked to make sure it was loaded, slid it home. Looked to Joe and Seri. "Either of you know how to shoot?"

"She does." Joe pointed at Seri. Morgan handed the gun to her.

"What am I going to do with this?"

"She's going to try and stop us once he gets someone out." Morgan slid the rifle off of his shoulder. "You and I are going to keep whatever she does off of him."

"And what am I… right, I'm going to be the spotter." Joe rubbed his hands as the four of them walked towards the stakes. "I started off this morning getting head in a nice warm bed."

"I was sleeping on a pool table." James replied. "For *me*, things are looking up."

*

"Isn't this the part where you threaten to destroy me?" Thea's tyrannosaur had taken care of the winged things and was now advancing on her grandmother, but she knew better than to relax. "Make a big speech about how pointless it is to try and stop you?"

"I learned English reading magazines that Thomas gave me." Robia grimaced, feeling the Cerberus dissipate as thunder boomed across the entire bay, sounding so close it was almost on top of her. "He was quite the reader. They called them pulps."

Thea raised her eyebrow. She hadn't expected the literature discussion.

"They often had the most lurid covers. Half naked women, strapped to altars. Similarly half naked men, quite muscular. Not always. Stories varied. I mention this for a reason. I had all day to get ready for what I was *really* going to summon."

She waved her hands and a line of dried blood seethed into fire, and the two of them were inside the ring of it, even Thea's summoning cut off from her. She dismissed it, wanting the power back for use, wondering what the game was.

"You're a big Johnny Cash fan?"

"Some of his music isn't bad. Not really my taste. I was born to people who traveled up and down the Adriatic coast, we had a fiddle. My father played it." She shook her head. "The things you remember. We don't have to fight."

"We don't." Thea took a half step closer, getting ready to try simply charging the woman.

"I want what you want. You think I enjoy hurting people?

That I get satisfaction out of it?"

"Yeah. That's exactly what I think." She looked up at the floating lights above them. "I think you treated your own children like *things*."

"They would have been safe forever, part of something far greater than you can imagine."

"Can you save me the fucking speech?" Thea charged her, snapping into a perfect side kick. It would have made Scott positively envious. It didn't connect, smashing into *nothing* and rebounding, sending Thea rolling away. She came up, her face livid with frustration.

"You want your cousins to live. Your Thomas. You want them safe from me." Robia smiled. "I want much the same thing. The people I love best. And thanks to these," she gestured to the urns. "I can have what I want. You can't come within ten feet of me, so you can stop trying to beat me into submission. It would be better for you to listen."

"Maybe I can't, but I bet I can make something that can."

"And I'll make something, and we'll be stuck in here. I can make this," She gestured and a weird looking horse appeared. At first she had no idea why *that* was what she'd called, until she saw the fangs set in its mouth, the clawed feet. Thea gestured in turn and a green and orange striped tiger in red barding appeared, roaring in defiance. Robia only smiled at her. "And while you and I play in here, my real summoning counts down out there."

The horse monster galloped at them, and Thea's armored tiger leapt at it, slashing as it reared and tried to kick, clawed feet whistling through the air. The sounds it made were disturbing.

"You see, I studied the rite you and your boy were working on. It's a fascinating thing. Utterly mad. Born of desperation. It would have killed him and there wouldn't have been any result. The longer someone's dead, the more exponential the amount of life required to redress things. The dead need life."

"So I heard." Thea grimaced as her armored cat took a shearing kick to the side that ripped down its flank, missing the barding entirely. It wasn't enough to disable, just enough to cause pain.

"Those out there? Not enough. Not even for *his* purposes. But I started thinking about what *would* do the trick. If I'd had my way I'd have killed Thomas' son, used his life to save Thomas. But he refused me." Her face lost some of its stolen youth with that admission. "I've never understood. We could have lived forever."

"He loved his son. Some people do."

The old woman grimaced. Thea thought it was about what she'd said, but she turned her attention away for a moment and Thea's summoned tiger took the opportunity to bear down the flesh-eating horse monster, pin it to the ground and crush its windpipe between its jaws. Thea was starting to feel dizzy, released the tiger as soon as the horse was dead.

"Your cousins. Of course." She gestured. "A distraction at best. Let them free all of them. I've taken enough by now anyway."

"So your plan is to keep me trapped in here and talk me to death?" Thea was expecting more talking, another summoning, maybe some ranting. But what she got was a cold smile, and the ground shuddering, lurching. She nearly lost her footing.

"I need many, many thousands. Perhaps hundreds of thousands. Enough to breach the barrier between life and death, force it open. Enough to rebuild Thomas' shattered body, or house him in another. And enough to seize *yours*. Then he and I can go from here. If you'd been willing to listen to my offer, I would have been willing to spare the others."

Thomas was nearly past the house when the ground started shaking, throwing him into the snow. He thought at first that Dassalia had summoned an earthquake of some kind, or maybe a god of same – perhaps Typhon or Poseidon, she seemed to like Greek myths. But the shaking subsided, and he pulled himself to his feet.

Then he noticed the cove was frothing, bubbling. The spur of land and rock that enclosed it cracked, cracked again and again as the land shuddered and subsided. The cove was now open to the bay, but the bubbling only increased.

The water began to part as a black shape, impossibly vast,

towering wings mantled over its enormous bulk. It rose from the water, until it dwarfed the tallest hill on the island itself, and still it rose until it became the tallest point in the state, easily nine hundred feet tall. It spread its enormous wings, and Thomas realized that even at night on December 24th the thing was clearly visible on both sides of the bay, that there was no way this thing wasn't being seen, and believed in, by thousands.

The head atop the mountain of a body swiveled, looking down at the farm as it strode out of the water. The ground groaned in protest with every step. It was like a hill of scaly rugose flesh, with gigantic red eyes set in a face like a giant squid or octopus.

Thea stared up at it, unable to process what she was looking at. In the field, they'd barely managed to free seven or eight of the islanders, and only James was still able to focus on the task, Joe and Seri both frozen in horror. Morgan was contemplating putting the rifle in his own mouth rather than letting that thing get a hold of him.

Out in the water, Bishop was staring at the thing's back, as waves threatened to swamp his boat.

"You see why I stayed here?" Dassalia cackled. "Where else would I *go*? Where else was *that* born? And now it will walk across the bay and kill and kill until enough have died. And nothing can possibly stop it. No *one* can stop it. Your body will be mine, your Thomas will provide mine with a home. All you accomplished was to push me to this moment."

Thea turned and concentrated as hard as she could and the already cracked and sundered ground pitched hard, ripping a hole in Dassalia's ring of fire. She ran, not bothering to look back at the old woman – there was no time to fling herself against the nothing that surrounded her. She instead looked for, and saw, Thomas standing there staring up at the thing as it pulled itself free of the water.

"What *is* that?"

"It's Cthulhu." He shook his head. "She actually called fucking Cthulhu."

"What the hell is Cthulhu?" She shook *her* head. "Never mind. What can beat it?"

"I don't know? God? Maybe if Yahweh, or the Archangel Michael stepped out of Heaven right now?" The ground shook again as it stepped on and crushed the hill leading up to the farm.

"Can we *do* God?"

"I don't…" He stopped. Looked up one more time. "We need something that would care. Something that would stand up to it. A modern myth bigger than that one."

"Okay, so who? What? I'm blank here."

They heard another step and the gigantic clawed feet crushed the stone wall. Hundreds of feet above them eyes the size of a tractor trailer regarded them. If they had any advantage it was the sheer ponderousness of the creature, its massive size. Dassalia couldn't imagine it moving quickly, and so it didn't.

"Remember when you called Santa?"

"You want me to call Santa to fight *that*?"

"No." He dropped to the snow. Began tracing a shape in the snow, a pentagonal shield. He drew what looked like stylized fish in the center, a large one swimming to the left, a smaller one below it swimming to the right. It looked familiar to her. She realized the negative space had an S shape to it, looked back to Thomas.

"You're kidding."

"I'm going to need your help on this one. It'll take both of us."

"You can't be serious."

Another massive step and the whole farm shook as it crushed the barn.

"It's that or a flying turtle."

"What do I…" He kissed her, and she kissed him back because it was what they *did*, and then he smiled at her. "Just focus on it. Everything you have, everything you can think of. I'll handle the rest."

*

"Someone help me!" James screamed. "I can't get the ropes off and keep it from killing them at the same time!"

"Should we be running?" Seri said even as she untied the rope. "Would that help?"

"If that thing decides to kill us we're already dead." Morgan replied. "How the fuck..."

Joe was staring *past* the nightmare thing and over at where he could see Thea and Thomas standing in its shadow. They were doing something in the snow. He wondered where Dassalia was, but figured it probably took a lot of concentration to keep *that* thing going. It was looking between the field of stakes and the little house he'd spent a week in, as if trying to decide what to destroy first.

So it was Joe who saw it happen first. Thea's eyes were closed, concentrating on the symbol and on everything she'd ever even *heard* about it representing, from the old cartoons she'd watched as a kid with her dad to the record Joe had gotten for Christmas one year. The movie Karl had taken her to see when it was playing at the planetarium.

You'll believe a man can fly.

Thomas was thinking about his grandfather, who had shared so much of his weird, awful life with his grandson. Death camps. The war in general. His taste in books. One thing his grandfather Willrew had left him was a collection of old Golden Age comics, on yellowing paper. He'd caged one for the idea for the ritual. Another had been about a lone survivor from a distant planet. A star child. His name ending in El, like the divine. *Who is like God*? Red and blue. Able to leap tall buildings in a single bound.

The creature noticed them just as the symbol in the snow burst forth into bright yellow light. The light of the sun. It took a step that covered the distance of a football field and dropped that enormous clawed foot right on top of them.

Joe didn't even have time to scream. He just saw the foot drop, and saw it *stop*. Thomas was standing there, holding the monster's foot above his head. Thea had already gotten away, was running back around the shattered barn. Thomas staggered, fell to one knee as nine hundred feet of vast cyclopean terror tried to grind him into the ground. But he wasn't crushed.

"Joe, what..."

"Keep untying them, Seri." Joe didn't turn his head. "Shit is about to get *really fucking weird.*"

Chapter Twenty Four

Magic Words

Dassalia wasn't sure what was happening.

Everything had gone exactly as she'd planned it. Even Thea's escape from the ring of fire didn't really matter. Where could she go? When the Great Old One walked the land in Providence, the deaths would feed a rite powerful enough to allow Dassalia to steal her body at any distance. And if she was forced to kill the girl, well, she wouldn't be dead very long.

But then she felt a rite. Now the mountain-sized beast's tentacled head was there, above its gargantuan body, but it was standing still? Why? It was such a vast thing, it was difficult to prod it to action, but she needed it to move, to head west across the bay, to make landfall.

"Where were we?" Thea's voice. The girl was standing there, panting.

"Back to waste your time?"

"Oh, I don't think so. Sure, you got the power to call that thing up in advance." She started walking right at her. "And I'm willing to bet that it'll keep going without you, at this point. But it goes both ways, doesn't it? You can't steer something like *that* without concentration."

"This is pointless. You can't touch me."

"Right." Thea walked around her. Walked up to the cairn. "I can't touch *you*."

She lifted the largest rock off of the top of the thing, tossed it to the side.

"Stop that."

"Or?" She lifted another, tossed that aside as well. "You'll do what?"

"Stop it!"

"What? This?" She picked up another stone, dropped this one at Dassalia's feet. "Stop desecrating the grave? I mean, you didn't think anything to doing this to my mother, your daughter. Or my father. But when it's someone you care about..." She turned her back on the woman, looking at the cairn. "That big one in the middle. I bet if I pull that one out half of this thing will collapse."

Dassalia couldn't think clearly. Her pulse was pounding in her head, her fingernails buried in her hands. She knew this wasn't really hurting Thomas. At the moment he was dead. But somehow it hurt *her*. The little witch, born to be a tool, and now she was hurting because of her.

I matter. I count. You don't. You don't get to hurt me.

She was bleeding from her palms, and she seized that pain, made it a weapon.

"I said *stop it.*"

*

Thomas felt amazing.

Oh, he had nine hundred feet of green monster stepping on him. When he'd been younger, Thomas had read all the big Cthulhu mythos stories. Lovecraft himself, Robert Bloch's *The Shambler from the Stars*, but as much as he liked old HPL (if not for Lovecraft's work he'd never have dared attempt the rite), his true guilty pleasure was of the four color variety.

He shifted his weight and leapt, with leg muscles strong enough to throw him over a tall building. The creature staggered back. It was impossible to tell what it was thinking, even with a face the size of three billboards the complete lack of human features made it impenetrable. But that didn't matter to him. In that moment, he wasn't just himself. He was what Thea had called him to be, their combined skill and purpose.

He hung in the air for a moment, just letting himself realize it.

He was flying.

The monster's wing swept forward, as big as a building, and slammed into him while he was busy being excited. It was the kind of impact they use words like *catastrophic* and *nightmarish* to describe, and it sent him hurtling away towards the Mount Hope Bridge.

It turned those vast eyes towards the farm again.

The Great Old One was occupied by the hate that pulsed over the link between itself and she who brought it into existence. It trudged, one step covering a hundred yards, and would have slammed its foot down to shake the very earth beneath it. It likely would have knocked Thea prone.

Instead, it caught fire.

The fury of the sun spit from Thomas' eyes. Heat so intense it would have melted steel like wax under a blowtorch. The Great Old One was not made of steel, but as unnatural as it was, it could not resist the lance of raw focused heat, could not defy it. It shrieked, a sound utterly unlike anything any human being had ever heard or ever would again, as its eye caught on fire as well.

Then a figure moving at seven times the speed of sound slammed into the center of the creature's vast bulk, toppling it in mid step. It fell, hundreds of feet of ancient terror made by a man born in Providence, in the year 1890 sent hurtling towards the ground by the creation of two men born in 1914. He'd never tried an idea this *big* before, he realized, something billions could likely identify. He barely felt like himself, able to hear voices all over the state, see miles, look through the ground...

Distracted again. It was hard to focus. But *he* wouldn't have a hard time focusing.

The impact shook the entire island and made waves around it. Snow hurtled up into the air from it, and animals in the woods surrounding the farm that had not already fled its arrival turned tail at this latest sound. He could hear more ground scraping away as it used its massive claws to tear at the ground, to right itself.

Then the thing's head simply spun on the body. A creature with bones couldn't do that, but he had no idea if Cthulhu (just realizing that's what it was should have terrified him, but *he* wouldn't be afraid of it, so neither could Thomas be afraid) had bones. What it did have was a face full of tentacles.

These lashed out and grappled with him. He smashed several aside with his fists, but others seized him, pulled him in closer. He was surprised to see the creature had a maw – he honestly wasn't sure if it had one in the original story or not, but by now enough people had an idea of what Cthulhu was it hardly mattered. After all, in the *original* comics he could only jump 1/8th of a mile. Not fly.

He flew now.

The Great Old One was massive. Taller than the tallest hill in all of Rhode Island, in fact. It weighed a ludicrous amount, so much that it had caved in the ground where it had fallen. Perhaps hundreds of thousands of tons. Perhaps millions. He had no way of knowing.

He lifted it up. As well-known and powerful as the myth of the Great Old One was, it was known by, at best, a few million. *He* was known worldwide, and known to be able to do *anything*. So yes, he *could* lift Great Cthulhu by his face, and he did, flying it up into the air.

They were a hundred meters off of the ground when Seri managed to untie the last stake. Joe and Morgan had been taking turns pulling people away from the north pasture, helped by some of the people who were less ruined by what Dassalia had done. But they weren't fooled. None of them were unhurt. Being unhurt by this was impossible.

Even Morgan, who'd been willing to kill complete strangers to save his own ass (if he were being honest, it was fear that had motivated him) couldn't believe what he was seeing. Almost a hundred people, tortured and forever marked by what they'd been forced to do to themselves. His own brother, letting himself burn to free them, the shirt on his back blistered from the heat rising from that one last symbol Dassalia carved on him. Joe and Seria, as helpless as he was, working to free complete strangers. And in the air above them all a thing so vast it shouldn't be possible was dangling by its face.

"What the fuck do we do with everyone?" Morgan said to

Joe. They were walking a woman in her fifties in any direction that was away from the stakes. Joe had no answers for him.

"The house." Seri yelled. "Take them towards the house." It was the only idea they had. They turned, just glad to have something normal to focus on.

A blast of fire at the cairn. Sloppy. Thea easily turned it aside, bending the lines and whorls of power before it even reached her.

"It doesn't need to be *you*." Dassalia spit at her. "I can use Seri."

"Good luck. I'd like to see you *try* and take Seri. You'd get nowhere fast." Thea kicked the pile of stones, kicked it again, and it tumbled as the big one in the middle fell out the back. "Damn it, I knew I should have brought a shovel. Or were you just planning to force him to rip his own way out of the ground? It's pretty cold here. A lot of work."

"Shut up! You didn't... you can't touch him!" She was sputtering and Thea wondered at it. To be *that* insane. She'd called up a horror so vast it dwarfed *buildings.* Thea could see it being hauled into the air, dragged over the water to the east while it swept those astonishingly vast wings, like runways beating in the air, hundreds of feet across. The howling wind intensified with each stroke, the moonlight blotted out.

"Touch him? I wasn't planning on it." Thea put her finger to her chin, affected a pose of contemplation. "I guess I could *piss* on him..."

She hadn't known what would happen when she pushed hard enough. She'd thought the woman might summon something big enough to break her link to the... whatever the hell it was. What she hadn't expected was that she'd simply grab one of the rocks from the cairn and charge her, swinging the thing at her head. She still managed to do a block and step, getting around her, and only then realized it.

She'd put her hand on the woman's arm.

They stood there for a moment. Dassalia panting, holding

the rock. Wanting to bash her brains in. Thea's hand warm from where she'd shoved her off balance.

"Well, now." Thea didn't work out like Thomas did, but every day she made sure to exercise, to perform her moves, keep her training sharp. She knew she was strong, *really* strong, not stolen youth ripped from someone else's pain. She knew she could win a fistfight, even with the old woman clutching a rock.

She lowered her hands.

Dassalia frowned, hefting the rock up higher.

"Two things could happen here. I could come over there, take that rock from you and crush your head with it. I could kill you. Or you could start trying to call up something to maul me with, and I'd do likewise, and who knows where that would end up. You've already lost control of your monster."

"I can get it back, I just need..."

"Listen to me." Thea took a half step closer. "I don't know what made you this. I get a sense of things, because I talked to Raifa, but I don't know. But I know what it's like to love someone, now. I know what it's like to lose the people you care about, thanks to you. We don't have to do this."

Thea had no idea what she was doing. She just knew she had to *try*. The cold was swirling around them, snow blown and blasted into the air. She focused all her attention on the old woman, who was visibly aging right in front of her, going gray even as she clutched the rock.

"There's nothing else for us to do." She looked, even *sounded* sad. "You don't understand. The web... it wasn't supposed to kill them. That wasn't the goal. And then they started dying and it was too much. Once you go that far there's no coming back. I saw it before I was fourteen, when Raifa was..." A choking sound, the rock gripped in withered fingers. "I need what you have."

"I'm asking you to stop." Thea adjusted herself. "Raifa asked you to stop. He rejected your offer." She pointed to the ruined cairn. "Absolutely everyone who ever loved you wanted this to stop."

"You destroyed it."

"It's just *rocks*." Thea could feel cold in every inch of her skin, in her bones, a cold that had nothing to do with winter. She stared into her grandmother's eyes and *hoped*. "He's the same as he was, and as he will be. The only trace of him left is the man trying to stop the thing you just did. All you're doing is hurting people for *nothing*. You can't have him back. You can't fix any of it."

The rock quivered. Dassalia staring at her, no longer seeing her, trapped inside herself. Thea *prayed*, for the first time in years she actually prayed that it could stop here. That she wouldn't have to do it.

"Perhaps you're right. Perhaps I can't."

The fingers around the rock tightened.

For all her advantages Thea barely managed to move her head in time to avoid being brained as Dassalia hurled the rock at her with inhuman strength, then leapt at her, her fingernails long and jagged like claws. She took a slash across her chest and right shoulder that went right through her shirt and her coat, staggering back as Dassalia tried to come in again. As much as the slashes hurt, she was prepared for the next swing, grabbed hold of the woman's wrist as it came in and twisted it around, pinning it behind her back and hauling her up off of the ground in the process.

They were both screaming. Thea had no idea what either of them was saying as she pushed her way forward, holding that arm so tightly against the woman's back it might have already broken. Her chest pulsed with every beat of her heart as blood welled up. The other hand was trying to slash around behind her, but the angle was all wrong.

Thea dropped them both into the snow. Robia Dassalia looked up to see a plaque at eye level. The name *Thomas Willrew Sr.* raised from the coppery metal. She had no idea what it was actually made of.

"I asked you to stop." Thea was panting raggedly. "I asked you. You didn't."

"I never will." She was shrieking each word, still trying to get her hand free, kicking and writhing as Thea increased the pressure. "Stop me now. I'll come back. I'll come back and I'll make it work next time. I'll *make it*."

"No you won't." Thea swallowed. "But you'll ruin lives trying."

"They don't matter. *You* don't matter. *I* matter! *Someone has to pay for all of it!*"

"Yes." Thea felt an implacable calm descend, the pain of her wounded chest receding. Her fingers closed on something cold and hard in the snow next to her. "Someone does."

*

They were out over the bay, past the cove when it released him and fell. It didn't drop very far, less than a hundred meters, but the weight was like dropping an aircraft carrier, and the water exploded outward from where it impacted.

The part of him that was Thomas was shocked. The part of him that wasn't moved instantly, swooping down to the water and underneath the nearby boat Bishop was in and lifting it out of the water before the waves could swamp it. He flew back to the island, placing the boat in the cove.

From Bishop's perspective, life simply made absolutely no sense. He'd seen a titanic form float overhead, pounding the air with giant wings, then crash into the bay and send water rolling in his direction. The deepest part of the bay was about 180 feet. He knew that because he'd been interested in scuba diving as a teenager, and he knew that thing was easily many hundreds of feet taller than *that*. It could stand on the bottom of the East Passage and tower over the Mount Hope Bridge.

It wasn't possible. Even by the incredibly loose standards he'd grown to accept. And of course then the boat started flying and he'd given up completely.

He stepped out of the boat's cabin (it was really more of a motor yacht than anything else, and he realized his dad would likely kill him if a giant dragon octopus ate the boat) and watched the thing looming over the whole east bay. Then Thomas came up out of the water and hovered... *hovered*... over the boat looking at it.

"Tommy?"

"Yeah." Bishop looked up. Thomas' eyes were glowing red. He sounded off, but then again, he was flying and his eyes were glowing so maybe that's what happens.

"Is that…"

"Yep."

"And you're…."

"Yes I am."

"Okay." Bishop blinked a few times. "I'm going to beach my dad's expensive boat and go up to see Joe in case we're all about to die."

"We're not." Thomas turned to face Bishop and smiled. "Thea's got this."

The monster turned, huge eyes making Bishop feel very much like it was staring right at him. Then it began walking towards the island again, rising out of the water as it came out of the deep channel.

"It's coming back."

"It won't get here." He rose up into the air. He felt so unbelievably sure of himself. He could *say* things like that, and mean them. Suddenly the part of him that was Thomas Willrew was very scared of what was going to happen if Thea didn't end this soon.

The other simply flew at the approaching leviathan. The water parted underneath him as the air cracked, split by his wake.

*

It would have been simple.

Thea had her pinned. She had the rock in her hand. She could have easily done it, just brought the rock down, crushed her head. It might have taken two or three hits, but in the end, she could easily beat the brains out of the skull of the woman writhing in the hold. She knew this.

She was weeping openly.

Above her the spirits of her aunts and uncles, four of them

utter strangers to her, related to her only by blood ties. But among them floated her uncle Paolo, Seri and Joe's father, and there she was, as she'd been the night in the kitchen. The sad eyes of her mother, trapped forever in Dassalia's web.

It wasn't supposed to kill them. That wasn't the goal.

Thea thought back to what her mother had said to her that night. She met the ghost's eyes, ignored the woman trying to get free – she'd break her arm before she broke that hold – and remembered.

Learn everything. Wake fully and see. If you do, you're of no use to her. But a threat, you'll be a threat.

Wake fully and see.

She watched them dancing above her and realized even dead they hung in the web. Dassalia's web.

"That's why you don't care if I kill you." She hissed in the woman's ear. "If I'd killed you at the house, you wouldn't really have cared, it just made you angry that I'd *try*. If you die here... you'll just go into the web. You'll just hang around and wait for one of us to get dragged in."

"There's no way out for any of us." Dassalia hissed back. "Make it easier. Just let me have what I want, because I *will* have it. One way or another. You're all marked. You. Seria. Joseph. Byron, Morgan, even James, doubly mine because I put my mark on him. There's no way out."

She heard a noise at a vast distance, a sound like a colossal *thud*, loud as thunder. Thomas was still out there fighting. The monster god thing had to be stopped, but for all his borrowed power he couldn't, not really. He could just hold it there. He'd trusted her to deal with it, to deal with her wicked grandmother once and for all. Joe and Seri were counting on her. Even Bry and her less than ideal brothers, really. All marked, all forced into a thing before they'd really even been born.

"The carousel," Thea whispered. "Round and round."

"What are you..." Dassalia felt it too late. Thea was building to something, a symbol becoming a bridge in her mind. She tried to use her own personal sun-wheel image to counter, but the wheel within a wheel was too similar to Thea's spinning circle, with steeds to ride. The snow and broken shards of wood and rock from the barn the monster had stepped on began to rise into the air.

Thea looked up and saw Ramses, placidly chewing on some grass. The great horse had returned even after the mountain sized monster had stomped the barn flat, and it met her eyes, struck at the snow with its hoof. She remembered the painted horses, her mother riding with her. Looked up at the ghost drifting in the air and cried out without words to get in the way.

Then they were all together.

In front of the house, James Williams had been led panting to the snow covered lawn. There were dozens of people. Seri had taken the keys and let herself in, feeling the house judge her, remember her. They brought in as many people as they could, the sickest and weakest. Every available space was filled, the two ground floor bedrooms, the living room, the upstairs bedroom. It wasn't even close to enough.

"What the hell is happening?" Seri turned to the man. She didn't know him. "What was that... why were we all..."

"After." She tried to look reassuring. "We can worry about it after." Another sound like thunder. Whatever was happening in the bay she had no desire to *see* it. She could only hope that someone, it would all end soon.

She was on her way back outside with some blankets when the dizziness hit her. She stumbled on the stairs, began to fall, and then someone caught her. She looked up with swimming eyes into Bishop's face, blinked in surprise.

"Bish?"

"Hey, hey. Easy." Bishop rarely showed off how strong he was, but he easily picked her up off of her feet and led her down the stairs. Joe was already lying on his back, gasping.

"Joey, what's..."

"She's doing something. To us. Williams..." Joe pointed to where Morgan and James already lay in the snow, out cold. People were tending to *them* now. Everyone was confused and exhausted and terrified, Seri could *see* it, and she didn't *want* to see it but she couldn't pretend it wasn't there anymore, the colors of people's hearts and minds, the power of their needs and wants and beliefs. She could see it all. And she could see Joe, like a floodlight in her face he was shining, rioting color shifting across him even as he clawed at consciousness. "Seri, let go. We have to go."

"We'll *die*."

"I'm here." Bishop said because it was all he could think to say. "I'm right here. I'll watch you." He put his hand on Joe's shoulder. "Just come back please. I need to introduce you to my folks."

"I thought they'd freak out."

"That's *why*." Bishop smiled, tried to make it a joke, but let the truth be in there.

Then they weren't there at all.

Thea made the trip first. Fully inside the web she almost drowned in Dassalia's suppressed emotions. The woman was shrieking at her, screaming everything, an entire life's worth of it. Images of barbed wire, of barely human shapes starved and denied water while their bowels voided over and over again, the smell of it. Being cleaned with a hose. Experiments on 'animal heat', tests to determine pain tolerances. One test, to see if the sisters could feel each other across long distances or through walls. No one bothered to tell her whether it was a success or not. Her huge bearded bear of a father, ground into filthy soil, starved to death. Taken away. Her mother. Gone. Gone and no one bothering to tell her where or why. Soon it would be her turn.

Each of them in the web was a point of light. She could see them, knew them, knew their lives. Her aunt Maria, who she'd never met, she now knew her quirky sense of humor and her longing for a home she'd never seen or been told about. The very chunk of rock Thea's body still lay atop. Marco, one of two twin brothers, never married because he feared his own mother so much. Her uncle Paolo, who'd loved his wife and his sister and their children, and if he hadn't loved Greg Mendel he was at least glad his sister was happy. She could feel them all.

"This is the web." Dassalia floated in nothing before her,

perfect. Beautiful, even, untouched by everything Thea had seen and experienced. "This is what you're fighting. In here there's no pain, no fear, no doubt. No *want*. Just everything you ever were, forever. I know my children better than any mother ever has. I'll know you that way, too. Your loves and hates, they'll be *my* loves and hates. We'll all be one person."

"One person." Thea shook her head. "I'm sorry, I'm *truly* sorry for what you went through. That no one helped you."

"Thomas helped me."

"And you repaid him with that." Thea pointed to the memory because all of their memories were there, exposed, easy to see and feel. Dassalia ripping open the world and showing Thomas Sr. the face of broken, blackened shells, tearing the illusion of her away and showing him who she really was. Destroying what little of comfort was left to him.

"I would have brought him *in*." Dassalia's frustration and fury were nearly physical things inside the web. Thea almost visualized it as an actual spider web but fought that off, knowing to imagine it would create it. The less concrete it was the better. "He would have lived forever."

"This isn't living. It's *hiding*." Thea looked at the image of a young woman screaming and screaming as her sister died in her arms. Felt the first prickling as the girl's refusal to accept it bent the world around her. "You have no idea how much I wish this had never happened. But it doesn't change anything. We don't get to hurt other people just because someone else hurt us. My mother deserved your *love*, not… this."

"I…" Dassalia couldn't lie in the web. There was no point. She *was* her children here. All that was left of them was hers, she'd sampled each of them in turn. She could say there was no pain in the web, but there had been so much pain to make it. "I can't *stop*."

Perhaps you can be stopped. Raifa's voice. And with that the calliope music started, and they found themselves in Roger Williams Park, at the foot of the carousel. Thea started. She hadn't imagined it, hadn't…

"No, you didn't," Raifa, as perfect in youth and beauty as her sister, as much the mother and grandmother, was simply there. "At last we're all here."

"No!" Robia recoiled. "No, no, not in here, Raifa, I don't want to!"

"But it's time." Thea could see that they were twins, identical ones, but there was on Raifa's face a look of understanding so great that it made pity seem inconsequential. "Robi, you can't fight this anymore. I should have died. But you didn't let me. It's past time."

"I can *fix* it."

"Look around you, love." All around them were people that Thea didn't know and yet recognized. Her mother and her nine brothers and sisters, and their many children. She could see Joe and Seri, even the Williams boys, even poor little Bry in a white dress with flowers behind her ear. They laughed and talked and *were*, and it made Thea want to weep to see her mother again. To see her *happy*. "This is what it could have been. What you couldn't accept, the love and yes, the disappointments. This is what we threw away. But it's not too late for them to wrestle something good out of our mistakes."

"Raffy, *please*."

"I love you, Robi. Please. Please let me go. Let *this* go. It's not how we're supposed to be."

"*I don't want to die!*"

"We're already dead, Robi."

There was a long moment of silence that wasn't silence, as low voices murmured around them, as people rode the carousel and nattered on about trifling nonsense. The sun was bright. Thea waited, hoped.

"Will I get to see you again? Or him? Or..." Robia Dassalia's voice cracked. "I don't want to be alone."

"I don't know, Robi. But if it's possible, I'll be there for you." Raifa Dassalia put her hands out, took her sister's fingers in hers. "I love you, Robi. I always did."

"Raffy." There's the moment of collapse in someone's voice when they finally surrender to the inevitable. It's never a moment of triumph to hear that sound and Thea Mendel took no pleasure in hearing the final breaking of a long cracked heart giving up her dream. Even if it was twisted and awful, she'd clutched it to herself for so long, it was harder than death to let it go and Thea knew it. She met those blue eyes as the woman who was her grandmother turned to face her.

"You win."

"It ends." Thea said. "Winning doesn't matter. Just let it end."

"Please fix his grave. He didn't deserve that... what you did. He didn't deserve that."

"I know." Thea nodded, because she *did* know. She looked across the space, the not real not place, and saw her mother again, smiling at her. Remembered the night they'd taken her out of the house. Remembered the night she'd seen her drinking Thomas' blood from a bowl. And managed to find a smile to give back, to love her mother again.

Then she rolled off of the dead old woman and into the snow, tears streaking her face, gasping as she felt something that had been part of her life for years just unravel. The web simply *wasn't*, and without it she was lighter, stronger, raw but healing.

She saw the wind blowing dust away where Dassalia had been, watched as her body unraveled into smoke and was gone. Knew that there was nothing left of her, or Raifa. Looked up and saw there were no ghosts drifting in the air above her.

She was alone with the toppled cairn and the rock in her hand. She looked at it for a moment, opened her hand, and sent it drifting to settle back at the base of the pile of rocks. Concentrated a moment, and watched each rock drift in place, a simple thing, but a promise. She might not have done it for Dassalia, but Thomas shouldn't have to see another grave knocked over. It took a few moments to float each stone in place, the magic stolen from an old movie. When it was done, she lifted the urns out of the snow, looked at them.

"Let's get you back to where you belong."

She wiped at her face. She wanted very badly to see Joe and Seri, and Thomas, and tell them she loved them. To show them.

*

Of course it was a horrid thing. Of course it was. It was a monster so huge that the entire bay wasn't deep enough to hide it. It slashed at where he was with talons larger than a building, vast inhuman eyes that promised knowledge that would destroy sanity. That was what it *was*, the very concepts that made it up. It was unstoppable, unknowable, horrific, madness given form.

He was punching it.

He knew if he didn't stop soon, what he was hosting inside him would obliterate him. There wouldn't be a *Thomas* anymore, just the idea, the concept of the star child. And *he* knew it too, and he wouldn't do that. Any other idea Thomas might have chosen, the danger was that it would choose to stay. But *he* wouldn't do that, wouldn't let Thomas die for him.

Cthulhu made landfall on the south end, near the ferry dock and the lighthouse, which it vastly towered over. A few more steps and it would probably destroy the thing. Thomas flew around it and blew on it, and it started freezing, which was just *ridiculous,* but it worked. He could blow on things and they'd get so cold that they'd freeze instantly. Of course the Great Old One could ignore death itself, so a little cold wasn't going to stop it. Neither were the intense blasts or pure heat from Thomas' eyes.

It caught him in one of those massive hands and squeezed, trying to crush him. It was uncomfortable, and he couldn't catch his breath from the pressure, but he was invulnerable. He'd always wondered exactly how that worked. What does it mean, to be invulnerable?

Apparently it meant that Cthulhu couldn't crush you.

He managed to force its ghastly fingers apart and stared up at those eyes, and *his* eyes spat forth heat so intense that red lights blazed forth and the air caught fire. The monster god made another of those astonishing *sounds*. As far as Thomas knew, an octopus was almost entirely silent. This wasn't. As it made that sound that made birds flee for miles and dogs start barking in Massachusetts, he kept burning it, carving a symbol onto its face with the lasers from his eyes. A star with a flaming eye at the center.

He'd finally remembered how *The Call of Cthulhu* ended. The monster staggered back towards the water and he flung himself forward, accelerating to nigh-impossible speeds and ramming himself through the creature's head. Just like in the story, the head exploded as he went through it, and immediately started to reform as the monster's body shot tendrils of matter up to replace the lost head.

He froze the stump with five hundred mile an hour wind colder than any ever seen on the surface of the planet, colder than mythical borean gods. Headless, the monster stomped around blinded, but hardly defeated. It didn't know *how* to be defeated.

He closed his eyes for a moment, letting himself rest. He'd have to...

There was a sound like a mudslide and he opened his eyes, prepared to lash out with fire from his eyes. What he saw made it unnecessary. The magic sustaining the Great Old One, or the simulacrum of it at least, was dissipating. He didn't know how, but that didn't matter, he could see it. Great Cthulhu or not, without the rite Dassalia had put together, without her presence, it had nothing holding it in place. It dissolved in front of him.

She did it.

He rocketed across the seven miles of Wolfshead Island in less than five seconds, the air booming behind him. Arced to land, saw many people huddled cold on his lawn. He gently used the heat from his eyes to warm them, just enough to nudge them all above freezing.

He staggered to a landing, nearly fell ass over end and managed to right himself. Saw Ramses eating in the field to the left of where the barn used to be, John a little further off. Wondered at it, at the horses being so close to home considering what had happened.

He looked through the crowd of people, many of them

people he'd known distantly all of his life. None of them knowing what had just happened, what they'd just seen. He could feel the other utterly gone from him now, could feel the cold again, feel aches and pains in his body. No more flying. No more fire from his eyes. Just a man.

"Little Tom," he swiveled, seeing Paul huddled under a blanket on the steps of his house. Several of the people around him were staring.

"Paul."

"Can you tell me what just happened? What... who was that woman? What..."

"I can tell you, but it's not going to make a lot of sense." He felt the ones who were in better shape watching, listening. "The important thing is it's over."

Paul just stared at him for a while. He met Paul's eyes because he owed the man that much. But he had no idea how to answer the man's question, so he waited. Paul just nodded, too tired to press, and ultimately probably not wanting to know. Thomas moved on, looking around his ridiculously full house, looking for the only reason he desperately needed to see.

She was leaning up against the stone wall, the part that hadn't been knocked down when Cthulhu had walked onto the farm. He thought about that statement, left it alone. Seri and Joe were on either side of her, talking to her and to Bishop, even occasionally talking to Morgan and James Williams who were lying on the ground a little further down from the wall. Morgan actually had his arm around James' shoulder, who looked to have actually been crying.

His eyes went to Thea. Her shirt and jacket were torn, there were healing scratches on her that looked like they'd been deep, would leave marks. She smiled when she saw him, looked exhausted but got up and headed towards him.

"Hi."

"Hello." She put her arms around his neck. "Are you okay?"

"Yes. Very much so now." He bent down and they kissed for a while, relieved to be able to do that again, touch and be touched by each other. When they parted she rested her head against his chest. "You?"

"It's over. She's gone." She exhaled. "I love you."

"I love you too." They both looked up at the sky. There were helicopters, likely trying to figure out what had just happened, why so many people had reported an impossible thing. "What should we tell people?"

"I vote for a Christmas miracle." She exhaled. "Happy birthday, Tommy."

"It is, isn't it?" He held on to her. At that moment she was everything he had ever or would ever want. The feel of her fingers in his hair as she pulled his head back down to touch his lips with hers beat anything. Even flying.

Epilogue

New Year's Eve

James Williams was loading his meager possessions into the cheap Dodge Avenger he'd bought three days before.

"You sure you have everything you want?"

"I have everything I think of as mine." It had all fit into two bags. Less than a month ago, that would have bothered James immensely. Now he didn't give a fuck. He turned to look at Bry, still a little confused about seeing someone he thought of as his little brother in a dress. But after seeing into Bry's heart in that weird vision when the bitch died, he knew that Bry would only be happy this way. "So, I'm really sorry I melted those dolls of yours that time."

"It's okay." Bry went up on her toes and hugged James around the waist. "You going to write?"

"When I figure out where I'm going, sure."

"You don't have to..."

"Morg. Look. You and I... we can't hang around each other without me wanting to stab you in the back and you wanting to slap me in the face. That's just the way it is. We're family. We're always going to be family. And we'll be better family with a *lot* of miles between us." He cracked his neck. "Plus I don't want to give that big sonofabitch an excuse to break my goddamn neck for me."

"I can see that." Morgan laughed a little at that. "You *are* a cocksucker after all."

"Fuck you too, Morg." He took a last look around the salvage yard. "How'd you get the money to buy me out anyway?"

"Been saving for a rainy day. Kind of a bugout fund. Now that she's gone... well." Morgan put his hands in his pockets. "I might sell this shithole anyway. I never much wanted to work in a salvage yard, that was dad."

"Yeah." James nodded. "Look, no point in dragging this out." He looked over his shoulder at where Seri was sitting on her car, watching. "You're not…"

"What?" Morgan looked back, saw Seri. "Christ, she's our *cousin*."

"I'm just saying…"

"We're figuring out what's best for Bry, that's all. Boy, you need to get your mind right. That's gross."

"Yeah yeah." He slid into the car, started it up. It sounded like you'd expect a car you bought on a used car lot two days after Christmas to sound. "You're a shithead but try not to get dead, Morg."

"You first." Morgan watched as James pulled out of the salvage yard and drove away.

"What did you mean 'what's best for me'?" Bry looked up at Morgan.

"Just that. You need to go back to school."

"Ugh."

"Bry, you're *ten*."

"They're all going to be weird and want me to use the boy's toilet and wear pants." She stuck out her tongue. And kept sticking it out until it was close to a foot long.

"Hey. Stop that."

"Sorry."

"We talked about that. Don't do that in public."

"I can do more than that, I can change…"

"Bry. I know you can, okay?" Morgan rubbed his forehead. He and Bry were almost to Seri's car. "Also, it might be better if you don't live with me."

"But you're my *brother*."

"Yeah, and my track record speaks volumes." He looked to Seri. "Look, we're all going to have to talk it over, okay? For one thing, we're probably going to have to ask Thea to help us cheat on some paperwork for you."

"We can talk about it later, sweetie." Seri bent down and

kissed Bry's head. The girl beamed and got in the back seat, leaving Seri and Morgan awkwardly standing around.

"What was that bit where you..."

"Oh, that was him being cute." Morgan leaned up against the back of her car, facing the salvage yard. "He insinuated that you and I..."

Seri blinked for several seconds.

"Oh my *God*."

"This is what I said."

"We're *cousins*."

"Yes, I know."

"We're not even *distant* cousins. We have the same grandmother for fuck's sake."

"I imparted this exact message to him."

"And you tried to break into my house and kidnap me once!"

"I may not have brought up that part."

"That part is *extremely* important." She blew hair out of her face. "I mean, okay, I'm mostly over it..."

"Mostly."

"But it's still a big deal."

"You know, I wasn't working up to asking you out or anything, you can relax."

She looked over at him, gauging his sincerity. He seemed to mean it.

"So what's up for you now?"

"Me? I'm going to go home, empty out what little I want to keep, and then go see a realtor about selling it, as is, fixer upper. See if I can get away with that. Because between you and me that first floor is a fucking lost cause, might as well gut the place and start over."

"Then what?"

"No idea." He rubbed his face. "Maybe I'll go west. Never been outside of the state, unless you count crossing into Seekonk or a day trip to Boston or some shit."

"You know, I don't want to cut Bry off from you, or James."

"I think James is making that decision for you. As for me..."

He straightened up. "I have to figure out how not to be an asshole."

"It's not that hard. Just don't do asshole things."

"I spent the past six years doing exactly that. Because I was scared. I don't want to be scared anymore." His eyes unfocused, remembering seeing his mother and her sister and brothers in that weird carousel place, seeing them as they could have been. "They all could have been happy."

"Maybe they are now."

"Maybe they are. But one way or another, if I want to be happy, I have to figure out what to do with myself. I'm not ditching Bry, but... she's better off with you lot than with me."

"We'll talk about it."

"We'll do that." He nodded. "I'll talk to you later, Seria."

"Goodbye, Morgan." She watched him nod into the car, and then walk off towards where he'd left his truck parked. Exhaled. *If I want to be happy, I have to figure out what to do with myself.* She thought about that one for a very long time. Then she took out her cellphone and dialed a number.

She expected it to go to voicemail but he answered it on the fourth ring.

"Seri."

"David." She looked over the junkyard. "We need to talk."

*

"So what do we know?"

"Dassalia's gone." Mercy Brown was lounging in a patio chair looking at the last hazy purple edge of sunset as it crested the trees. She missed seeing the sun huge and red in the sky, but that would be like dousing herself in kerosene and playing with matches. "My source tells me she's been dealt with."

"Source?"

"A boy." Mercy smiled at her mother. "We're getting to know each other."

"Not another Stuart. Mercy, you know I love all my children, but we don't need another reluctant convert."

"For now it's just light socialization and some back and forth exchange of information. But he's got something. That right combination of regret, anger and ruthlessness. And he's attracted to me." Mercy was letting the hunger build. She'd have to go hunting soon, but for now the need for blood was merely a pleasant ache, not a compulsion. "If I do it right, I think he'd come over willingly."

Akivasha said nothing. Mercy was still a little sensitive about the subject of Stuart and his unwillingness to adopt their ways. There was no point to antagonizing her eldest daughter.

"It's a beautiful night."

"Yes." Akivasha sniffed the air. "With her gone, we'll need to be careful. Those things might try and encroach again."

"I could see if the new ones are willing to deal."

"Carefully. I would be lost without you, darling." Akivasha's gentle kiss sent tremors of longing and helpless love through Mercy. Suspecting that her mother controlled her utterly did nothing to lessen the emotion. She felt like a child again, the first night she'd seen that dark form gliding through the trees.

"I will, of course."

"Good." Akivasha settled back in her chair. "I'm so glad we live here. It's so hard to see the stars from the cities now."

Mercy looked up, understanding the implied command and exposing her throat to her mother. She didn't bite it, of course. But she could, and they all knew that. It was just the way things were. The strongest ruled.

*

Thea was working the new heavy bag they'd installed in the basement. The pool table had ended up on the back of a truck along with the ruins of the old garage and a lot of Thomas' other basement junk neither of them had any interest in. He was outside hammering things. Thea liked watching him work, but didn't really care about carpentry, so eventually she'd come downstairs and started punching and kicking.

She still had a lot of questions she'd never get answers to –

was there anything after that place, were her parents together again, what had *happened* to Robia and Raifa at the end – but at least it was over.

A rapid series of kicks and strikes followed. Paul had managed to get the rest of the islanders to just sort of act like nothing had happened. Their cars were parked to the north, they'd all eventually gotten in and gone home. The Coast Guard and various city and town harbor patrols had tried to find a giant monster, and there were a few grainy pictures of it out there (and a couple of a flying man) but if anyone connected them to it, no one had come asking yet.

Thomas and Thea had spent Christmas day cheating to get the barn back. The horses were comfortable again, at least. John had been a very patient horse. Ramses had not, clearly irritated with the interruption of his busy eating schedule.

Thomas wanted to find a buyer for the horses, because he hated the idea of asking Paul to take care of them after what the man had been through. For now things were as they had been. Thea had decided to hope for the best.

She slammed her hands several times into the top of the bag where someone's head might be. Then she did a few leg strikes. She heard the creaking on the stairs long before she saw him come around the corner, shirtless and ducking his head as he walked into the big room.

"We should get you some other stuff."

"Speed bag would be nice." She rested on the bag, looking at him. "How're Bishop and Joe?"

"Making Bishop's parents terribly uncomfortable from what I gather." Thomas let his teeth show, which he did rarely when smiling. "I gather Bish insisted they share a room."

"Oooh, so much for his parents' willing self-delusion."

"So I have the basic frame up. Gonna be a bit before I can actually get the walls finished, but it's getting there."

"Why not just cheat again?"

"Daedalus seemed a trifle pissed off that I just wanted a barn."

"I still think you should have let him design it the way he wanted it."

"It would have been six stories, made of marble and with a labyrinth in it." He walked over towards her. "The horses wouldn't have liked that."

"It would have made our eventual minotaur storage easier." She leaned in, took a brief sniff. "You're all sweaty."

"So are you."

"I wasn't complaining." She started taking off her gloves. "I have an idea. See if you like it."

"I'm listening." He was unbuttoning his plaid shirt.

"Ooh, you're thinking ahead, that's good. I was thinking we go upstairs, and we can be sweaty together. Maybe even get sweatier."

"This is one of your better ideas." He pulled his thermal undershirt over his head and she let herself just admire him for a moment, the breadth of his chest, his arms. He'd trimmed his beard down to a goatee, but it was getting stubbly again, which she liked in certain activities.

She stepped closer, pulling off her t-shirt and undoing her sports bra. "No fair getting naked first."

"Best for last and all that." Their mouths were close enough to kiss but they held off, enjoying just playing for the moment. "I…"

"*Iloveyou!*" She hopped up and down in glee. "I said it first!"

"Yes you did." He dipped, putting his arms under her knees and lifting her up. She made a delighted little sound, somewhere between a laugh and a purr. "Here's your reward."

Getting up the stairs was a bit tricky while they were busy kissing and even biting each other, but they managed after a few minutes. The door was sticking, but a hard shove of his shoulder sent it flying open. She laughed into his mouth.

"Impatient?"

"Always a little around you." He was breathing heavy, much heavier than he needed to from carrying her. "You make me want to run everywhere, do everything fast so I can get back to you."

"That one was good. You keep doing that." The phone picked

that moment to ring, just as she finished the word *that*. Thomas snarled at it. "Shit, put me down."

"Christ, *why?*"

"Oh, calm down. You're getting laid and you know it, you can wait a few minutes." She laughed at the expression on his face, as mutinous as a small child told he had to wait for candy until after dinner. Still, he put her down and she snatched up her cell. "Thea Mendel."

"Right. Thea." The voice on the other end of the phone was familiar, but she didn't quite place it. "Evvie told me you were selling your house?"

"I am." She nodded, then realized she was on the phone and resisted the urge to slap her own forehead. "And who is this?"

"Uh, I'm Evvie's employer. My name's Stuart." She heard him make some noise, then take a breath and try again. "Uh, we met..."

"Yes, you're the vampire who doesn't like being a vampire, I remember you Stuart." She side eyed to Thomas, who had a look on his face best described as utterly lost. "Am I to take it you're in the market for a house?"

"Well, someone reminded me that, people like *me*, we can't come into a house uninvited so..."

"That actually makes sense." She looked over at Thomas. "Well, I'm about to have sex with my fiancée for a few hours. I assume you'll be up all night?"

"Yeah."

"Excellent. I'll call you back at this number if that's acceptable."

"Uh, sure, that'll be fine..."

"Okay then bye." She hung up the phone. Thomas was laughing now.

"You really did that to Stuart?"

"I really did. Still, looks like I actually might be able to scrape together a college fund now." She put her arms around his neck. "Weren't we on our way to do something?"

"Apparently for a few hours." He brushed his lips against her throat, and she moaned as the gooseflesh settled in. "I suppose we'd best get started."

"Yes." She bit his collarbone, loving the sound of his breathing speeding up, the feel of the sound playing through him. "We had best."

Thank you for reading Nameless!

For news on my upcoming books sign up for my Otherworlds Publishing Newsletter: Otherworlds.pub/Newsletter-Signup/

***

Keep reading for a preview of the next book in the series, Heartless, available now!

The drive to Exeter had been uneventful, and as to be expected for any drive from anywhere in Rhode Island to anywhere else in Rhode Island, reasonably short. They were pulling up in front of the old farmhouse within a half hour, with sunset a recent thing.

"This the address?" Thea was peering over the wheel of Thomas' 1969 Camaro. "Doesn't look like much."

"They're all the same around here." The car creaked as he opened the door and stepped out, the suspension groaning in relief. Thea decided it was time to be paranoid, so she concentrated for a moment and opened what old mystics would have called her third eye. For her it was just seeing in a different way, seeing life as a glowing tapestry of filaments bound together by will. Thomas gleamed in it, blazing, radiant. She loved looking at him this way, seeing the leashed power of his frame translated into a seething mass of pointillist brightness.

She could tell by the flash around his eyes that he was doing it too, like twin gemstones set in his face, shining verdant into the dark around them.

"There's something over there." He wasn't whispering, but his voice was pitched lower than usual. She looked in the direction of the barn and saw it. Just for a second before it went behind or inside the barn, but something that left a stain of purple-blackness, filaments the color of a bruise. Something truly dysfunctional.

She nodded to him and they made their way up the drive towards the building. It reminded Thea a bit of the farm on Thomas' grandfather's old acreage, the one where she'd finally freed herself and Joe and Seri and even their Williams relations from a horror. She hoped there wasn't one here, but that stain wasn't fading as they got closer. It had left reeking fluid smeared across the barn door, fluid that looked utterly wrong when viewed with her true sight.

"Smear's heading out, not in."

"How the hell do you know that?"

"I've worked in a slaughterhouse, remember?" Technically it

was just his own farm's killing floor, but he'd spent summers there and one of the things that happens to cattle on a working farm is they get killed and eaten. He'd never liked it, but it was the same if you brought up your meat, hunted for it, or bought it in a store. Something died so you could eat it. This, however, felt different.

Thea looked in the barn and saw why.

Everything inside it was dead. There was a broken mule with its guts torn out and its limbs at angles limbs don't go, several dead sheep that looked crushed, and masses of feathers and blood that might have been chickens once. Even Thomas, for all his farm-taught dispassion, hissed at the sight.

"Let's go," Thea said while walking around the door. "We need to find it *now*." She was breathing through her mouth to avoid the smell. They hadn't been dead long, and the reek of their panicked deaths was that of any fresh death, their blood pooling on the floor.

Thomas took point. The stain they could both see was apparent now, the blood dripping from whatever had killed everything in the barn, the wrongness that of their brutal and unnecessary deaths. Death, pain, fear were as powerful a source as any, and here they'd been spattered like paint by an uncaring child.

"We're heading towards that house." Thea whispered. Thomas just nodded.

They saw it once they got around a small stand of trees between the house and the barn. It stood massive, naked and coated in hairy hide around its shoulders and head, easily nine feet tall. Most of it was the body of a grotesquely proportioned man – thick arms and legs, corded with muscles that seemed out of place on human limbs. Thomas himself was a large and (if Thea said so herself) heroically-proportioned man, but he looked like a child next to this thing.

It dropped to its haunches to squat over something, and it took Thea a moment to see what it was. The fading life in it was just enough for her to see that it was a Holstein, a dairy cow. She remembered a trip out to a farm in East Greenwich when she was a child, seeing cows just like it in a barn. It had been a pleasant memory.

The head on the creature was that of a bull, but not like any bull Thea had ever seen. It was enormous, with huge curving horns that looked more like spears pointed forward. It reached out its massive hands and wrenched hard at the cow's neck, snapping bone. Thea couldn't contain herself another second.

"Hey, Ferdinand Kruger!" She stepped forward, putting herself in what little light there was from the overcast dusk sky. "Get the fuck off of her, you already killed her!"

It made a bellowing noise that did not sound like anything either a bull nor a human could have produced and stood to its full height, whirling to point those nearly three-foot-long horns at them both.

Thomas hadn't spoken yet. He was looking at it, at the lines and knots of mottled power. It dripped blood from its recent kills, but it hadn't used the death, just caused it. It wasn't a maker of magic, just made *by* it, a myth given limbs. He could see that there was no *there* there, no being, just a calling.

"It's a summoned thing." It was regarding the two of them. "Can you keep it busy?"

"Oh, I'll do more than keep it *busy*. You don't hurry up, there won't be anything left for you to play with." She was humming a song under her breath, remembered from after school on the couch with her late mother. The smell of her mom's hair, the smell of dinner as dad puttered in the kitchen, an oasis for a girl who'd never fit in anywhere.

The beast (the Minotaur, Thea realized, the myth incarnated in front of her, the monster which ate fourteen Athenians every seven years) had finally decided to kill them. It leapt forward, a very strong leap that cleared yards in a single bound.

A horn blared from the path to the left, between the house and the barn, and bright light spilled over the creature. The bull head turned in time to see a red tractor trailer with the cab over the engine come out of the darkness and smash full into it, bearing it backwards into the tree in the center of the space between the house and barn.

The creature didn't die. Amazingly, it actually began pushing the massive truck *back*. Thea grunted as the feedback came. Her way of summoning was slightly different than her grandmother's had been. She felt more of what she called, but could more easily direct them, more fully control them. The muscles of her arms and neck, well defined and athletic, stood out in tension.

Thomas was studying the Minotaur, trying to figure out if there was a link he could follow. It didn't look like there was. Whoever had called it up had just let it go, let it wander and destroy as it saw fit. That disturbed him. A summoning wasn't an easy thing to sustain. How...

"Thomas?" Thea concentrated her will, and the truck changed. One second it was that same red truck with the flat square front, and then with a mechanical sound it unfolded like an origami of metal, arms and legs and a head appearing from it. "How much longer do I need to keep playing with it?"

"Not...is that...you didn't."

"Why wouldn't I? I loved that show. Peter Cullen's voice. I like deep voices." She smiled, a bit of a grimace as the Minotaur slashed those horns across the front grill of the robot. "You can write him a thank you later for setting me up for you."

Thomas didn't reply. He'd seen something...a kind of knot in the filaments, a means to set up a summoning so that it drew power directly from the other world where spirits and myths were concrete. You could call it various things – the Astral, the Ether, the Dreamland or Otherworld. He whistled to himself at the purity of it, how *elegant* it was.

"I have got to show you this. Can you look at the thing?"

"I *am* looking at it!" The robot produced a giant glowing axe from its hand and swung a blow that managed to slash across the thing's face. "Kind of hard not to when I'm attacking it with a giant robot."

"Look at the center. The interlocking whorls of power." She did as the robot managed a kick that sent the minotaur back, giving her breathing space to focus on it.

"Huh, like Celtic knotwork."

"Or Vedic. The Endless Knot, but not quite the same."

"It's powering itself." She whistled. "It's not being controlled. How is that possible?"

"I don't know yet." The Minotaur charged back in, driving its horns into the robot's side, causing an explosion of sparks. Thea bit her own tongue to keep from crying out.

"No time. It's *strong*. I'd need a few minutes to work up something more solid. This was a fast call. I need help." Neither of them had actually expected there to be anything here, which she now realized had been a mistake. Her ribcage felt like fire from the goring to her summon.

"I'm on it." He had an idea, smiled to himself. Thomas didn't like summoning, himself. He could do it, but he preferred to embody concepts. It was more visceral, but took much less concentration. He dropped to one knee and began tracing crude symbols in the ground, remembering his own childhood. "Gonna borrow a page from your book."

"Just hurry it up before Babe here gets his hands on the Matrix."

Five figures in the dirt, crude but serviceable. He imagined black, blue, red, green and yellow, heard the metallic roar of each in his head. Fixed them. Remembered when he and Scott Poole (*whatever happened to Scottie I haven't seen that kid in a decade*) would sit on the couch and argue about it. Scott had always insisted 'He should just form the sword first thing, why doesn't he?'

Thomas slammed his hands together and an explosion of light radiated out between them, blazing brilliance as he pulled them apart, a massive two-handed blade shimmering into existence. Around him was an aura of shifting colors – black, red, blue, green, and yellow. He roared and five lions roared from him, shattering the air around them. People later reported hearing it in Connecticut.

The Minotaur danced around the axe, slashed again with its horns, but then the roar sounded and it turned to try and face him. The robot took advantage, grabbed hold of one of its horns and twisted, bending its head back.

Thomas leapt into the air, the glowing sword above his head.

With the Minotaur restrained, it was all about delivering the cut. He landed in a blast of light and sound, a shockwave of dust exploding all around him.

The summoning unravelled, its filaments severed completely. The knotwork undone by the world's oldest solution to a complex knot. Thomas stood up, the glowing blade quivering and then vanishing as he let the power flow back into where he'd drawn it from.

Thea was laughing as she dismissed her robot. They were both keyed up, as always. Even after what they'd seen, the magic always made their bodies sing, their thoughts race and burn. They embraced, so amazingly glad to be alive and together in that moment, to have someone who understood what it was. What it meant. Who they were.

"Let's go home." He breathed into her hair. "I need time with you."

"Should probably check in with the...oh, fuck it. We can call them from the house. Take me home, Tommy." She pulled his head down to kiss him, just brushing against his lips to feel the warmth, the life of him. "Get me the fuck away from this."

They made a circuit of the place, but found nothing alive. They looked at the house, but didn't go inside. If there had been anything alive inside it, they would have seen traces. It might simply have been deserted, or there might be dead people inside. Neither of them wanted to kick over that nest.

Thomas drove on the way home. The car wasn't an automatic so he couldn't really touch Thea, so she touched him instead, leaning her head on his shoulder. The drive home felt shorter than the drive there and they both breathed a little easier when they pulled into the driveway of the house, shining to their eyes with the layers of wards and protections they'd laid over it. When it came to weird shit, that house was fast becoming the safest place in the state.

As they stepped out of the car Thea's phone rang.

"Ah shit." She flipped it open. "Mendel."

"Did I do something wrong?" The voice on the other end

wasn't who she'd expected and she relaxed. Thomas could see it, knew who it had to be.

"Joey. What time is it there?"

"One in the freaking morning. I can't sleep."

"Can't call Bishop? I'm sure he'd be willing to pass the time with you." Thomas reached out to the house and told it they were home, felt the wards acknowledge them. He opened the door while Thea kept chatting with her cousin.

"I, ah, don't have a lot of privacy. I'm at a youth hostel in Edinburgh."

"Why?"

"It seemed the thing to do. I just got done watching *Pulp Fiction* with a bunch of Australians." He snorted into the phone. "They asked me if I knew Uma Thurman."

"Seriously?" Thea watched Thomas peel his jacket off and hang it up on a hook, then remove his shirt. His lovely back, tapering down to a glorious tight little ass (for his size, anyway) in jeans that did little to hide it from her. *Christ* but her libido was always charged up after a summoning, and even without that, ogling Tommy was one of her favorite pastimes. "They're aware it's a big country, right?"

"Who knows? I decided not to ask if they all knew Paul Hogan."

"Joey, I love you, and I'm very glad to hear your voice." Thea was playing with her hair, recently cut back to above her shoulders. "But you're cramping my style here."

"God, haven't you two gotten that out of your systems yet?"

"I hope not." She made a growling sound into the phone. "So unless you need something besides a friendly voice..."

"I, ah, did have a request."

"Make it fast." Thomas was walking around the den without his shirt and Thea was getting all sorts of ideas about what to do with him.

"Could you guys check up on Bishop? Make sure he's okay? He came over to visit in April and that was great, but it's October now, and..."

"I got you. We see him once a week, you know. He seems fine. Anxious for you to get back, but fine." Thea didn't say *the poor guy's backed up pretty hard,* but she was thinking it. "But sure, we can do that."

"Thanks. I know it's...well. Thank you."

"You're welcome and goodbye, cos." Thea hung up and dropped the phone on the counter. "My cousin's traipsing around Scotland."

"I liked the place when I was there. He must be on his free week. We got one every few months to go do whatever we wanted, explore. I went to Scotland and Wales with mine." Thea pulled her jacket off, tossed it on the counter next to her phone, then reached down and pulled her shirt up over her head in one motion. Thomas' eyes widened in appreciation.

"We'll have to go sometime so you can show me." She walked over to the couch and pushed Thomas down onto it, straddling him. "Right now, you need to stop talking and do other things with that beautiful mouth of yours."

He decided to do as he was told.

Printed in Great Britain
by Amazon

77539874R00253